JOHN LE CARRÉ'S
A MOST WANTED MAN

• *New York Times* Notable Book •
• *New York Times* bestseller •
• #1 *San Francisco Chronicle* bestseller •
• #1 *Los Angeles Times* bestseller •

Now a major motion picture!

Praise for the masterful twenty-first novel from "the venerable lion of the espionage and political thriller" (*Chicago Sun-Times*)

"In *A Most Wanted Man,* you are, unlike in the modern world, in thrillingly deft, safe hands. . . . What le Carré has always done terrifically is to capture the nuances of the spying game. His spooks are wonderful. . . ."

—*The Guardian*

"One of the best novels he's ever written. Maybe the best. . . . This is le Carré's strongest, most powerful novel, which has a great deal to do with its near perfect narrative pace and the pleasure of its prose, but even more to do with the emotions of its audience."

—*The New York Times Book Review*

JOHN LE CARRÉ

A MOST WANTED MAN

POCKET BOOKS

NEW YORK   LONDON   TORONTO   SYDNEY   NEW DELHI

Pocket Books
A Division of Simon & Schuster, Inc.
1230 Avenue of the Americas
New York, NY 10020

This book is a work of fiction. Any references to historical events, real people, or real places are used fictitiously. Other names, characters, places, and events are products of the author's imagination, and any resemblance to actual events or places or persons, living or dead, is entirely coincidental.

This Pocket Books paperback edition July 2014

POCKET and colophon are registered trademarks of Simon & Schuster, Inc.

For information about special discounts for bulk purchases, please contact Simon & Schuster Special Sales at 1-866-506-1949 or business@simonandschuster.com.

The Simon & Schuster Speakers Bureau can bring authors to your live event. For more information or to book an event, contact the Simon & Schuster Speakers Bureau at 1-866-248-3049 or visit our website at www.simonspeakers.com.

Manufactured in the United States of America

10 9 8 7 6 5 4 3 2 1

ISBN 978-1-4767-4478-0
ISBN 978-1-4391-2321-8 (ebook)

For my grandchildren,
born and unborn

The golden rule is, to help those we love
to escape from us.

FRIEDRICH VON HÜGEL

A MOST WANTED MAN

1

A Turkish heavyweight boxing champion saun-
tering down a Hamburg street with his mother
on his arm can scarcely be blamed for failing to
notice that he is being shadowed by a skinny boy
in a black coat.

Big Melik, as he was known to his admiring
neighborhood, was a giant of a fellow, shaggy,
unkempt and genial, with a broad natural grin
and black hair bound back in a ponytail and a
rolling, free-and-easy gait that, even without his
mother, took up half the pavement. At the age
of twenty he was in his own small world a
celebrity, and not only for his prowess in the
boxing ring: elected youth representative of his
Islamic sports club, three times runner-up in the
North German Championship hundred-meter
butterfly stroke and, as if all that weren't
enough, star goalkeeper of his Saturday soccer
team.

Like most very large people, he was also more

accustomed to being looked at than looking, which is another reason why the skinny boy got away with shadowing him for three successive days and nights.

The two men first made eye contact as Melik and his mother, Leyla, emerged from the al-Umma Travel Shop, fresh from buying air tickets for Melik's sister's wedding in their home village outside Ankara. Melik felt someone's gaze fixed on him, glanced round and came face-to-face with a tall, desperately thin boy of his own height with a straggly beard, eyes reddened and deep-set, and a long black coat that could have held three magicians. He had a black-and-white kaffiyeh round his neck and a tourist's camel-skin saddlebag slung over his shoulder. He stared at Melik, then at Leyla. Then he came back to Melik, never blinking, but appealing to him with his fiery, sunken eyes.

Yet the boy's air of desperation need not have troubled Melik all that much since the travel shop was situated at the edge of the main railway station concourse, where every variety of lost soul—German vagrants, Asians, Arabs, Africans, and Turkish like himself but less fortunate—hung around all day long, not to mention legless men on electric carts, drug sellers and their customers, beggars and their dogs, and a seventy-year-old cowboy in a Stetson and silver-studded leather riding breeches. Few had work, and a sprinkling had no business standing on German soil at all, but were at best tolerated under a deliberate policy of destitution, pending their summary deportation, usually at dawn. Only new arrivals or the willfully foolhardy took the risk. Cannier illegals gave the station a wide berth.

A further good reason to ignore the boy was the classical music that the station authorities boom at full blast over this section of the concourse from a battery of well-aimed loudspeakers. Its purpose, far from spreading feelings of peace and well-being among its listeners, is to send them packing.

Despite these impediments the skinny boy's face imprinted itself on Melik's consciousness and for a fleeting moment he felt embarrassed by his own happiness. Why on earth should he? Something splendid had just occurred, and he couldn't wait to phone his sister and tell her that their mother, Leyla, after six months of tending her dying husband, and a year of mourning her heart out for him, was bubbling over with pleasure at the prospect of attending her daughter's wedding, and fussing about what to wear, and whether the dowry was big enough, and the groom as handsome as everybody, including Melik's sister, said he was.

So why shouldn't Melik chatter along with his

own mother? Which he did, enthusiastically, all the way home. It was the skinny boy's stillness, he decided later. Those lines of age in a face as young as mine. His look of winter on a lovely spring day.

That was the Thursday.

And on the Friday evening, when Melik and Leyla came out of mosque together, there he was again, the same boy, the same kaffiyeh and outsized overcoat, huddled in the shadow of a grimy doorway. This time Melik noticed that there was a sideways list to his skinny body, as if he'd been knocked off true and remained at that angle until somebody told him he could straighten up. And the fiery stare burning even more brightly than on the previous day. Melik met his gaze head-on, wished he hadn't and looked away.

And this second encounter was all the less probable because Leyla and Melik scarcely ever went to mosque, not even a moderate Turkish-language one. Since 9/11, Hamburg's mosques had become dangerous places. Go to the wrong one, or the right one and get the wrong imam, and you could find yourself and your family on a police watch list for the rest of your life. Nobody doubted that practically every prayer row contained an informant who was earning his way with the authorities. Nobody was likely to forget, be he Muslim, police spy or both, that the city-state of Hamburg had been unwitting host to three of the 9/11 hijackers, not to mention their fellow cell-members and plotters; or that Mohammed Atta, who steered the first plane into the Twin Towers, had worshiped his wrathful god in a humble Hamburg mosque.

It was also a fact that since her husband's death Leyla and her son had become less observant of their faith. Yes, of course the old man had been a Muslim, and a laic too. But he was a militant supporter of workers' rights, which was why he had been driven out of his homeland. The only reason they had gone to mosque at all was that Leyla in her impulsive way had felt a sudden need. She was happy. The weight of her grief was lifting. Yet the first anniversary of her husband's death was approaching. She needed to have a dialogue with him and share the good news. They had already missed the main Friday prayer, and could just as well have prayed at home. But Leyla's whim was law. Arguing correctly that personal invocations stand a better chance of being heard if they are offered in the evening, she had insisted on attending the last prayer hour of the day, which incidentally meant that the mosque was as good as empty.

So clearly Melik's second encounter with the skinny boy, like the first, was mere chance. For what else could it be? Or so, in his plain way, the good-hearted Melik reasoned.

The next day being a Saturday, Melik took a bus across town to visit his affluent paternal uncle at the family candle factory. Relationships between his uncle and his father had at times been strained, but since his father's death he had learned to respect his uncle's friendship. Jumping aboard the bus, whom should he see but the skinny boy sitting below him in the glass shelter, watching him depart? And six hours later, when he returned to the same bus stop, the boy was still there, wrapped in his kaffiyeh and magician's overcoat, crouched in the same corner of the shelter, waiting.

At the sight of him Melik, who as a rule of life was pledged to love all mankind equally, was seized by an uncharitable aversion. He felt that the skinny boy was accusing him of something and he resented it. Worse, there was an air of superiority about him, despite his miserable condition. What did he think he was achieving with that ridiculous black coat, anyway? That it made him invisible or something? Or was he trying to imply that he was so unfamiliar with our Western ways that he had no idea of the image he created? Either way, Melik determined to shake him off. So instead of going up to him and asking him whether he needed help, or was ill, which in other circumstances he might have done, he struck out for home at full stride, confident that the skinny boy stood no chance of keeping up with him.

The day was unseasonably hot for spring, and the sun was beating off the crowded pavement. Yet the skinny boy contrived by some kind of miracle to keep pace with Melik, limping and panting, wheezing and sweating, and now and then jumping in the air as if in pain, but still managing to draw up alongside him at pedestrian crossings.

And when Melik let himself into the tiny brick house that, after decades of family scrimping, his mother now owned almost free of debt, he had only to wait a few breaths before the front doorbell chimed its carillon. And when he returned downstairs, there stood the skinny boy on the doorstep with his saddlebag over his shoulder and his eyes blazing from the effort of the walk, and sweat pouring down his face like summer rain, and in his trembling hand he held a piece of brown cardboard on which was written in Turkish: *I am a Muslim medical student. I am tired and I wish to stay in your house. Issa.* And as if to ram the message home, round his wrist a bracelet of fine gold, and dangling from it, a tiny gold replica of the Koran.

But Melik by now had a full head of outrage. All right, he wasn't the greatest intellect his school had ever seen but he objected to feeling guilty and inferior, and being followed and preyed upon by a beggar with attitude. When his father died Melik had proudly assumed the role of master of the house and his mother's protector and, as a further assertion of his authority, done what his father had not succeeded in doing before his death: as a second-generation Turkish resident, he had launched himself and his mother on the long, stony road to German citizenship, where every aspect of a family's lifestyle was taken under the microscope, and eight years of unblemished behavior were the first prerequisite. The last thing he or his mother needed was some deranged vagrant claiming to be a medical student and begging on their doorstep.

"Get the hell out of here," he ordered the skinny boy roughly in Turkish, shaping up to him in the doorway. "Get out of here, stop following us and don't come back."

Meeting no reaction from the haggard face except a wince as if it had been struck, Melik repeated his instruction in German. But when he made to slam the door, he discovered Leyla standing on the stair behind him, looking over his shoulder at the boy and at the cardboard notice shaking uncontrollably in his hand.

And he saw that she already had tears of pity in her eyes.

Sunday passed and on the Monday morning Melik found excuses not to show up at his cousin's greengrocery business in Wellingsbüttel. He must stay home and train for the Amateur Open Boxing Championship, he told his mother. He must work out in the gym and in the Olympic pool. But in reality he had decided she was not safe to be left alone with an elongated psycho with delusions of grandeur who, when he wasn't praying or staring at the wall, prowled about the house, fondly touching everything as if he remembered it from long ago. Leyla was a peerless woman, in her son's judgment, but since her husband's death volatile and guided solely by her feelings. Those whom she chose to love could do no wrong. Issa's softness of manner, his timidity and sudden rushes of dawning happiness, made him an instant member of that select company.

On the Monday and again on the Tuesday, Issa did little except sleep, pray and bathe himself. To communicate he spoke broken Turkish with a peculiar, guttural accent, furtively, in bursts, as though talking were forbidden, and yet still in some unfathomable way, to Melik's ear, didactic. Otherwise he ate. Where on earth did he put all that food? At any hour of the day, Melik would walk into the kitchen and there he was, head bowed over a bowl of lamb and rice and vegetables, spoon never still, eyes slipping from side to side lest somebody snatch his food away. When he'd finished, he'd wipe the bowl clean with a piece of bread, eat the bread and, with a muttered "Thanks be to God" and a faint smirk on his face as if he had a secret that was too good to share with them, take the bowl to the sink and wash it under the tap, a thing Leyla would never in a month of Sundays have allowed her own son or husband to do. The kitchen was her domain. Men keep out.

"So when are you reckoning to start your medical studies, Issa?" Melik asked him casually, in his mother's hearing.

"God willing, it will be soon. I must be strong. I must not be beggar."

"You'll need a residence permit, you know. *And* a student's ID. Not to mention like a hundred thousand euros for board and lodging. And a neat little two-seater to take your girlfriends out."

"God is all-merciful. When I am not beggar, He will provide."

Such self-assurance went beyond mere piety in Melik's view.

"He's costing us real money, Mother," he declared, barging into the kitchen while Issa was safely in the attic. "The way he eats. All those baths."

"No more than you, Melik."

"No, but he's not me, is he? We don't know who he is."

"Issa is our guest. When he is restored to health, with Allah's help we shall consider his future," his mother replied loftily.

Issa's implausible efforts at self-effacement only made him more conspicuous in Melik's eyes. Sidling his way down the cramped corridor, or preparing to climb the stepladder to the attic where Leyla had made up a bed for him, he employed what Melik regarded as exaggerated circumspection, seeking permission with his doe eyes, and flattening himself against the wall when Melik or Leyla needed to pass.

"Issa has been in prison," Leyla announced complacently one morning.

Melik was appalled. "Do you know that for a fact? We're harboring a jailbird? Do the police know that for a fact? Did he *tell* you?"

"He said that in prison in Istanbul they give only one piece of bread and a bowl of rice a day," said Leyla, and before Melik could protest any more, added one of her late husband's favorite nostrums: "We honor the guest and go to the assistance of those in distress. No work of charity will go unrewarded in Paradise," she intoned.

"Wasn't your own father in prison in Turkey, Melik? Not everyone who goes to prison is a criminal. For people like Issa and your father, prison is a badge of honor."

But Melik knew she had other thoughts up her sleeve that she was less inclined to reveal. Allah had answered her prayers. He had sent her a second son to make up for the husband she had lost. The fact that he was an illegal half-crazed jailbird with delusions about himself was of no apparent interest to her.

He was from Chechnya.

That much they established on the third evening when Leyla astonished them both by trilling out a couple of sentences of Chechen, a thing Melik never in his life had heard her do. Issa's haggard face lit up with a sudden amazed smile that vanished equally quickly, and thereafter he seemed to be struck mute. Yet Leyla's explanation of her linguistic skills turned out to be simple. As a young girl in Turkey she had played with Chechen children in her village and picked up snippets of their language. She guessed Issa was Chechen from the moment she set eyes on him but kept her counsel because with Chechens you never knew.

He was from Chechnya, and his mother was

dead and all he had to remember her by was the golden bracelet with the Koran attached to it that she had placed round his wrist before she died. But when she died and how she died, and how old he was when he inherited her bracelet were questions he either failed to understand or didn't wish to.

"Chechens are hated everywhere," Leyla explained to Melik, while Issa kept his head down and went on eating. "But not by us. Do you hear me, Melik?"

"Of course I hear you, Mother."

"Everyone persecutes Chechens except us," she continued. "It is normal all over Russia and the world. Not only Chechens, but Russian Muslims everywhere. Putin persecutes them and Mr. Bush encourages him. As long as Putin calls it his war on terror, he can do with the Chechens whatever he wishes, and nobody will stop him. Is that not so, Issa?"

But Issa's brief moment of pleasure had long passed. The shadows had returned to his wracked face, the spark of suffering to his doe eyes, and a haggard hand closed protectively over the bracelet. *Speak,* damn you, Melik urged him indignantly but not aloud. If somebody surprises me by talking Turkish at me, I speak Turkish back, it's only polite! So why don't you answer my mother with a few obliging words of

Chechen, or are you too busy knocking back her free food?

He had other worries. Carrying out a security inspection of the attic that Issa now treated as his sovereign territory—stealthily, as Issa was in the kitchen, talking as usual to his mother—he had made certain revealing discoveries: hoarded scraps of food as though Issa was planning his escape; a gilt-framed miniature head-and-shoulder photograph of Melik's betrothed sister at eighteen, purloined from his mother's treasured collection of family portraits in the living room; and his father's magnifying glass, lying across a copy of the Hamburg Yellow Pages, open at the section devoted to the city's many banks.

"God gave your sister a tender smile," Leyla pronounced contentedly, in answer to Melik's outraged protests that they were harboring a sexual deviant as well as an illegal. "Her smile will lighten Issa's heart."

Issa was from Chechnya then, whether or not he spoke the language. Both his parents were dead, but when asked about them he was as puzzled as his hosts were, gazing sweetly into a corner of the room with his eyebrows raised. He was state-less, homeless, an ex-prisoner and illegal, but

Allah would provide the means for him to study medicine once he was no longer a beggar.

Well, Melik too had once dreamed of becoming a doctor and had even extracted from his father and uncles a shared undertaking to finance his training, a thing that would have entailed the family real sacrifice. And if he'd been a bit better at exams and maybe played fewer games, that's where he'd be today: at medical school, a first-year student working his heart out for the honor of his family. It was therefore understandable that Issa's airy assumption that Allah would somehow enable him to do what Melik had conspicuously failed to do should have prompted him to throw aside Leyla's warnings and, as best his generous heart allowed, launch himself on a searching examination of his unwanted guest.

The house was his. Leyla had gone shopping and would not be back until midafternoon.

"You've studied medicine then, have you?" he suggested, sitting himself down beside Issa for greater intimacy, and fancying himself the wiliest interrogator in the world. "Nice."

"I was in hospitals, sir."

"As a student?"

"I was sick, sir."

Why all these *sir*'s? Were they from prison too?

"Being a patient's not like being a doctor,

though, is it? A doctor has to know what's wrong with people. A patient sits there and waits for the doctor to put it right."

Issa considered this statement in the complicated way that he considered all statements of whatever size, now smirking into space, now scratching at his beard with his spidery fingers, and finally smiling brilliantly without answering.

"How old are you?" Melik demanded, becoming more blunt than he had planned. "If you don't mind my asking"—sarcastically.

"Twenty-three, sir." But again only after prolonged consideration.

"That's quite old then, isn't it? Even if you got your residence tomorrow, you wouldn't be a qualified doctor till you were thirty-five or something. Plus learning German. You'd have to pay for that too."

"Also God willing I shall marry good wife and have many children, two boys, two girls."

"Not my sister, though. She's getting married next month, I'm afraid."

"God willing she will have many sons, sir."

Melik considered his next line of attack and plunged: "How did you get to Hamburg in the first place?" he asked.

"It is immaterial."

Immaterial? Where did he get *that* word from? And in Turkish?

"Didn't you know that they treat refugees worse in this town than anywhere in Germany?"

"Hamburg will be my home, sir. It is where they bring me. It is Allah's divine command."

"*Who* brought you? Who's *they*?"

"It was combination, sir."

"Combination of what?"

"Maybe Turkish people. Maybe Chechen people. We pay them. They take us to boat. Put us in container. Container had little air."

Issa was beginning to sweat, but Melik had gone too far to pull back now.

"*We*? Who's *we*?"

"Was group, sir. From Istanbul. Bad group. Bad men. I do not respect these men." The superior tone again, even in faltering Turkish.

"How many of you?"

"Maybe twenty. Container was cold. After few hours, very cold. This ship would go to Denmark. I was happy."

"You mean Copenhagen, right? Copenhagen in Denmark. The capital."

"Yes"—brightening as if Copenhagen was a good idea—"to *Copenhagen*. In Copenhagen, I would be arranged. I would be free from bad men. But this ship did not go immediately Copenhagen. This ship must go first Sweden. To *Gothenburg*. Yes?"

"There's a Swedish port called Gothenburg, I believe," Melik conceded.

"In Gothenburg, ship will dock, ship will take cargo, then go Copenhagen. When ship arrive in Gothenburg we are very sick, very hungry. On ship they tell to us: 'Make no noise. Swedes hard. Swedes kill you.' We make no noise. But Swedes do not like our container. Swedes have dog." He reflects awhile. " 'What is your name, please?' " he intones, but loud enough to make Melik sit up. " 'What papers, please? You are from prison? What crimes, please? You escape from prison? How, please?' Doctors are efficient. I admire these doctors. They let us sleep. I am grateful to these doctors. One day I will be such a doctor. But God willing I must escape. To escape to Sweden is no chance. There is NATO wire. Many guards. But there is also toilet. From toilet is window. After window is gate to harbor. My friend can open this gate. My friend is from boat. I go back to boat. Boat takes me to Copenhagen. At last, I say. In Copenhagen was lorry for Hamburg. Sir, I love God. But the West I also love. In West I shall be free to worship Him."

"A *lorry* brought you to Hamburg?"

"Was arranged."

"A *Chechen* lorry?"

"My friend must first take me to road."

"Your friend from the crew? That friend? The same guy?"

"No, sir. Was different friend. To reach road was difficult. Before lorry, we must sleep one night in field." He looked up, and an expression of pure joy momentarily suffused his haggard features. "Was stars. God is merciful. Praise be to Him."

Wrestling with the improbabilities of this story, humbled by its fervor yet infuriated as much by its omissions as his own incapacity to overcome them, Melik felt his frustration spread to his arms and fists, and his fighter's nerves tighten in his stomach.

"Where did it drop you off then, this magic lorry that showed up out of nowhere? Where did it drop you?"

But Issa was no longer listening, if he had been listening at all. Suddenly—or suddenly to the honest if uncomprehending eyes of Melik—whatever had been building up in him erupted. He rose drunkenly to his feet and with a hand cupped to his mouth hobbled stooping to the door, wrestled it open although it wasn't locked and lurched down the corridor to the bathroom. Moments later, the house was filled with a howling and retching, the like of which Melik hadn't heard since his father's death. Gradually it ceased, to be followed by a slopping of water, an opening and closing of the bathroom door and a creaking of the attic steps as Issa scaled the ladder. After which a deep, troubling silence descended, broken each quarter hour by the chirping of Leyla's electronic bird clock.

At four the same afternoon, Leyla returned laden with shopping and, interpreting the atmosphere for what it was, berated Melik for transgressing his duties as host and dishonoring his father's name. She too then withdrew to her room, where she remained in rampant isolation until it was time for her to prepare the evening meal. Soon smells of cooking pervaded the house, but Melik remained on his bed. At eight-thirty she banged the brass dinner gong, a precious wedding gift that to Melik always sounded like a reproach. Knowing she brooked no delay at such moments, he slunk to the kitchen, avoiding her eye.

"Issa, dear, come down, please!" Leyla shouted and, receiving no response, grabbed hold of her late husband's walking stick and thumped the ceiling with its rubber ferrule, her eyes accusingly on Melik, who, under her frosty gaze, braved the climb to the attic.

Issa was lying on his mattress in his underpants, drenched in sweat and hunched on his side. He had taken his mother's bracelet from his wrist and was clutching it in his sweated hand. Round his neck he wore a grimy leather purse tied with a thong. His eyes were wide open, yet he seemed unaware of Melik's presence. Reaching out to touch his shoulder, Melik drew back in dismay. Issa's upper body was a slough of crisscross blue-and-orange bruises. Some appeared to be whiplashes, others bludgeon marks. On the soles of his feet—the same feet that had pounded the Hamburg pavements—Melik made out suppurating holes the size of cigarette burns. Locking his arms round Issa, and binding a blanket round his waist for propriety, Melik lifted him tenderly and lowered the passive Issa through the attic trap and into Leyla's waiting arms.

"Put him in my bed," Melik whispered through his tears. "I'll sleep on the floor. I don't care. I'll even give him my sister to smile at him," he added, remembering the purloined miniature in the attic, and went back up the ladder to fetch it.

Issa's beaten body lay wrapped in Melik's bathrobe, his bruised legs jutting out of the end of Melik's bed, the gold chain still clutched in his hand, his unflinching gaze fixed resolutely on Melik's wall of fame: press photographs of the champ triumphant, his boxing belts and winning

gloves. On the floor beside him squatted Melik
himself. He had wanted to call a doctor at his
own expense, but Leyla had forbidden him to
summon anyone. Too dangerous. For Issa, but
for us too. What about our citizenship application? By morning, his temperature will come
down and he'll start to recover.

But his temperature didn't come down.

Muffled in a full scarf and traveling partway by
cab to discourage her imagined pursuers, Leyla
paid an unannounced visit to a mosque on the
other side of town where a new Turkish doctor
was said to worship. Three hours later she returned home in a rage. The new young doctor
was a fool and a fraud. He knew nothing. He
lacked the most elementary qualifications. He
had no sense of his religious responsibilities. Very
likely, he was not a doctor at all.

Meanwhile, in her absence, Issa's temperature
had after all come down a little, and she was able
to draw upon the rudimentary nursing skills she
had acquired in the days before the family could
afford a doctor or dared to visit one. If Issa had
suffered internal injuries, she pronounced, he
would never have been able to gulp down all that
food, so she was not afraid to give him aspirin for
his subsiding fever, or run up one of her broths
made from rice water laced with Turkish herbal
potions.

Knowing that Issa in health or death would never permit her to touch his bare body, she provided Melik with towels, a poultice for his brow and a bowl of cool water to sponge him every hour. To achieve this, the remorse-stricken Melik felt obliged to unfasten the leather purse at Issa's neck.

Only after long hesitation, and strictly in the interests of his sick guest—or so he assured himself—and not until Issa had turned his face to the other wall and fallen into a half sleep broken by mutterings in Russian, did he untie the thong and loosen the throat of the purse.

His first find was a bunch of faded Russian newspaper clippings, rolled up and held together with an elastic band. Removing the band, he spread them out on the floor. Common to each was a photograph of a Red Army officer in uniform. He was brutish, broad-browed, thick-jowled and looked to be in his midsixties. Two cuttings were memorial announcements, decked with Orthodox crosses and regimental insignia.

Melik's second find was a wad of U.S. fifty-dollar bills, brand-new, ten of them, held together by a money clip. At the sight of them, all his old suspicions came flooding back. A starving, homeless, penniless, beaten fugitive has *five hundred untouched dollars* in his purse? Did he steal them? Forge them? Was this why he had been in prison? Was this what was left over after he had paid off the people smugglers of Istanbul, the obliging crew member who had hidden him and the lorry driver who had spirited him from Copenhagen to Hamburg? If he's got five hundred left now, however much did he set out with? Maybe his medical fantasies aren't so ill-placed after all.

His third find was a grimy white envelope squeezed into a ball as if somebody had meant to throw it away, then changed his mind: no stamp, no address and the flap ripped open. Flattening the envelope, he fished out a crumpled one-page typed letter in Cyrillic script. It had a printed address, a date and the name of the sender—or so he assumed—in large black print along the top. Below the unreadable text was an unreadable signature in blue ink, followed by a handwritten six-figure number, but written very carefully, each figure inked over several times, as if to say *remember this*.

His last find was a key, a small pipestem key, no larger than one knuckle joint of his boxer's hand. It was machine-turned and had complex teeth on three sides: too small for a prison door, he reckoned, too small for the gate in Gothenburg leading back to the ship. But just right for handcuffs.

Replacing Issa's belongings in the purse, Melik

slipped it under the sweat-soaked pillow for him to discover when he woke. But by next morning, the guilty feelings that had taken hold of him wouldn't let him go. All through his night's vigil, stretched on the floor with Issa one step above him on the bed, he had been tormented by images of his guest's martyred limbs, and the realization of his own inadequacy.

As a fighter he knew pain, or thought he did. As a Turkish street kid he had taken beatings as well as handing them out. In a recent championship bout, a hail of punches had sent him reeling into the red dark from which boxers fear not to return. Swimming against native Germans, he had tested the extreme limits of his endurance, or thought he had.

Yet compared with Issa he was untried.

Issa is a man and I am still a boy. I always wanted a brother and here he is delivered to my doorstep, and I rejected him. He suffered like a true defender of his beliefs while I courted cheap glory in the boxing ring.

By the early hours of dawn, the erratic breathing that had kept Melik on tenterhooks all night settled to a steady rasp. Replacing the poultice, he was relieved to establish that Issa's fever had subsided. By midmorning, he was propped semi-upright like a pasha amid a golden pile of Leyla's tasseled velvet cushions from the drawing room, and she was feeding him a life-giving mash of her own concoction and his mother's gold chain was back on his wrist.

Sick with shame, Melik waited for Leyla to close the door behind her. Kneeling at Issa's side, he hung his head.

"I looked in your purse," he said. "I am deeply ashamed of what I have done. May merciful Allah forgive me."

Issa entered one of his eternal silences, then laid an emaciated hand on Melik's shoulder.

"Never confess, my friend," he advised drowsily, clasping Melik's hand. "If you confess, they will keep you there forever."

2

It was six o'clock in the evening of the following Friday as the private banking house of Brue Frères PLC, formerly of Glasgow, Rio de Janeiro and Vienna, and presently of Hamburg, put itself to bed for the weekend.

On the dot of five-thirty, a muscular janitor had closed the front doors of the pretty terraced villa beside the Binnen Alster lake. Within minutes, the chief cashier had locked the strong room and alarmed it, the senior secretary had waved off the last of her girls and checked their computers and wastepaper baskets, and the bank's longest-serving member, Frau Ellenberger, had switched over the telephones, jammed on her beret, unchained her bicycle from its iron hoop in the courtyard and pedaled away to collect her great-niece from dancing class.

But not before pausing to administer a playful rebuke to her employer, Mr. Tommy Brue, the bank's sole surviving partner and bearer of its famous name: "Mr. Tommy, you are worse than us Germans," she protested in her perfectly learned English, popping her head round the door of his sanctum. "Why do you torture yourself with work? Springtime is upon us! Have you not seen the crocuses and magnolia? You are sixty now, remember. You should go home and drink a glass of wine with Mrs. Brue in your beautiful garden! If you don't, you will be *'worn to a raveling,'*" she cautioned, more to parade her love of Beatrix Potter than out of any expectation of mending her employer's ways.

Brue raised his right hand and rotated it in genial parody of a papal blessing.

"Go well, Frau Elli," he urged, in sardonic resignation. "If my employees refuse to work for me during the week, I have no choice but to work for them at weekends. *Tschüss,*" he added, blowing her a kiss.

"And *Tschüss* to you, Mr. Tommy, and my regards to your good wife."

"I shall pass them on."

The reality, as both knew, was different. With the phones and corridors silent, and no clients clamoring for his attention, and his wife, Mitzi, out on her bridge night with her friends the von Essens, Brue's kingdom was his own. He could survey the outgoing week, he could usher in the new. He could consult, if the mood was on him, his immortal soul.

In deference to the unseasonably hot weather, Brue was in shirtsleeves and braces. The jacket of his tailor-made suit was neatly draped over an elderly wooden clotheshorse beside the door: *Randall's of Glasgow,* it read, tailors to the Brues for four generations. The desk at which he labored was the same one that Duncan Brue, the bank's founder, had taken on board with him when, in 1908, he set sail from Scotland with nothing but hope in his heart and fifty gold sovereigns in his pocket.

The outsized mahogany bookcase that filled the whole of one wall was similarly the stuff of family legend. Behind its ornate glass front reposed row upon row of leather-bound masterpieces of world culture: Dante, Goethe, Plato, Socrates, Tolstoy, Dickens, Shakespeare and, somewhat mysteriously, Jack London. The bookcase had been accepted by Brue's grandfather in part repayment of a bad debt, so too the books. Had he felt obliged to read them? Legend said not. He had banked them.

And on the wall directly opposite Brue, like a traffic warning permanently in his path, hung the original, hand-painted, gilt-framed family tree.

The roots of its ancient oak struck deep into the shores of the silvery river Tay. The branches spread eastward into Old Europe and westward into the New World. Golden acorns marked the cities where foreign marriages had enriched the Brue bloodline, not to mention its disposable reserves.

And Brue himself was a worthy descendant of this noble lineage, even if he was its last. In his heart of hearts he might know that Frères, as the family alone referred to it, was an oasis of discarded practices. Frères would see him out, but Frères had run its natural course. True, there was daughter Georgie by his first wife, Sue, but Georgie's most recent known address was an ashram outside San Francisco. Banking had never loomed large on her agenda.

Yet in appearance Brue was anything but obsolete. He was well-built and cautiously good-looking, with a broad freckled brow and a Scotsman's mop of wiry red-brown hair that he had somehow tamed and parted. He had the assurance of wealth but none of its arrogance. His facial features, when not battened down for professional inscrutability, were affable and, despite a lifetime in banking or because of it, refreshingly unlined. When Germans called him typically English he would let out a hearty laugh and promise to bear the insult with Scottish fortitude. If he was a dying species, he was also secretly rather pleased with himself on account of it: Tommy Brue, salt of the earth, good man on a dark night, no highflier but all the better for it, first-rate wife, marvelous value at the dinner table and plays a decent game of golf. Or so the word went, he believed, and so it should.

Having taken a last look at the closing markets and calculated their impact on the bank's holdings—the usual Friday-night sag, nothing to get hot under the collar about—Brue shut down his computer and ran an eye over the stack of folders that Frau Ellenberger had earmarked for his attention.

All week long he had wrestled with the nigh-incomprehensible complexities of the modern banker's world, where knowing who you were actually lending money to was about as likely as knowing the man who had printed it. His priorities for these Friday séances, by contrast, were determined as much by mood as necessity. If Brue was feeling benign, he might spend the evening reorganizing a client's charitable trust at no charge; if skittish, a stud farm, a health spa or a chain of casinos. Or if it was the season for number crunching, a skill he had acquired by hard industry rather than family genes, he would likely play himself Mahler while he pondered the prospectuses of brokers, venture capital houses and competing pension funds.

Tonight, however, he enjoyed no such freedom of choice. A valued client had become the target of an investigation by the Hamburg Stock Exchange, and although Brue had been assured by Haug von Westerheim, the committee's chairman, that no summons would materialize, he felt obliged to immerse himself in the latest twists of the affair. But first, sitting back in his chair, he relived the improbable moment when old Haug had breached his own iron rules of confidentiality:

In the marbled splendor of the Anglo-German Club a sumptuous black-tie dinner is at its height. The best and brightest of Hamburg's financial community are celebrating one of their own. Tommy Brue is sixty tonight, and he'd better believe it, for as his father Edward Amadeus liked to say: *Tommy, my son, arithmetic is the one part of our business that doesn't lie.* The mood is euphoric, the food good, the wine better, the rich are happy and Haug von Westerheim, septuagenarian fleet owner, power broker, Anglophile and wit, is proposing Brue's health.

"Tommy, dear boy, we have decided you have been reading too much Oscar Wilde," he pipes in English, champagne flute in hand as he stands before a portrait of the Queen when young. "You heard of Dorian Gray perhaps? We think so. We think you have taken a leaf out of Dorian Gray's book. We think that in the vaults of your bank is the hideous portrait of Tommy at his true age today. Meanwhile, unlike your dear Queen, you decline to age graciously, but sit smiling at us like a twenty-five-year-old elf, exactly as you smiled at us when you arrived here from Vienna seven years ago in order to deprive us of our hard-earned riches."

The applause continues as Westerheim takes the elegant hand of Brue's wife, Mitzi, and, with additional gallantry because she is Viennese, kisses it, and informs the gathering that her beauty, unlike Brue's, is indeed eternal. Swept up with honest emotion, Brue rises from his seat with the intention of grasping Westerheim's hand in return, but the old man, intoxicated as much by his triumph as the wine, enfolds him in a bear hug, and whispers huskily into his ear: "Tommy, dear boy . . . that inquiry about a certain client of yours . . . it shall be attended to . . . first we postpone for technical reasons . . . then we drop it in the Elbe . . . happy birthday, Tommy, my friend . . . you are a decent fellow . . ."

Pulling on his half-frame spectacles, Brue studied anew the charges against his client. Another banker, he supposed, would by now have called Westerheim and thanked him for his quiet word, thereby holding him to it. But Brue hadn't done that. He couldn't bring himself to saddle the old boy with a rash promise made in the heat of his sixtieth birthday.

Taking up a pen, he scribbled a note to Frau Ellenberger: *First thing Monday, kindly call Ethics Committee Secretariat and ask whether a date has been set. Thanks! TB.*

Done, he thought. Now the old boy can choose in peace whether to push ahead with the hearing or kill it.

The second of the evening's must-do's was Mad Marianne, as Brue called her, but only to Frau Ellenberger. The surviving widow of a prosperous Hamburg timber merchant, Marianne was Brue Frères's longest-running soap opera, the client who makes all the clichés of private banking come true. In tonight's episode, she has recently undergone a religious conversion at the hands of a thirty-year-old Danish Lutheran pastor, and is on the brink of renouncing her worldly goods—more pertinently, one-thirtieth of the bank's reserves—in favor of a mysterious not-for-profit foundation under his pastoral control.

The results of a private inquiry commissioned by Brue on his own initiative lie before him and are not encouraging. The pastor was recently charged with fraud but acquitted when witnesses failed to come forward. He has fathered love children by several women. But how is poor Brue the banker to break this to his besotted client without losing her account? Mad Marianne has a low tolerance of bad news at the best of times, as he has more than once discovered to his cost. It has taken all his charm—short of the ultimate, he would assure you!—to stop her moving her account to some sweet-tongued child at Goldman Sachs. There is a son who stands to lose a fortune and Marianne has moments of adoring him, but—another twist!—he is presently in rehab in the Taunus hills. A discreet trip to Frankfurt may prove to be the answer . . .

Brue scribbles a second note to his ever-loyal Frau Ellenberger: *Please contact director of clinic, and establish whether boy is in a fit state to receive visitor (me!)*.

Distracted by the mutterings of the telephone system beside his desk, Brue glanced at the pin lights. If the incoming call was on his unlisted hotline, he'd take it. It wasn't, so he turned to the Frères's draft six-monthly report, which, though healthy, needed sparkle. He had not engaged with it long before the telephone system again distracted him.

Was this a new message, or had the earlier mutterings somehow insinuated themselves into

his memory? At seven on a Friday evening? The
open line? Must be a wrong number. Giving in
to curiosity, he touched the replay button. First
came an electronic beep, cut off by Frau Ellenberger courteously advising the caller in German, then English, to leave a message or call
again during business hours.

Then a woman's voice, young, German, and
pure as a choirboy's.

The staple of your private banker's life, Brue
liked to pontificate after a scotch or two in ami-
able company, was not, as one might reasonably
expect, cash. It wasn't bull markets, bear markets, hedge funds or derivatives. It was cock-up.
It was the persistent, he would go so far as to say
the *permanent* sound, not to put too fine an edge
on it, of excrement hitting your proverbial fan.
So if you didn't happen to like living in a state of
unremitting siege, the odds were that private
banking wasn't for you. He had made the same
point with some success in his prepared speech in
reply to old Westerheim.

And as a veteran of such cock-ups, Brue over
the years had developed two distinct responses to
the moment of impact. If he was in a board
meeting with the eyes of the world on him, he
would rise to his feet, shove his thumbs into his

waistband and meander round the room wearing an expression of exemplary calm.

Unobserved, he was more likely to favor his second option, which was to freeze in the position in which the news had hit him, flicking at his lower lip with his forefinger, which was what he did now while he played the message a second time and then a third, starting with the initial beep.

"Good evening. My name is Annabel Richter, I am a lawyer, and I wish to speak personally to Mr. Tommy Brue as soon as possible on behalf of a client I represent."

Represent but do not name, Brue methodically notes for the third time. A crisp, but southerly German tone, educated and impatient of circumlocution.

"My client has instructed me to pass his best wishes to a Mr."—she pauses, as if consulting a script—"to a Mr. *Lipizzaner*. I repeat that. The name is *Lipizzaner*. Like the horses, yes, Mr. Brue? Those famous white horses of the Spanish Riding School in Vienna, where your bank was formerly situated? I think your bank knows Lipizzaners very well."

Her tone lifts. A factual message about white horses becomes a choirboy in distress.

"Mr. Brue, my client has *very* little time at his disposal. I naturally do not wish to say more on the telephone. It is also possible you are more familiar with his position than I am, which will expedite matters. I would therefore be grateful if you would call me back on my cell phone on receipt of this message so that we can make an appointment to meet."

She could have stopped there, but she doesn't. The choirboy's song takes on a sharper edge:

"If it's late at night, that's acceptable, Mr. Brue. Even *very* late. I saw a light just now as I went past your office. Maybe you personally are no longer at work, but someone else is. If so, please will that person kindly pass this message to Mr. Tommy Brue as a matter of urgency, because nobody but Mr. Tommy Brue is empowered to act in the matter. Thank you for your time."

And thank you for *your* time, Frau Annabel Richter, thought Brue, rising to his feet and, with thumb and finger still fastened on his lower lip, heading for the bay window as if it were the nearest means of escape.

Yes indeed, my bank knows Lipizzaners *very* well, madam, if by *bank* you mean myself and my one confidante, Frau Elli, and not another living soul. My *bank* would pay top dollar to see the last of its surviving Lipizzaners gallop over the horizon, back to Vienna where they came from, never to return. Perhaps you know that too.

A sickening thought came at him. Or perhaps it had been with him these seven years, and only now decided to step out of the shadows. Would *top dollar* actually be what you're after, Frau Annabel Richter—you and your sainted client who is so short of time?

Is this a blackmail job you're pulling, by any remote chance?

And are you perhaps, with your choirboy purity, and your air of professional high purpose, dropping a hint to me—you and your accomplice, sorry, *client*—that Lipizzaner horses possess the curious property of being born jet black and only turning white with age—which was how they came to lend their name to a certain type of exotic bank account inspired by the eminent Edward Amadeus Brue, OBE, my beloved late father whom in all other respects I continue to revere as the very pillar of banking probity, during his final salad days in Vienna when black money from the collapsing Evil Empire was hemorrhaging through the fast-fraying Iron Curtain by the truckload?

Brue took a slow tour round the room.

But why on earth did you do it, dear father of mine?

Why, when all your life you traded on your

good name and that of your forebears, and lived by it in private as well as in public, in the highest traditions of Scottish caution, canniness and dependability: Why put all that at risk for the sake of a bunch of crooks and carpetbaggers from the East whose one achievement had been to plunder their country's assets at the moment when it had most need of them?

Why throw open your bank to them—your beloved bank, your most precious thing? *Why* offer safe haven to their ill-gained loot, along with unprecedented terms of secrecy and protection?

Why stretch every norm and regulation to its snapping point and beyond, in a desperate, and as Brue had perceived it, even at the time, reckless attempt to set himself up as Vienna's banker of choice to a bunch of Russian gangsters?

All right, you hated communism and communism was on its deathbed. You couldn't wait for the funeral. But the crooks you were being so nice to were part of the regime!

No names needed, comrades! Just give us your loot for five years and we'll give you a number! And when you next come and see us your Lipizzaners will be lily-white, full-grown, runaway investments! We do it just like the Swissies, but we're Brits so we do it better!

Except we don't, thought Brue sadly, hands linked behind his back as he paused to peer out the bay window.

We don't, because great men who lose their marbles in old age die; because money relocates itself and so do banks; and because strange people called regulators appear on the scene and the past goes away. Except that it never quite does, does it? A few words from a choirboy voice and it all comes galloping home.

Fifty feet beneath him the armored cavalry of Europe's richest city roared homeward to embrace its children, eat, watch television, make love and go to sleep. On the lake, skiffs and small yachts skimmed through the red dusk.

She's out there, he thought. She saw my light burning.

She's out there practicing her scales with her so-called client while they argue the toss about how much they're going to sting me for not blowing the whistle on the Lipizzaner accounts.

It is also possible that you are more familiar with my client's position than I am.

Well, it's also possible I'm not, Frau Annabel Richter. And to be frank I don't want to be, although it looks as though I must.

And since you will tell me nothing more about your client by way of the telephone—a reticence that I appreciate—and since I possess no super-sensory powers and am therefore unlikely to identify him from among the half dozen Lipizzaner survivors—assuming there are any—who have not been shot, jailed or have simply forgotten in their cups where in heaven they locked away those odd few million, I have no alternative, in the best tradition of blackmail, but to accede to your request.

He dialed her number.

"Richter."

"This is Tommy Brue of Brue's Bank. Good evening, Frau Richter."

"Good evening, Mr. Brue. I would like to speak to you just as soon as it is convenient, please."

Like now, for instance. With a bit less melody, and a bit more cutting edge, than when she had been pleading for his attention.

The Atlantic Hotel lay ten minutes' walk from the bank, along a crowded gravel footpath that skirted the lake. Beside it a second path ticked and hissed to the oaths of homebound cyclists. A chill breeze had got up, and the sky had turned blue-black. Long drops of rain were starting to fall. In Hamburg, they call them bundles of thread. Seven years ago when Brue was new to the city, his progress through the throng might have been retarded by the last of his British diffidence. Tonight he cut his own furrow, and kept an elbow ready for predatory umbrellas.

At the hotel entrance, a red-cloaked doorman raised his top hat to him. In the lobby, Herr Schwarz the concierge glided to his side and led him to the table that Brue favored for clients who preferred to talk their business away from the bank. It lay in the farthest corner between a marble column and oil paintings of Hanseatic ships, under the liverish gaze of the second Kaiser Wilhelm, rendered in sea-blue tiles.

"I'm expecting a lady I haven't had the pleasure of meeting before, Peter," Brue confided, with a smile of male complicity. "A Frau Richter. I have a suspicion she's young. Kindly make sure she's also beautiful."

"I shall do my best," Herr Schwarz promised gravely, richer by twenty euros.

Out of nowhere, Brue was reminded of a painful conversation he had had with his daughter, Georgie, when she was all of nine years old. He had been explaining that Mummy and Daddy still loved each other, but were going to live apart. It was better to live apart in a loving relationship than quarrel, he had told her, on the advice of a psychiatrist he loathed. And how two happy homes were better than one unhappy one. And how Georgie would be able to see Mummy and Daddy as often as she wanted, just not together like before. But Georgie was more interested in her new puppy.

"If you'd only got one Austrian schilling left in the whole world, what would you do with it?" she demanded, thoughtfully scratching its tummy.

"Why, invest it, of course, darling. What would *you* do?"

"Tip someone," she replied.

Mystified more by himself than by Georgie, Brue tried to work out why he should be punishing himself with the story now. Must be the similarity of their voices, he decided, with an eye to the swing doors. Will she be wired? Will her "client," if she's bringing him, be wired? Well, if so, they'll be out of luck.

He reminded himself of the last time he'd met a blackmailer: another hotel, another woman, British and living in Vienna. Prevailed upon by a Frères client who wouldn't trust his problem to anyone else, Brue had met her for tea in the discreet pavilions of the Sacher. She was a stately madame, dressed in widow's weeds. Her girl was called Sophie.

"She's one of my best, Sophie is, so naturally I'm ashamed," she had explained from under the brim of her black straw hat. "Only she's thinking of going to the newspapers, you see. I've told her not to, but she won't listen, her being so young. He's got some rough ways with him, your friend has, not all of them nice. Well, nobody wants to read about themselves, do they? Not in the newspapers. Not when they're managing director of a big public company, it's hurtful."

But Brue had taken prior counsel from the Viennese chief of police, who happened also to be a Frères client. On the policeman's advice, he meekly consented to a swingeing sum of hush-money while Vienna's plainclothes detectives recorded the conversation from a nearby table.

This time round, however, he had no chief of police on his side. The intended target was not a client, but himself.

In the great hall of the Atlantic, as in the street outside, it was rush hour. From his vantage point Brue observed at his supposed ease the arriving and departing guests. Some wore furs and boas, some the funereal uniform of the modern executive, others the torn jeans of millionaire hobos.

A procession of elderly men in dinner jackets and women in sequined ball dresses emerged from an inner corridor, led by a page boy pushing a trolley of bouquets wrapped in cellophane. Somebody rich and old is having a birthday, thought Brue, and wondered for a moment whether it was one of his clients and had Frau

Elli sent a bottle? Probably no older than me, he
thought bravely.

Did people really think of him as old? Probably they did. His first wife, Sue, used to complain that he had been *born* old. Well, sixty had
always been in the contract, if you were lucky
enough to get there. What was it Georgie had
once said to him, when she started going Bud-
dhist? "The cause of death is birth."

He glanced at his gold wristwatch, a gift from
Edward Amadeus on his twenty-first. In two minutes she'll be late, but lawyers and bankers are
never late; nor, he presumed, are blackmailers.

On the other side of the swing doors a mistral
was gusting down the street. The top-hatted
doorman's cloak flapped like useless wings as he
scurried from one limousine to another. A dramatic rainstorm broke as cars and people vanished in a milky mist. Out of it, like the sole
survivor of an avalanche, stepped a small, stocky
figure in shapeless clothes and a scarf wound
round her head and neck. For an appalled moment Brue fancied she had slung a child across
her shoulders, until he realized it was a man-
sized rucksack.

She mounted the steps, let the swing doors take
her, stepped into the lobby and stopped. She was
holding up the passage of people behind her but if
she knew, she didn't care. She removed her rain-

spotted spectacles, pulled an end of the scarf from
the depths of her anorak, polished the spectacles
and replaced them on her nose. Herr Schwarz addressed her, she gave him a curt nod. Both peered
in Brue's direction. Herr Schwarz made to escort
her, but she shook her head. Shifting her rucksack
to one shoulder, she advanced on him between the
tables, eyes fixed straight ahead of her, ignoring
the other guests on her way.

No makeup, not a square inch of flesh from
the throat down, Brue recorded as he rose to
greet her. Firm, fluid movement of a small, capa-
ble body inside the frumpish gear. A bit martial,
but women these days were. Round spectacles,
frameless, catching the chandeliers. No blink
rate. Child's skin. About thirty years younger
than me and a foot shorter, but blackmailers
come in all sizes and get a little younger every
day. A choirboy face to go with the choirboy
voice. No visible accomplice. Navy blue jeans,
army boots. A pocket beauty in disguise. Tough
but vulnerable; hellbent on concealing her female
warmth and not succeeding. Georgie.

"Frau Richter? Marvelous. I'm Tommy Brue.
What can I get for you?"

The hand so small that he instinctively relaxed
his grasp.

"Do they have water here?" she asked, glowering up at him through her spectacles.

"Of course." He beckoned a waiter. "Did you walk?"

"Cycled. Still, please. No lemon. Room temperature."

She sat opposite him, upright at the center of her leather throne, hands braced against its arms, knees tight together and her rucksack at her feet while she studied him: first his hands, then his gold watch and his shoes, then his eyes, but only briefly. She seemed to see nothing that surprised her. And Brue in return subjecting her to an equally searching inspection, if a more furtive one: the tutored way she sipped her water, elbow in, forearm across the upper body; her self-confidence in the rich surroundings that she appeared determined to disapprove of; her covert air of breeding; the hidden stylist who can't quite hide.

She had removed her headscarf to reveal a woolen beret. An errant hank of gold-brown hair hung across her brow. She returned it to captivity before taking a pull of water and resuming her inspection of him. Her eyes, enlarged by the spectacles, were gray-green and unflinching. *Honey-flecked*, he remembered: Where had he read that? In one of the dozen novels always at Mitzi's bedside. A small, high bosom, deliberately illegible.

Brue extracted a calling card from a pocket in the blue silk lining of his Randall's jacket and, with his courteous smile, handed it to her across the table.

"Why *Frères?*" she demanded. No rings, fingernails childishly short.

"It was my great-grandfather's idea."

"Was he French?"

"I'm afraid not. He just wanted to be," Brue replied, trotting out his stock answer. "He was Scottish. A lot of Scots feel closer to France than England."

"Did he have brothers?"

"No. Neither do I, I'm afraid."

She ducked to her rucksack, unzipped a compartment and then another. Over her shoulder, Brue noted in fast order: paper tissues, a bottle of contact lens lotion, a cell phone, keys, a legal pad, credit cards and a buff file flagged and numbered like a barrister's brief. No identifiable tape recorder or microphone, but with the technology these days, how could you be sure? And anyway, under that garb, she could be wearing a twenty-five-pound bomb belt.

She handed him a card.

SANCTUARY NORTH, Brue read. *A Charitable Christian Foundation for the protection of stateless and displaced persons in the Region of North Germany.* Offices in the east of town. Phone and fax numbers, e-mail. Commerzbank account number. Have a quiet word with their city manager on Monday if I need to, check her credit rating. *Annabel Richter, Legal Counsel. Never believe a beautiful woman, Tommy. They're a criminal class, the best there is.* His father's words, coming back to haunt him.

"You'd better take a look at this too," she said, thrusting an identity card at him.

"Oh come, why should I do that?" he protested, although the same thought had occurred to him.

"Maybe I'm not who I say I am."

"Really? Who else might you be?"

"Some of my clients get people coming to them claiming to be lawyers when they're not."

"How shocking. My goodness. I do hope that never happens to me. Well, of course, it may have done, mayn't it? And I wouldn't know. Awful thought," he declared with false levity, but if he expected her to join him in it, he was disappointed.

Her photograph showed her with her hair let down, older spectacles and the same face without the glower. Annabel Richter born Freiburg im Breisgau, 1977, which made her about as young as she could be for a German lawyer, if that was what she was. She had slumped back in her chair like a boxer relaxing between rounds, while continuing to watch him through her granny spectacles down the line of her bulked-out, buttoned-down, prim little body.

"Heard of us?" she demanded.

"I'm sorry?"

"Sanctuary North. Have you heard of our work? Has word of it reached you at all?"

"I'm afraid not."

Slowly shaking her head, she gazed round the lobby in disbelief. At the elderly couples in their finery. At the raucous young rich in the bar. At the house pianist playing love songs nobody was listening to.

"And your charity is financed by whom?" Brue inquired in his most practical tone.

She shrugged. "Couple of churches. State of Hamburg when it's feeling virtuous. We get by."

"And how long have you been in business—your organization, I mean?"

"We're not in business. We're pro bono. Five years."

"And you yourself?"

"Two. Give or take."

"Full-time? You have no other practice?" Meaning, Are you moonlighting? Are you doing a bit of blackmail on the side?

She had tired of his questioning.

"I have a client, Mr. Brue. Officially he's represented by Sanctuary North. However, as of a short time ago he has formally empowered me as his personal lawyer in all matters relating to your bank, and given his consent for me to get in touch with you. Which I am now doing."

"Consent?" His screwed-on smile widening.

"Instructions. What's the difference? As I indicated to you on the phone, my client's situation in Hamburg is sensitive. There are limits to what he is willing to tell me, also limits to what I am able to tell you. My belief, after spending a number of hours in his company, is that the little he tells me is true. Not all the truth, but maybe a small part of it, edited for my consumption, but true all the same. That's a judgment we have to make in my organization. We have to be content with the little we get and work with it. We'd rather be fooled than cynical. That's who we are. That's what we stand for," she added defiantly, leaving Brue with the unspoken accusation that he would prefer things the other way round.

"I hear what you're saying," he assured her. "I respect it." He was fencing. He knew how to do that.

"Our clients are not what you would consider *normal* clients, Mr. Brue."

"Really? I'm not at all sure I've met a normal client." A joke that she again refused to share.

"Our clients are basically more like what Frantz Fanon called the wretched of the earth. You know the book?"

"Heard of, but not actually read, I'm afraid."

"They're effectively stateless. They're frequently in trauma. They're as frightened of us as they are of the world they have entered and the world they have left behind."

"I see." He didn't.

"My client believes, rightly or wrongly, that you are his salvation, Mr. Brue. You're why he came to Hamburg. Thanks to you, he will be able to remain in Germany, obtain legal status and study. Without you he will return to hell."

Brue considered an "Oh dear" or a "How very sad" but meeting her unyielding gaze, thought better of it.

"He believes he has only to mention Mr. Lipizzaner and present you with a certain reference number—referencing who or what I do not know, and perhaps he doesn't either—and abracadabra, all doors will be open to him."

"May I ask how long he has been here?"

"Call it a couple of weeks."

"And he took this long to get in touch with me, although I was the reason for his coming, allegedly? I find that a little hard to understand."

"He arrived here in bad shape and terrified, not

knowing a single human being. It's his first time in the West. He speaks no word of German."

He started to say "I see" again, but changed his mind.

"Also, for reasons I cannot begin to unravel, he detests the fact that this approach to you is in any way necessary. Half the time at least, he would prefer to remain in denial and starve. Unfortunately, given his situation here, you're his only chance."

It was Brue's turn, but for what? *When you're in a hole, don't dig, Tommy, just put up more defenses.* His father again.

"Forgive me, Frau Richter," he began respectfully, though in no way conceding he had done anything requiring her forgiveness. "Who or what precisely gave your client the information—the *impression,* I prefer to say—that my bank could perform this miracle for him?"

"It's not only the bank, Mr. Brue. It's you personally."

"I'm afraid I'm somewhat puzzled as to how that can be. I was asking you about the source of his information."

"Maybe a lawyer told him. Another of *us,*" she added self-deprecatingly.

He selected a different approach. "And in

what *language,* may I ask, did you elicit this information from your client?"

"About Mr. Lipizzaner?"

"About other things too. My name, for one."

Her young face was hard as rock. "My client would say your question was immaterial."

"May I ask whether there were intermediaries present when he instructed you? A qualified interpreter, for instance? Or are you able to communicate with him directly?"

The hank of hair had once more escaped her beret, but this time she grabbed hold of it and twisted it while she scowled round the room. "Russian," she said—and with a sudden surge of interest in him: "Do *you* speak Russian?"

"Tolerably. Quite well, actually," he replied.

The admission seemed to trigger some kind of female self-awareness in her, for she smiled and, for the first time, faced him directly.

"Where did you learn it?"

"I? Oh, Paris, I'm afraid. Very decadent."

"*Paris!* Why Paris?"

"Sent there by my father. It was something he insisted on. Three years at the Sorbonne and a lot of bearded émigré poets. How about you?"

The moment of connection had passed. She was delving in her rucksack. "He's given me a reference," she said. "Some special number that will chime Mr. Lipizzaner's bells. Maybe it chimes yours too."

She ripped a page off her legal pad and gave it to him. Six digits, handwritten, he assumed by herself. Beginning with 77, which was how Lipizzaners were denoted.

"Does it fit?" she demanded, challenging him with her unforgiving stare.

"Does what fit what?"

"Is the number I have just given you a reference in use at Brue Frères Bank? Or is it not?" As if addressing a recalcitrant child.

Brue considered her question—or more accurately, how to avoid it. "Well now, Frau Richter, you place heavy emphasis on client confidentiality as I do," he began easily. "My bank doesn't broadcast the identity of its customers, or the nature of their transactions. I'm sure you respect that. We disclose nothing we're not obliged to disclose in law. If you say Mr. Lipizzaner to me, I hear you. If you quote a reference number to me, I consult our records." He paused to allow some acknowledgment but her face was set in resolute opposition. "You yourself, I am sure, are as honest as the day," he went on. "Of course you are. However, you'd be surprised how many tricksters there are in the world." He signaled to the waiter.

"He's not a trickster, Mr. Brue."

"Of course not. He's your client."

They were standing. Who had stood first, he didn't know. Probably she had. He hadn't expected their meeting to be so short and, despite the chaos raging in him, he found himself wishing it were longer. "I'll call you when I've completed my researches. How's that?"

"When?"

"It depends. If I draw a blank, then very little time at all."

"Tonight?"

"Possibly."

"Are you going back to your bank now?"

"Why not? If it's a compassionate situation, as you seem to suggest, one does what one can. Obviously. We all do."

"He's drowning. All you have to do is hold out your hand."

"Yes, well, I'm afraid that's a cry I hear rather often in my profession."

His tone sparked her anger. "He *trusts* you," she said.

"How can he, if we've never met?"

"All right, he *doesn't* trust you. But his father did. And you're all he's got."

"Well, it's very confusing. For both of us, I'm sure."

Shouldering her rucksack, she marched off down the lobby to the swing doors. On the other

side of them, the top-hatted doorman was waiting
with her bicycle. The rain was still pelting down.
She extracted a shell hat from the wooden box
strapped to the handlebars, set it on her head,
buckled it, then pulled on a pair of waterproof
trousers. Without a glance or wave, she was gone.

The Frères strong room lay in a semi-basement
at the back of the building. Twelve feet by eight
were the dimensions, and there had been bad
jokes with the architect about how many default-
ing creditors it could contain, hence its house
nickname of oubliette. With the advance of
modern technology, other private banks might
have dispensed altogether with archives and even
strong rooms, but Frères carried its history on its
back and here was what remained of it, shipped
by secure lorry from Vienna and laid to rest in a
white-painted brick mausoleum pulsing with de-
humidifiers and guarded by consoles of lights
and digits that required a code, a thumbprint
and a couple of soothing words. The insurance
company had urged iris recognition, but something in Brue had revolted.

Once inside, he picked his way down an alley
of musty safe boxes to a steel cabinet perched
against the end wall. Entering a code, he opened
it and worked through the hanging folders until,

consulting the page torn from Annabel Richter's notebook, he found the folder he was looking for. It was colored a faded orange and held together by clips of sprung metal. A panel on its spine gave the reference but no name. By the sallow glow of the ceiling lights he turned the pages at an even speed, not so much reading as scanning them. Again groping inside the cabinet, he emerged this time with a shoebox of dog-eared cards. He flicked through them and extracted the card that bore the same reference as the file.

KARPOV, he read. *Grigori Borisovich, Colonel Red Army. 1982. Founder Member.*

Your vintage year, he thought. My poisoned chalice. Never heard of a Karpov, but I wouldn't have done, would I? The Lipizzaners were your private stable.

"All movements on this account and all client instructions to be reported immediately and personally to EAB before any action is taken. Edward Amadeus Brue," he read.

Personally to you. Russian crooks being your personal preserve. Lesser crooks—investment managers, insurance brokers, banking colleagues—may sit in the waiting room for half an hour and end up settling for the chief cashier, but Russian crooks, on your personal orders, go direct to EAB.

Not printed. Not rubber-stamped by Frau Elli, at that time your young, devoted and very private secretary, but hand-inscribed by you in fine blue strokes of your ubiquitous fountain pen, ending with your signature in full, lest the casual reader—not, God knows, that there ever was one—happened to be unaware that EAB stood for Edward Amadeus Brue, OBE, the banker who throughout his life never bent the rules, until the end of it, when he broke them all.

Relocking the cabinet, then the strong room, Brue wedged the file under his arm and climbed the elegant staircase to the room where two hours earlier his weekend peace had been so brutally disturbed. The detritus of Mad Marianne strewn across his desk seemed a year ago, the ethical concerns of the Hamburg Stock Exchange irrelevant.

And yet again: *Why?*

You didn't need the money, dear father of mine, none of us did. All you needed was to stay as you were: the rich, respected doyen of the Viennese banking world, soundness your watchword.

And when I barged into your office one evening and asked Frau Ellenberger to leave us alone—Fräulein, as she then was, and a jolly pretty fräulein too—and purposefully closed the door behind her, and poured us both a large scotch, and told you I was sick to the heart of hearing us referred to as Mafia Frères, what did you do?

You screwed on your banker's smile—all right, a painful version of it, I grant you—and you patted me on the shoulder and told me there were secrets in this world that even a man's beloved son is better off not knowing.

Your words. A total snow job. Even Fräulein Ellenberger knew more than I did, but you'd sworn her to silence from the day she began her noviciate.

And you had the last laugh as well, didn't you? You were dying by then, but that was another of your secrets I wasn't allowed to share. Just when it was beginning to look like a close-run race between the Grim Reaper and the Viennese authorities as to who would get you first, enter old Westerheim's beloved Queen of England, who out of a clear blue sky had decided, for no reason known to mortal man, to command you to the British embassy, where with due pomp her loyal ambassador would appoint you a Member of the Order of the British Empire, an honor, I was afterwards informed, although you never *personally* told me, that you had coveted all your life.

And at the investiture you wept.

And so did I.

And so would your wife, my mother, have

wept if she'd been around, but in her case the Grim Reaper had won long ago.

And by the time you joined her in the Happy Bank in the Sky, which with a return to your fabled prudence you accomplished a mere two months later, the move to Hamburg looked more attractive than ever.

Our clients are not what you would consider normal *clients, Mr. Brue.*

Chin in hand, Brue flipped back and forth through the skimpy, tight-lipped file. The index had been doctored, papers removed to protect the holder's identity. An encounter report—only Lipizzaners had them—recorded the time and place of meetings between rogue client and rogue banker, but not the subject matter.

The account owner's capital was invested in a Bahamian offshore management fund, standard practice for Lipizzaners.

The management fund belonged to a Liechtenstein foundation.

The account owner's share of the Liechtenstein foundation was in the form of bearer bonds lodged with Frères.

These bonds were to be surrendered to the approved claimant on production of the relevant account number, satisfactory papers of identity and what was coyly defined as "the necessary instrument of access."

For further details, see account owner's personal file, except that you can't because it went up in smoke on the same day that Edward Amadeus Brue, OBE, formally handed his son the keys to the bank.

In short, no formal transfer and, as near as made no odds, no due process: just a "hullo-it's-me" from the lucky owner of the reference number, a driving license and the so-called *instrument,* and an undeclared slide of junk bonds from one grimy paw to another had taken place—your money launderer's dream scenario.

"Except," Brue muttered aloud.

Except that, in the case of Colonel Grigori Borisovich Karpov, formerly of the Red Army, the "approved claimant"—if that's what he turns out to be—is one of the wretched of the earth who detests the fact that his approach is necessary, and half the time would rather starve. He's also drowning, and all I have to do is hold out my hand. He believes that I am his salvation, and without me he will return to hell.

But it was Annabel Richter's hand he was remembering: no rings, the fingernails childishly short.

The traffic had died. Friday. Mitzi's bridge
night. Brue glanced at his watch. Good lord,
where had the time gone? However did it get so
late? But what's late? Sometimes their games
went on into the wee hours. He hoped she was
winning. It mattered to her. Not the money, the
winning. His daughter, Georgie, was all the other
way. A softie, Georgie was. Never happy unless
she was losing. Dump her blindfold in a roomful
of chaps and, if there's one of them who's a sure-
fire no-hoper, you can bet your boots she'll have
palled up with him in minutes.

And Annabel Richter of Sanctuary North,
which are you? A winner or a loser? If you're saving the world, probably the latter. But you'll go
down with all guns blazing, that's for sure. Edward Amadeus would have loved you.

Without further thought Brue once more dialed her cell phone.

3

The first intimation of Issa's presence in the city penetrated the cramped quarters of the Foreign Acquisitions Unit of Hamburg's grandly named Office for the Protection of the Constitution—in plain language, domestic intelligence service—on the late afternoon of his fourth day of roaming the city, at about the moment when he was shivering and perspiring on Leyla's doorstep, begging to come in.

The Unit, as it was disparagingly known to its reluctant hosts, was housed not in the main body of the protectors' out-of-town complex, but on the farthest side of the courtyard from it, and as close to the razor-wire perimeter as anyone could get without actually cutting himself. The unlovely home of the sixteen-strong team, with its skimpy complement of researchers, watchers, listeners and drivers, was a disused former SS riding stables with a defunct clock tower and an unobstructed view of car tires and garden allotments gone wild.

Wished on the protectors by Berlin's recently formed Joint Steering Committee, which claimed as its mission the remodeling of Germany's fragmented and famously inept intelligence community, the Unit was regarded as the harbinger of a plan to do away with precious demarcations in the name of a streamlined, integrated organization. Though on paper under local command and lacking the powers granted to the Federal Police, they were accountable neither to the protectors' Hamburg station, nor to their headquarters in Cologne, but to the same vaporous, all-powerful body in Berlin that had imposed them on the protectors in the first place.

Of whom or what was this omnipotent body in Berlin then composed? Its very existence struck fear into the heart of Germany's entrenched espiocracy. In name, true, Joint Steering was no more than a bunch of top players drafted from each of the main services, and charged with improving cooperation between them in the wake of a string of near-miss terror plots on German soil. After a gestation period of six months—thus the official version—its recommendations would be passed to the twin power centers of German intelligence, the Ministry of the Interior and the Office of the Chancellor, for their consideration, and that would be pretty well that.

Or not. For in reality, Joint Steering's remit

was of earth-shaking significance: no less than
the creation of a brand-new system of command-
and-control covering all major and minor intelligence services and, untypically of the Federal
German system until now, presided over by a
new-style intelligence coordinator—czar—with
unprecedented powers.

Who then would this awesome new coordinator be?

No one doubted that he would be selected
from the shadowy ranks of Joint Steering itself.
But from which faction? With Germany's political stability caught in the limbo of a capricious
coalition, which way would he lean? What alle-
giances, what agenda would the coordinator
bring to his formidable task? What promises had
he to keep? And whose voice exactly would he be
listening to when he wielded his new broom?

Would the Federal Police, for example, continue to outstrip the beleaguered protectors in
their long-running power battle for primacy in
the field of domestic intelligence? Would the
Federal Foreign Intelligence Service remain the
only body authorized to operate covertly abroad?
And if so, would it finally purge itself of the dead
wood of ex-soldiers and quasi-diplomats who
cluttered its overseas stations? Fine men, all,
when it came to defending German embassies in
times of civil riot, no doubt, but a lot less adept

at the nuanced business of recruiting and running undercover networks.

No wonder then if, infected by the mood of suspicion and anxiety that swept through the entire German intelligence community, relations between the mysterious interlopers from Berlin and their reluctant Hamburg hosts were at best frigid, affecting even the smallest aspects of their daily intercourse; or that the interest aroused by Issa's appearance on one side of the courtyard should not necessarily be reciprocated on the other. Without the imaginative—some said *over*imaginative—eye of the Unit's volatile Günther Bachmann, indeed, the surreptitious arrival of the man who called himself Issa might never have been spotted at all.

And this Günther Bachmann fellow from Berlin— who was *he,* exactly when he was at home?

If there are people in the world for whom espionage was ever the only possible calling, Bachmann was such a person. The polyglot offspring of a string of mixed marriages contracted by a flamboyant German-Ukrainian woman, and reputedly the only officer of his service not to possess an academic qualification beyond summary expulsion from his secondary school, Bachmann had by the age of thirty run away to sea, trekked the Hindu

Kush, been imprisoned in Colombia and written a thousand-page unpublishable novel.

Yet somehow, in the course of notching up these improbable experiences, he had discovered both his nationhood and his true calling: first as the occasional agent of some far-flung German outpost, then as a covert overseas official without diplomatic rank; in Warsaw for his Polish; in Aden, Beirut, Baghdad and Mogadishu for his Arabic; and in Berlin for his sins, while he cooled his heels after fathering a near-epic scandal of which only the sketchiest outlines had ever reached the gossip mill: excessive zeal, said the rumors; a blackmail attempt too far; a suicide, a German ambassador hastily recalled.

Then cautiously, under yet another name, back to Beirut, to do once more what he had always done better than anyone, if not necessarily according to the book—but since when had "the book" been necessary equipment in Beirut?—namely to trawl, recruit and run, by any means, live agents in the field, which is the gold standard of real intelligence gathering. Eventually even Beirut became too hot for him, and a desk in Hamburg seemed suddenly the safest place—if not to Bachmann, then to his masters in Berlin.

But Bachmann was never the one to be put out to grass. Those who said that Hamburg was a punishment posting didn't know what they were talking about. Now stuck in his midforties, he was a scruffy, explosive mongrel of a man, stocky in the shoulders and frequently with ash on the lapels of his jacket until it was brushed off by the egregious Erna Frey, his long-standing workmate and assistant. He was driven, charismatic and compelling, a workaholic with a knockout smile. He had a mop of sandy hair that was too young for the crisscross wrinkles on his brow. Like an actor, he could blandish, charm or intimidate. He could be sweet-tongued and foul-mouthed in the same sentence.

"I want to keep him loose and keep him walking," he told Erna Frey as they stood shoulder to shoulder in the researchers' dank den in the SS riding stables, watching Maximilian, their star hacker, conjuring successive images of Issa onto his screens. "I want him to talk to whoever he was told to talk to and pray where he was told to pray and sleep wherever they told him to sleep. I don't want anybody interfering with him before we do. Least of all those arseholes across the courtyard."

The first sighting of Issa, if it could be called one, had been of no apparent interest to anybody. It was a search notice issued under European treaty rules by Swedish police headquarters in Stockholm advising all signatories that an illegal Russian immigrant, name, photograph, particulars supplied, had evaded Swedish custody, present whereabouts unknown. A single day might produce half a dozen such notices. In the protectors' operations center across the courtyard, it was duly acknowledged, downloaded, added to rows of similar notices adorning the walls of the recreation room and ignored.

Yet Issa's features must have lodged themselves on the retina of Maximilian's inner eye, because over the next hours, as the atmosphere inside Bachmann's researchers' den thickened, team members from other corners of the stables began to trickle in to share the excitement. At the age of twenty-seven, Maximilian had a near-total stammer, a memory like a twelve-volume lexicon and an intuition for cobbling together extraneous scraps of information. But it was long past suppertime before he flopped back in his chair and linked his long, freckled fingers behind his ginger head.

"Play it again, please, Maximilian," Bachmann ordered, breaking the churchlike silence with a rare snatch of English.

Maximilian blushed and played it again:

Issa's Swedish police mug shot, full-face, both profiles, with WANTED blazoned over it and his name in capitals like a warning: KARPOV, Issa.

A ten-line text in thick type describing him as an escaped Muslim militant, born Grozny,

Chechnya, twenty-three years ago, reportedly violent, approach with caution.

Lips pressed tight together. No smile offered or permitted.

Eyes stretched wide open in pain after days and nights in the stinking blackness of the container. Unshaven, emaciated, desperate.

"How do we know he gave his real name?" Bachmann asked.

"He didn't." Erna Frey this time, while Maximilian was still struggling to answer. "He gave a Chechen name but his mates from the container ratted on him. 'He's Issa Karpov,' they said. 'The escaped Russian aristocrat.'"

"Aristocrat?"

"It's in the report. His mates decided he was stuck-up. Special somehow. How you can be stuck-up in a container is a secret we have yet to learn."

Maximilian had overcome his stammer. "The Swedish police reckon he went back to the ship and paid off the crew," he burst out, in a great splash of words. "And the ship's last port of call was *Copenhagen*"—the word becoming a positive triumph of will over nature.

Muddied footage of thin bearded man in long dark overcoat, kaffiyeh and zigzag-patterned skullcap dismounting from the rear of lorry at dead of night.

Lorry driver waves.

Departing passenger does not wave back.

Familiar landmarks of Hamburg's main station concourse, rank upon rank of pastel-yellow cabs.

Same thin figure stretched horizontal on station bench.

Same thin figure sitting up, speaking to gesticulating fat man, accepting paper beaker of refreshment from him, sipping from it.

Cross-cut comparisons between Issa's mug shot and enhanced stills of thin bearded man on station bench.

Another still of same thin bearded man standing full length on station concourse.

"The Swedes measured him," Maximilian said, after a couple of tries. "He's tall. Pushing two meters."

On the screen, a virtual measuring stick appears beside the bearded man lying down, then sitting up. The measuring stick reads one meter ninety-three.

"What in heaven's name made you pick on the Hamburg railway station footage?" Bachmann protested. "Somebody gives you a mug shot from Sweden of a man who's gone to Denmark, and you trawl the drunken layabouts at Hamburg railway station? I think I should have you arrested for being psychic!"

Scarlet with pleasure, Maximilian flung up a

hand needlessly for attention, and with the other again clicked on his screen:

Enlarged image of same lorry in railway station concourse, side view, no markings.

Enlarged image of same lorry, rear view. Maximilian zooms in on vehicle registration plate. It is partly covered by a knot of black rag. One side of a European Union emblem and first two figures of a Danish registration visible. Maximilian struggles to speak and fails. His pretty girlfriend, the half-Arab Niki from audio section, speaks for him.

"The Swedes questioned the other stowaways about him," she says while Maximilian nods. "He was on his way to Hamburg. Nowhere else would do. Everything was going to come right for him in Hamburg."

"Did he say *how*?"

"No. He went all secretive and mysterious. His companions thought he was a nutter."

"By the time they got out of that container they were all nutters. What languages does he speak?"

"Russian."

"Just Russian. Not Chechen?"

"Not according to the Swedes. Maybe they didn't try him."

"But *Issa*'s his first name. As in *Jesus*. Jesus Karpov. He's got a Russian surname and a Muslim first name. How in hell did he come by that?"

"Niki didn't christen him, Günther dear," Erna Frey murmurs.

"And no patronymic," Bachmann complains. "What happened to his Russian patronymic? Did he leave it behind him in jail?"

Instead of answering him, Niki took back the story on her lover's behalf: "Maximilian had a brainwave, Günther. He reckoned that if Copenhagen was the ship's next port of call, and Hamburg was the boy's destination, how about checking the video footage on the Hamburg station platform whenever a Copenhagen train came in?"

Sparing as always of his praise, Bachmann affected not to hear her. "Was Issa No-patronymic Karpov the only one to get out of that Danish lorry with the concealed registration plate?"

"He was alone. Right, Maximilian? Solo." Enthusiastic nods from Maximilian. "Nobody else got out of the Danish lorry and the driver stayed inside his cab."

"So tell me who the fat old bastard is."

"Fat bastard?" Niki was thrown momentarily off balance.

"The fat bastard with the paper beaker. An elderly fat bastard talked to our boy on the railway concourse. He wore a black seafarer's cap. Am I the only person to have seen that fat bastard? I am not. Our boy *talked back* to the said elderly fat bastard. In what language did they talk? Russian? Chechen? Arabic? Latin? Ancient Greek? Or does our boy speak German and we don't know it?"

Maximilian again has his arm up. With his other hand he is clicking on footage of the elderly fat bastard, bringing him closer. He plays him in real time, then in slow motion: a bald, burly old man with a military bearing and cavalry boots, ceremoniously proffering a polystyrene or paper beaker. Something quaintly dignified, almost priestly about his gestures. And yes, the elderly fat bastard and our boy are definitely talking back and forth.

"Now show me his wrist."

"Wrist?"

"The boy's," Bachmann snapped. "The boy's right wrist, for Christ's sake, as he takes the coffee. Show it me close."

A fine bracelet, gold or silver. A tiny open book dangling from it.

"Where's Karl? I need Karl," Bachmann shouts, swinging round and opening his arms as if he's been robbed. But Karl is standing right before him: Karl the onetime street kid from Dresden with three juvenile convictions and a degree in social studies. Karl of the timid, help-me smile.

"Go down to the railway station for me, please, Karl. Maybe the chance encounter between the elderly fat bastard and our boy was not chance.

Maybe our boy was getting orders or meeting his connect. Or maybe we're looking at a sad old guy whose best thing in life is giving beakers of coffee to handsome young bums in railway stations at two o'clock in the morning. Talk to the good people who run the mission there for down-and-outs. Ask them whether they know who was it gave our boy that beaker of something in the middle of the night. Maybe he's a regular. Don't show them any photographs or you'll scare them. Use your sweet tongue and steer clear of the railway police. Have a nice fairy story at your fingertips. Maybe the fat old bastard is your long-lost uncle. Maybe you owe him money. Just don't break any porcelain. Be quiet, be invisible, the way you can. Right?"

"Clear."

Bachmann is addressing all of them—Niki, her friend Laura, a couple of street watchers who had followed Karl upstairs, Maximilian, Erna Frey:

"So here's where we are, my friends. We're looking for a man who has no patronymic and no relationship with normality. His record tells us he's a militant Chechen-Russian who does violent crime and bribes his way out of Turkish jail—and what the hell was he doing there anyway?—gives the slip to the Swedish port police, buys himself back onto the boat he comes off, smuggles himself out of Copenhagen docks, charters himself a lorry to Hamburg, accepts a beaker of refreshment from an elderly fat bastard whom he engages in conversation in Christ knows whose language, and wears a gold Koran bracelet. Such a man deserves our considerable respect. Amen?"

Upon which, he stomps back to his office, closely followed as ever by Erna Frey.

Were they married?

In every known respect, Bachmann and Erna Frey were opposites, so perhaps they were. While Bachmann loathed exercise, smoked, swore, drank too much whisky and could settle to nothing if it wasn't work, Erna Frey was tall, fit and frugal, with cropped, sensible hair and a purposeful stride. Saddled with the Christian name of a maiden aunt, and dispatched by wealthy parents to Hamburg's elite convent school for daughters of the eminent, she had emerged laden with the strict German virtues of chastity, industry, piety, sincerity and honor—until a mordant sense of humor and a healthy skepticism put paid to all of them. Another woman might have traded her antiquated first name for a newer model. Not Erna. At tennis tournaments she sliced and volleyed her way to victory over opponents of both sexes. On alpine excursions she outstripped men half her age. Her greatest passion, however, was lone sailing, and she was known to be storing away every penny she earned to buy herself a round-the-world yacht.

Yet at work, this ill-matched pair were husband and wife, sharing the same room, telephones, files, computers and each other's smells and habits. When Bachmann in defiance of regulation lit up one of his odious Russian cigarettes, Erna Frey would cough demonstratively and fling open the windows. But there her protest ended. Bachmann could go on puffing till the room filled up like a fish smokery and she wouldn't say another word. Did they sleep together? According to rumor, they had given sex a try and declared it a disaster area. Yet on nights when they were staying late, they had no hesitation in bunking down together in the cramped emergency bedroom at the end of the corridor.

And when the fledgling team assembled for the first time in the hastily redecorated upper gallery of the stables that was their new home, to be welcomed by Bachmann's favorite choice of Baden wine and Erna Frey's home-cooked wild boar and red berries, the two of them together were so uxorious, interacting so intuitively and well, that it would have come as no surprise to their guests to see them holding hands: until, that is, the moment when Bachmann took it on himself to explain to his newly mustered troops just what the hell it was they had been put on earth to do. His address, by turn ribald and messianic, was part idiosyncratic history lesson and part call to battle. Inevitably, it came to be known as Bachmann's Cantata. It ran as follows:

"When 9/11 happened, there were two ground zeros," he announced, addressing them now from one side of the gallery, now from the back, before popping up like a squat djinni beneath the rafters in front of them, hands punching out the words as he spoke them. "One ground zero was in New York. The other ground zero that you don't hear so much about was right here in Hamburg."

He jabbed an arm at the window.

"That courtyard out there was a hundred feet high in rubble, all of it paper. And our pathetic barons of the German intelligence community were raking through it trying to find out where the hell they'd gone so terribly wrong. We had geniuses from all over the hemisphere fly to this town to offer advice and cover their arses. Top protectors of our sacred constitution from Cologne, God protect us from protectors"—laughter, which he ignored—"espiocrats from our own distinguished foreign intelligence service, fine ladies and gentlemen from our omniscient Bundestag intelligence oversight committee, Americans from more agencies than I ever heard of—sixteen of them at last count—falling over each other to dump the shit on anybody's doorstep but their own. I tell you: so many wise arseholes gave of their wisdom in those weeks that the poor bastards who were trying to run the shop and sweep up the rubble couldn't help wishing they'd dropped by a few weeks earlier. That way there'd have been no Mohammed Atta and no howling monkeys from the media pissing on them."

He took a tour round the gallery, elbows out, fists clenched.

"Hamburg screwed up. Everybody else had screwed up, but Hamburg took the fall." He was buffooning, playing both sides of an imaginary press conference: "'Sir, can you tell us, please: How many Arab speakers precisely does your organization have operating here in town at this time?'" he squawked, hopping to his left. "'At last count, one and a half.'" Hopping to his right: "'Sir, who precisely have you been bugging and following around town in the months leading up to Armageddon?'" Another hop: "'Well, madam, now I come to think of it . . . a couple of Chinese gentlemen suspected of stealing our fine industrial secrets . . . adolescent neo-Nazis who paint swastikas on Jewish gravestones . . . the next generation of the Red Army Fraktion . . . oh, and twenty-eight geriatric ex-communists who want to bring back the dear old GDR.'"

He vanished from view to resurface at the far end of the gallery, a somber man.

"Hamburg is a guilty city," he announced quietly. "Consciously, unconsciously. Maybe Hamburg even *pulled* those hijackers. Did they pick us? Or did we pick them? What signals does Hamburg send out to your average Islamist anti-Zionist terrorist bent on fucking up the Western world? Centuries of anti-Semitism? Hamburg has them. Concentration camps just up the road? Hamburg had them. All right, I'll grant you: Hitler wasn't born in Blankenese. But don't think he couldn't have been. The Baader-Meinhof gang? Ulrike Meinhof, born not far from here, was Hamburg's proud adopted daughter. She even got herself Arab trained. Partied with their crazies and went hijacking with them. Maybe Ulrike was some kind of signal. Too many Arabs love Germans for the wrong reasons. Maybe our hijackers did. We never asked them. And now we never shall."

He let the silence last awhile, then seemed to take heart.

"And then there's the *good* news about Hamburg," he resumed cheerfully. "We're sea people. We're a world-wise, liberal-left, wide-open city-state. We're world-class traders with a world-class port and a world-class nose for profit. Our foreigners aren't strangers to us. We're not some one-horse inland town where foreigners look like Martians. They're part of our landscape. For centuries, millions of Mohammed Atta lookalikes have drunk our beer, screwed our hookers and gone back on their ships. And we haven't said hello and good-bye to them, or asked them what they're doing here, because we take them for granted. We're Germany, but we're *aside* from Germany. We're *better* than Germany. We're Hamburg, but we're also New York. Okay, we don't have Twin Towers. But then neither does New York anymore. But we're *attractive*. We still *smell* right to the wrong people."

Another silence while he weighed what he had just said. "But if we're talking *signals,* I think I'd blame our newfound, arse-licking tolerance of religious and ethnic diversity. Because a guilty city making amends for its past sins—parading its inexhaustible, amazing, indiscriminate tolerance—well, that's a signal of a kind too. It's practically an invitation to come and test us out."

He was homing in on his pet subject, the one they were all waiting for, the reason they had been dragged out of Berlin or Munich and relegated to a run-down SS stables in Hamburg. He was chafing against the dismal failure of Western intelligence services—and the German service most of all—to recruit a single decent live source against the Islamist target.

"You think everything changed after 9/11?" he demanded, furious with them, or himself. "You think that on 9/12, our fine foreign intelligence service, fired by a global vision of the terror threat, put on their kaffiyehs and went down to the souks of Aden and Mogadishu and Cairo and Baghdad and Kandahar and bought themselves a little retail information about where and when the next bomb would go off and who would be pushing the button? Okay, we all know the bad joke: you can't buy an Arab, but you can rent one. We couldn't even *rent* one, for fuck's sake! With a couple of noble exceptions I won't bore you with, we had *shit* for live sources then. And we have *shit* for live sources now.

"Oh sure, we had any number of gallant German journalists and businessmen and aid workers on our payroll, and even some who weren't German, but only too happy to sell us their industrial waste for an untaxable second income. But they're not *live sources*. They're not venal, disenchanted, radical imams, or Islamist kids halfway to the bomb belt. They're not Osama's sleepers, or his talent spotters, or his couriers or his quartermasters or paymasters, not even at fifty removes. They're just nice dinner guests."

He waited till the laughter had subsided.

"And when we woke up to what we hadn't got, we couldn't find it."

We, they noticed. *We* in Beirut. *We* in Mogadishu and Aden. The Bachmann royal *we.* Bachmann had found live sources, real ones, good ones, all the secret world said so. Bought them or rented them, who cared? But perhaps he had lost them too. Or perhaps security obliged him to disown them.

"We thought we could *charm* them across the line to us. We thought we could *lure* them with our good faces and fat wallets. We sat in car parks all fucking night, waiting for high-level defectors to get into the backseat and cut a deal with us. Nobody showed up. We trawled the airwaves to break their codes. They hadn't *got* any fucking codes. Why not? Because we weren't fighting the Cold War anymore. We were fighting off-cuts of a nation called Islam with a population of one and a half billion and a passive infrastructure to match. We thought we could do it the way we'd done it before, and we were plain, stupid, fucking *wrong.*"

His anger subsided as he allowed himself a diversion. "Listen. I've been there," he confided. "Before I worked the Arab target, I played games with my Soviet opposite numbers. I bought people and sold them. I doubled and redoubled joes till I couldn't see up my own arse. But nobody sawed my head off. Nobody blew up my wife and children while they were sunbathing in Bali or riding to school on a train to Madrid or London. The rules had changed. Our problem was, *we* hadn't," he ended with a snap, and strode off to another part of the gallery to announce another switch of mood.

"And even *after* 9/11, our beloved Fatherland—forgive me, *Heimat*—was *immune,* of course it was!" he declared with a hoot of bitter laughter. "We Germans could go *naked* anywhere! *Still!* Nobody would touch us because we were so wonderfully *German* and immune. Okay, we'd harbored a few Islamist terrorists, and a trio of them had gone off and blown up the Twin Towers and the Pentagon. So what? It was what they'd come here to do, and they'd done it. Problem solved. They'd struck at the heart of the Great Satan, and they'd killed themselves in the process. We were their *launchpad,* for Christ's sake, not their target! Why should *we* worry? So we lit candles for the poor Americans. And we *prayed* for the poor Americans. And we showed them a lot of *free solidarity.* But I don't need to tell you there were plenty of arseholes around in this country who didn't mind too much about Fortress America getting a dose of its own medicine, and some of those arseholes were sitting quite high up in Berlin, and still are. And when the Iraq war came along, and we good Germans stayed aloof from it, that made us even *more* immune. Madrid happened. Okay. London happened. Okay. But no Berlin, no Munich, no Hamburg. We were too fucking immune for *any* of it."

Selecting a corner of the gallery he spoke diagonally at them in a more confiding voice.

"But there were two tiny problems, my friends. The first tiny problem was that Germany was providing America with five-star military bases under leftover treaties from the days when they owned us because they'd defeated us. Remember the fine black banner that our elected masters hung on the Brandenburg gate? *We mourn along with you.* It didn't arrive there by mistake. The second tiny problem was our unflinching, unqualified, guilt-ridden support for the State of Israel. We supported them against the Egyptians, the Syrians and the Palestinians. Against Hamas and Hezbollah. And when Israel bombed the living shit out of Lebanon, we Germans duly consulted our unquiet consciences and talked only about how gallant little Israel could be defended. And we sent our gallant little boys in uniform to Lebanon to do exactly that—which did not endear us to those Lebanese and other Arabs who felt we had hastened to the protection of a bully on the rampage who was acting with the permission and encouragement of Messrs. Bush, Blair and several other brave world statesmen who, for reasons of modesty, preferred that their names not be included in the roll of honor.

"And the next damn thing we knew, there were a couple of Lebanese bombs on our German railway system that, if they'd gone off, would have made London and Madrid look like a rehearsal for the real thing. After that, even our own politicians accepted there was a price to be paid for giving the finger to the Americans in public and kissing their arses in private. German cities were victims-in-waiting. And that's how they are tonight."

He scanned the room, studying their faces one by one. Maximilian's hand had gone up, registering an objection. So had Niki's next to him. Others followed. This pleased him, and he smiled broadly.

"Okay. Don't bother to say it. You're telling me that those Lebanese guys who planted the bombs didn't even *know* about the latest wreck of Lebanon when they started their plotting, is that right?"

The hands went down. It was right.

"They were pissed off by a couple of very bad Danish cartoons of the Prophet Mohammed that some German newspapers reprinted because they thought they were being brave and setting us free, okay?"

Okay.

"So am I wrong? No, I am *not* wrong! What pulled their triggers doesn't matter a fuck. What *does* matter is, the threat we are dealing with doesn't see the difference between personal and collective guilt. It doesn't say: '*You're* good and *I'm* good, and Erna here is no good at all.' It says: 'You're all a bunch of no-good apostates and blasphemers and murderers and fornicators and God-haters, so fuck the lot of us.' For those guys, and all the guys we'd like to meet who share their perceptions, it's the western hemisphere versus Islam, and no stops between."

And then he went to the heart of it.

"The sources that we newly assembled pariahs here in Hamburg will be looking for have to be conjured into life. They don't know they exist till we tell them. They won't come to us. We find them. We stay small. We stay on the street. We do detail, not grand vision. We have no preconceived target to direct them at. We find a man, we develop him, we see what he's got, and we take him as far as he'll go. Or woman. We work the people nobody else reaches. The baggy little guys from the mosques who speak three words of German. We befriend them and befriend their friends. We watch for the quiet incomer, the invisible nomad on his way to somewhere who is passed from house to house and mosque to mosque.

"We comb the undead files of Herr Arni Mohr and his fellow protectors across the courtyard, we revisit old cases that started with a flourish and fizzled out when the prospect took fright or resettled in another town where the local outstation was so fucking dumb it didn't know how to handle him and didn't want to. We ignore the protests of our hosts, and we track these former prospects down. We take their temperature again. We make the weather."

He had one last word of caution, though it too was typically anarchic.

"And remember, please, that we are illegal. How illegal, not being a fine lawyer like so many of our august colleagues, I don't truthfully know. But from all they tell me, we can't so much as wipe our arses without prior consent in writing from a board of high judges, the Holy See, Joint Steering in Berlin and our beloved Federal Police, who don't know spying from shit, but have all the powers that the intelligence services are rightly deprived of so that we don't become the Gestapo by mistake. Now let's do some real work. I need a drink."

The all-night bar was called Hampelmanns and it was situated in a cobbled side street close by the station concourse. A wrought-iron dancing man in a pointed hat dangled over the ill-lit porch, and tonight, as on most other nights apparently, it was host to the gentleman known initially to Günther Bachmann's team as the elderly fat bastard.

The gentleman's unspectacular surname, as they now knew, was Müller but to his fellow habitués at Hampelmanns he was known exclusively as the Admiral. He was a returnee from ten years of Soviet captivity as a reward for his career as a submariner in Hitler's Northern Fleet. Karl the reformed street kid from Dresden had tracked him down and, having phoned through his name and whereabouts, kept a silent watch on him from an adjoining table. Maximilian the stammering computer genius had magicked up his date of birth, personal history and police record, all within a matter of minutes. And now Bachmann himself was negotiating the smoky brick staircase that descended to the cellar bar. As he did so, Karl the street kid slipped past him into the night. The time was 3 A.M.

At first, Bachmann could see only the people sitting closest to the shafts of light from the stairwell. Then he made out an electric candle on each table and gradually the faces round them. Two gaunt men in black ties and suits were playing chess. At the bar, a lone woman invited him to buy her a drink. "Another time, thank you, dear,"

Bachmann replied. In an alcove four boys, naked to the waist, were enjoying a game of billiards, watched by two dead-eyed girls. A second alcove was given over to stuffed foxes, silver shields and faded miniature flags with crossed rifles. And in a third, surrounded by model warships in dusty glass cases, ships' knots, tattered hatbands and mottled photographs of submariners in their prime, sat three very old men at a round table that would have seated twelve. Two were thin and frail, which should have given authority to the third, whose glossy bald pate, barrel chest and belly made him the equal of his two companions put together. But authority, at first glance, was not what the Admiral was about. His huge motionless hands, cupped before him on the table, seemed unable to grasp the memories that haunted him. The small eyes, which had long retreated into his creaseless head, appeared to be turned inward.

With a nod to encompass all three men, Bachmann quietly sat himself at the Admiral's side and from his back pocket drew a black wallet displaying his photograph and the address of a quasi-official missing persons agency based in Kiel that did not exist. It was one of several workaday identities that he liked to carry with him for contingencies.

"We're looking for that poor young Russian kid

you bumped into at the railway station the other night," he explained. "Young and tall and hungry. Dignified fellow. Wore a skullcap. Remember him?"

The Admiral woke sufficiently from his reveries to turn his huge head and examine Bachmann while the rest of his body remained rock-still.

"Who's *we*?" he inquired at last, after he had taken in Bachmann's humble leather jacket, shirt and tie, and his air of decent concern that—almost legitimately—was his stock-in-trade.

"The boy's not well," Bachmann explained. "We're afraid he's going to harm himself. Or other people. The health workers in my office are really worried about him. They want to get to him before anything bad happens. He's young but he's had a hard life. Like you," he added.

The Admiral appeared not to hear him.

"You a pimp?" he asked.

Bachmann shook his head.

"Cop?"

"If I can get to him before the cops do, I'll be doing him a favor," he said, while the Admiral continued to stare at him. "I'll do *you* a favor too," he continued. "One hundred euros cash for everything you remember about him. No comebacks, I guarantee."

The Admiral lifted a large hand and, having wiped it speculatively across his mouth, rose to

his full height and, without a glance for his silent
companions, moved to the next alcove, which was
empty and in near darkness.

The Admiral ate decorously, using a lot of paper
napkins to preserve the cleanliness of his fingers,
and adding liberal doses of Tabasco that he kept
in his jacket pocket. Bachmann had ordered a
bottle of vodka. The Admiral had added bread,
gherkins, sausage, salt herrings and a plate of
Tilsit cheese to the order.

"They came to me," he said at last.

"Who did?"

"The mission people. They all know the Admiral."

"Where were you?"

"In the mission house. Where else?"

"Sleeping?"

The Admiral pulled a wry smile as if sleep was
something other people did. "I'm a Russian
speaker. A harbor rat from Hamburg docks, but
I speak better Russian than German. How did
that happen?"

"Siberia," Bachmann suggested, and the vast
head rocked in silent agreement.

"The mission doesn't speak Russian. But the
Admiral does." He gave himself a huge pull of
vodka. "Wants to become a doctor."

"The boy?"

"Here in Hamburg. Wants to save mankind. Who from? Mankind, of course. A Tartar. So he said. A *Mussulman*. Been commanded by Allah to come to Hamburg and study so that he can save mankind."

"Any reason why Allah picked him out?"

"Make up for all the poor devils his father slaughtered."

"Did he say who the poor devils were?"

"Russians kill everybody, my friend. Priests, children, women, the whole fucking universe."

"Were they fellow Muslims that his father killed?"

"He did not specify the victims."

"Did he say what his father's profession was? How he managed to kill so many poor devils in the first place?"

The Admiral took another swallow of vodka. Then another. Then replenished his glass. "He was curious to know where the rich bankers of Hamburg have their offices."

To Bachmann the practiced interrogator, no piece of information, however outrageous, must ever appear surprising. "What did you tell him?"

"I laughed. I can do that. 'What do you want a banker for? Do you need to cash a check? Maybe I can help you.' "

Bachmann shared the joke. "So how did he take that one?"

" 'Check? What is check?' Then he asked me whether they lived in their offices or had private houses as well."

"And you said?"

" 'Look,' I told him. 'You're a polite fellow, and Allah has told you to become a doctor. So stop asking a lot of stupid questions about bankers. Come and relax in our fleabitten hostel, sleep on a real bed and meet some of the other fine gentlemen who want to save mankind.' "

"And did he?"

"Shoved fifty dollars into my hand. A crazy starving Tartar kid gives an old campnik a brand-new fifty-dollar bill for a beaker of lousy soup."

Having taken Bachmann's money also, and stuffed his pockets with whatever was left on the table, ending with the vodka bottle, the Admiral returned to his seamates in the adjoining ward-room.

For several days after this encounter Bachmann lapsed into one of his cherished silences from which Erna Frey made no attempt to retrieve him. Even the news that the Danes had arrested the driver of the lorry on charges of people-smuggling failed at first hearing to spark him.

"His chauffeur?" he repeated. "The lorry driver who dropped him at Hamburg railway station? *That* chauffeur?"

"Yes, *that* chauffeur," Erna Frey retorted. "As of two hours ago. I sent it through to you, but you were too busy. Copenhagen to Joint in Berlin, Joint to us. It's rather informative."

"A Danish national?"

"Correct."

"Of Danish origin?"

"Correct."

"But a Muslim convert?"

"Nothing of the kind. Look at your e-mails for once. He's a Lutheran and the son of one. His only sin is to have a brother in organized crime."

Now she had him.

"The bad brother telephoned the good brother two weeks ago and told him there was a rich young man who'd lost his passport and was about to arrive in Copenhagen as a passenger in a certain cargo ship from Istanbul."

"Rich?" Bachmann leapt in. "Rich *how*?"

"The fee would be five thousand dollars up front for getting him out of the docks, and another five on safe delivery to Hamburg."

"Payable who by?"

"The young man."

"Himself, on safe delivery? Out of his own pocket? Five thousand?"

"It would seem so. The good brother was broke so he was a fool and took the job. He never knew his passenger's name and he doesn't speak Russian."

"Where's the bad brother?"

"In jail too. Naturally. They're keeping them apart."

"What does he say?"

"He's frightened stiff and he'd rather stay in prison than have the Russian mafia take a week to kill him."

"This mafia boss: Is he a plain Russian or a Muslim Russian?"

"The bad brother's Moscow connect—according to the bad brother—is a respectable, thoroughbred, high-rolling Russian gangster, engaged in the best class of organized crime. He has no time for Muslims of any sort, and would prefer to see the whole lot of them drowned in the Volga. His contract with our driver's brother was a favor for a friend. Who the said friend is, or was, is not for a humble Danish crook to inquire."

She sat back and with lowered eyelids waited for Bachmann to come to heel.

"What does Joint say about it?" he asked.

"Joint burbles. Joint is fixated on a high-stepping imam, currently living in Moscow, who filters money to dubious Islamic charities. The Russians know he does it. He knows they know he does it. Why they let him do it is beyond the wit of man. Joint is determined to believe that the imam is the mafia boss's missing friend. This despite the fact that, so far as anyone knows, he has no record of funding escape lines for runaway Russian-Chechen vagrants on their way to study medicine in Hamburg. Oh, and he gave him his coat."

"Who did?"

"The good brother who drove our boy to Hamburg took pity on him and feared he would catch his death of cold in the chilly north. So he gave him his overcoat to keep him warm. A long black one. I have another gem for you."

"Which is?"

"Herr Igor across the courtyard has an ultra-secret source buried inside the Russian Orthodox community in Cologne."

"And?"

"According to Igor's intrepid source, reclusive Orthodox nuns in a town not far from Hamburg recently gave shelter to a young Russian Muslim male who was starving and a little crazy."

"Rich?"

"His wealth has not been established."

"But polite?"

"Very. Igor is meeting his source tonight under conditions of extreme secrecy to discuss payment for the rest of the story."

"Igor's an arsehole and his stories are a load of shit," Bachmann pronounced, bundling together the papers on his desk and stuffing them into an old, scuffed briefcase that nobody would want to steal.

"Where are you going?" Erna Frey demanded.

"Across the courtyard."

"Whatever for?"

"To tell the gallant protectors that he's our case. To tell them to keep the police off our backs. To make sure that, if by any unlikely chance the police *do* find him, they will kindly *not* send in Armed Response and start a small war, but stay out of sight and inform us immediately. I need this boy to do what he came to do for as long as he can do it."

"You've forgotten your keys," Erna Frey said.

4

*If you're not taking the S-Bahn, please do not arrive at
the café by taxi.*

Annabel Richter had been equally uncompro-
mising about Brue's clothes. *For my client, men in
suits are secret policemen. Kindly wear something informal.* The best he had been able to manage was
gray flannels and the sports coat by Randall's of
Glasgow that he wore for the golf club, and an
Aquascutum raincoat in case there was another
deluge. As a gesture, he had dispensed with a tie.

Darkness of a sort had fallen over the city. The
earlier downpour had left the night sky clear. A
cool breeze was washing off the lake as he
climbed into the cab and recited her directions to
the driver. Standing alone on a strange pavement
in a humble part of town, he felt momentarily deprived, but rallied when he saw her promised
street sign. The fruit stalls of the halal grocer's
shop were a blaze of red and green. The white
lights of the kebab house next door shone all

across the street. Inside it, at a corner table of bright purple, sat Annabel Richter with a bottle of still water before her and a discarded bowl of what looked to Brue like school tapioca with brown sugar sprinkled over the top.

At a table next to her, four old men were playing dominoes. At another, a young couple in their best suit and frock were nervously courting. Her anorak hung over her chair. She wore a shapeless pullover and the same high-necked blouse. A cell phone lay on the table, the rucksack at her feet. Sitting down opposite her, he caught a scent of something warm in her hair.

"Do I pass?" he asked.

She ran an eye over his sports coat and flannels. "What did you find in your archives?"

"That there's a prima facie case for further inquiry."

"That's all you're going to tell me?"

"At this stage, yes, I'm afraid."

"Then let me tell you a couple of things you don't know."

"I'm sure there are many."

"He's a Muslim. That's number one. Devout. So it's tough for him when he's got to deal with a woman lawyer."

"But tougher for you, surely?"

"He asks me to wear a headscarf. I wear one. He asks me to respect his traditions. I respect them. He uses his Muslim name: Issa. As I told you, he speaks Russian; otherwise bad Turkish with his hosts."

"And who are his hosts, if I may ask?"

"A Turkish widow and her son. Her husband was a client of Sanctuary North. We nearly got him citizenship but he died. Now the son is trying on behalf of the family, which means starting all over again, and taking each member of the family separately, which is why he's running scared and why he called us. They love Issa but they want him off their hands. They think they're going to be thrown out of the country for harboring an illegal immigrant. Nothing will persuade them otherwise, and these days they may be right. They've also got air tickets to Turkey for her daughter's wedding and there's no way they're going to leave him in the house alone. They don't know your name. Issa knows it but hasn't repeated it, and won't. You're somebody who's in a position to help Issa, that's all you are. Are you comfortable with that description?"

"I believe so."

"Only believe?"

"I'm comfortable with it."

"I've also told them, because I had to, that you won't reveal any of their names to the authorities."

"Why on earth should I do that?"

Ignoring his offers of assistance, she clambered into her anorak and slung her rucksack over one shoulder. Heading for the door, Brue noticed an oversized young man prowling the pavement. Following him at a respectful distance, they entered a side street. The boy seemed to grow bigger the farther he got away from them. At a pharmacy the boy took a swift look up and down the road at the cars, at the windows of the houses and at two middle-aged women studying the window of a jeweler's. To one side of the window stood a brides' shop with a dream wedding couple clutching wax flowers, and to the other a thickly varnished front door with an illuminated bell button.

About to cross the road, Annabel stopped, half unslung her rucksack, extracted her headscarf, put it over her head, then carefully pulled down two corners and tied them at her throat. Under the streetlight, her face looked strained and older than her age.

The oversized boy unlocked the door, shooed them in and held out an immense hand. Brue shook it but didn't say his name. The woman Leyla was small and sturdy and dressed to receive, in a headscarf and high heels and a black suit with a ruff. She stared at Brue, then uneasily took his hand, her eyes all the time on her son. Follow-

ing Leyla into the living room, Brue knew he had
entered a house of fear.

The wallpaper was puce, the upholstery gold.
Lace antimacassars were draped over the chair
arms. In the glass base of a table lamp, globules
of plasma rotated, parted and rejoined. Leyla
had awarded Brue the presidential throne. My
late husband's, she had explained, pulling nervously at her headscarf. For thirty years, my
husband wouldn't sit on any other chair, she had
said. It was ornate, hideous and exquisitely uncomfortable. Brue dutifully admired it. He had
one not unlike it in his office: inherited from his
grandfather, and hell on earth to sit on. He
thought of saying something to that effect, but
elected not to. I'm somebody in a position to
help. That's all I am, he told me himself. On
dishes of best china Leyla had laid out triangles
of baklava in syrup, and a lemon cream cake cut
into slices. Brue accepted a piece of cake and a
glass of apple tea.

"Marvelous," he declared, when he had tasted
the cake, but nobody seemed to hear him.

The two women, the one beautiful, the other
dumpy, both grim, sat on a velveteen sofa.
Melik stood with his back against the door.
"Issa will be down in a minute," he said, look-

ing upward at the ceiling, listening. "Issa's preparing himself. Issa's nervous. He may be praying. He'll come."

"Those policemen could hardly wait till Frau Richter had left the house," Leyla burst out to Brue, venting a grouse that had evidently been gnawing at her. "I closed the front door behind her, I took the dishes to the kitchen, and five minutes later, there they were, ringing my bell. They showed me their identity cards and I wrote down their names, just the way my husband used to. Plainclothes. Didn't I, Melik?"

She thrust a writing block into Brue's hands. One sergeant, one constable, names supplied. Not knowing what to do with it, he rose and showed it to Annabel, who handed it back to Leyla beside her.

"They waited till Mother was alone in the house," Melik put in from the door. "I had a swimming date with the team. Two-hundred-meter relay."

Brue offered a nod of earnest sympathy. It was a long time since he had attended a meeting where he was not in charge.

"An old one and a young one," Leyla said, resuming her complaint. "Issa was in the attic, thanks be to God. When he heard the doorbell, he pulled up the steps and closed the trapdoor. He's been up there ever since. He says they come back. They pretend they've gone away, then they come back and deport you."

"They're just doing their job," Annabel said. "They're visiting people all across the Turkish community. They're calling it outreach."

"First they said it was about my son's Islamic sports club, then it was about my daughter's wedding in Turkey next month, and are we sure we're entitled to return to Germany afterwards? 'Of course we're sure!' I said. 'Not if you obtained German residence on humanitarian grounds,' they said. 'That was twenty years ago!' I told them."

"Leyla, you're upsetting yourself unnecessarily," Annabel said sternly. "It's a hearts-and-minds operation to separate decent Muslims from the few bad apples, that's all it is. Calm down."

Was the choirboy voice a notch too sure of itself? Brue suspected that it was.

"You want to hear something funny?" Melik asked Brue, his expression anything but humorous. "You're going to help him, so maybe you should hear this. He's not like any Muslim I ever met. He may be a believer, but he doesn't *think* like a Muslim, he doesn't *act* like a Muslim."

His mother snapped at him in Turkish, but to no avail.

"When he was weak—all right?—when he was lying in my bed, recovering? I read him verses from the Koran. My father's copy. In Turkish. Then he wanted to read it for himself. In Turkish. He knew enough to recognize the holy words, he said. So I go to the table where I keep it—*open,* okay?—I say *Bismillah,* the way my father taught me—I made like I was going to kiss it but I *didn't,* he taught me that too, I just touched it with my forehead, and I gave it into his hands. 'Here you are, Issa,' I said. 'Here's my dad's Koran. Reading it in bed is not how you should do it normally, but you're sick, so maybe it's okay.' When I come back into the room an hour later, where is it? *Lying on the floor.* My dad's copy of the Koran and it's lying on the floor. For any decent Muslim, never mind my dad, that's *unthinkable*! So I thought: All right. I'm not angry. He's sick and it fell from his grasp when he had no strength. I forgive him. It's right to be generous-hearted. But when I yelled at him, he just reached down and picked it up—with *one hand only,* not two—and gave it me like it was"—at first he could find no suitable comparison—"like it was any book in a shop! Who would *do* that? *Nobody!* Whether he's Chechen or Turkish or Arab or—I mean, he's my brother, all right? I love the man. He's a true hero. But on the floor. One hand. Without a prayer. Without *anything.*"

Leyla had heard enough.

"Who are *you* to bad-mouth your brother,

Melik?" she snapped at him, also in German for the benefit of her audience. "Playing dirty rap music all night in your bedroom! What d'you think your father would make of *that*?"

From the direction of the hall Brue heard cautious feet descending a rickety ladder.

"Plus he took my sister's photograph and put it in his room," Melik said. "Just took it. In my dad's time I should kill him or something. He's my brother but he's weird."

The choirboy voice of Annabel Richter took command.

"You've missed your baking day, Leyla," she said with a meaningful glance towards the frosted screen that separated the kitchen area from the drawing room.

"That's their fault."

"Then why don't you do some baking now?" Annabel suggested calmly. "That way the neighbors will know you've nothing to hide." She turned to Melik, who had taken up a position at the side of the window. "It's nice that you're keeping watch. Please continue to do that. If the doorbell goes, whoever they are, they can't come in. Tell them you're having a conference with your sports promoters. All right?"

"All right."

"If it's the police again, they must either come another time or speak to me."

"He's not a real Chechen either. He just pretends to be," Melik said.

The door opened and a silhouette as tall as Melik's but half his width advanced by slow steps into the room. Brue stood up, his banker's smile aloft and his banker's hand outstretched. Out of the corner of his eye he saw that Annabel was also standing, but had not come forward.

"Issa, this is the gentleman you have asked to meet," Annabel said in classic Russian. "I am confident that he is who he says he is. He has come specially to see you tonight, at your request, and he has told nobody. He speaks Russian and needs to ask you some important questions. We are all grateful to him and I am sure that, for your own sake and for the sake of Leyla and Melik, you will cooperate with him all you can. I shall be listening, and representing your interests whenever I consider it necessary."

Issa had drawn up at the center of Leyla's gold carpet, arms to his sides, awaiting orders. When none came, he lifted his head, placed his right hand over his heart and fixed Brue with an adoring look.

"Thank you most respectfully, sir," he murmured, through lips that seemed to smile despite him. "I am privileged, sir. You are a good man, as I have been assured. It is visible in your features and your beautiful clothes. You have also a beautiful limousine?"

"Well, a Mercedes."

For reasons of ceremony or self-protection, Issa had donned his black overcoat and slung his camel-skin bag over his shoulder. He had shaved. The two weeks of Leyla's motherly attentions had smoothed the crevices in his cheeks, giving him, to Brue's eye, a seraphic unreality: *This pretty slip of a boy has been tortured?* For a moment, Brue believed none of him. The radiant smile, the stilted style of speech, too flowery by half, the air of false composure, were all the classic equipment of an imposter. But then as they sat down to face each other at Leyla's table, Brue saw the film of sweat on Issa's forehead, and when he looked lower he saw that his hands had remet each other, wrist-to-wrist on the table, as though waiting to be chained. He saw the fine gold chain round his wrist, and the talismanic golden Koran hanging from it to protect him. And he knew that he was looking at a destroyed child.

But he remained master of his feelings. Should he count himself inferior to somebody merely because that somebody has been tortured? Must he suspend judgment for the same reason? A point of principle was involved here.

"Well now, and welcome," he began brightly, in a carefully well-learned Russian, curiously comparable with Issa's own. "I gather we have little time. So we must be brief but we must be effective. I may call you Issa?"

"Agreed, sir." The smile again, followed by a glance for Melik at his window and a dropping of the eyes away from Annabel, who had taken up a place in the far corner of the room, where she sat sideways, with a folder set chastely on her averted knees.

"And you will call me nothing," said Brue. "I believe that is agreed. Yes?"

"It is agreed, sir," Issa responded with alacrity. "All your wishes are agreed! You permit me to make a statement, please?"

"Of course."

"It will be short!"

"Please."

"I wish only to be a medical student. I wish to live a life of order and assist all mankind for the glory of Allah."

"Yes, well, that's very admirable and I'm sure we shall come to that," said Brue and, as a sign of his businesslike intentions, drew a leather-backed notepad from one inside pocket, and a gold rollerball pen from another. "But meanwhile, let's get down a few elementary facts, if you don't mind. Starting with your full names."

But this evidently wasn't what Issa wanted to hear.

"Sir!"

"Yes, Issa."

"You have read the work of the great French thinker Jean-Paul Sartre, sir?"

"I can't say I have."

"Like Sartre, I have a nostalgia for the future. When I have a future, I shall have no past. I shall have only God and my future."

Brue felt Annabel's eyes on him. When he couldn't see them, he still felt them. Or thought he did.

"However, tonight we are obliged to address the present," he countered glossily. "So why don't you just let me have your full names?"— pen poised to receive them.

"Salim," Issa answered after a moment's indecision.

"Any others?"

"Mahmoud."

"So Issa Salim Mahmoud."

"Yes, sir."

"And are those your given names or names that you have chosen for yourself?"

"They are chosen of God, sir."

"Quite so." Brue smiled to himself deliberately, partly to ease the tension, partly to show he was in command. "Then let me ask you this

one, may I? We are talking Russian. You are
Russian. Before God chose your present names,
did you have a *Russian* name? And a Russian
patronymic to go with it? What names, for example, might one find on your birth certificate, I
wonder?"

Having consulted Annabel with lowered eyes,
Issa plunged a skeletal hand inside his overcoat,
then his shirtfront, and drew out a grimy purse
of chamois leather. And from it two faded press
cuttings, which he passed across the table.

"Karpov," Brue ruminated aloud when he had
read them. "Karpov is who? Karpov is your *family* name? Why do you give me these pieces of
newspaper?"

"It is not material, sir. Please. I cannot," Issa
muttered, shaking his sweated head. His hands
had rejoined each other. His long thin fingers
were fondling the gold Koran at his wrist.

"Well, for me I'm afraid it *is* material," Brue
said, as kindly as he was able without relinquish-
ing the upper hand. "I'm afraid it's very material
indeed. Are you telling me that Colonel Grigori
Borisovich Karpov is, or was, a relative of yours?
Is that what you are telling me?" He turned to
Annabel, whom in his mind he had been addressing all along. "This is really rather difficult, Frau
Richter," he complained in German, starting
stiffly, then instinctively moderating his tone. "If

your client has a claim to make, he must either say who he is and make it, or withdraw, surely. He can't expect me to play both sides of the net."

A moment of confusion intervened while from the kitchen Leyla called something plaintive to Melik in Turkish, and Melik said something soothing in return.

"Issa," Annabel said when they had all settled again. "It is my professional opinion that, however painful it is to you, you should try to answer the gentleman's question."

"Sir. As God is great, I wish only to live a life of order," Issa repeated in a strangled voice.

"All the same, I'm afraid I need an answer to my question."

"It is logically true that Karpov is my father, sir," Issa confessed at last with a mirthless smile. "He did all that was necessary in nature to secure that title, I am sure. But I was never Karpov's son. I am not now Karpov's son. God willing, sir, I shall never in my life be Colonel Grigori Borisovich Karpov's son."

"But Colonel Karpov is *dead*, it appears," Brue pointed out, with more brutality than he intended, waving a hand towards the press cuttings lying on the table between them.

"He is dead, sir, and God willing he is in hell and will remain in hell for all eternity."

"And before he died—at the time when you

were born, I should rather say—what first name did he give you in addition to your patronymic, which is presumably *Grigorevich*?"

Issa was hanging his head, rolling it from side to side.

"He chose the purest," he said, lifting his head and sneering at Brue in a knowing way.

"Purest in what sense?"

"Of all Russian names in the world, the most Russian. I was his *Ivan,* sir. His sweet little Ivan from Chechnya."

Never one to allow a bad moment to fester, Brue decided on a change of topic.

"I understand you came here from *Turkey.* By an informal route, shall we say?" Brue suggested, in the sort of cheery tone he might have used at a cocktail party. Leyla, contrary to Annabel's instructions, had returned from the kitchen area.

"I was in Turkish prison, sir." He had unfastened the gold bracelet he was wearing and was holding it in his hand, agitating it while he spoke.

"And for how long, if I may ask?"

"One hundred and eleven and a half days exactly, sir. In Turkish prison, there is every incentive to study the arithmetic of time," Issa exclaimed, with a harsh, unearthly laugh. "And before Turkey I was in prison in Russia, you see! Actually in three prisons, for an aggregate period of eight hundred and fourteen days and seven hours. If you wish, I will list my prisons for you in their order of quality," he ran on wildly, his voice rising in lyrical insistence. "I am quite a connoisseur, I assure you, sir! There was one prison so popular they had to split it in three pieces. Oh yes! In one part we slept, in another we were tortured and in the third part there was a hospital for us to recover. The torture was efficient, and after torture one sleeps well, but unfortunately the hospital was substandard. That is a problem with our modern Russian state, I would say! The nurses were qualified in sleep deprivation but noticeably deficient in other medical skills. Permit me an observation, sir. To be a good torturer, it is extremely necessary to be of a compassionate disposition. Without a fellow feeling for one's subject, one cannot ascend to the true heights of the art. I have encountered only one or two who are in the top class."

Brue waited for a moment in case there was more, but Issa, his dark eyes wide with excitement, was waiting on Brue. And yet again it was Leyla who inadvertently succeeded in breaking the tension. Troubled by Issa's state of emotional excitement, if unable to understand its cause, she scurried back to the kitchen and fetched a glass of cordial, which she placed before him on the table, while fixing first Brue and then Annabel with a reproachful scowl.

"And may one ask *why* you were in prison in the first place?" Brue resumed.

"Oh yes, sir! Please ask! You are most welcome," Issa cried, now with the recklessness of a condemned scholar speaking from the scaffold. "To be a Chechen is crime enough, sir, I assure you. We Chechen are born extremely guilty. Ever since czarist times, our noses have been culpably flat and our hair and skin criminally dark. This is an enduring offense to public order, sir!"

"But your nose is not flat, if I may say so."

"To my regret, sir."

"But one way or another you made it to Turkey, and from Turkey you escaped," Brue suggested soothingly. "And came all the way to Hamburg. That was quite an achievement, surely."

"It was the will of Allah."

"But with some assistance from yourself, I suspect."

"If a man has money, sir, as you will know better than I, everything is possible."

"Ah, but *whose* money?" Brue demanded archly, darting in swiftly now that money was in the air. "Who provided the money to pay for your many brilliant escapes, I wonder?"

"I would say, sir"—Issa replied after prolonged soul searching, in which Brue half expected the answer to be Allah again—"I would
say his name is very likely to be Anatoly."

"Anatoly?" Brue repeated, after allowing the
name to resonate in his head—and in some distant chamber of his late father's past.

"Anatoly is correct, sir. Anatoly is the man
who pays for everything. But especially for escapes. You know this man, sir?" he interjected
eagerly. "He is a friend of yours?"

"I'm afraid not."

"For Anatoly, money is the purpose of all life.
And death too, I would say."

Brue was on the point of pursuing this when
Melik spoke up from his post at the window.

"They're still there," he growled in German,
peering through the edge of the curtain. "Those
two old women. They're not interested in the
jewelry anymore. One's reading the notices in
the window of the pharmacist's shop, the other's
in a doorway talking on her mobile. They're too
ugly to be hookers, even for round here."

"It's just two ordinary women," Annabel retorted sternly, going to the window and looking
out, while Leyla cupped her hands before her
face and closed her eyes in supplication. "You're
being dramatic, Melik."

But this was not good enough for Issa, who

having caught the sense of Melik's words, was already standing with his saddlebag slung across his chest.

"What do you see there?" he appealed to Annabel in a shrill voice, swinging round accusingly to face her. "Is it your KGB again?"

"It's nobody, Issa. If there's a problem, we'll take care of you. That's what we're here for."

And once again, Brue had a sense that the choirboy voice was trying a little too hard to be nonchalant.

"So now, this *Anatoly,*" Brue resumed with determined purpose, when peace of a kind had been restored and Leyla, on Annabel's insistence, dispatched to make fresh apple tea. "He must be a pretty good friend of yours, by the sounds of it."

"Sir, we indeed may say that this Anatoly is a good friend to prisoners, no question," Issa agreed with exaggerated alacrity. "It also unfortunately happens that he is the friend of rapists, murderers, gangsters and crusaders. Anatoly is broad-minded in his friendships, I would say," he added, pushing away sweat with the back of his hand while he managed a rather dreadful grin.

"Was he a good friend to Colonel Karpov also?"

"I would say that Anatoly is the best friend a

murderer and rapist could possibly have, sir. For Karpov, he acquired places for me at the best Moscow schools, even when I had been rejected for disciplinary reasons."

"And it was Anatoly who paid for your escape from prison. Why did he do that, I wonder? Had you earned his gratitude in some way?"

"Karpov paid."

"Forgive me. You just said Anatoly paid."

"But forgive *me,* sir! Please forgive this technical error! You are correct to rebuke me. I hope this will not appear in my record," he ran on recklessly, this time including Annabel in his appeal. "*Karpov* paid. That is the unavoidable truth, sir. The money came from the precious gold trinkets round the necks and wrists of Chechnya's dead, that is very correct. But it was Anatoly who bribed the prison governors and the guards. It was Anatoly who gave me the letter of introduction to your admirable self. Anatoly is a wise and pragmatic counselor who knows very well how to do business with corrupt prison officials without offending their standards of probity."

"Letter of introduction?" Brue repeated. "Nobody has shown *me* any letter." He turned to Annabel, but to no avail. She could freeze her face as well as he could. Better.

"It is a mafia letter, sir. It is written by the mafia lawyer Anatoly regarding the death of the murderer and rapist Colonel Grigori Borisovich Karpov, formerly of the Red Army."

"To whom?"

"To me, sir."

"Do you have it with you?"

"Against my heart, always." Slipping the bracelet back on his wrist, he hauled the purse from the recesses of his black coat once more and handed Brue a crumpled letter. A printed heading in Roman and Cyrillic script gave the name and address of a firm of lawyers in Moscow. The text was typed in Russian and began *My dear Issa.* It lamented that Issa's father had died of a stroke in the company of beloved comrades in arms. He had been buried with military honors. No reference to a Karpov, but the names *Tommy Brue* and *Brue Frères* typed in bold and the word *Lipizzaner* followed by the number of the account inked across the bottom. Signed Anatoly, no surname.

"And what exactly did this gentleman *Anatoly* tell you that my bank and I might do for you?"

Through the frosted screen came sounds of Leyla noisily clanking cups and saucers.

"You will protect me, sir. You will enfold me in your protection, as Anatoly himself did. You are a good and powerful man, an oligarch of your fine city. You will appoint me a medical student in your university. Thanks to your great bank, I shall become a doctor in the service of God and humanity, and live an ordered life according to a solemn oath given to the criminal and murderer Karpov by your revered father, and passed to his son on his death. You are your father's son, I believe."

Brue gave a deft smile. "Unlike you, yes, I am indeed my father's son," he conceded, and was rewarded with another overbrilliant smile as Issa's haunted gaze slid towards Annabel, held her for a moment as if in thrall to her and then abandoned her.

"Your father made many fine promises to this Colonel Karpov, sir!" Issa blurted, springing to his feet again as fear and excitement once more got the better of him. He drew a hasty gulp of breath, grimaced wildly and adopted the rasping, autocratic tone of Brue's imaginary father: "'Grigori, my friend! When your little boy Ivan comes to me, though let us hope it will be many years hence, my bank will treat him as our kin and blood,'" he cried, flinging out an arm and clawing at the air with his fingertips in order to entrench the sacred vow. " 'If I am no longer on this earth, then it will be my son, Tommy, who honors your Ivan, this I swear to you. This is my heart's solemn promise, Grigori my friend, and it is the promise also of Mr. Lipizzaner.'" His voice came crookedly down to earth. "Such, sir, were

the words of your revered father as they were repeated to me by the mafia lawyer Anatoly, who
out of a perverse love of my father has been my
savior through many misfortunes," he ended, as
his voice cracked, and his breathing came in
rasps.

In the fraught silence that followed it was
Melik's turn to make his feelings felt:

"You want to look out," he warned Brue
roughly in German. "If you wind him up too
tight, he'll have a fit." And in case Brue hadn't
understood the point: "Take it easy with him,
okay? He's my brother."

When Brue at last spoke, he did so in German,
in words of studied casualness directed not at
Issa but at Annabel.

"And do we have that solemn promise in writing anywhere, Frau Richter, or must we depend
solely on the hearsay evidence of Mr. Anatoly, as
relayed to us by your client?"

"All we have in writing is the name and reference number of an account at your bank," she
replied tautly.

Brue affected to ruminate. "Let me explain
my little problem to you, Issa," he suggested in
Russian, selecting from among the voices
screaming in his head the tone of a reasonable

man doing his sums. "We have an Anatoly, who you tell me is or was your father's lawyer. We have a Colonel Karpov, who you tell me is your natural father, although you otherwise disown him. But we don't have *you,* do we? You have no papers, and you have by your own account a substantial prison record which does not exactly inspire confidence in a banker, whatever the reason."

"I am a Muslim, sir!" Issa protested, his voice soaring in agitation as he again glanced at Annabel for support. "I am a Chechen black-arse! Why do I have to have a reason to go to prison?"

"I need to be *persuaded,* you see," Brue continued implacably, ignoring Melik's scowl. "I need to know how you came to be in possession of privileged information concerning a valued client of my bank. I need, if I may, to dig a little deeper into your family circumstances, starting, where all good and bad things start in this world, with your *mother.*" He was being cruel and knew it, even wished it. Melik's warning notwithstanding, Issa's grotesque mimicry of Edward Amadeus had sickened him. "Who is she, your dear mother, or who was she? Have you siblings, alive or deceased?"

At first Issa did not speak at all. His spindly body was stretched forward, elbows on the table, the bracelet now halfway down his emaciated forearm, long hands sheltering his head inside the upturned collar of his black coat. Suddenly the child's face emerged and became a man's.

"My mother is dead, sir. Most dead. My mother died many times. She died on the day that Karpov's fine troops seized her from her village and drove her to the barracks for Karpov to defile her. She was fifteen years old. She died on the day the elders of her tribe decreed that she had collaborated in her defilement, and ordered that one of her brothers be sent to kill her in the tradition of our people. She died every day she waited to bear me, knowing that as soon as she had brought me into the world, she would be obliged to leave it, and that her child would be sent to a military orphanage for the children of violated Chechen mothers. She was correct in anticipating her death, but not in anticipating the actions of the man who had caused it. When Karpov's regiment was recalled to Moscow, he elected to take the boy with him as a trophy."

"You were by then how old?"

"Sir, the boy was seven years old. Old enough to have glimpsed the forests, hills and rivers of Chechnya. Old enough to return to them whenever God allowed him. Sir, I wish to make a further statement."

"Please do."

"You are a gracious and important man, sir. You are an honorable Englishman, not a Russian barbarian. The Chechens once dreamed that they would acquire an English queen to protect them from the Russian tyrant. I will accept your protection as promised to Karpov by your respected father, and in God's name I thank you from my heart. But if it is Karpov's money we are speaking of, I must regretfully refuse it. Not one euro, not one dollar, not one ruble, not one English pound, please. It is the money of imperialist robbers and infidels and crusaders. It is money that has grown in usury, which is against our divine law. It is money that was essential to my difficult journey here, but I will touch no more of it. Kindly obtain for me a German passport and a permit of residence, and a place where I can study medicine and pray in humility. That is all I ask, sir. I thank you."

His upper body flopped forward onto the table as his head buried itself in his folded arms. Leyla darted from the kitchen to console him as he heaved and sobbed. Melik placed himself in front of Brue as if to shield Issa from further assault. Annabel was also standing, but for reasons of decorum had not presumed to approach her client.

"And I thank you too, Issa," Brue replied after

a prolonged hush. "Frau Richter, I wonder whether we might have a word alone, please."

They were standing two feet apart in Melik's bedroom next to a punchball. If she had been a foot taller they would have been face-to-face. Her honey-flecked gaze was rock steady behind her spectacles. Her breathing was slow and deliberate, and so, he realized, was his own. With one hand she unknotted her scarf and exposed her features, challenging him to throw the first punch. But she had Georgie's fearlessness and her own unassailable beauty, and part of him knew already that he was lost.

"How much of this did you know?" he demanded, in a voice that was scarcely familiar to him.

"That's my client's business, not yours."

"He's a claimant, but he's not a claimant. What am I supposed to do? He's withdrawn his claim but he wants my protection."

"That's right."

"I don't *do* protection. I'm a bank. I don't *do* permits of residence. I don't *do* German passports or places at medical school!" He was gesturing naturally, a thing he seldom did. With each *do* he was hammering his right fist into his left palm.

"As far as my client's concerned, you're a high official," she retorted. "You own a bank, so you own the town. Your father and his father were crooks together. That makes you blood brothers. Of course you'll protect him."

"My father was *not* a crook!" He collected himself. "All right, your emotions are engaged. So it seems are mine. So they should be. Your client is a tragic case, and you are a—"

"A mere woman?"

"A conscientious lawyer doing your best for your client."

"He's your client too, Mr. Brue."

In any other circumstances Brue would vigorously have disputed this, but he let it go. "The man has been tortured and for all I know his mind is disturbed in consequence," he said. "Unfortunately that doesn't mean he's telling the truth. Who's to say he hasn't appropriated the belongings and identity of a fellow prisoner in order to stake a bogus claim to somebody else's birthright?—have I said something amusing?"

She was smiling, but only in vindication. "You just admitted it's his birthright."

"I admitted nothing of the kind!" Brue retorted, incensed. "I said the absolute reverse. I said it might well *not* be his birthright! And even if it *is* his birthright, and he won't claim it, what's the difference?"

"The difference is, Mr. Brue, that without your fucking bank, my client wouldn't be here."

An armed truce followed while each appraised her startling choice of vocabulary. He was trying to be aggressive, but not feeling it. To the contrary, he had increasingly the feeling of going over to her side.

"Frau Richter."

"Mr. Brue."

"I will not concede, without overwhelming evidence, that my bank—my father—provided aid and comfort to Russian crooks."

"What *will* you concede?"

"First your client must make a claim."

"He won't. He has five hundred dollars left over from what Anatoly gave him and he won't touch them. He intends to give them to Leyla when he leaves here."

"If he won't claim, then I have nothing to respond to and the entire situation is—academic. Less than academic. Void."

She considered this, but not for long. "All right. Suppose he claims. *Then* what?"

Sensing she was wrong-footing him, he hesitated. "Well, first, obviously, I would need minimum, basic proofs."

"What's minimum?"

Brue was extrapolating. He was taking refuge behind the regulations that Lipizzaners had been set up to avoid. This is now, not then, he was assuring himself. This is me aged sixty, not Edward Amadeus in his years of wild dotage.

"Proof of his identity, obviously, starting with his birth certificate."

"Where would you get that from?"

"Assuming he has no means of providing it, I would request the assistance of the Russian embassy in Berlin."

"After that?"

"I would need proof of the father's death and a sight of any will he made, together with a notarized affidavit from his lawyer, obviously."

She said nothing.

"You can hardly expect me to rely on a couple of chewed-up press cuttings and a dubious letter."

Still nothing.

"That would be the normal procedure," he continued bravely, only too aware that normal procedures did not apply. "Once the necessary proofs had been obtained, I would recommend that you take your client to a German court and seek a formal probate or court order. My bank operates here on license. A condition of that license is that I abide by the jurisdiction of the State of Hamburg and the Federal Republic."

Another unnerving pause while she took a reading of him with her steadfast eyes.

"Those are the rules, then. Yes?" she asked.

"Some of them."

"What would happen if you bent them? Suppose a smart Russian exec in a thousand-dollar suit had flown in first-class from Moscow to collect his portion—'Hi, Mr. Tommy. It's me, Karpov's kid. Your dad and mine were drinking buddies. Where's my money?' What would you do then?"

"Precisely as I am doing now," he retorted with spirit, but without conviction.

Now it was Annabel Richter who was the defeated one, and Tommy Brue the victor. Her face had softened in resignation. She took a slow breath.

"All right. Help me. I'm out of my depth. Tell me what to do."

"What you always do, I imagine. Throw yourself on the mercy of the German authorities and have his situation normalized. The sooner the better, by the look of things."

"Normalized how? He's young, younger than me. Suppose they *don't* normalize his situation? How many more of his best years are they going to beat out of him?"

"Well, that's your world, isn't it? Fortunately, it's not mine."

"It's both our worlds," she snapped, as the color shot to her face and stayed there. "You just don't care to live in it. You want the best bit of the story? I don't think you do. Here it is anyway. You said take him to a court. Seek a formal probate. The moment I do that, he's very likely dead. Okay? *Dead.* He came here via Sweden. Sweden, then Denmark, then Hamburg. His ship wasn't meant to stop in Sweden, but it did. Ships do that sometimes. The Swedes arrested him. He was so screwed up from prison and the journey that they thought he couldn't stand up. Somehow he ran. Money helped. He's deliberately hazy about it. Before he ran, the Swedish police took his photograph and fingerprints. You know what that means?"

"Not yet."

She had recovered her equilibrium, but with difficulty. "It means that his fingerprints and photograph are on every police website. It means that under the Dublin treaty of 1990, which you have no doubt read from cover to cover, the Germans have no option but to post him back to Sweden express. No appeal, no due process. He's an escaped prisoner and illegal immigrant to Sweden, wanted in Russia and Turkey, with a record of Muslim activism. It's the Swedes, not the Germans, who get to deport him."

"The Swedes are as human as anyone else, I take it."

"Yes. They are. In the matter of illegal immigrants they're particularly human. As far as the Swedes are concerned he's an illegal immigrant and an absconded terrorist on the run, *period*. If the Turks want him back to serve the rest of his sentence—plus an extra few years for bribing his way out of jail—the Swedes will give him to the Turks and to hell with him. All right, there's a thousand-to-one chance that some Swedish saint will intercede, but I don't set much store by saints. When the Turks have had their fun with him, they'll give him to the Russians for more of the same. On the other hand, the Turks may feel they've had the best of him and pass, in which case the Swedes will give him straight to the Russians. Whichever they do, it's more prisons and more torture. You've seen him. How much more of it can he take? . . . Are you listening to me? I can't tell. I don't know your face."

He didn't know it himself. He didn't know how it should look, or what to inject into it by way of feeling.

"You speak as if there are no grounds for a simple compassionate appeal," he complained lamely, while she went on staring at him.

"Last year I had a client called Magomed. He was a twenty-three-year-old Chechen who'd been tortured by the Russians. Nothing personal, nothing very scientific, just a lot of beatings. But he was a soft kid, a bit crazy like Issa. Beatings hadn't suited him. Maybe he'd had one beating too many. We applied for asylum, played the compassion card. He liked the zoo. I was worried for him, so Sanctuary broke the bank and hired a hotshot lawyer who said the compassionate case was overwhelming, then went to sleep on it. Theoretically Germany has strict laws about where it can't send people. While we were waiting for the verdict, we planned another day at the zoo. Magomed didn't have Issa's track record. He wasn't a militant or a suspected Islamist. He wasn't wanted by Interpol. Five in the morning, they dragged him out of his hostel bed and put him on a plane to St. Petersburg. They had to gag him. His screams were the last anybody has heard of him." She blushed, unaccountably, and took a breath.

"In my law school we talked a great deal about law over life," she said. "It's a verity of our German history: law not to protect life, but to abuse it. We did it to the Jews. In its current American form it licenses torture and state kidnapping. And it's infectious. Your own country is not immune, neither is mine. I am not the servant of that kind of law. I'm the servant of Issa Karpov. He's my client. If that embarrasses you, I'm not sorry."

But it seemed to embarrass her, for she was by now scarlet in the face.

"How aware is your client of his situation?" Brue asked, after a prolonged silence.

"It's my job to tell him, so I've told him."

"How did he take it?"

"What's bad news for us isn't necessarily bad news for him. He was interested, but he's confident you'll fix it. The house is being watched, perhaps you hadn't noticed. Those hearts-and-minds policemen who paid Leyla a courtesy call—sure, they do hearts and minds all right."

"I thought you knew them."

"Everybody at Sanctuary knows them. They're the sniffer dogs."

Partly to escape her stare and partly to gain a moment's respite, Brue took a tour round the room.

"I have a question for your client," he said, turning to confront her. "Perhaps you can answer it for him. Under the terms relating to his supposed late father's account, there's something called an *instrument*. An *instrument* would be an essential part of any claim."

"Is it a key?"

"It might be."

"A small one with teeth on three sides?"

"Conceivably."

"I'll ask him," she said.

Was she smiling? It seemed to Brue that a spark of complicity had passed between them, and he prayed it had.

"That's if he makes a claim, obviously," he added sternly. "Only *if* he can be persuaded to. Otherwise we're back where we started."

"Is it a lot of money?"

"If he claims, if his claim is successful, no doubt he'll tell you how much is involved," he replied primly.

But here, out of the blue, either his good heart became too much for him, or he just forgot for a moment that he was a hardheaded banker born and bred. An eerie sensation swept over him that someone else—someone real, someone prepared to embrace spontaneous humanity rather than treat it as a threat to sound financial management—had commandeered him and was speaking out of him:

"But if there's anything personal I can do in the meantime—to help, I mean—quite honestly, anything at all within reason—I'd really be very happy to. Delighted, in fact. I'd regard it as a privilege."

She was watching him with such stillness that he began to wonder whether he had spoken at all.

"Help how, exactly?" she asked.

He had nowhere to go but forward, which was

as well, because he was already going there. "Within reason, any way I could. I'd be guided by you. Totally. I'm assuming he's genuine. I have to do that, obviously."

"We both have to assume that," she said impatiently. "I'm trying to find out what you were talking about when you said you'd really like to help."

Brue had no better idea what he had been talking about than she did, but he knew that her stare no longer accused him: rather, that he had said something that suited her purposes in some way, even if the realization was only now dawning in her mind.

"I suppose I was really thinking *money,*" he said a little shamefacedly.

"Could you lend him money now, for instance, up front, against his future expectations?"

The banker in him came briefly awake again. "Through the bank? No. Not while his expectations are unsubstantiated, and he won't claim. That would be out of the question."

"So what kind of money are you talking about?"

"Has your organization no funds for contingencies of this sort?"

"Sanctuary North has about enough funds at the moment to pay his fare to the nearest deportation center."

"And no—facility—where he can be accommodated temporarily?"

"Without the police finding him in five minutes, no."

Brue hadn't quite given up. "And if he's really ill? If he pleads sick? Nobody deports a seriously sick man, surely."

"If he pleads sick—which half of them do—which we did in Magomed's case—and the doctors agree he's not fit to travel, he'll be treated in a secure hospital till he's fit enough to be deported. Let me ask you again: What kind of money were you thinking of?"

"Well, the sum would rather depend on actual *need,* I suppose," said Brue, back to playing the banker. "If you can give me *some* idea of what you propose to do with it—"

"I can't. It's client confidential."

"Of course. And it should be. Clearly. But if we're talking of, well, relatively modest money, just to tide him over—"

"Not that modest—"

"—then in that case, given the circumstances, it would be money lent out of my own personal resources. To your client, obviously. Via yourself, but for his use."

"Does it have to be secured?"

"Good lord, no!" Why was he so shocked? "Simply an informal loan that one hopes in due course to get back—or not, so to speak. Depending on the amount that you have in mind, obviously. But no. No security asked for or needed."

He'd said it. And now that he'd said it, he knew he believed it, and was ready to say it again, and if need be, again after that.

It was her turn to be uncertain. "It could be—well—a lot."

"Ah, but that depends on how much a lot *is*," he could not resist replying, with the banker's smile that tells you that what may sound a lot to *you* may not sound a lot to *him*.

"If he doesn't end up needing it, I'll give it you back. You've got to believe that."

"I've no doubt of it. Now what sum are we thinking of?"

What was she calculating? How much he was good for, or how much for what she had in mind? And how long had she had it in mind? From the moment they came in here, or only when he put the idea into her head?

"For what he needs to do—if I can persuade him to do it—I reckon it's not going to be less than—thirty thousand euros," she said, gabbling the sum as if to make it smaller.

Brue's head was swirling, but not in a way to alarm. She's not a dubious entrepreneur. She's not an overdrawn client or a bad debt or a brilliant loser with a crazy idea. The crazy idea was mine, or rather: it was mine and it wasn't crazy.

"How soon do you want it?" he asked, before he could stop himself—another stock question.

"Very soon. Within a couple of days at most. Things could go fast for him. If they do, I'll have to have the money fast."

"And today's Friday. So why not do it now, then there's no missing the bus? And since you'll be giving back what you don't use, let's chuck in a bit in reserve too, shall we?" As if they were making something together, which was how in his out-of-body state he felt.

As ever, Brue had a checkbook handy, issued by a major clearing bank. But where on earth was his pen? He patted his pockets, only to remember that he had left it with his notepad on the table in the living room. She handed him her own, and looked on while he made out a check to Annabel Richter in the order of fifty thousand euros, dated today, Friday. On a calling card, of which he had half a dozen secreted in his Randall's jacket, he wrote out his cell phone number and as an afterthought—might as well be hanged twice!—his direct number at the bank.

"And you'll call me, I imagine," he added in an embarrassed mumble, when he discovered that she was still staring at him. "The name is Tommy, by the way."

In the drawing room, Issa had been persuaded to lean his head back on the sofa while Leyla laid a poultice on his brow.

"Best you don't come back here," Melik growled, escorting Brue to the front door. "Best you don't remember the name of the street. We don't remember you, and you don't remember us. Deal?"

"Deal," said Brue.

"Von Essens cheat," Mitzi announced, unfastening her sapphire earrings while she watched herself in her dressing mirror and Brue watched her from the bed. At the age of fifty, thanks to high maintenance and the attentions of a fashionable surgeon, she was still a ravishing thirty-nine, or almost.

"Von Essens play all the tricks in the book," she went on, critically examining the cords on her neck. "Fingers to the face, fingers on the cards, scratch your head, yawn, mirrors. And that tarty little maid of theirs pushing drinks and looking over our shoulders when she's not making eyes at Bernhard."

It was two in the morning. Sometimes they spoke German, sometimes English, and for fun a mix. Tonight it was German, or Mitzi's soft, Viennese version of it.

"So you lost," Brue suggested.

"And von Essens' house smells," she added, ignoring him. "Considering that it's built on top of a sewage system, no wonder. Bernhard should never have played the king. He's so rash. If he'd held his nerve we could have taken the rubber. It's time he grew up."

Bernhard, her regular partner, and not only at bridge, one suspects. But what can one do? Life's a botch. Old Westerheim hit it on the head when he called her the best First Lady in Hamburg.

"Did you work late again, Tommy?" Mitzi called from the bathroom.

"Fairly."

"Poor you."

One day, he thought, you'll really ask me where I've been, and what I've been up to. Except you never will. You won't ask me anything you don't want to be asked yourself. Wise girl. Wiser than me by a mile. Give you your head and you'd turn the bank round in a couple of years.

"You sound sharp," she complained, emerging in her nightdress. "You're not Friday night at all. You're flushed and busy. Have you taken your sleeping pill?"

"Yes, but it hasn't worked."

"Have you been drinking?"

"Couple of scotches."

"Are you worried about something?"

"Of course not. Everything's fine."

"Good. Maybe after sixty we want only to stay awake."

"Maybe we do."

She put the light out.

"And Bernhard wants to fly us up to his house in Sylt for lunch tomorrow. He's got two spare seats. Do you want to come?"

"Sounds fun."

Yes, Mitzi, I am flushed and busy. No, I am not Friday night. I just gave away the best fifty thousand euros of my life, and have yet to work out why. Buy time for him? What are you going to do with him? Get him a suite at the Atlantic?

This Friday night I walked all the way home on my own. No cab, no limousine. Lighter by fifty thousand euros, and feeling better for it. Was I followed? I don't think so. Not by the time I got lost in Eppendorf.

I marched through flat, straight roads that all looked the same, and my head refused to tell me where to go. But that wasn't fear. That wasn't me shaking off my pursuers, even if there were any. That was my compass going on the blink.

This Friday night I hit the same crossroads three times, and if I were standing there now, I still wouldn't know which way to turn.

Look back on my eventless life, what do I see? Escape. Whether it's been woman trouble, or bank trouble or Georgie trouble, dear old Tommy's always been halfway out of the door by the time the balloon goes up. It wasn't him, it was two other people, he wasn't there and, anyway, they hit him first: that was dear old Tommy for you.

Whereas Annabel—if I may call you so— well, you're all the other way, aren't you? You're a collision girl. The real thing—which presumably is why I'm thinking *Annabel, Annabel,* when I should be thinking: *Edward Amadeus,* you mad, dead, beloved man, and just look at the mess you've left me in!

But I'm not in a mess. I'm a happy investor. I haven't bought *out,* I've bought *in.* That fifty grand was my ticket of entry. I'm a partner in whatever plan you've got up your sleeve. And the name is Tommy, by the way.

Who've you got, Annabel? Who do you talk to—now, this minute? Who do you share yourself with when you hit the bottom of the sea?

One of Georgie's radical blowhards with long hair, no fifty grand and no manners?

Or some older, richer man of the world who can talk you down when you go off-scale?

Fathers, he thought as the pill began to take hold of him. Mine and Issa's. Brothers in crime, riding into the sunset on pitch-black Lipizzaners that refuse to turn white.

And *your* father, who's he when he's at home? Another one of me? Rejected and reviled—with justice? Only loved, if at all, from a range of eight thousand miles? But he's part of you all the same, I can feel it. I can feel it in your self-assurance, in your whiff of social arrogance, even when you're saving the wretched of the earth.

Issa, he thought. Her foundling. Her tortured man-child. Her black-arsed Chechen who is only half a Chechen, but insists he's a whole one, while he spouts ironies at me like those bearded Russian émigrés who used to hang around Montparnasse, every one of them a genius.

Issa's the chap who should go walkabout in Eppendorf, not me.

5

Günther Bachmann was at first annoyed, then alarmed, to be summarily bidden to the ample presence of Herr Arnold Mohr, head of the protectors' Hamburg station, at midday on a Sunday when Mohr, an ostentatious Christian, should by rights have been parading his family at one of the city's best churches. Bachmann had spent the night plowing through background files on Chechen *jihadis,* prepared for him by Erna Frey, who, in a rare burst of self-indulgence, had taken herself off to Hanover for a niece's wedding. His reading complete, he had been thinking of flying up to Copenhagen and having a couple of beers with the Danish security crowd, whom he liked; and, if they let him, a word with the good-brother lorry driver who had smuggled Issa to Hamburg and made him a present of his overcoat. He had gone so far as to call his connection there: *No problem, Günther, we'll send you a car to the airport.*

Instead of which, he now found himself apprehensively prowling his office in the stables while Erna Frey, still in her festive clothes, sat primly at her desk laboring at a monthly summary of costings she was preparing for Berlin.

"Keller's here," she informed him without lifting her head.

"*Keller?* Which Keller?" Bachmann retorted irritably. "Hans Keller from Moscow? Paul Keller from Amman?"

"Dr. Otto Keller, the most protective of all protectors, flew in from Cologne one hour ago. Look out of the window and you can admire his helicopter cluttering up the car park."

Bachmann looked as he was told and let out an exclamation of disgust. "What the hell does Uncle Otto want from us this time? Have we jumped another traffic light? Bugged his mother?"

"The meeting is top secret, operational and terribly urgent," Erna Frey replied, calmly continuing with her work. "That's all I can winkle out of them."

Bachmann's heart sank. "Meaning, they've found my boy?"

"If by your boy you mean Issa Karpov, rumor has it that they're warm."

Bachmann clapped a hand to his brow in despair. "They *can't* have arrested him. Arni swore the police wouldn't do that without consulting us first. *Your case, Günther. Your case, old boy, but we confer.* That was the pact." A different thought occurred to him, an even more appalling one: "Don't tell me the police arrested him just to show Arni who was boss!"

Erna Frey remained unmoved. "My Deep Throat—in the form of one very bad tennis player in Arni's very incompetent counterespionage section—assures me that the protectors are warm. That's the entire sum of her message. She'll never forgive me for beating her six–love in two straight sets, so she brings me gifts of gossip from the canteen. Then she tells me I mustn't tell you, so naturally I'm telling you," she said and, watched by Bachmann, again returned to her calculations.

"Why so sour this morning?" he demanded of her back. "That's my job."

"I loathe weddings. I consider them unnatural and insulting. Every time I attend one, I see another good woman go to the wall."

"How about the poor bloody *groom?*"

"As far as I'm concerned, the poor bloody groom *is* the wall. Keller wishes the meeting to be principals only. You, Mohr, Keller."

"No policemen?"

"None advertised."

Mollified, Bachmann resumed his study of the

courtyard. "Then it's two against one, the shining-white protectors versus one excommunicated black sheep."

"Well, just remember you're all fighting the same enemy," said Erna Frey tartly. "One another."

Her skepticism shocked him, since it was much like his own.

"And you're coming with me," he retorted.

"Don't be ridiculous. I detest Keller. Keller detests me. I shall be a liability and speak out of turn."

But under his unflinching eye she was already closing down her computer.

Bachmann had reason to be concerned. Rumors from Berlin abounded, some wild, others disconcertingly plausible. What was certain was that the old demarcations between rival services were indeed disappearing, and that Joint Steering, far from being the advisory body of wise men that it was designed to be, had become a house bitterly divided against itself. The running feud between those determined to defend civil rights at all costs, and those determined to curtail them in the name of greater national security, was approaching critical mass.

In the leftist corner, if such antiquated distinctions still counted for anything, presided the urbane Michael Axelrod of Foreign Intelligence. Axelrod was a keen European, an Arabist and—with reservations—Bachmann's mentor; and in the rightist corner, the archconservative Dieter Burgdorf from the Ministry of the Interior, Axelrod's rival to fill the post of intelligence czar once the foundations of the new structure had been laid: Burgdorf, the unashamed friend of Washington's neoconservatives, and the German intelligence community's most vocal evangelist for greater integration with its American counterpart.

Yet for the coming three months these two men, who could scarcely have had less in common, were committed to sharing equal power and exercising a duty of consensus. And as the two generals grew further apart, so did the troops they commanded, each jockeying and maneuvering to gain real or imaginary advantage. Since Burgdorf was from the interior ministry, and Mohr and Keller were employed by the domestic intelligence services, then logically it was to the highly personable and shamelessly ambitious Burgdorf that they would look for favor; and since the debonair but slightly older Axelrod was from Foreign Intelligence, and Bachmann was his protégé and colleague, then logically Bachmann was Axelrod's vassal heart and soul. Yet with the borders between the two services in flux, and the reach of the Federal Police adding to the confusion, and the ley lines of Berlin's power not yet drawn, who could tell anymore what was logical?

Which, in less refined language, was what Bachmann was cursing the world for as he and Erna Frey made their way across the courtyard to be greeted by Arni Mohr with his schoolboy forelock bouncing as he waddled towards them, fleshy hands outstretched and slippy eyes searching beyond them lest someone more important should be coming through the door after them.

"Günther, my dear friend! So good of you to sacrifice your precious Sunday! Frau Frey, what a pleasant surprise! And dressed so finely! We shall have another set of papers run off for you immediately"—lowering his voice for security reasons—"returnable after our little meeting, please. Each set numbered. Nothing goes outside the building. No, no, after you, Günther, please! I am at home here!"

Dr. Otto Keller sat alone at the long mahogany conference table, crouched over a box file, fastidiously exploring its contents with the tips of his long white fingers. Seeing the three of them enter, he lifted his head, noted the addition of Erna Frey in her wedding outfit and resumed his

reading. A second box file had been set in front
of the chair ordained for Bachmann. The code
word FELIX was stamped on the cover in black,
informing him that, whatever might have been
previously agreed, Issa Karpov was Mohr's baby,
and this was how Mohr had christened him—
and classified him top-secret-and-beyond while
he was about it. From a side door a woman in a
black skirt flitted in with a third file for Erna
Frey, and vanished. Shoulder to shoulder, Bachmann and Erna Frey dutifully embarked on their
homework while Mohr and Keller invigilated.

URGENT RECOMMENDATION:
That the internationally wanted
Islamist fugitive FELIX and those
connected with him be the object of an
immediate and comprehensive investiga-
tion by state and federal police and
protection agencies with a view to
public prosecution. Mohr.

REPORT NUMBER ONE
Respectfully submitted by field agent
[name deleted] of the Hamburg Office
of Protection:
    Source is a Turkish doctor recently
arrived in Hamburg and attached to
a medical practice serving Muslim

patients. On arrival in Germany,
source reached an understanding with
this agent that he would be vigilant
on behalf of this office. Motivation:
the favorable opinion of the state
authorities. Payment: on results only.
Source's statement:

"Last Friday I attended midday prayer
at the Othman Mosque, well known to
you for its moderate stance. I was
about to leave the mosque when I was
approached by a Turkish woman who was
not familiar to me. She desired to
speak to me confidentially regarding a
matter of urgency, but not in my
surgery or in the street. I would
describe her as aged fifty-five,
stout, dressed in a full gray scarf,
suspected blond, volatile.

"Halfway up the staircase leading
to the mosque there is an office
set aside for the convenience of imams
and visiting dignitaries. It was
unoccupied. Once inside, she began
talking volubly but not in my opinion
honestly. By her voice, she was of
peasant stock, from the northeastern
part of Turkey. I would say that
her statement contained factual

contradictions. Also she wept a lot, I
believe in order to arouse my sympathy. My impression was of a cunning
woman with an agenda.

"Her story, which I do not believe,
was as follows: She is a legal
resident in Hamburg but not a citizen.
She has a nephew staying with her, a
devout Muslim like herself. He is an
excitable boy, turned twenty-one, who
suffers from attacks of hysteria, high
fever and vomiting, also mental
stress. Many of his problems derive
from his childhood, when he was
frequently beaten by the police for
being a disturbing element, also
confined to a special hospital for
delinquents where he was abused.
Though he consumes large quantities of
food at any hour of the day or night
he remains emaciated and highly
stressed, pacing his room at night and
talking to himself. During fits
of nervous excitement he shows signs
of anger and makes menacing gestures
but she is not afraid of him, since
she has a son who is a champion
heavyweight boxer. Nobody ever got the
better of her son in a physical fight.

However, she would be grateful if I
would prescribe a sedative that would
enable him to sleep and recover his
psychological stability. He is a good
boy, and determined to become a doctor
like myself.

"I suggested that she bring the boy
to surgery, but she said he would
never come: first because he was too
ill, then because it would be
impossible to persuade him, and then
because it would be too dangerous for
all of them and she would not allow
it. These three separate excuses did
not seem to me compatible, and
reinforced my belief that she was
lying.

"When I asked why it would be
dangerous, she became even more
agitated. Her nephew was completely
illegal, she said, although by now she
no longer called him her nephew but
her guest. He could not go out into
the street without risking arrest,
also the deportation of herself and
her son, now that her late husband was
not around to bribe the police.

"When I offered to come and visit
the boy in her home, she refused me on

the grounds that it would be too
dangerous for me professionally, also
that she did not wish to endanger
herself by giving me her address.

"When I asked where the boy's
parents were, she replied that so far
as she could understand him, both were
dead. First the father had killed
the mother, then the father had been
buried in his military uniform. This
accounted for the boy's distress. When
I asked why she had difficulty
understanding her nephew, she replied
that in his dementia he spoke only
Russian. She then offered me two
hundred euros from her handbag for a
prescription. When I declined to accept
her money or write the prescription,
she emitted an exasperated shout and
ran down the stairs.

"I have inquired in the mosque. Nobody appears to know this strange
woman. As a believer in inclusiveness
and an opponent of all acts of terror,
I feel it my duty to make these facts
known to the authorities, since I
suspect that she is deliberately
harboring an undesirable and possibly
radical individual."

"Happy so far, Günther?" Mohr asked, his too-small eyes greedily upon him. "You get the idea?"

"Is this the whole statement?" Bachmann demanded.

"Abridged. The whole statement is longer."

"Can I see it?"

"Source protection, Günther, source protection."

Dr. Otto Keller appeared not to be listening. Perhaps he felt he oughtn't to be. Like so many of his kind, he was by philosophy and training a lawyer. His life's priority, far from encouraging his subordinates, was to throw the law book at them, the only weapon he knew.

```
REPORT NUMBER TWO
Extract of report compiled by field
agent [name deleted] of the Federal
Criminal Office at the request of the
Office for the Protection:
  "Orders were to identify a legally
resident heavyweight champion Turkish
boxer, who was not a citizen, whose
father was dead and whose mother
answered source's description.
Searches revealed Melik Oktay, aged
twenty, known as Big Melik, as
possible trace. Melik Oktay is
reigning heavyweight champion and this
year's captain of the Turkish Tigers
```

Sports Association. Photographs
displayed in the gymnasium of the
Altona Muslim Sports Center show Big
Melik with a black ribbon of mourning
stitched to his boxing shorts. Melik
Oktay is the son of Turkish legal
residents Gül and Leyla. Gül Oktay
died in 2007 and was buried according
to custom in the Muslim cemetery in
Hamburg-Bergedorf. Melik and his
widowed mother Leyla continue to
occupy a freehold family residence at
no. 26 Heidering, Hamburg.

APPENDIX:
Summary of Personal Record of OKTAY
Melik born Hamburg, 1987.
Aged thirteen, subject reported to be
ringleader of a gang of non-German
adolescents calling themselves the
Genghis Kids. Involved in violent
street clashes with anti-foreign
street elements of same age. Twice
detained and placed under warning
order. Father offers caution money
against son's future behavior. Offer
refused.

At school debate subject, aged
fourteen, advocates expulsion of

American troops from all Muslim lands,
including Turkey and Saudi Arabia.

Aged fifteen, subject enters
period of not shaving and favoring
Islamic-style dress.

Aged sixteen, subject gains titles
of under-18 all-Islamic boxing and
swimming champion. Elected captain of
his Muslim sports club. Subject
shaves, reverts to Western dress.
Enters Muslim rock group as drummer.

Mosque attendance: Subject reportedly
came under the influence of the Sunni
imam at the Abu Bakr Mosque in the
Viereckstrasse. After the imam's
deportation to Syria, and closure of
mosque in December 2006, no known
further adherence to radical Islamic
beliefs.

"They go under," Mohr explained, as Bachmann set aside the report and made to take up
the next one.

"Under what?" Bachmann replied, genuinely
mystified.

"Like the communists used to. They get the
indoctrination at a cadre meeting, they become
fanatics. Then they go under, and pretend

they're not fanatic anymore. They are *sleepers,*" he said, as if he had invented the term all alone. "That sports club—we have it from a top reliable informant who has infiltrated himself as a member and supplies us with first-class material, no exaggerations—that sports club where this Oktay is so admired, in my informant's opinion, it is a *cover organization.* They box and wrestle and train and get fit and talk about girls. And maybe they don't compromise themselves with fanatical statements when they are in large groups because they always know we will be listening. But in secret—in twos and threes—over coffee together and at the Oktays' house—they are Islamists. Militants. And now and then—we have this from the same excellent informant—this or that member of the group—a *selected* one—slips away. And where has he gone? To Afghanistan! To Pakistan! To the madrassas. To the training camps! And when he comes back—he's trained. Trained, but a *sleeper.* Read the rest, Frau Frey. Don't judge prematurely until you've read the rest, please. We must remain objective. We must not be prejudiced."

"I thought we agreed this was my case, Arni," Bachmann said.

"It is, Günther! We did! It's your case! That's why you're here, my friend! *Your case* doesn't mean we have to blind ourselves and put our hands over our ears. We watch, we listen—but we don't disturb your case, okay? We run parallel to you. We don't cross your lines, you don't cross ours. We pool what we know. This Melik Oktay will soon be going to Turkey for a *wedding*—theoretically. With the mother too, naturally. And of course we checked. Such a wedding will take place. His sister's. No question. But *after* the wedding—or before—where will he vanish to? Maybe only for a few days, but he goes. And the mother, what does she do? Find more boys that she can bring together, maybe. All right. I agree. It's circumstantial. It's hypothetical. But we are paid to think hypothetically. So we do. Hypothetically and objectively. No prejudices."

REPORT NUMBER THREE
Operation FELIX. Report of the
Hamburg Street Surveillance Team of
the Office for the Protection of the
Constitution.

Bachmann had passed through his anger threshold and entered a state of operational calm. Whether he liked it or not, this was information. It had been obtained in defiance of their agreement, and sprung on him too late for him to do anything about it. Well, in his time he'd done that to a few people himself. There was substance here, and he wanted it.

<u>Possible retrospective sighting date:</u> <u>seventeen days ago:</u> A man answering FELIX's description was observed loitering outside Hamburg's largest mosque. Security video images unclear. Subject inspecting worshipers entering and leaving mosque. Subject elects middle-aged couple as they walk towards their car, follows them at ten-meter distance. When asked in Farsi what he wants, subject turns and flees. Couple has since identified FELIX from wanted photograph.
<u>Agent's note:</u> Wrong mosque? Mosque is Shiite. Is FELIX Sunni?
<u>Desk officer's note:</u> Sources report similar figure lurking outside two other mosques, both Sunni, later in day. Sources unable to identify FELIX positively.

"Who the hell's the boy looking for?" Bachmann muttered aloud, to Erna Frey, who by now was a good couple of pages ahead of him. No answer.

REPORT NUMBER THREE (CONTINUED):

Melik Oktay is temporarily employed in his cousin's wholesale greengrocery business. He also works part-time at the candle factory of his uncle. Discreet inquiries under a pretext reveal that for the last two weeks his attendance has been unsatisfactory on the following grounds:

He is ill with a cold.

He needs to train for an upcoming boxing event.

He has an unexpected houseguest whom he must honor.

His mother is in depression.

Leyla Oktay is reported by neighbors to have displayed excitable behavior over the same period, telling them that Allah has made her a precious gift but refusing to explain what it is. She shops extravagantly but does not allow anyone to enter her house on the grounds that she is nursing a sick relative. Though politically naive, she is described as "deep," "secretive" and, by one neighbor, as "radical, manipulative and harboring concealed resentments against the West."

"But now look here what happened," Mohr urged Bachmann.

Bachmann was still trying to adjust to the situation. Mohr, without so much as a by-your-leave from him, had put a full-scale watch on the Oktays' house.

Mohr had invited the Hamburg police public relations department to make a so-called goodwill visit on the off chance of getting a sight of the mysterious houseguest. Mohr was an offense against every known tenet of intelligence good housekeeping, but Mohr also had loot from his rampage.

```
OPERATION FELIX
Report Number Four, relating to the
night of Friday, 18 April.
"At approximately 20.40 hours the
subject Melik Oktay left his house at
no. 26 Heidering . . . At 21.10 subject
returned, followed at a distance of
fifteen meters by a small, fair-headed
woman aged approx. twenty-five carrying
a large rucksack, contents unknown."
```

Of course they bloody well were, thought Bachmann . . .

```
"Accompanying her was a large-built
man aged between fifty-five and
```

sixty-five, dark-haired, could be
ethnic German, could be Turkish or
Arab of light skin. While Melik
unlocked the front door of his house,
the fair-headed woman put on a
headscarf in the Muslim manner.
Accompanied by the older man, she
crossed the street. Both were then
admitted to the house by Leyla, mother
of Melik, wearing a smart dress."

"Any pictures?" Bachmann snapped.

"The team weren't *prepared,* Günther! Why should they be? It was a *windfall*! Two tired women, their second shift, pedestrians, nine o'clock, it's dark. Nobody told them this was their big night."

"So no pictures."

Bachmann read on:

"At five minutes past midnight
large-built man emerged alone from no.
26 and proceeded down the street and
out of sight."

"Anyone house him?" Bachmann demanded, glancing ahead at the next page.

"This fellow was a trained operator, Günther, the best!" Mohr explained excitedly. "Used the little alleys, doubled back on his tracks, how do you follow a man like that through empty streets at one in the morning? We had six cars on drive-by. We could have had twenty. He gave us all the slip!" he ended proudly. "Also we did not wish to flush him, you understand. When a man is trained and surveillance-conscious, one must be circumspect. Tactful."

REPORT NUMBER FOUR (CONTINUED):
"02.30. Animated vocal exchange
occurring inside no. 26. Leyla Oktay's
voice the most penetrating. Precise
words could not be distinguished by
our operatives. Languages spoken were
Turkish, German and one other,
believed Slavonic. Unknown female
voice intervening at intervals,
possibly translating."

"They actually *heard* this?" Bachmann asked still reading.

"A fresh team in a van," Mohr said with satisfaction. "I ordered them in personally. No time to apply directional mikes, but they heard it all."

"At 4 A.M., unknown young female
previously described emerged from
house wearing headscarf and carrying

rucksack. Accompanied by man not
previously seen by our agents,
description as follows: nearly
two meters tall, skullcap and long
dark overcoat, early twenties,
long-striding, agitated in manner,
light-colored bag over shoulder.
Front door closed after them by Melik
Oktay. Couple disappeared, walking at
high speed down small streets."

"So you lost them," Bachmann said.

"Only temporarily, Günther! Just for an hour, maybe. But we quickly pieced it together. They did some fast walking, a bit of metro, a taxi, walked again. Typical countersurveillance methods. Like the big fellow before them."

"What about their phones?"

"Your next page, Günther. All laid out for you. Cell phones on the left, landlines on the right. Melik Oktay to Annabel Richter. Annabel Richter to Melik Oktay. Nine calls in all. Annabel Richter to Thomas Brue. Thomas Brue to Annabel Richter. Three calls in one day. The Friday. At this stage we can only give calls made, no conversations. Maybe retrospectively we can recover some of the conversations. Tomorrow, if Dr. Keller permits, we shall put in a bid with signals intelligence. Everything must proceed legally, that goes without saying. But what was in those bags, tell me? What was in those bags, Frau Frey? What had those two suspect individuals collected from the Oktay safe house, and where were they taking it in the middle of the night, and for what purpose?"

"Richter?" Bachmann asked, glancing up from his reading.

"A lawyer and Russian speaker, Günther. Excellent family. Works for Sanctuary North, a Hamburg foundation. Some of them a bit leftish, but never mind. Do-gooders. Assistance for asylum seekers and illegal immigrants, getting residence for them, helping them with their applications. *Et cetera.*"

It was the *et cetera* that gave the dismissive edge.

"And Brue?"

"Banker. British. Hamburg-based."

"What sort of banker?"

"Private. For the best people only. Fleet owners. Big tonnage."

"Anyone got any idea what he was doing there?"

"A total mystery, Günther. Soon maybe we shall be asking him. With Dr. Keller's approval, naturally. This bank had some problems in *Vienna,*" he added. "A bit of a *dark* character, by the sound of him. Are you ready?"

"For what?"

Holding up an impresario's index finger for silence, Mohr delved in a briefcase and retrieved a brown envelope. From the envelope he drew a couple of pages of electronic type. Bachmann stole a look at Keller: not a flicker. Erna Frey had closed her folder and was sitting back, tense with anger, glowering at the floor.

"From Russia with Love," Mohr announced in creaking English, setting out the pages before him. "Fresh from our translation section this morning. You permit me, Frau Frey?"

"I permit you, Herr Mohr."

He began reading.

"'In 2003, an investigation was launched by organs of Russian state security into unprovoked armed attacks by militant bandits on law-enforcement officers in the region of Nalchik, capital of the Russian republic of Kabardino-Balkaria,'" Mohr intoned, in a voice pregnant with significance. He looked up, making sure he had their attention.

"'The ringleader of the criminal group, which consisted entirely of dissident *jihadists* from neighboring Chechnya, was identified as one Dombitov, director of a local mosque known for propagating *extreme radical views.* Stored in the memory of this Dombitov's cell phone were the name and telephone number of'"—pause—

"'subject *Felix*'"—huge emphasis—"'together with the names and numbers of other *criminal members* of the gang. Under interrogation, Dombitov confessed that all names in his cell phone belonged to a militant Salafi group committed to violent acts with the aid of'"—significant pause—"'explosive devices, homemade, low quality, but highly effective.'"

Erna Frey's head lifted slightly. "They were tortured," she explained, in a deliberately matter-of-fact tone. "We spoke to Amnesty. We do not ignore open sources, Herr Mohr. According to Amnesty's eyewitnesses, they beat them and put electrodes on them. First they tortured Dombitov, then they tortured everybody he'd named, which was everybody who'd attended his mosque. There wasn't an ounce of real evidence against any of them."

Mohr was visibly annoyed. "You have read this, Frau Frey?"

"Yes, Herr Mohr."

"You have cut across my authority and gone directly to my translators, Frau Frey?"

"Our researcher downloaded the Russian police report last night, Herr Mohr."

"You speak Russian?"

"Yes. Herr Bachmann speaks it also."

Mohr had recovered himself. "Then you know the record of this Felix."

The irritable voice of Dr. Keller interposed itself: "Read it, please. Read it now you've started."

As Mohr resumed, Bachmann reached out his foot and put it softly on Erna Frey's. But she took her own foot away, and he knew there was no restraining her.

"'The inflammatory opinions and terrorist activities of Felix were confirmed by his accomplices, who described him as *a bad shepherd*,'" Mohr read doggedly. "'The criminal Felix was accordingly placed in a pretrial detention center for fourteen months while he faced two charges of attacking the local road police station, and a further charge of inciting his fellow Muslims to commit terrorist acts. He confessed his guilt on all charges.'"

"He was forced to," Erna Frey said, her voice thickening.

"You are suggesting that this is *all* fabrication, Frau Frey?" Mohr demanded. "You are unaware that we have excellent working relations with Russia in the fields of crime and terror?"

Receiving no answer, Mohr continued.

"'In 2005, equipped with false papers in the name of Nogerov, the criminal Felix was arrested by officers of state security regarding the sabotage of a gas pipeline in the region of Bugulma in the Russian republic of Tatarstan. Swift action by the local organs identified the presence of a group of antisocial dissidents living in squalid conditions in an isolated barn close to the scene of the outrage.' "

"The pipeline was old and rotten, like every other pipeline in Russia," Erna Frey explained, in a tone of superhuman forbearance. "The manager of the local power station was a drunk who bribed the police to call it sabotage. The police hauled in the nearest group of Muslim dropouts and forced them to denounce Felix as the ringleader. According to Human Rights Watch, the police put a store of explosives under the floorboards of the barn, discovered it, then rounded up the group, tortured them one by one and made the others watch. The longest anyone lasted was two days. They asked Felix whether he thought he could beat the record. He tried, but didn't make it."

Bachmann was praying that she might stop there but her righteous fury drove her to continue.

"The barn was nowhere *near* the scene of the explosion, Herr Mohr. It was in a field forty kilometers up the road and the kids hadn't a bicycle or a bus fare between them, let alone a car. It was the month of Ramadan. When the police came to get them they were playing an improvised game of hockey with homemade sticks to cheer themselves up, Herr Mohr."

* * *

Now, it was Dr. Otto Keller of Cologne who was leading the meeting.

"So you contest this report, Bachmann?"

"Yes and no."

"What's the yes?"

"Other people will not contest it in the same way, if at all."

"What people?"

"The people who are predisposed to believe it."

"And for you there is no middle way? You don't allow that the case against Felix might be *partially* true? For instance, that he is a *jihadi,* as they suggest?"

"If we're going to use him, all the better if he is."

"So a dyed-in-the-wool *jihadi* will be happy to collaborate with you? Is that what you're saying, Bachmann? We have not had much success so far in that field."

"I mean he may not *have* to collaborate with us," Bachmann retorted, feeling his throat tighten. "It may be better that he doesn't. We let him go his own way, with our help."

"This is total speculation, naturally."

"As Felix stands now, he makes no sense. You have our report on the man known as the Admiral who was summoned to help him at the railway station. You have the report on Felix's lorry

driver. The boy's escape must have cost a fortune
but he sleeps on the street. He's a Chechen, but
he's not a real Chechen. If he was, he'd go looking for other Chechens. He's Muslim but he
can't tell the difference between a Sunni and a
Shiite mosque. In one night he's visited by a civil
rights lawyer and a British banker. It had to be
Hamburg for him. Why? He's here with a mission. What is it?"

Mohr leapt in. "With a mission! Yes! A mission to make contact with a terrorist woman and
her son and establish a sleeper cell of *jihadi*
clean-skins here in Hamburg! He's a terrorist on
the run, he hides out with a Turkish thug who
was inspired by an Islamist rabble-rouser and
grew a beard, then cut it off and pretended to go
Western. He slips away with a German woman
lawyer in the middle of the night, carrying God
knows what in his bag, and you want to *exploit
him unconsciously*?"

Issuing his judgment from the throne, Keller's
arid voice had the starkness of a death sentence:

"No responsible security officer can ignore a clear
and present threat in order to humor a vague
operational ambition. It is my view that a search-
and-find operation resulting in high-profile arrests
will serve as a deterrent to Islamist sympathizers,
and restore confidence in those responsible for
seeking them out. Some cases cry out for a solid

conclusion. This is such a case. I'm therefore proposing you set aside whatever interests you may
imagine you have invested in this case, and we
pass it over to the Federal Police for due process
under the Constitution."

"You mean *arrest*?"

"I mean whatever the case merits under the
law."

And whatever wins you brownie points with
your far right-wing friend Burgdorf of Joint
Steering, thought Bachmann. Whatever annoints
you as the intelligence superbrain behind the
plonking Federal Police. And leaves me nowhere,
which is where you want me to be.

But for once he managed not to say all this.

Side by side, Erna Frey and Bachmann walked
back across the courtyard to their unit's humble
riding stables. Reaching his office, Bachmann
slung his jacket over the arm of the sofa, and
called Michael Axelrod at Joint on the encrypted
line.

"Tell him it was all my fault," Erna Frey said,
head in hands.

But to their shared surprise, Axelrod sounded
a great deal less disturbed than he should have
been.

"Have you two eaten?" he inquired, in his

usual debonair way, when he had heard Bachmann out. "Then get yourselves a sandwich and
stay where you are."

They waited for Keller's helicopter to take off,
but it didn't, which only depressed them further.
They had no appetite for sandwiches. It was four
in the afternoon by the time the encrypted
phone rang.

"You've got ten days," Axelrod said. "If you
haven't got a good argument after ten days, they
get their arrest. That's the way things work up
here. Ten days, not eleven. You'd better be
lucky."

6

I'm doing this for my client Magomed, she told herself as she fought for clarity in the mayhem of her mind.

I'm doing it for my client Issa.

I'm doing it for life over law.

I'm doing it for me.

I'm doing it because Brue the banker gave me money, and the money gave me the idea. But that's not true at all! The idea was growing inside me long before Brue's money. Brue's money only tipped the scales. The moment I sat down with Issa and heard his story, I knew that this was where the system stops, that this was the unsavable life I must save, that I must think of myself not as a lawyer but as a doctor like my brother Hugo and ask myself: What is my duty to this injured man, what sort of a German lawyer am I if I leave him in the legal gutter to bleed to death like Magomed?

As long as I think like that, I'll keep my courage.

It was crack of dawn. Sullen strips of blue-black cloud were smeared across the pink city sky. Annabel was leading by a meter and Issa, contrary to Muslim manners, was stalking close behind her in his long black overcoat, and the two of them in her imagining were a pair of eternal refugees: she with a rucksack, he with his saddle-bag. The yammer of their final scene in Leyla's house was still ringing in her head:

With Melik standing mutely beside her, Leyla has suddenly no *idea* why Issa is leaving! Her screams are cries to heaven. She didn't even know he *was* leaving! Why had nobody *told* her? Where in God's name is Annabel taking him at this time of night? Friends? *What* friends? If she'd known, she'd have prepared food for his journey! Issa is her son, her gift from Allah, her house is his house, he can stay forever!

Five hundred dollars? Leyla won't accept a penny of them! She has done nothing for money, only for Allah, and for love of Issa. And where in Allah's name did he get the money from anyway? That rich Russian who came and went? Besides, nobody accepts fifty-dollar bills these days! They're all forged. And if Issa wants to give her money, why has he hoarded it for two weeks instead of coming out with it straightaway like a man?

After which Melik, all tears himself now, must beg Issa's forgiveness and pledge his eternal friendship, and in evidence of which bestow on him his precious Azan pager, the Muslim novelty, given to him by a beloved uncle, that electronically signals the prayer hours.

"Take it, my dear brother. It is yours, keep it beside you at all times. It's foolproof. You'll never miss."

And while he demonstrates how it works—Issa being unversed in such things—Annabel stands in Melik's place beside the window and resumes her watch of the frozen food van parked fifty meters down the road, and still nobody has got out of it, which was why, the moment they reached the street, she turned not to left or right but, under full view of the van, marched him at random across the road and down an alley and, as luck would have it, through a narrow gateway to a wider, parallel road with traffic and a bus stop. At first Issa was stiff with fear and Annabel had to pull at his coat sleeve—only the sleeve, mind, not his actual arm, not even through the cloth—to get him moving.

"Do you know where we are going, Annabel?"

"Of course I do."

But we go there cautiously. We don't take the rational route. The nearest underground station is ten minutes' walk away.

"We shall not talk together on the train, Issa. If someone addresses you, point at your mouth and shake your head." And, observing his acquiescence, she thought: I'm just another of Anatoly's mafiosi arranging his latest escape.

The train was packed with migrant office cleaners. Directed by Annabel, Issa took his place among them, head down like the rest, while she stared into the black window, watching his reflection. We are not a couple. We are two single people who just happen to be in the same carriage, and that's how we are in life, and we'd both better believe it. At each stop he raised his eyes to her, but she ignored him until the fourth. A line of cream-colored cabs stood in the station forecourt. Taking the first, she opened the back door, climbed in and left it open for him to join her. But to her momentary horror he vanished, to reappear on the front seat beside the driver, presumably so that he could avoid physical contact with her. His skullcap was pulled so low over his brow that all that was left for her to contemplate was his muffled head and the mystery of what was going on inside it. At a crossroads five hundred meters from her street she paid the driver off and again they walked. There's still time, she thought, as the bridge came into sight and her courage failed again. All I have to do is walk him over the bridge, turn him in at the police station, earn the thanks of a grateful community and live out the rest of my life in shame.

Annabel's mother was a district judge, her father a retired lawyer-diplomat in the German foreign service. Her sister, Heidi, was married to a public prosecutor. Only her elder brother, Hugo, whom she adored, had managed to beat the legal rap and become, first a general practitioner, and now a brilliant if wayward psychiatrist who claimed to be the last pure Freudian on earth.

That Annabel, the family rebel, had ever succumbed to the law herself was a continuing mystery to her. Was it to please her parents? Never. Perhaps she had imagined that by entering their profession she could demonstrate her difference from them in language they understood; that she would wrench the law out of the grasp of the rich and easy, and take it to the people who had most need of it. If so, nineteen months at the Sanctuary had told her how wrong she was.

Sitting out the pitiful kangaroo tribunals, biting her lip as she listened to her clients' horror stories being picked over by low-ranking bureaucrats whose experience of the outside world amounted to two weeks in Ibiza, she must have known a moment would come—a client would come—that would cause her to abandon every professional and legal principle she had ever reluctantly embraced.

And she was right. Come the day, come the client: Issa.

Except that before Issa, Magomed had come, and it was Magomed—stupid, trusting, abused, not particularly truthful Magomed—who had taught her, never again.

Never again the too-late dawn rush to the airport; or the plane for Petersburg standing on the runway with its passenger door open; or the trussed figure of her client being bundled up the steps; or the hands—were they real or imagined?—the cuffed hands helplessly waving goodbye to her through the cabin window.

Therefore don't tell her that she had made an impulsive, spur-of-the-moment decision about Issa. Her decision had been taken that day at Hamburg airport, as she watched Magomed's tumbrel disappear into low cloud. As soon as she had set eyes on Issa last week in Leyla's house and prised his story out of him, she had known: This is the one I have been waiting for ever since Magomed.

First, forcing herself to observe the family forum's rules of engagement, she had calmly set out for herself the *givens* of the case:

From the moment he landed in Sweden, Issa became unsavable.

There is no legal process available to him that offers more than an outside hope of salvation.

The poor, brave people who are harboring him are putting themselves at risk. He can't stay here much longer.

After that, she had made straight for the practicalities: How in *pure terms,* how in *reality,* given the situation as it stands, does Annabel Richter, law graduate of the universities of Tübingen and Berlin, perform her solemn duty to her client?

How best does she hide, house, and feed said client, it also being a precept of the family forum that the fact that you can only do a little is no excuse for doing nothing?

We lawyers are not put on earth to be icebergs, Annabel, her father liked to preach: he of all men! *Our job is to acknowledge our feelings and control them.*

Yes, dear Father. But has it ever occurred to you that by *controlling* them you destroy them? How many times can we say sorry before we don't feel sorry anymore?

And what—forgive me—do you mean exactly by *control*? Do you mean, finding the right *legal* reasons for doing the wrong thing? And if you do, isn't that what our brilliant German lawyers did during the Great Historical Vacuum, otherwise known as the Nazi era—all twelve years of it—that for some reason finds so little mention in our forum's deliberations? Well, from this moment on, *I* control my feelings.

In life—you liked to warn me when I had grievously sinned against you—I can do anything I wish, just as long as I'm prepared to pay full price for it. Well, Father dear, I'm prepared. I'll pay full price. If that means good-bye to my beautiful but brief career, I'll pay that too.

And it so happens that by an act of benign Providence, if that's what we believe in, I am in temporary possession of two apartments: one that I can't wait to see the back of, the other a gem on the harbor front that I bought with the last of my beloved grandmother's money just six weeks ago, and am in the throes of refurbishing.

And if that was not enough, Providence, or guilt or a sudden surge of unexpected compassion—she had no time to fathom which—had provided her with money. Brue's money: on account of which there was not merely a short-term plan—an emergency plan of strictly limited duration and convenience—but, thanks to Brue's munificence, a longer-term plan; a plan that allowed her time to cast around for solutions; a plan that, prudently implemented with help from her beloved brother, Hugo, would not only keep Issa safely hidden from his pursuers, but set him on the path to recovery.

"And you'll call me, I imagine," Brue had said, as if he, like Issa, needed to be rescued by her.

From what? Emotional deadness? Was Brue drowning too? Did she only have to hold out her hand to him as well?

They had reached her house. Turning, she saw Issa cowering in the darkness of an overhanging lime tree, his bag clutched in the folds of his black coat.

"What's the matter?"

"Your KGB," he muttered.

"Where?"

"They followed us from the taxi. First in a big car, then in a small one. One man, one woman."

"They were just two cars that happened to pass by."

"These cars had radio."

"In Germany all cars have radios. Some have telephones as well. Please, Issa. And keep your voice down. We don't want to wake everyone up."

Glancing up and down the road but seeing nothing out of the ordinary, she descended the steps to the front door, unlocked it and nodded him forward, but he shied to one side and insisted on entering after her, and at a distance.

She had left the flat in a hurry. Her double bed

was unmade, the pillow crushed, her pajamas
strewn across it. The wardrobe had two sides, to
the left her own clothes, to the right, Karsten's.
She had thrown Karsten out three months ago,
but he'd never had the guts to fetch them. Or
perhaps he thought that by leaving them there he
was asserting his right of return. Well, screw
him. One top-brand buckskin jacket, one pair of
designer jeans, three shirts, one pair of soft
leather moccasins. She dumped them on the bed.

"These are your husband's, Annabel?" Issa inquired from the doorway.

"No."

"They are whose, please?"

"They belonged to a man I had a relationship
with."

"He is dead, Annabel?"

"We broke up"—wishing by now she hadn't
told him to call her by her first name, although
with clients she always did, and kept her surname to herself.

"Why did you break up, Annabel?"

"Because we weren't suited to each other."

"Why were you not suited? Did you not love
each other? Perhaps you were too severe towards
him, Annabel. That is possible. You can be very
severe. I have noticed this."

At first she didn't know whether to laugh out
loud or slap him down. But when she looked at

him for guidance, she saw only puzzlement in his eyes as well as fear, and she remembered that, in the world he had escaped from, there was no such thing as privacy. Simultaneously, a second thought overcame her and she was both ashamed and disconcerted by it: that she was the first woman he'd been alone with after years of confinement, and they were standing in her bedroom in the early hours of the morning.

"Would you lift that bag down for me, please, Issa?"

Taking a large step back to make way for him, she wondered whether she should have put her cell phone in her jacket pocket, though God knew who she was going to ring if things got heavy. Karsten's holdall was gathering dust on top of the wardrobe. Issa lifted it down and laid it on the bed beside the clothes. She shoved the clothes into it and fetched her rolled-up sleeping bag from the bottom of the airing cupboard.

"Was he a lawyer like you, Annabel? This man you had a relationship with?"

"It doesn't matter what he was. It's not your business, and it's over."

Now it was she who wished urgently for greater distance between them. In the kitchen he was too tall for her and too present, however much he hung back. She set a bin bag on the table and brusquely held up items for his approval: Wholegrain bread, Issa? Yes, Annabel. Green tea? Cheese? Live yogurt from the funky organic shop ten minutes' cycle ride away that she determinedly patronized in opposition to the supermarket up the road? Yes, Annabel, to all of it.

"I can't give you meat, okay? I don't eat it."

But what she wanted to say was: Nothing's going on here. All that's happening is I'm sticking my neck out for you. I'm your lawyer and that's all I am, and I'm doing this for the principle, not the man.

They carted their luggage to the crossroads. A cab appeared and she directed it to a point above the harbor front. Then for the second time, she walked him the rest of the way.

Her new apartment was eight rickety flights of wooden staircase high, set in the loft of an old dockside warehouse that according to its owner was the only building the British had had the grace to leave to posterity when they bombed the rest of Hamburg into oblivion. It was a shiplike attic fourteen meters by six with iron rafters and a grand arched window that looked down onto the harbor; and a bathroom crammed into one eave and a kitchen in the other. She had first seen it at an open house, with half of Hamburg's young rich tripping over themselves to buy it, but the owner had taken a shine to her and, unlike her present landlord, he was gay and didn't want to get her into bed.

By the same evening, the flat was miraculously hers, a Karsten-free life in the making, and for the last six weeks she had been cosseting it, fussing over its wiring and plasterwork and paintwork, replacing rotting floorboards, and in the evenings, after another sickening tribunal or another lost battle with authority, racing down here on her bicycle, just to stand at the arched window with her elbows on the sill and watch the sun go down, and the cranes and cargo ships and ferries interweaving and relating in the way that human beings should, respectfully and without crashing into one another, and the gulls swirling and warring, and the kids rampaging on the playground.

And in what she knew to be a rosy surge of optimism, she would congratulate herself on the woman she was about to become, married to her work and her family at the Sanctuary—Lisa, Maria, André, Max, Horst and doughty Ursula, their boss—men and women who like herself were dedicated to fighting the good fight for people whom the accidents of life had earmarked for the scrap heap.

Or put another way: coming home exhausted and as empty as the flat that awaited her, knowing that however hard she had pushed herself all day, there was only herself to look forward to at night. But even nothing was better than Karsten.

They climbed the stairs slowly, Annabel leading, and at each floor she put down her bin bag of provisions and made sure Issa was struggling after her with the holdall and the bedroll. She would have shared more of the load with him but every time she tried he waved her angrily away, although after two flights he was looking like an old, thin child, and after three his breathing was coming in rasps that echoed up and down the stairwell.

The din they were making alarmed her until she remembered it was Saturday and there were no other tenants. All the other floors were given over to fancy offices of haute couture, designer furniture and gourmet food companies: worlds she told herself that she had resolutely left behind.

Issa had stopped halfway up the last flight and was staring past her, his face stiff with fear and incomprehension. The door to her loft was of old hammered iron with heavy bolts. Its giant padlock would have secured the Bastille. She hurried down to him and this time accidentally seized his arm, only to feel him recoil.

"We're not locking you up, Issa," she said. "We're trying to keep you free."

"From your KGB?"

"From everyone. Just do as I say."

He slowly shook his head, then in an act of terrible submission lowered it, and step after step, but so laboriously that his feet might have been chained together, he followed her up the last of the stairs. Then stopped again, head still bowed and feet together, while he waited for her to unlock the door. But all her instincts told her not to.

"Issa?"

No reply. Stretching out her right hand until it was directly in his eyeline, she laid the key on her open palm and offered it to him the way she had offered carrots to her horse when she was small.

"Here. *You* open it. I'm not your jailer. Take the key and unlock the door for us. Please."

For a lifetime, as it seemed to her, he remained staring downward at her open hand, and at the rusted key lying on it. But either the prospect of taking it from her was too much for him, or he was fearful of making contact with her bare flesh, for abruptly his head, then his whole upper body, turned away from her in rejection. But Annabel refused to be rejected.

"Do you want *me* to open it?" she demanded. "I need to know, please, Issa. Are you telling me I may open this door? Do I have your permission? Answer me, please, Issa. You're my client. I need your instructions. Issa, we're going to stand here and get very cold and tired until you *instruct* me to open this door. Do you hear me, Issa? Where's your bracelet?"

It was in his hand.

"Put it back on your wrist. You're not in danger here."

He put the bracelet back on his wrist.

"Now tell me to open the door."

"Open."

"Say it louder. Open the door, please, Annabel."

"Open the door, please."

"Annabel."

"Annabel."

"Now watch me unlock the door at your request, please. There. Done. I go in first and you follow me. Not like prison at all. No, leave the door open behind you, please. We won't close it until we need to."

It was three days since she had been here. A swift look round told her that the builders were more advanced than she had feared. The plastering was nearly complete, the tiles she had ordered were stacked and waiting, the old bathtub her mother had found in Stuttgart was in place, fitted with the brass taps Annabel had bought at the flea market. The water supply was restored, or why would the builders have left their coffee cups in the sink? The telephone she had ordered was in its blister pack at the center of the floor, waiting to be connected.

Issa had discovered the arched window. Stock-still, his back to her as he contemplated the lightening sky, he was tall again.

"It's only for a day or two while I make other arrangements," she called to him lightly down the room. "This is where we keep you safe for your own good. I'll bring you books and food and visit you every day."

"I cannot fly?" he inquired, his gaze still on the sky.

"I'm afraid not. You can't go outside either. Not until we're ready to move you."

"You and Mr. Tommy?"

"Me and Mr. Tommy."

"He will visit also?"

"He's consulting his files. That's what he has to do. I'm not a banker, neither are you. Not everything can be solved at once. We have to move one step at a time."

"Mr. Tommy is an important gentleman. When I am appointed a doctor, I shall invite him to the ceremony. He has a good heart and speaks Russian like a Romanov. Where did he learn to do this?"

"In Paris, I believe."

"Is that where you learned your Russian also, Annabel?"

This time, at least, it wasn't about Karsten. He had stopped sweating. His voice was calm again.

"I learned my Russian in Moscow," she said.

"You were at school in Moscow, Annabel? That is most interesting! I too was at school in Moscow. Only for a short time, it is true. What school, please? What number? Maybe I am familiar with this school. Did they accept Chechen students?"—clearly excited to be making a connection between his world and hers, imagining perhaps that they were school friends.

"It didn't have a number."

"Why not, Annabel?"

"It wasn't that kind of school."

"What kind of school is it that doesn't have a number? Was it a KGB school?"

"No, it most certainly was not! It was a private school." In her sudden weariness she heard herself telling him the rest. "It was a private school for the children of foreign officials living in Moscow. So I attended it."

"Your father was a foreign official living in Moscow? What kind of official, Annabel?"

She was backtracking. "I happened to be staying in the house of an official foreign family. I was eligible to attend this private school, and that's where I learned to speak Russian."

And that's more than I meant to tell you, because not even you are going to drag out of me the fact, unknown even to the Sanctuary, that my father was legal attaché to the German embassy in Moscow.

A beeper was screaming and it was not her own. Fearing they had set off some clever alarm left behind by the builders, she peered anxiously round the room for the source, but it was Issa's electronic pager, given him by Melik, summoning him to the first prayer hour of the day.

Yet he remained at the window. Why? Was he looking for his KGB followers? No. He was plotting the direction of Mecca by the dawn light before his pencil-thin body folded to the bare floorboards.

"You will please leave the room, Annabel," he said.

Waiting in the kitchen, she cleared a space and unpacked the bin bag. Sitting on a stool with one elbow on the decorators' table and her fist bunched against her cheek, she lapsed into a daze in which, by an act of self-transposition, she found herself staring, as often when she was tired, at her father's collection of small paintings by Flemish masters that hung in the drawing room of the family estate outside Freiburg.

"Bought at auction in Munich by your grandfather, darling," her mother had replied when, as a rebellious fourteen-year-old, Annabel had launched her one-woman investigation into the paintings' provenance. "The way your father likes to collect his icons."

"How much for?"

"In today's money, they're no doubt worth a great deal. But back in those days, pennies."

"Bought at auction *when*?" she had demanded. "Bought who *from*? Who did the paintings belong to before Grandpa bought them for pennies at an auction in Munich?"

"Why don't you ask your father, darling?" her mother suggested, altogether too sweetly for Annabel's suspicious ear. "It's *his* father, not mine."

But when Annabel asked her father, he became someone she didn't know. "Those times are over and done with," he had retorted, in an official tone he had never used to her before. "Your grandfather had a nose for art, he paid the going price. For all I know, they're fakes. Never dare ask that question again."

And I never did, she remembered. Not in all the family forums since, whether out of love, or fear or, worst of all, submission to the family discipline she was in revolt against, had she dared ask that question again. And her parents considered themselves radicals! They were rebels, or had been: sixty-eighters who had manned the barricades at student protests, and carried banners urging the Americans to get out of Europe! "You young of today don't know what real protest is about!" they liked to tell her laughingly, when she overstepped the mark.

Taking a notebook from her rucksack, she began jotting herself a must-do list by the glow from the skylight. Her lists were as much a family joke as her intransigence. One minute she was this chaotic snail with her whole disorganized life in her rucksack, the next she was this German over-organizer who made herself lists about the lists she was going to make.

```
Soap.
Towels.
More food.
Sweet and savory.
Fresh milk.
Loo paper.
Russian medical journals: where to
    find?
My cassette player. Classical only,
    no trash.
```

And no, I won't buy a bloody iPod, I refuse to be a slave to consumerism.

Unsure whether Issa was still at prayer, she softly returned to the big room. It was empty. She ran to the window. It was locked, no broken glass. She swung round and, with the light be-hind her, looked back into the room.

He was standing two meters above her on top of a builder's ladder. Like some Soviet-era statue, he was holding a giant pair of scissors in one hand and in the other a paper airplane he must have cut from the roll of lining paper at the foot of the ladder.

"One day, I shall be a great aeronautical engi-neer like Tupolev," he announced, without look-ing down at her.

"No more doctor?" Annabel called up, humor-ing him as she might a suicide.

"Doctor also. And maybe, if I have time, lawyer. I wish to acquire the Five Excellences. Do you know the Five Excellences? If you do not, you are not cultivated. I have already a good grounding in music, literature and physics. Maybe you will convert to Islam and I will marry you and attend to your education. That will be a good solution for both of us. But you must not be severe. Look, Annabel."

Articulating his long body forward to a point where he defied the laws of gravity, he gently laid his paper airplane on the still air.

He's simply another client, she repeated to her-self angrily as she closed the door behind her and snapped shut the aged padlock.

A client who's in need of special attention, granted. Unorthodox attention. Illegal attention. But a client for all that. And soon he'll get the medical care he needs as well.

He's a case. A legal case. With a file. All right, a patient too. He's a damaged and traumatized child who's had no childhood, and I'm his lawyer and his nanny and his only connection with the world.

He's a child but he knows more about pain and captivity and the worst of life than I ever will. He's arrogant and helpless, and half the time what he's saying bears no relation to what he's thinking.

He's trying to please me and he doesn't know how. He's saying the right words, but he's not the man who should be saying them: Marry me, Annabel. Watch my paper airplane, Annabel. Convert to Islam, Annabel. Don't be severe, Annabel. I want to be a lawyer, a doctor and a great aeronautical engineer and a few other things that will occur to me before I'm shipped back to Sweden for onward transportation to the gulag, Annabel. You will please leave the room, Annabel.

On the harbor front, dawn had turned to early morning. She mounted a pedestrian walkway that ran alongside the harbor wall. In the past weeks while she waited for her new apartment to materialize she had walked here often, notching up the shops she would use and the fish cafés where she would meet her friends, and fantasizing about the routes she would take to work: one day, ride all the way, the next put her bike on the ferry, stay aboard three stops, hop off and ride again, but now all she could think of was Issa's parting words after she had prepared him for being locked up again:

"If I sleep, I shall return to prison, Annabel."

Back in her old flat, Annabel moved with the elaborate precision for which the family forum never ceased to tease her. She had been frightened and refused to admit it. Now she could celebrate her victory over fear.

First she basked in the shower she had promised herself, and washed her hair while she was at it. Her near exhaustion of an hour ago had been replaced by a thirst for action.

Once showered, she dressed for the road: knee-length Lycra shorts, trainers, a light blouse for a hot day, Sherpa waistcoat, and—on the bamboo table next to the door—her shell hat and leather gloves. Her need for physical exercise was insatiable. Without it, she was convinced, she would turn to blubber in a week.

Next, she e-mailed her builders and tradesmen with the same urgent message: *Very sorry, friends, please absolutely no work at new flat until further no-*

tice. Unforeseen legal problems over lease, all will be re-solved in next few days. Will recompense you fully for any loss of earnings. Tschüss, *Annabel Richter.*

And to the shopping list lying at her side she added *new padlock,* because people don't necessarily read their weekend e-mails before setting off to work on a Monday.

Her cell phone was ringing. Eight o'clock. Every Saturday morning, public holidays included, at the stroke of eight, Frau Dr. Richter called her daughter, Annabel. On Sundays she called Annabel's sister, Heidi, because Heidi was the elder. Family ethic did not allow that either daughter could be lying in late or making love on a Saturday or a Sunday, or on any other morning.

First, her mother's "State of the Nation" address. Annabel was already smiling.

"I am being totally indiscreet, but Heidi thinks she may be pregnant again, she will know for certain on Tuesday. Until then, the news is embargoed, Annabel. You understand?"

"I understand, Mother, and how lovely for you. Your fourth grandchild already, and you still a child yourself!"

"As soon as it's official, you may congratulate her, naturally."

Annabel forbore from saying that Heidi was furious, and only her husband's entreaties had prevented her from having an abortion.

"And your brother, Hugo, has been offered a job in the human psychology wing of a large teaching hospital in Cologne, but says he isn't sure they are real Freudians, so he may not take it. Really, he's too stupid sometimes."

"Cologne might suit Hugo fine," Annabel said, without adding that she spoke to Hugo three times a week on average, and knew very well what his plans were: namely to stay put in Berlin until his torrid love affair with a married woman ten years his senior had either burned itself out or blown up in his face, or—which with Hugo was pretty much the norm—both.

"And your papa has agreed to deliver the keynote speech to a conference of international jurists in Turin. So being him, he has already started writing it, and I shan't get a word out of him till September. Have you made it up with Karsten yet?"

"We're working on it."

"Good."

A small pause.

"How did your tests go, Mother?" Annabel asked.

"Idiotic as usual, my dear. When somebody tells me the results are negative, I'm depressed because I'm a natural optimist. Then I have to think myself round."

"Were they negative?"

"There was one small positive voice, but it was immediately drowned out by the negatives."

"Which one was positive?"

"My stupid liver."

"Have you told Papa?"

"He's a man, darling. He'll either tell me to have another glass of wine, or he'll think I'm dying. Go for your cycle ride."

Now for her master plan.

Hugo's life, as ever, was precariously poised. His lady-love's husband was an itinerant businessman of some kind with the inconsiderate habit of coming home at weekends. Accordingly, Hugo spent his Saturday and Sunday nights at his hospital, on call in the staff hostel, and seeing his patients by day. The trick therefore was to catch him after 8 A.M. when his night shift ended, and before 10 A.M. when he began his rounds. The time now was eight-twenty, and therefore ideal.

For security reasons, she required a public telephone and, for her ease of mind, a place she was familiar with. She selected a former hunting lodge turned café in the deer park at Blankenese, normally fifteen minutes of hard cycling away. She made the distance in twelve and had to order a herbal tea and sit and stare at it while she got her breath back. In the corridor leading to the lavatories was an old-fashioned red English phone box. At the counter, she negotiated a handful of coins in readiness.

As usual with Hugo, they talked half in banter, half in earnest. Perhaps because she was feeling so earnest she overdid the banter.

I've got this nightmare client, Hugo, she began. Highly intelligent but a psychological wreck. Speaks Russian only.

He needs to chill out and be looked after professionally.

His personal circumstances are dire and can't be described over the phone.

"I think you would be the first to agree he's in serious need of help," she said, trying not to make it sound like a plea. But addressing Hugo's soft heart was a mistake.

"Would I? I'm not sure I would at all. What are his alleged symptoms?" he demanded sharply, in his professional voice.

She had written them down. "Delusions. One minute he thinks he's going to run the world, the next he's shivering like a mouse."

"We all are. What is he—a politician?"

She let out a hoot of laughter, but had the uncomfortable feeling Hugo wasn't joking.

"Unpredictable outbursts of rage, abject dependence one minute, then all his own man again.

Does that make sense? I'm not a doctor, Hugo. He's worse than that. He really needs help. Now. Urgently. With total confidentiality built in. Aren't there places like that? There must be."

"Good ones, no. Not that I know of. Not for what you want. Is he dangerous?"

"Why should he be?"

"Do you see signs of violence in him?"

"He plays music to himself. He sits for hours and looks out of the window. He makes paper airplanes. I don't think that's violent."

"How high's the window?"

"Hugo, shut up!"

"Does he look at you strangely? I'm asking you. It's a serious question."

"He doesn't *look*. I mean, he looks away. Most of the time he just looks away." She collected herself. "All right then, a *nearly* good place. Somewhere that will take him in, keep an eye on him, not ask a lot of questions and just—give him the space, help him put himself together."

She was talking too much.

"Has he got money?" Hugo demanded.

"Yes. Plenty. Any amount."

"Where from?"

"All the rich married women he sleeps with."

"Is he spending it wildly? Buying Rolls-Royces and pearl necklaces?"

"He doesn't really know he's *got* any money,"

she replied, starting to get desperate. "But he *has*. He's all right. I mean financially. Other people have got it for him. Christ, Hugo. Does it really have to be this difficult?"

"He speaks only Russian?"

"I told you."

"And you're fucking him?"

"No!"

"Do you intend to?"

"Hugo, be sensible for once, for heaven's sake."

"I *am* being sensible. That's what's making you cross."

"Look, all I need—all he needs—the bottom line is, can we get him into somewhere fast—say within a week—even if it's not perfection? If it's just adequate and *very* private. Not even the people at the Sanctuary know we're having this conversation. That's how private it's got to be."

"Where are you?"

"In a phone box. My cell phone's shot."

"Today's the weekend, in case you haven't noticed." She waited. "And Monday's a conference all day. Call me on my cell phone on Monday evening, nine-ish. Annabel?"

"What?"

"Nothing. I'll rake around. Call me."

7

"Frau Elli," Brue began skittishly.

The trip to Sylt and the lunch at Bernhard's beach house had gone off predictably, with the usual social mix of senile rich and bored youth, lobster and champagne, and a trek over the dunes during which Brue repeatedly consulted his cell phone in case he had missed a call from Annabel Richter, but alas he hadn't. By evening bad weather had closed the airfield, obliging the Brues to bunk down in the guest cottage, which in turn prompted Bernhard's wife, Hildegard, stoned on cocaine, to render exaggerated apologies for not being able to offer Mitzi sleeping arrangements better suited to her appetites. A row threatened, but deft Brue as usual quelled it. On Sunday he had played bad golf, lost a thousand euros and afterwards been forced to eat liver dumplings and drink Obstler with an elderly shipping baron. Now at last it was Monday morning, the nine o'clock meeting of senior staff had ended, and

Brue had invited Frau Ellenberger to be so good
as to remain behind if she had a moment, which
was a move he had been planning all weekend.

"It is but a small thing I ask of you, Frau Elli,"
he began in stagey English.

"Mr. Tommy, be it never so small, I am yours
to command," she answered in the same vein.

These absurd rituals, played out over a quarter
of a century, first by Brue's father in Vienna and
now by the son, were supposed to celebrate the
unbroken chain of Frères.

"If I were to say *Karpov* to you, Frau Elli—
Grigori Borisovich Karpov—and if I were to add
the word *Lipizzaner*—how do you suppose you
might react?"

The joke was long over by the time he had completed his question.

"I think I would be sad, Herr Tommy," she
said in German.

"Sad *how,* exactly? Sad for Vienna? For your
little flat in the Operngasse that your mother so
loved?"

"For your good father."

"And for what he asked of you in respect of
Lipizzaners, perhaps?"

"The Lipizzaner accounts were not correct,"
she said, eyes down.

It was a conversation they should have had
seven years ago, but Brue had never believed in

lifting stones unnecessarily, least of all when he had a shrewd idea of what he might find underneath.

"But you have nonetheless continued—very loyally—to manage them," he suggested gently.

"I do *not* manage them, Herr Tommy. I have made it my business to know as little as possible about how they are managed. That is the task of the Liechtenstein fund manager. That is his province and that, I assume, is how he earns his living, whatever we may think of his ethics. I do only what I promised your father I would do."

"And that included, I believe, stripping the personal files of past or present Lipizzaner account holders."

"Yes."

"Is that what you did in the case of Karpov?"

"Yes."

"And the papers in this file, therefore"—he held it up—"are all the papers that remain to us?"

"Yes."

"In the world. In the oubliette, in the cellar in Glasgow, here in Hamburg."

"Yes," she said with emphasis, after a small hesitation that did not escape Brue's notice.

"And apart from these papers, do you have any *personal* memory of Karpov—from those days—from the odd thing my father may have said or not said about him?"

"Your father treated the Karpov account with . . ."

"With—?"

"*Respect,* Herr Tommy," she replied, blushing.

"But my father treated all clients with respect, surely?"

"Your father spoke of Karpov as a man whose sins should be forgiven, even in advance. He was not always so indulgent towards our clients."

"Did he say *why* they should be forgiven?"

"Karpov was special. All Lipizzaners were special but Karpov was very special."

"Did he say what the sins were that should be forgiven in advance?"

"No."

"Did he suggest there might be—how shall I put it?—an untidy love life to deal with? Children out of wedlock scattered around, and so forth?"

"Such things were widely implied."

"But not specifically addressed? No mention of a beloved illegitimate son, for instance, who might step off the street one day and announce himself?"

"Many such contingencies were spoken of regarding the Lipizzaners. I cannot say I have a particular memory regarding one of them."

"And *Anatoly.* Why is Anatoly a name to me? Is it something I overheard? 'Anatoly will fix it?' "

"There was an Anatoly who was a go-between, I believe," Frau Elli replied reluctantly.

"Going between—?"

"Between Mr. Edward and Colonel Karpov, when Karpov was not available, or did not wish to be."

"As Karpov's lawyer then?"

"As"—she hesitated—"as his *enabler*. Anatoly's services extended beyond the merely legal."

"Or *illegal*," Brue suggested but, receiving no recognition for his wit, made one of his tours of the room. "And without putting you to the bother of opening up the oubliette, can you tell me, in broad-brush terms, not for publication, what percentage of the overall Liechtenstein fund is owned by the Karpov account?"

"Each Lipizzaner account holder was awarded shares in proportion to his investment."

"So I gather."

"If the account holder chose at any time to increase his investment, then the shareholding increased also."

"That sounds like sense."

"Colonel Karpov was one of the earliest of the Lipizzaners, and the richest. Your father called him our founder member. In four years his investment was increased nine times."

"By Karpov?"

"By credit transfers into his account. Whether Karpov himself made the payments, or others made them on his behalf, was not known. The credit notes, once they were effective, were destroyed."

"By you?"

"By your father."

"Any straight cash deposits at all? Banknotes in a suitcase, as it were? Old-style? Back in Vienna days?"

"Not in my presence."

"How about when you weren't there?"

"Sums of cash were from time to time credited to the account."

"By Karpov himself?"

"I believe so."

"And by third parties?"

"Possibly."

"Such as Anatoly?"

"The signatories were not required to identify themselves formally. Cash was passed across the counter, the beneficiary's account was indicated, a receipt was issued in whatever name was given by the depositor."

Another tour while Brue reflected on the uses of the passive voice.

"And when, do you suppose, did the last credit transfer hit the Karpov account?"

"My understanding is, the credits continue to come in, even to the present day."

"Literally the present day—or just until recently, say?"

"It is not my place to know, Herr Tommy."

And not your day either, thought Brue. "And the value of the Liechtenstein fund amounted to *what,* roughly, by the time we left Vienna—before it was divvied out among the shareholders, obviously?"

"By the time we left Vienna there was only one shareholder, Herr Tommy. Colonel Karpov stood alone. The others had fallen by the wayside."

"Really? And how did *that* happen?"

"It is not known to me, Herr Tommy. My understanding is, the other Lipizzaners were either bought out by Karpov or disappeared by natural means."

"Or *un*natural?"

"That's all I am able to say, Herr Tommy."

"Give me a ballpark figure. Off the top of your head," Brue urged.

"I cannot speak for our Liechtenstein trust manager, Herr Tommy. That is not something within my competence."

"A Frau Richter rang me, you see," Brue explained, in the tone of a fellow coming clean. "A *lawyer.* I expect you picked up her message this morning when you were going through the weekend crop."

"I did indeed, Herr Tommy."

"She had some questions to ask of me regard-

ing . . . a certain client of hers, and ours, allegedly. Pressing questions."

"So I understood, Herr Tommy."

He had decided. All right. She was being
sticky. She was of an age. And where Lipizzaners
were concerned, she had always been sticky. But
he would make an ally of her, tell her the whole
story, win her round. If he couldn't take Frau Elli
into his confidence, then who on earth?

"Frau Elli."

"Herr Tommy."

"I think it would be very nice if you and I had
a heart-to-heart talk about—well, shoes and
ships and—"

He smiled and broke off, waiting for her to
come in with one of her favorite Lewis Carroll
quotes, but in vain.

"So what I suggest *is,*" he went on, like someone who has had a jolly good idea, "a *big* pot of
your lovely Viennese coffee and some of your
mother's homemade Easter biscuits, and two
cups. And while you're about it, tell the switchboard I'm in conference and so are you."

But the tête-à-tête Brue had proposed did not
run its course. Frau Ellenberger did indeed come
back with the coffee—though it took longer to
prepare than a man might decently expect—and
she was, as ever, the soul of courtesy. When called
upon to smile, she smiled. Her mother's Easter

biscuits were incomparable. But the moment Brue attempted to draw her out further on Colonel Karpov, she rose to her feet and, staring before her like a child at a school concert, delivered herself of a formal statement.

"Herr Brue, I regret to inform you that I am advised that the Lipizzaner accounts transgress the outer borders of legality. In view of my junior position in the bank at the time, and the undertakings I gave your late father, I am also advised that I must not discuss these matters with you anymore."

"Of course, of course," said Brue airily, who prided himself on being at his best when suffering a reversal. "Fully understood and accepted, Frau Elli. The bank thanks you."

"And Mr. Foreman called," she said at the door, when Brue hurried after her to help her with the coffee tray.

Why was she talking with her back to him? Why was the back of her neck scarlet?

"Again? What on earth for?"

"He was confirming your lunch today."

"He confirmed it on Friday, for heaven's sake!"

"He needed to know whether you had any dietary requirements. La Scala specializes in fish, apparently."

"I know it specializes in fish. I dine there once a month at least. I also know it's *not* open for lunch."

"It appears that Mr. Foreman has made an arrangement with the manager. And he's bringing his business partner, a Mr. Lantern."

"His ray of light," Brue suggested, mordantly pleased by his own wit. But she was still avoiding him as if he had the evil eye, and Brue for his part was wondering what manner of man was this who could persuade Mario the proprietor of La Scala to open his premises for lunch on a Monday of all days, tiny though the restaurant was.

Frau Ellenberger had finally agreed to face him.

"Mr. Foreman comes with solid credentials, Herr Tommy," she said, with an emphasis he couldn't read. "You asked me to check him out, so I did. *Mr. Foreman* is personally recommended by your own firm of London solicitors, and by a *major* city bank. He is flying from London *specially*."

"With his ray of light?"

"Mr. Lantern will come separately from Berlin, where I understand he is based. They are proposing an exploratory luncheon with no commitment on either side. Their project is a substantial one and will require an extensive feasibility study."

"And I have known this for how long?"

"One week exactly, Herr Tommy. We discussed it at this hour last Monday, thank you."

Why on earth the *thank you*? Brue wondered. "Has the world gone mad or have I, Frau Elli?"

"That's what your father used to say, Herr Tommy," Frau Ellenberger replied primly, and Brue went back to thinking about Annabel: that vibrant, sovereign young woman on a bicycle, who was not dependent on social occasions for her identity.

To his surprise and relief, Messrs. Foreman and Lantern turned out to be rather amusing company. By the time he arrived at La Scala, they had charmed Mario into pointing them to Brue's favorite table in the window, and advising them which Etruscan white Brue favored so that they could have it ready for him. And there it was now, nestling uncorked in an ice bucket.

Afterwards, Brue puzzled about just how they knew La Scala was his favorite watering hole, but he assumed that since most of banking Hamburg knew he ate there, they did too. Or maybe Foreman had succeeded in charming the information out of Frau Ellenberger, because charm was what Foreman had in bucketfuls. Sometimes you meet a twin, and relate to him immediately. Foreman was Brue's height and Brue's age, and had Brue's shape of head. He was tweedy, in a patrician sort of way that Brue admired, with merry eyes and a smile that was so disarming it made you smile too. And a confiding, low-pitched voice that had learned to take the world as it came.

"Tommy Brue! Well done, sir, well done, all of us," he murmured, rising to his feet as Brue came through the door. "Meet Ian Lantern, my partner in crime. Mind if we call you Tommy? I'm another Edward, I'm afraid, like your dear papa. Ted for short, though. He would never have put up with that, would he? It was Edward or nothing for him."

"Or when in doubt, *sir,*" Brue countered, to their collective enjoyment.

Did he take any particular note of this first proprietorial reference to his father? Deep down in himself, where Brue had never lost his balance—or never until Friday night? Not that he was aware of. Edward Amadeus OBE had been a legend in his lifetime and was a legend still. Brue was well used to hearing people speak of him as if they knew him, and he took it as a compliment.

His first impression of Lantern was equally favorable. Young Englishmen, in Brue's limited experience of the breed, didn't come like Lantern these days. He was small and trim and well turned out in a charcoal suit with sloping shoulders and one button to the jacket, all in the style of your upwardly mobile executive when Brue had been one himself. His light brown hair was cropped army-style short. He was softly and thoughtfully spoken and had an engaging courtesy. But like Foreman, he radiated a quiet self-assurance that told you he was nobody's man. He also had what Brue had learned to call a classless accent, which touched the democrat in him.

"Jolly good of you to think of us, Ian," he said heartily, to make the instant bridge. "We private bankers get to feel a bit marginalized these days, what with all the big boys strutting their stuff."

"It's a privilege to meet you, Tommy, and that's a fact," Lantern responded, giving Brue's hand a second sporting squeeze as if he couldn't bear to let it go. "We've heard all these great things about you, haven't we, Ted? Not a dissenting voice anywhere."

"Nary a one," Foreman quaintly confirmed, on which note they sat down, and Mario scurried over with a giant bass that he swore had been killed in their honor and which, after a bit of banter, they agreed he should bake in sea salt. And why not a couple of scallops in garlic sauce while they were waiting?

Our lunch, they insisted.

Absolutely mine, Brue protested. Bankers always pay.

But he was outnumbered. And besides, it was their idea. So Brue did exactly what he knew he was supposed to do: he sat back and prepared to enjoy himself, in the full knowledge that Messrs.

Foreman and Lantern were in all probability out to fleece him, as were most people he did business with. Well, let them try. If they were predators, they were at least civilized predators, which God knows wasn't always the case. After a gruesome weekend and not a peep out of Annabel, let alone his unsettling nondialogue with Frau Elli, he was not disposed to be critical.

And he *liked* Brits, dammit. As an expatriate, he nursed a powerful nostalgia for the land of his birth. His eight dismal years of Scottish boarding school had left a void in him that no amount of foreign living could fill: which probably explained why, from the outset, he got on so swimmingly with Foreman, while little Lantern, like an enraptured elf, switched his respectful smile from one player to the other.

"Ian doesn't touch it, I'm afraid," Foreman said, apologizing for his companion's disinclination to drink the wine that Mario had poured for him. "One of the new breed. Not like us old farts at all. To old farts! Cheers!"

And cheers also to Annabel Richter, who insists on riding her bicycle through my head whenever she feels the urge.

Afterwards again, Brue struggled to remember what on earth they had talked about for so long before the bombshell hit. They did mutual friends in London, and probably, but not certainly, it occurred to Brue that the mutual friends knew Foreman rather better than Foreman knew the mutual friends. But if so, he made little of it. People who networked did it all the time. There was nothing sinister about it. He said he supposed they should be talking business, although neither of his hosts seemed in any hurry to do so. And he'd done his usual material about the integrity and soundness of Frères, and duly speculated about whether Wall Street was in adequate health, what with the subprime mortgage stuff—Frères, thank God, had trodden warily on that front!—and whether the rise in commodity prices would affect the move towards soft assets on the global market, and would the Asian bubble reinflate itself or stay down there, and did China's domestic boom mean we should be scouting around elsewhere for cheaper labor? Subjects in which Brue was tolerably well-versed from his reading of the financial prints, but about which in reality he had no opinion whatever: a fact that enabled him to indulge in further musings about Annabel Richter without troubling his audience.

And then there was the Arab stuff. Which of the two of them brought the subject up, Brue never worked out. Was it Ted, who was right in thinking that Brue's father had been one of the first British bankers to woo back disaffected Arab investors after the 1956 mess—or was it Ian? Never mind: whichever of them had set up the hare, the other one chased it. And yes it was indeed true, Brue conceded cautiously, mentioning no names, that one or two of the lesser members of the Saudi and Kuwaiti households held accounts with Frères, although Brue himself, being more of a European chap, had never quite shared his father's enthusiasm for that market.

"But no hard feelings?" Foreman asked solicitously. "No bad blood or anything?"

Good lord, no, God forbid, Brue replied. Everything sweet as pie. A few had died, some had moved away and some had stayed. It was just that rich Arabs liked to bank where other rich Arabs banked, and Frères today wasn't really in a position to offer that size of golden umbrella.

At the time they had appeared satisfied with his answer. In retrospect it was as if the question had been hanging around on their checklist, and they had artificially shoehorned it into the conversation. And perhaps subconsciously it was this awareness that caused him, if belatedly, to turn the conversation upon themselves.

"So now, how about you gents? You know our reputation or you wouldn't be here. How can we help you? Or as we like to put it, what can we do

for you that the big fellows can't?"— Because
without my fucking bank, you wouldn't be here.

Foreman gave up eating and dabbed at his lips
with his napkin while he peered around at the
empty tables for an answer, then at Lantern who,
by contrast, seemed not to have heard anything.
With his nicely groomed jockey's hands, he was
performing a surgical operation on his sea bass,
skin to one side of his plate, bones the other, and
a little pyramid of flesh that he was stacking in
the middle.

"Mind awfully if I ask you to turn that thing
off a moment?" Foreman asked quietly. "Makes
me bloody nervous, quite honestly."

Brue realized that Foreman was referring to
the cell phone he had set beside him on the off
chance that Annabel called. After a moment's
puzzlement, he switched it off and dropped it in
his pocket, by which time Foreman was leaning
across the table at him.

"Now buckle your seat belt for a moment and
listen," he advised in a confiding murmur. "We're
from British Intelligence, okay? Spooks. Ian
here's from the Berlin embassy, I'm London-side.
Our names are kosher. If you don't like 'em,
check 'em with Ian's ambassador. My patch is
Russia. Has been for the last twenty-eight years,
God help me. That's how I came to know your
revered late father, Edward Amadeus. My name

was Findlay in those days, as far as he was concerned. Perhaps you heard your old man talk about me now and then?"

"I'm afraid not."

"Marvelous. That's Edward Amadeus for you. Silent to the end. Not to put too fine a point on it, I'm the chap who got him his OBE."

Brue might reasonably have expected Foreman to break off at this point, allowing him an opportunity to ask a few clarifying questions from among the few thousand coursing in his head, but Foreman had no intention of offering such respite. Having made a breach in Brue's defenses, he was pressing forward to entrench his victory. True, he was sitting comfortably back in his seat by now, with his fingertips together and a benign, even pastoral expression on his weathered features, to all outward appearance the picture of a mellow luncheon guest offering his observations on the state of the universe. His voice, adjusted for short range, was light-toned and mysteriously happy. There was music playing in the kitchen—lute as far as Brue could make it out—and Foreman spoke beneath it. He was painting a picture of a time that was as dead and gone as Brue's father but, like his father's ghost, wouldn't lie down: last years of the Cold War, Tommy, when the Soviet knight was dying in his armor and the whole of Russia stank of decay.

He didn't talk about the greater loyalty of the Russians who had spied for him, their ideals or their higher motives: If you were trying to induce a ranking Soviet to risk his neck for capitalism, then believe me, Tommy, you had to offer him what capitalism was all about: money and sackloads of it.

And you didn't just offer him money by itself either, because for as long as he worked for you he couldn't spend it, couldn't flaunt it, couldn't slip it to his kids or his wife or his lover. If he tried, he was a bloody fool and deserved to be caught, which he usually was. So you offered your spy-to-be a package.

And a key component of this package was a sound, flexible Western bank with plenty of tradition behind it, because you know as well as I do, Tommy, your Russian loves tradition. Another key component was a waterproof system for transferring his hard-earned loot to his heirs and assigns without the formalities that normally attach: probate, estate duty, full disclosure and the inevitable questions about where said loot came from, all the stuff you know about, Tommy.

"So it was chicken and egg," he went on in the same endearing tone while Brue struggled to collect his thoughts. "In this case, the egg came first. A golden egg. A walk-in Red Army colonel who'd seen which way the wind was blowing decided to sell off his assets before the Big Crash. He reasoned the way you fellows reason. The share price of Sovs Incorporated was on the slide, so he wanted to sell his stocks and shares before they became a drug on the market. And he had a lot to sell. He also had some interesting friends to introduce to us. Like-minded chaps who would strangle their own mothers for a spot of the hard currency. I'll call him Vladimir, okay?" he suggested.

And I'll call him Grigori Borisovich Karpov, Brue was thinking. And so will Annabel. After the first shock waves, an unexpected calm had settled over him.

"Vladimir was a shit, but he was our shit, as the saying doesn't quite go. Cunning as they come, venal to his boots, but alpha-plus access to military secrets. In our job, that's a recipe for pure love. He sat on three intelligence commit-tees, he'd served with Soviet special forces in Africa, Cuba, Afghanistan and Chechnya and run every kind of racket you can think of and some you can't. He knew every bent brother offi-cer, the scams *they* got up to, how to threaten them and how to buy them. He was running a Red Army mafia five years before anyone outside Russia knew they had mafias: blood, oil, dia-monds, heroin out of Afghanistan by way of Red air-force cargo planes. When his unit was demobilized, Vladimir had his boys put on Armani suits but keep their guns. How else were they going to negotiate the competition?"

Brue was doing what he had by now decided to do: saying nothing, looking attentive but detached and secretly wondering why Foreman was telling him all this, and in such detail, and beaming all his considerable befriending powers at him, as if the three of them were already brothers in an enterprise yet to be unveiled.

"Our problem was—not the first time it's happened in our business or the last—that in order to keep Vladimir happy, we not only had to bank his money and add to it, we had to *launder* it for him as well."

Surprisingly, as Brue was now getting to know him, Foreman seemed to feel that this needed some justification.

"Well, I mean, if *we* didn't do it, the Americans would have done it and fucked up. Which was how we came to have a quiet word with your papa. Vladimir liked Vienna. He'd done a couple of delegations there. He liked the waltzes and the whorehouses and the Wiener schnitzels. What better place for him to visit his money, from time to time, than dear old Vienna? And your papa was, well, just marvelously receptive. Mustard, in fact. That's one of the amusing things about this caper. The more respectable chaps are in their public lives, the faster they come running when we spies whistle. The moment we suggested Lipizzaners, he was away. If we'd given your old man his head, he'd have turned his whole bank into a substation of the Service. We're rather hoping that, when we explain our little problem to you, you'll feel the same way, aren't we, Ian? Not the substation bit"—jolly laughter from both men—"we're not going that route, thank God! Just, well, a helping hand here and there."

"We're counting on you, Tommy," Lantern agreed, with his soft Northern accent and the ever-ready smile of a small man trying to please.

And once again Foreman might decently have called a break, but he was approaching the nub of his story and wished no diversion. Mario was hovering with the dessert menu. Brue was hovering too, but in his father's sanctum in Vienna with the door locked, furiously scripting the last part of the unfinished row he had had with him about the Lipizzaner accounts: *So you were a British spy, they now tell me. Selling Frères down the river for a British medal. Pity you didn't feel able to tell me yourself.*

Vladimir's last posting was Chechnya, Foreman was saying. And if Brue took everything he'd ever heard about that hellhole and multiplied it by ten, he'd have a rough idea of what it was like: the Russians pounding the place into ashes, and the Chechens returning the compliment whenever they got a chance.

"But for Vladimir and his lot it was one long happy party," he confided in the same intimate tone, as if the story had lain deep inside him for years, and only Brue's presence here had succeeded in coaxing it out of him. "Bombing, boozing, raping and looting. Syphoning off the oil and selling it to the highest bidder. Then lining up the locals and shooting them in reprisal for what you've done, and getting promoted for your trouble." This time Foreman did allow a pause, if only to signal a change of direction in his story. "Anyway, that was the *backcloth,* Tommy. And it was against this *backcloth* that Vladimir fell in love. He'd got wives all over the globe, but this one for some reason got under his skin. Some Chechen beauty he'd grabbed, installed in the officers' compound in Grozny, then fallen for in a big way. And she for him, or so he convinced himself. Love and Vladimir didn't sit well together, I'll admit, or not the way you and I might understand the word. But for Vladimir she was the real thing at last. Or so he told me. In his cups. In Moscow. While enjoying a spot of well-earned leave from the Chechen front."

Foreman had become a player in his own narrative. His face had softened, and his confiding voice also. And Brue was being invited to enter the circle of his strange affections, dragging Annabel and her bicycle with him.

"In our business, Tommy, as we get older, those are the bits of our lives we'd give our eyes to talk about, and never can. I'll bet it's much the same in your world?"

Brue offered some platitudinous reply.

"You're banged up in a stinking safe flat in subtopian Moscow with your joe. You've got embassy cover and it's taken you all day to get there unnoticed. You've got an hour maximum with him and you're listening for footsteps on the stairs. He's pushing microfilm at you across the table, and you're trying to debrief and brief him at the same time. 'Why did General So-and-So say that to you? Tell me about the rocket site at So-and-So. How do you like our new signals procedure?' But your joe's not listening. He's got tears running down his cheeks and all he wants to tell you about is this amazing girl he's raped. And now, God help him, she loves him and she's bearing him a child. And he's the happiest man in the world. He never knew it could be like this. So I'm happy for him. We drink to her. Here's to Yelena, or whatever her name is. And here's to the baby, God bless it. That's my job, or used to be. Half spy and all welfare officer. I've got seven months to go. Lord alone knows what I'll do with myself. The private security firms are all over me, but I think I'd rather reflect on times past," he added disarmingly, and smiled a sad smile that Brue dutifully attempted to reciprocate.

"So that was Vladimir in love," Foreman resumed more cheerfully. "And like all great loves it didn't last. As soon as she'd had her baby boy, her family smuggled one of her brothers into the camp to kill her. Vladimir was desolate, well he would be. When his unit was posted back to Moscow and disbanded, he took the kid with him. The reigning wife in Moscow wasn't at all happy. Told Vladimir she resented having a black-arse bastard dumped on her. But Vladimir didn't give up on him. He loved the boy born to him by the love of his life, and he'd made him heir to his slush fund, and nothing was going to change that."

Was the story over? Foreman's eyebrows lifted and he gave a shrug as if to say: Way of the world, what can one do?

"So now?" Brue asked.

"So now the great wheel of history has turned full circle, Tommy. The past's the past, Vladimir's son has attained man's estate and is on his way to visit the son of Edward Amadeus and claim his portion."

This time, Brue was not as easily won as they seemed to expect. He was growing into the part, whatever the part was.

"Forgive me," he began, after invoking the banker's moment of sober reflection. "I don't wish to spoil your fun, but I'm pretty sure that if I went back to the bank now, and called up the Lipizzaner files, and established which client most closely resembles the description you have provided, together with the provisions he has made for his heir—"

He needed to say no more. From a jacket pocket, Foreman extracted a white envelope that reminded Brue of the little white boxes of sticky wedding cake wrapped in doily that his daughter, Georgie, had sent to absent friends to celebrate her brief marriage to a fifty-year-old artist called Millard. Inside the envelope was a piece of blank card on which the name KARPOV was written in ballpoint pen. On the reverse side, the name Lipizzaner.

"Ring a bell?" Foreman inquired.

"The name?"

"That's right. Not the horse. The chap."

But Brue would not be stampeded. Some mulish objection was forming in him, and it went way beyond his banker's duty of discretion. It went way beyond the occasional fits of Scots cussedness that came over him unannounced, and which he was always quick to redress. It was multistranded, and in due course he would separate the strands, but he knew that Annabel Richter was woven in there somehow, and she needed his protection, which meant that Issa needed it too. Meanwhile he would respond in the way that came most naturally to him. He would hedge-hog, as Edward Amadeus used to call it. He would hunker down and put up his quills. He would tell the minimum, and he would let them fill the silences for themselves.

"I would have to consult my chief cashier. Lipizzaners are something of a world apart at Frères," he said. "That was how my father wished them to be."

"You're telling *me* he did!" Foreman exclaimed. "Your proverbial grave was a bloody *chatterbox* where E.A. was concerned! Exactly what I said to Ian here before you showed up. Didn't I, Ian?"

"His words, Tommy. Literally," said little Lantern with his pretty smile.

"Then perhaps you know more about them than I do," Brue suggested. "The Lipizzaners are something of a gray area to me, I'm afraid. They have been a thorn in my bank's side for two decades and more."

Lantern, unlike Foreman, didn't lean across the table to confide in Brue, but his Northern voice, like Foreman's, knew how to stay beneath the level of the music.

"Tommy. Give us the form here. If the boy in

question—or somebody delegated by him and equipped with the necessary password or reference—walked into your bank—right?"

"I'm listening." And so is Annabel, intently.

"And this person made a claim on a Lipizzaner account—cleaned it out, say—at what point would this come to your knowledge? Would it be straight away? A couple of days later? How would it work?"

Brue the hedgehog left the question unanswered for so long that Lantern might have wondered whether he had grasped it.

"First of all, one assumes he would make an appointment and state his business," he said warily.

"And if he did?"

"In that case, my senior assistant, Frau Ellenberger, would alert me in advance. And all being well, I would make myself available. If there was a personal element—I'm not sure it would apply in this case, but let's suppose for argument's sake it does—if *his* father knew *my* father, for instance, and he let this be known—then obviously one would make a point of receiving him more warmly. Frères set considerable store by that kind of continuity." He allowed time for this to sink in. "If, on the other hand, there was *no* appointment, and I was in conference, or away from my desk, then it's possible, though unlikely, that the business would be transacted without my knowledge. Which would be unfortunate. I would regret that."

Judging by Brue's preoccupied air, he seemed to be regretting it already.

"Lipizzaners are, of course, very much a separate category," he went on disapprovingly. "And not a very happy one, frankly. If we think of them much at all, I suppose we have come to regard those that have remained to us over time as either dormant, or lockaway. No direct correspondence with clients. All papers and accounts kept at the bank. That sort of thing," he added with disdain.

Foreman and Lantern exchanged glances, apparently uncertain who should go next, and how far. Somewhat to Brue's surprise, Lantern decided he would.

"We need to talk urgently to the boy, you see, Tommy," he explained, his Midland murmur sinking even lower. "We need to talk to him privately and immediately. Off the record and as soon as he appears. Before he talks to anyone else. But it's got to be natural. The very *last* thing we want him to think is that anyone is looking out of the window for him, or the staff have been in any way alerted, or there's some kind of agenda out there for him, at the bank or anywhere else. That would kill everything stone dead, right, Ted?"

"Totally," Foreman confirmed in his newfound role as second fiddle.

"He strolls in, he announces himself, sees whoever he would normally see. He makes his claim, does his business, and while he's doing it, you press the button to us. That's all we're asking for at this stage," Lantern said.

"I press the button *how*, exactly?"

Foreman again, as Lantern's adjutant: "You call Ian's number in Berlin. Right away. Even before you shake the boy's hand, or he's brought upstairs to have a coffee in your office. 'The boy's here.' That's all you need to say. Ian will do the rest. He has people. His phones are manned round the clock."

"Twenty-four seven," Lantern confirmed, passing Brue his card across the table.

A nearly royal crest in black and white. *British Embassy, Berlin. Ian K. Lantern, Counselor, Defense & Liaison.* A cluster of phone numbers. One of them underlined in blue ballpoint and starred. How did they know my office was upstairs? The same way that Annabel did—by bicycling past my window? Avoiding eye contact with his hosts, Brue put Lantern's card in his pocket alongside the card marked *Karpov* and *Lipizzaner*.

"So the scenario you're proposing is presumably this," he suggested. "Correct me if I'm wrong. A brand-new client enters my bank. He's the son of an important client, now deceased. And he makes a claim for—certainly a substantial sum of money. And instead of advising him, as I might, on how we could best look after it for him, and invest it, I deliver him into your hands without so much as consulting him."

"Wrong, Tommy," Lantern corrected him. The smile was unchanged.

"Why?"

"Not *instead of.* In addition to. We want you to do both. First tip us off, then behave as if you hadn't. He doesn't know you've told us. Life goes on completely normally."

"So cheat."

"If that's what you want to call it."

"For how long?"

"I'm afraid that's our business, Tommy."

Perhaps Lantern had sounded more abrupt than he intended, or perhaps Foreman as the older man only thought he did, and felt he ought to put it right.

"Ian just needs to have this very private, very helpful talk with the boy, Tommy. You won't be harming a hair of your new client's head. If we could tell you the whole story, you'd know you were giving him a considerable helping hand."

He's drowning. All you have to do is hold out your hand, a choirboy voice was telling him.

"All the same, I think you'll agree it's a very

tall order for a banker," Brue insisted, while the two men conferred with each other with their eyes. This time it was Foreman who got the job of answering him.

"Let's just say it's an untidy bit of history that's got to be sorted, Tommy. Would you settle for that? Some messy loose ends a certain late client of yours left lying about."

"If we don't catch them now, they could come back to haunt *all of us* in a pretty serious way, Tommy," Lantern agreed earnestly. The loose ends, he apparently meant. The haunting loose ends.

"*All* of us?" Brue repeated.

After another glance for Lantern, Foreman pulled a resigned shrug, indicating that, having gone this far, he might as well go the whole hog and be damned.

"I'm not sure I'm briefed to say this, Tommy. But I will. There's a bit of a question mark in London about how all of this might impact on your bank if we leave it unattended, if you follow me."

Lantern was quick to add his own personal assurance. "We're doing absolutely everything we can, Tommy. At the highest level."

"Can't get any higher," Foreman agreed.

"Just one more thing, Tommy," Lantern put in, by way of what could have been a warning. "It's just possible you'll get some strange Germans sniffing around. If that *should* happen, we would once more ask you to give us a bell *right* away so that we can sort it out. Which of course we will, without delay. Provided you give us the chance."

"What on earth would the Germans want?" Brue asked, thinking that one German at least was already sniffing around, but she was not the sort of German they were warning him against.

"Maybe they're not too fond of British bankers operating black bank accounts on their patch," Lantern suggested, with a pretty lift of his young eyebrows.

In the taxi, Brue checked his mobile, then called Frau Ellenberger. No, not a word from her, Herr Tommy. Not on your direct line either.

There was a place, a precious place, open to the general public yet private to himself, that Brue repaired to when his life became oppressive. It was a small museum dedicated to the work of Ernst Barlach, sculptor. Brue was no art buff, and Barlach had been no more than a name in his head, and a pretty hazy one at that, until a day two years ago, when a flat-voiced Georgie informed him over the transatlantic telephone that her six-day-old baby boy was dead. On hearing the news, he had walked into the street, hailed the first taxi and told the driver, who was elderly and, to judge by the name on his license, Croatian, to take him somewhere private, he wasn't particular where. Half an hour later, without another word passing between them, they drew up at a low brick building at the far end of a great park. For a sickening moment Brue believed he had been delivered to a crematorium, but a woman was selling tickets at a desk, so he bought one and entered a glazed courtyard inhabited by nobody but mythic figures from the middle world.

One was in monk's habit, floating. Another was lost to depression, a third to contemplation or despair. Another was screaming, but whether from pain or pleasure it was not possible to tell. What was evident to Brue, however, was that each figure was as alone as he was, and that each was communicating something; but nobody was listening, each was searching for a solace that was not available, which was a kind of solace of its own.

And that taken all in all, Barlach's message to the world was one of deeply perplexed pity for its suffering, which was why, ever since that day, Brue had come here maybe a dozen times, either when he was in temporary despair—"the black dog," as Edward Amadeus used to call it—or when things were going seriously awry at the bank, or for instance when Mitzi told him, practically in as many words, that he didn't match up to her exacting standards as a lover, a thing he had more or less assumed, but would have preferred not to hear. But he had never before come here in quite the state of delayed anger and perplexity as now.

I kept faith, he told Barlach's familiars. I stood up for her, and I dissembled. I lied the way they lied: by omission. Their lies contained so many omissions that by the time they'd finished telling them, the lies were all I could hear. Spies' lies, not spoken aloud but, like empty centers, described by what wasn't said:

Issa never was, is not now, a Muslim, they lied.

Issa was never a Chechen activist. He was never anybody's activist, they lied.

Issa is just an ordinary, run-of-the-mill spy's son, like me, on his way to claim his dirty legacy *from* me, they lied.

And he *certainly* hasn't been tortured or imprisoned, or jumped jail, God no!

And he is not *remotely* connected with an alleged Islamist terrorist on the run who is wanted by the Swedes and featured on every police website—including, therefore, it is a fair presumption, the website of the omniscient British Secret Service.

No to all of that! Issa's problem—if it's his problem at all—is to do with untidy history, whatever that might be. It's about some messy loose ends that our fathers left lying about, and which make us, in some undefined way, jointly culpable.

But mercifully, if I do everything I'm told, Messrs. Foreman and Lantern, with the assistance of their highest level, will save my skin. And while they're about it, they'll save me from the Germans too.

Yet Brue was not at odds with himself as he bade farewell to Barlach and strolled into the sunlit park. He had not misstepped. A Barlachian cry of both pain and pleasure swelled in him as he woke to the reality of his feelings. Ever since their meeting at the Atlantic, which was eons ago, Annabel Richter had been an instructive, he might almost say a *moral* force. From that moment on, he had seen and thought nothing without referring it to her in his mind: Is this the right way to go, would Annabel approve?

At first he had seen himself as the put-upon victim of a hostile takeover. Then he had sneered at himself: me, an adolescent of sixty, grappling

with my waning testosterone. At no point had
the dread word *love,* whatever that had meant to
him, entered the dialogue he was having with
himself. Love was Georgie. All the rest—the
sticky hot-breath stuff, the eternal protesta-
tions—frankly, that was for the other fellows.
Cut through the posturing, and he wondered
whether it was for the other fellows either, but
that was their business. All the same, when somebody half your age barges into your life and ap-
points herself your moral mentor, you sit up and
listen, you have to. And if she happens to be the
most attractive and interesting woman, and the
most impossible love to have come your way *ever,*
then all the more so.

And sex? By the time he married Mitzi, he had
recognized he was punching above his weight. He
bore her no grudge for this, nor she him, apparently. Pressed to take a view, he would probably
argue that she had kept him in the style to which
he was accustomed and sent him the bill, which
was fair-do's. He could hardly blame her for having appetites he failed to satisfy.

Now at last he was able to understand himself. He had mistaken his need. He had invested
himself in the wrong market. It wasn't copula-
tion he had been looking for. It was *this.* And
now he had found *this,* which was an important
and rather astonishing clarification of his nature

for him. Waning testosterone was not the issue.
The issue was *this,* and *this* was Annabel.

And it was for *this,* as much as for any other
reason, that he had lied to Messrs. Lantern and
Foreman. They had talked about his father as if
he was their property. They had bullied the son
in the name of the father, and thought they
owned him too. They had strayed too close to
ground that was his and Annabel's alone, and he
had kept them out. In doing so he had consciously and deliberately entered her danger
zone, which he now shared with her. And in consequence, his life had become vivid and precious
to him, for which he thanked her from the heart.

"And the house of Brue Frères is going under,
one hears," Mitzi remarked. It was the same
evening. They were sitting in the sunroom, admiring the garden. Brue was sipping old Calva-
dos, a gift from a French client.

"Are we really?" he replied lightly. "I didn't
know. Who does one hear that from, if I may
ask?"

"Bernhard, who got it from your geriatric
friend Haug von Westerheim, who is supposed
to know these things. Is it?"

"Not yet. Not that *I've* heard."

"Are *you* going under?"

"Not noticeably. Why?"

"You seem unable to control your signals. One minute you're leaping around like a puppy, the next you hate us all. Is it a woman, Tommy? I had the impression you'd rather given us up these days."

Even by the rules of the games they played—and didn't play—the question was unusually blunt, and Brue permitted himself an unusually long time to turn it round.

"A *man,* actually," he replied, mentally taking refuge in Issa; at which Mitzi produced a knowing smile and went back to her book.

8

The building was not a sanctuary—or not from the outside. It was a guilty, down-at-heel accomplice of Nazi times, squeezed onto the corner of a traffic junction and walled in by garish cigarette hoardings. The graffiti on its weeping walls offered tropical sunsets and obscenities. To one side squatted a tin café called Asyl, to the other an Africa-Asia trading mart for cast-off clothing. Inside, however, all was bustle, efficiency and determined optimism.

And so it was this sunny Monday spring morning as Annabel, with every effort to appear her normal self, manhandled her bicycle up the steps into its usual place in the entrance lobby, chained it to a downpipe, and followed the glitter-painted arrows: up the tiled staircase to the lobby where she waved and waited as usual for Wangaza the receptionist to spot her through the glass door and press the button that made the lock buzz; into the lobby, past the usual rows of men in brown suits and women in *hijabs,* and shadow-eyed children piling up building blocks in the glass-walled playpen, or feeding lettuce to the tortoise family, or wistfully poking their fingers through the wire perimeter of the rabbit house—and why was everyone so quiet this morning or was it always like this?—into the open plan where Lisa and Maria, our in-house Arabists, were already sitting head-to-head with their first clients of the day; a quick hello and a smile to each of them, enter the lawyers' corridor with its shafts of morning sunlight making it look more like a path to Paradise—and why was Ursula's door closed this early on a Monday and her red don't-enter light burning above it—Ursula who prided herself on keeping her door open to the entire world and urged everybody else to do the same? And so into her own office where she unharnessed her rucksack, dumped it onto the floor like the burden of guilt it had become, sat to her desk, closed her eyes and put her head into her hands for a moment, before taking refuge in her computer and peering sightlessly at its screen.

In the sudden quiet of her own office, in the very room where she had first received Ursula's referred call from Melik imploring her to come and visit this Russian-speaking friend of his who desperately needed her help, she looked back on the weekend as if it comprised her entire life.

The pieces still refused to settle. Over two days and nights she had visited him five times. Or was it six? Or seven if you included taking him there? Again on the Saturday evening. Twice on Sunday. Again this morning at crack of dawn when I interrupted him praying. How many times did that make?

But ask her to account for the actual hours she had spent with him, arrange them in some kind of rational order—what they had talked about as they walked their separate tightropes, where they had laughed and where they had retreated to their separate corners—everything merged, and incidents started changing places with each other.

Was it for Saturday supper that they had cooked potato and onion soup together on her camping stove in the dark, like children at a campfire?

"Why do you not put on the lights, Annabel? Are you in Chechnya expecting an air raid? Is it illegal to show lights tonight? In that case, all Hamburg is illegal."

"It's better not to attract attention unnecessarily, that's all."

"Sometimes the dark attracts more attention than the light," he observed after long reflection.

Nothing that was without its meaning for him; meanings from his world, not hers. Nothing that did not have the ring of hard-won profundity, arrived at in the face of despair.

Was it on the Sunday morning that she brought him Russian newspapers from the railway station kiosk—or afternoon? She remembered cycling to the station and spending a small fortune on *Ogonyok, Novi Mir* and *Kommersant,* and as an afterthought flowers from the station stall. Her first idea had been a begonia that he could tend. Then, given the plans she had for him, she decided it was better to buy cut flowers, but which? Did roses denote love to him? Heaven forbid. She compromised on tulips, only to find they didn't fit into the box on the front of her bicycle so she ended up carrying them one-handed like an Olympic torch all the way down to the harbor front only to find that half the petals had blown off.

And when they sat with the length of the attic between them listening to Tchaikovsky, and he suddenly jumped up, switched off the tape recorder and returned to his place on the packing case beneath the arched window in order to recite a heroic Chechen poem to her about mountains, rivers, forests and the thwarted love of a noble Chechen hunter—arbitrarily translating patches into Russian when he felt like it or, as she suspected, when he knew their meaning, which was not always the case, and clutching his gold bracelet while he orated—well, was that last night or Saturday?

And when was it that he described, by way of distracted reminiscence, a beating he had received while being hauled from room to room by two men he insisted on calling "the Japanese," though whether this was a true description of their ethnicity, or their prison nickname, and whether the beatings took place in Russia or in Turkey, he seemed unclear. He cared only about the rooms: in this room they beat my feet, in this one my body, in this one they electroed me.

Whenever it was, it was the moment when she felt most inclined to fall in love with him, when intimacy on such a scale became an act of stupendous generosity, and her whole being was responding to him: he is owed everything, he is humiliating himself so that I can know and heal him; what have I to give him in return? But no sooner had the answer threatened to present itself than she felt herself recoil absolutely, because that way lay the negation of the promise she had made to herself: to put his life—and not his love—before law.

She knew also that there were long passages when, like someone who has lived alone a lot, he

barely spoke, or not at all. But his silences were
not oppressive. She took them as some kind of
compliment, as a further act of trust. And when
they ended he became so garrulous that they were
like old friends remet, and she found herself responding to him in kind, chatting away about her
sister, Heidi, and her three babies, and about
Hugo the brilliant doctor she was so proud of—
Issa couldn't get enough about him—even about
her mother's cancer.

Just never her father, don't ask her why. Perhaps because of his old job as legal attaché in
Moscow. Or perhaps it was Colonel Karpov's
long shadow that she felt. Or perhaps she knew
that now at last it was she and not her father
who was controlling her life.

Yet she was Issa's lawyer, not merely his
keeper. Not once but half a dozen times she had
prevailed on him, besought him, practically *ordered* him, to make a formal claim to his inheritance, but always to no avail. What she expected
him to gain by claiming was something she
hardly dared think about. But who could doubt
that, if the size of his inheritance was as large as
Brue had hinted, all sorts of doors would mysteriously open to him? She had heard of cases—
some whispered here at the Sanctuary—of
wealthy Arabs and Asians whose records stank to
high heaven, yet they had received benign treat-

ment on the strength of a fine German property and a fine German bank account.

Get him cared for first, she told herself. When he's calm and strong, work on him in earnest. Wait for the Hugo solution.

And Brue? Realistically yet intuitively, she believed she had come to understand who he was: a lonely rich man in the last part of his life, looking for the dignity of love.

Her phone was ringing. Internal from Ursula.

"We're postponing our usual Monday meeting till two this afternoon, Annabel. Is that acceptable to you?"

"Fine."

Not fine. Ursula's crisp voice was a warning. She's got somebody in the room with her. She's talking for her audience.

"Herr Werner is here."

"Werner?"

"From the Office for the Protection of the Constitution. He wishes to ask you a few questions regarding a client of yours."

"He can't. I'm a lawyer. He's not allowed to ask and I'm not allowed to answer. He must know the law as well as you and I do." And when Ursula said nothing: "Which client of mine is he talking about, anyway?"

He's standing over her, she thought. He's listening to everything we say.

"Herr Werner has a Herr *Dinkelmann* with him, Annabel, also from the Office for Protection. They are very serious gentlemen and they wish to discuss with you urgently 'a feared public outrage that they believe is about to occur.'"

She is quoting their words, deliberately making a meal of them for my benefit.

Herr Werner was in his late twenties and fleshy, with small watery eyes and ash-blond eyebrows and a sheen to his pale, overfed complexion. As Annabel entered the room, Ursula was seated at her desk and Herr Werner was standing behind her, exactly as Annabel had pictured him, with his head tilted back and his mouth set in an imperious downward curve while he subjected Annabel to a prolonged optical body search: face, breasts, hips, legs and face again. The inspection complete, he took a stiff pace forward, helped himself to her hand and bent over it with a quarter-bow.

"Frau Richter. My name is Werner. I am one of those people who are paid to help the great German public sleep peacefully at night. Under the law, my office has responsibilities, but no executive powers. We are officials, not policemen.

You are a lawyer so you know this already. Allow me to present Herr *Dinkelmann* from our coordination unit," he went on, releasing her hand.

But Herr Dinkelmann from our coordination unit was at first invisible. He had sat himself in the corner behind Ursula's desk, and was only now emerging into view. He was mid-forties, sandy-haired and squat, with an air of apology about him that seemed to acknowledge that his best days were behind him. He wore a librarian's rumpled linen jacket, and an old tartan tie.

"Coordination?" Annabel repeated, with a sideways glance for Ursula. "Whatever do you coordinate, Herr Dinkelmann? Or are we not allowed to know?"

Ursula's smile was tepid at best, but the smile of Herr Dinkelmann was briefly delightful: a clown's smile, reaching right up into the cheekbones.

"Frau Richter, without me the uncoordinated world would fall apart immediately," he said in a cheerful tone, holding her hand a trifle longer than she considered necessary.

They sat four in a ring round the low pinewood table, with blue-eyed, stiff-backed Ursula, her prematurely gray hair swept into a bun, playing Mother. Ursula had such deep upholstered chairs that it was impossible to be pompous in them. On each chair lay one of her hand-embroidered cushions. Needlework is my anger management, she had told Annabel at one of their little chats. Industrial-sized coffee thermos, milk, sugar, mugs and a proud array of assorted waters. Ursula is a water gourmet like me. And midway between the coffee and the water tray, a high-gloss photograph of Issa, full face and both profiles.

But Annabel was the only person looking at Issa's photograph. Everybody else was looking at Annabel: Werner with a show of professional shrewdness, Dinkelmann with his clown's smile, and Ursula with the studied impassivity she adopted at moments of crisis.

"Do you recognize this man, Annabel?" Ursula inquired. "As a lawyer you don't have to say anything to these gentlemen unless you are yourself an object of investigation. You and I are both aware of that."

"But we know it also, Frau Meyer!" Herr Werner cried fulsomely. "Since day one of our training course! Lawyers are a no-go area. Keep your fingers off them, especially if they are ladies!" Relishing the innuendo. "And we do not forget that there is a legal requirement of confidentiality upon *you* too, Frau Richter, concerning your client. We respect that also. Totally, don't we, Dinkelmann?"

The clown's smile meekly confirmed *totally*.

"For us to attempt to persuade Frau Richter to violate her client's confidentiality would be *completely* illegal. For you too, Frau Meyer. Even *you* may not persuade hēr! Unless she is personally an object of investigation—which she is not, clearly. Not at this moment. She is a lawyer, she is a citizen, we assume a loyal one, a member of a distinguished legal family. Such a person is not an object of investigation, unless there are highly exceptional circumstances. That is the spirit of our Constitution, and we are its protectors in spirit and in law. So *naturally,* we know."

At long last, he stopped. And waited while he watched her. As they all did, with Dinkelmann the only one who was smiling.

"As a matter of fact, I *do* recognize this man," Annabel conceded, after a lengthy delay to signal her professional concerns. "He's one of our clients. A recent one"—addressing Ursula, and Ursula alone—"You haven't met him, but you passed him across to me because he's a Russian speaker." Calmly picking up the photograph, she affected to examine it more closely, and laid it down again.

"What is his *name,* please, Frau Richter?" Werner blurted into her left ear. "We are not pressing you. Maybe you are bound also to keep his name confidential. If so, we don't press you. Only that we have a potential public outrage that is about to occur. But never mind."

"His name is Issa Karpov. Or he says it is"— still firmly and deliberately to Ursula. "He's half Russian, half Chechen. Or says he is. With some clients, one can never be certain, as we both know all too well."

"Oh, but *we* can be certain, Frau Richter!" Werner contradicted her with unexpected vigor. "Issa Karpov is an Islamist Russian criminal with a long record of convictions for militant actions. He entered Germany illegally—smuggled by *other* criminals, maybe also Islamist—and has no rights in this country whatever."

"Everyone has rights, surely," Annabel suggested, in gentle reproof.

"Not in his situation, Frau Richter. Not in his situation."

"But Mr. Karpov has approached Sanctuary North in order to *regularize* his situation," Annabel objected.

Werner pretended to laugh. "Oh dear! Has your client not told you that when his ship landed in Gothenburg he escaped captivity in order to smuggle himself to Germany? Then in Copenhagen escaped again? After escaping from Turkey and before that Russia?"

"What my client has told me is a matter for

my client and myself, not to be divulged to third parties without his consent, Herr Werner."

Ursula had put on her most inscrutable expression. Herr Dinkelmann beside her was drawing his stubby fingers reflectively back and forth across his lips while he watched Annabel with a paternal smile.

"Frau Richter," Werner resumed, in a tone to suggest his patience was running short, "we are looking *urgently* for a *violent Islamist fugitive*. He is a desperate man, suspected of terrorist connections. It is our task to protect the public from him. And to protect *you also*, Frau Richter. You are a single, defenseless woman. Also very attractive, if I may say so. We therefore ask you, and Frau Meyer here, to assist us in doing our duty. Where is this man to be found, please? And second question, maybe first: *When did you last see him?* But only if you wish to answer, naturally. Maybe you don't mind that you are protecting a terrorist and enabling a public outrage to occur?"

Intending to seek Ursula's opinion on the propriety of this question, Annabel turned to address her, but the delay was already too much for Herr Werner to bear.

"No need to ask your director, Frau Richter! Let me come out with it, and then you can decide what is the correct response in the interests of your client. Nobody is forcing you. We have

witnesses to that. *What did you do with Issa Kar-*
pov after you left the house of Mrs. Leyla Oktay at four
o'clock on Saturday morning?"

So they knew.

They knew some, but not all.

They knew the outside but not the inside. Or
so she must believe. If they knew the inside, Issa
would be on the flight to Petersburg by now,
like Magomed, waving his manacled fists at her
from the cabin window.

"Frau Richter. I ask you again, please. What
did you do with Issa Karpov when you left the
Oktays' house?"

"I escorted him."

"On foot?"

"On foot."

"At four in the morning? You do this with all
your clients? Walk the streets with them at
dawn? Is this normal practice for an attractive
young woman lawyer? If I am asking you to
breach client confidentiality again, I withdraw
the question completely. You will hold up our
investigations but never mind. We shall get him
even if it's too late."

"Our discussion had run into the small hours,
which is not unusual with clients of Oriental or
Asiatic origin," Annabel continued, after due re-

flection. "There was tension in the Oktays' household. Mr. Karpov did not wish to trespass further on their hospitality. He is a man of considerable sensitivity. His irregular status was becoming an anxiety to them, and he was aware of this. They are also about to leave for Turkey on vacation."

She was still addressing her replies to Ursula, not Werner. She was phrasing them in short sentences, clearing each one with Ursula before she moved to the next. Ursula, sphinxlike, was squinting into the middle air with half-closed eyes while the relaxed Herr Dinkelmann seated beside her preserved his fond smile.

"Describe your route exactly, please, Frau Richter! Also methods of transportation. I have to warn you, you are potentially in a dangerous situation here, not only from Issa Karpov. We are not policemen but we have responsibilities. Go on, please."

"We went on foot to the Eppendorfer Baum, then took the underground."

"Where to? Please give the entire story, not piece by piece."

"My client was fraught and the train distressed him. After four stations we took a taxi."

"You took a taxi. Always one thing at a time. Why must you put out your facts like gold coins, Frau Richter? You took a taxi where to?"

"At first, we had no destination."

"You are joking! You gave the driver an address: a crossroads less than a kilometer from the American consulate! How can you say you had *no destination* when you gave a destination to the driver?"

"Very easily, Herr Werner. If you could enter for a moment into the mentality of many of our clients, you would understand that such things happen every day." She was brilliant. Not a word out of place. Not a foot fault. She had never been this good at the family forum's games of legal lying. "Mr. Karpov had a destination in mind, but for his own reasons he didn't wish to share it with me. Those crossroads lead in several directions. They also suited my own purpose very well, since I happen to live quite close to them."

"But you didn't take the taxi direct to your apartment! Why not? He could have walked from there, and you would have been safe and sound at home already. Or have we hit another insuperable obstacle in your story?"

"No, I most certainly did *not* take the taxi to my apartment." Straight into Werner's face.

"Why not?"

"Perhaps I didn't *go* to my apartment."

"Why not?"

"Perhaps I am disinclined to show my clients where I live. Perhaps I decided to go to the apartment of one of my many lovers, Herr Werner." Of whom you would so dearly like to be one, she was thinking.

"But you dismissed the taxi."

"Yes."

"And you walked. We may not know where to."

"Correct."

"And Karpov walked with you, clearly! He would not leave a pretty woman like you alone in the street at half past four in the morning. He is a sensitive man. Not dangerous at all. You said so. Yes?"

"No."

"No what?"

"No, he didn't walk with me."

"So he walked also, but in a different direction!"

"Correct. He set off north and vanished. I assume he entered a side road. I was more concerned that he should not follow me than in observing where he went."

"And after that?"

"What do you mean, *after that*?"

"You haven't seen him since? Had contact with him?"

"No."

"Not even through intermediaries?"

"No."

"But he gave you a phone number, naturally. Also an address. A desperate illegal immigrant does not obtain a talented young woman champion one day and dismiss her on the next, I assume."

"He gave me no phone number or address, Herr Werner. In our work, that's also quite normal. He has the phone number of the Sanctuary. I naturally hope we shall hear from him again, but we may not." Once more seeking Ursula's tacit confirmation, but receiving only the remotest nod. "That is the nature of our work here at the Sanctuary. Clients enter our lives and they disappear. They need time to talk to their companions in distress, to pray, to recover or go to ground. Perhaps Mr. Karpov has a wife and family who are already here. We are seldom admitted to the whole story. Perhaps he has friends, fellow Russians, fellow Chechens. Perhaps he has placed himself in the hands of a religious community. We don't know. Sometimes they come back next day, sometimes in six months, sometimes never."

Herr Werner was still considering how to launch his counterattack when his hitherto silent colleague decided to enter the conversation.

"So how about this other fellow who was at the Turks' house on Friday night?" he inquired, in the convivial tone of a man who liked a good party. "Big, stately fellow, nice clothes. Old as me. Older even. Is he also a lawyer for Karpov?"

Annabel was remembering her law tutor at Tübingen, discoursing on the arts of cross-examination. Never underestimate a witness's silence, he liked to say. There are eloquent silences, and guilty silences, and silences of genuine bewilderment and silences of creativity. The trick is to know what kind of silence you are hearing from your witness. But this silence was her own.

"Is this part of your coordination, Herr Dinkelmann?" she asked playfully, while desperately collecting her thoughts.

The clown's smile again, the perfect curve. "Don't flirt with me, Frau Richter. I'm too susceptible. Just tell me now: Who was this man? You brought him with you. He stayed in the house for hours on end. Then left on his own, poor fellow. Walked all over town, like he'd lost something. What was he looking for?" He appealed to Ursula. "Everybody *walks* in this story, Frau Meyer. It wears me out." Then back to Annabel, at his leisure: "Come on. Just tell me who he is. A name. Any name. Make one up."

But Annabel had put on her father's face, the one that said never mention this subject again.

"My client has a potential benefactor here in Hamburg. As a man of position, he wishes to remain anonymous for the time being. I have agreed to respect his wish."

"Let's all respect it. Did he speak, or just sit and watch, this anonymous benefactor?"

"Speak to whom?"

"To your boy. Issa. To you."

"He's not my boy."

"I'm asking you whether your client's anonymous benefactor participated in your conversation. I'm not asking you the topic of that conversation. I'm asking: Did he take part? Or is he deaf and dumb?"

"He took part."

"So it was a three-cornered conversation. You. The benefactor. Issa. You can tell me that. You're not breaking any rules. You sat there, the three of you, and you chewed the fat together. You can tell me yes or no."

"*Yes* then." And a shrug to go with it.

"A free exchange. There were issues to discuss between you that you can't reveal. But you discussed them in a free and unobstructed manner. Yes?"

"I don't know what you're trying to imply."

"You don't have to. Just answer this. Did you enjoy a full and uninhibited exchange between the three of you, an easy flow, with no obstructions?"

"This is ridiculous."

"Yes. It is. Did you?"

"Yes."

"So he speaks Russian, like you."

"I didn't say so."

"No, you really didn't. Somebody had to say it for you. I admire that. Your client is a fortunate boy."

Herr Werner was making a last effort to recover his ascendancy.

"So *that*'s where your Issa Karpov went when you left him to himself at four-thirty in the morning!" he cried. "He went to this *anonymous benefactor*! Maybe the terrorist paymaster, even! You left him at the crossroads in a rich area of town, and as soon as you were safely out of the way, he went to the house of his benefactor. Do you think that is a reasonable hypothesis?"

"It is as reasonable or unreasonable as any other hypothesis, Herr Werner," Annabel retorted.

And surprisingly it was the genial and passé Herr Dinkelmann, rather than his brash young superior, who decided that they had detained Frau Meyer and Frau Richter quite long enough.

"Annabel?"

They were alone, the two of them.

"Yes, Ursula."

"Perhaps it would be better if you gave this afternoon's meeting a miss. I suspect you may have important claims on your time. Do you have anything more you wish to tell me about our missing client?"

Annabel hadn't anything more to tell her.

"Good. Ours is a world of half-measures. Perfect solutions are not within our gift, however much we may wish otherwise. I think we have had this conversation before."

They had. About Magomed. We cannot expect an institution to deliver our personal utopias, Ursula had told her, when Annabel led a staff protest march on her office.

This was not panic. Annabel didn't panic. Not in her own book. She was responding to a critical situation that was in danger of unraveling.

From the Sanctuary she cycled at top speed to a petrol station at the edge of town, keeping an eye on the twin mirrors mounted on her handlebars for signs that she was being followed. What the signs would be she had no idea.

At the cash desk, she bought a handful of loose change.

She dialed Hugo's cell phone and got the answering service, which was what she had expected.

She dialed Information and got the number of the hospital where he worked.

Monday was a conference all day, he had told her. Call me on Monday evening. But Monday evening was now too late. The conference, she remembered, was about the restructuring of the hospital's mental health wing. She spoke first to a hospital switchboard operator and, after some hard bargaining, to the assistant to the hospital's administrator. She was Dr. Hugo Richter's sister, she said, it was an urgent family matter, could he possibly be called to the phone for a brief conversation?

"This had better be good, Annabel."

"My client's blown up in my face, Hugo. He needs a clinic now. I mean really *now*."

"What time is it?"

Hugo, the only doctor in the world who never has a watch.

"Ten-thirty. In the morning."

"I'll call you in the lunch break. Twelve-thirty. On your cell phone. Is it operative or have you still not charged it?"

She wanted to say, "No cell phone," but said, "Thanks, Hugo, really thanks," instead. "It's working fine," she added.

In the garage forecourt, two women were doing something to a battered yellow van. She dismissed them from her mind. Herr Werner's vans would be spotless. Filling time, she rode to her favorite shopping mall: the freshly pickled

herrings that he likes, plain dark organic choco-
late, Emmental cheese for what she prayed
would be their last evening in the apartment.
And her favorite brand of still water, which was
now his favorite too.

Hugo rang precisely at twelve-thirty as she
knew he would, wristwatch or no. She was sitting on a park bench with her bike propped
against a lamppost. He began aggressively,
which she hoped was a good sign.

"Am I supposed to be the doctor who's *referring*
him to this place? Sign a chit for him without
even knowing his name? Because that's a non-
starter. Anyway, you don't even *need* a false chit,"
he went on, before she could reply. "They'll have
some in-house quack who'll feel his pulse and di-
agnose a thousand euros a day. I've got two possi-
bilities. Five-star rip-off joints, both."

His first suggestion was in Königswinter,
which she discarded on the grounds of distance.
His second was ideal: a converted farmhouse near
Husum, by train just two hours north of Hamburg.

"Ask for Herr Dr. Fischer and put a clothes-
peg on your nose. Here's the number. And don't
thank me. I just hope he's worth it."

"He is," she said, and dialed the number.

Dr. Fischer understood the situation immediately.

He understood immediately that Annabel was speaking on behalf of a close friend, but did not presume to inquire into the nature of the friendship.

He understood immediately her views on the need for discretion on the telephone and shared them.

He understood that the unnamed patient spoke only Russian but foresaw no problem in this respect since several of his most experienced nurses came from what he delicately called the East.

He understood that the patient was in no way violent, but traumatized by a chain of unfortunate incidents best discussed face-to-face.

He took her point that a regimen of complete rest, plentiful food and escorted walks might well provide the needful cure. Such decisions would naturally depend upon a detailed assessment of his case.

He understood the need for urgency, and proposed an initial nonbinding interview between patient, carer and consultant.

Yes, indeed, tomorrow afternoon would do very well, would four o'clock be convenient? Then let us say four o'clock sharp.

And just a few more details. Was the patient competent to travel alone or did he perhaps require assistance? Trained assistants and suitable transport were on hand at extra charge.

He understood finally that Annabel might care to have an intimation of the clinic's basic fees, which, even without additional specialist attention, were astronomic. But thanks to Brue: yes, she said, her sick friend was fortunately in a position to make a substantial down payment.

"Until four o'clock tomorrow then, Frau Richter, when let us hope all outstanding formalities may be swiftly dispatched." And her name again? Her address? And her profession, please? And this was her regular cell phone number, wasn't it?

She had brought him her grandmother's chess set, a treasure. She wished she had thought of chess earlier. It was an activity sport for him. Before a move, he would sit motionless in the place where she guessed he sat all day when she wasn't there: on the sill of the arched brick window with his long legs folded to his chin and his spidery philosopher's hands linked round them. Then he would swoop, make his move, spring to his feet again and sashay to the other end of the attic to fly his paper airplanes and pirouette to the rhythms of Tchaikovsky while she contemplated her own move. Music, he had assured her, was not against Islamic law provided it did not intrude upon worship. Sometimes his religious statements sounded more like received wisdom than conviction.

"I'm arranging for you to go to a new place tomorrow, Issa," she said, picking a lighthearted moment. "Somewhere more comfortable where they can look after you properly. Good doctors, good food, all the decadent Western comforts."

The music had stopped, the scuffle of his feet also.

"To hide me, Annabel?"

"For a short time, yes."

"Will you be there also?"—as a hand sought his mother's bracelet.

"I'll be visiting. Often. I'll take you there and I'll visit you whenever I can. It's not so far away. Two hours by train"—casually, the way she had planned it.

"Will Leyla and Melik come?"

"I shouldn't think so. Not till you're legal."

"Is it a prison, this place where you are hiding me, Annabel?"

"No, it is *not* a prison!" She steadied herself. "It's a place to rest. A sort of"—she didn't mean to say the word, but said it anyway—"it's a special clinic where you can get your strength back while we wait for Mr. Brue."

"*Special* clinic?"

"Private. But terribly expensive; it has to be because it's so good. That's why we need to talk

again about the money Mr. Brue is holding for
you. Mr. Brue has kindly advanced us money for
you to stay there. That's another reason why you
must claim your inheritance. So that you can pay
back Mr. Brue."

"A *KGB* clinic?"

"Issa, we do *not* have KGB here!"

She was cursing her own stupidity. Clinic was
worse than prison to him.

He needed to pray. She retreated to the
kitchen. When she came back, he was perched in
his usual place on the windowsill.

"Did your mother ever teach you to sing,
Annabel?" he asked, in a thoughtful voice.

"When I was young, she took me to church. I
don't think she really taught me to sing, though.
I don't think anyone did. I don't think they
could. Not even the greatest teachers."

"It is enough for me that I hear you speak. Is
your mother a Catholic, Annabel?"

"Lutheran. A Christian, but not a Catholic."

"Are you also a Lutheran, Annabel?"

"I was brought up as one."

"Do you pray to Jesus, Annabel?"

"Not anymore."

"To the one God?"

She could bear no more of it. "Issa, listen to me."

"I am listening to you, Annabel."

"We can't escape this problem by not talking

about it. It's a good clinic. The good clinic will be a safe place for you. To stay at the good clinic we've *got* to have your money. Which means you've *got* to claim. I'm telling you this as your lawyer. If you don't claim, you won't be able to become a medical student here, or anywhere else in the world. Or whatever it is you decide to do with your life."

"God's word will prevail. It will be His will."

"No! It will be *yours*. However much you pray, it's *you* who's going to have to take the decision."

Would nothing persuade him? Apparently not.

"You are a woman, Annabel. You are not being rational. Mr. Tommy Brue loves his money. If I tell him to keep it, he will be grateful to me and continue to assist me. If I take the money away from him, he will not assist me, he will be angry. That is the logic of his position. For me it is also a convenient logic, since the money is filthy to me, and I refuse to dirty my hands with it. Do you wish the money for yourself?"

"Don't be ridiculous!"

"Then we have no use for it. You like it as little as I do. You are not yet ready to accept God's reality in your life, but you are moral. That speaks well for our relationship. We shall build upon this understanding."

Bereft, she buried her face in her hands, but the gesture seemed not to interest him.

"Kindly do not send me to this clinic, Annabel. I prefer it here in your house. When you have converted to Islam, this is where we must live. Tell this to Mr. Brue also. You must leave now, or you will be a provocation to me. It is better we don't shake hands. Go with God, Annabel."

She had left her bicycle in the entrance hall. Misted harbor lights were shining through the dusk, and she had to blink several times before they cleared. Remembering that the cycle path ran on the other side of the road, she took her place in the huddle of pedestrians waiting at the zebra crossing. Somebody was saying her name. She couldn't be sure the voice wasn't inside her head, but it couldn't have been because it was a woman's whereas the voice inside her head was Issa's. The external voice she was hearing, now that she listened to it properly, was talking to her about her sister.

"Annabel! My God! How *are* you? How's Heidi? Is it true she's pregnant again already?"

A burly woman of her own age. Green velveteen jacket, jeans. Short hair, no makeup, big smile. With her mind still struggling to return to the real world, Annabel temporized while she hunted for a connection: Freiburg? School? Skiing in Austria? The health club?

"Oh, I'm fine," she said. "Heidi's fine too. Are you out shopping?"

The pedestrian light turned to green. They crossed side by side with Annabel's bike between them.

"Hey, Annabel! What are you doing this side of town? Don't you live in Winterhude anymore?"

A second woman had drawn up on Annabel's left, the side with no bike. She was buxom with rosy cheeks and a gypsy headscarf. They had reached the curb and it was only the three of them. A strong hand closed round her wrist that held the bicycle. Another took hold of her left arm and, in a gesture that could have passed for affection, forced it behind her back. With the pain, Annabel had an absolutely clear recollection of the two women at the petrol station this morning.

"You get quietly into the car," the second woman explained, her lips in Annabel's ear. "You sit in the backseat at the center, please, no fuss. Everything friendly and normal. My friend will look after your bike."

The battered yellow van had its back doors open. A male driver and a male passenger sat in the front, staring ahead of them. With the woman's arm round her shoulder, Annabel allowed herself to be propelled onto the backseat. She heard the clunk of her bicycle behind her, followed by a thud. In the scramble, she hadn't noticed they had taken her rucksack. In leisurely time, the women sat themselves either side of her, took one of her hands each, slipped a handcuff round it and wedged it out of sight on the seat between their bodies.

"What are you going to do with him?" she whispered. "He's locked up! Who's going to feed him when I'm not there?"

A black Saab saloon drove off ahead of them. The van followed close behind it. Nobody was in a hurry.

9

Assemble your facts clearly and calmly.

You're a lawyer.

You may be an outraged woman with a volcano of fury in you waiting to erupt, but it's the lawyer, not the woman, who will speak for you.

This plonking iron lift you are riding in is conveying you upward, not downward. You know this from the feeling in your stomach, which is separate from other things you feel, such as nausea, and the aching pain of violation.

You are therefore about to be delivered to an upper floor and not a cellar, for which you are cautiously grateful.

This lift does not stop at intermediate floors. It has no controls, no mirrors, no window. It smells of diesel oil and field. It is a cattle lift. It smells of your school playing field in autumn.

Those who ride in this lift do so at the will of others. You are standing between two women who abducted you by pretending to be your friends. They were then assisted by a third woman who did not pretend to be your friend. Not one of them identified herself. Not one used any name in your hearing except your own.

Nobody, not even Issa, can describe to you what it feels like to lose your freedom but now you are beginning to learn.

You are a lawyer beginning to learn.

With the black Saab ahead of them to lead the way, they had made a stately procession past church steeples and dockyards, paused correctly at red lights, indicated right and left, traversed at moderate speed avenues of comfortable villas with lighted windows, entered an industrial wasteland, negotiated ruts of iron dragon's teeth that had lain down before them, slowed but not stopped at a guardhouse flanked by rolls of razor wire, watched the red-and-white boom rise at the instance of the Saab and arrived in a floodlit asphalt courtyard of parked cars and black-eyed office blocks on one side, and on the other an ancient riding stable that was a distant cousin of the stables on the family estate in Freiburg.

But the van didn't stop. Selecting the darker side of the courtyard it continued, slowly and, as it seemed to Annabel, furtively, to pull up a few meters short of the stable. Releasing her hands from the locks between the seat cushions, her captors pulled her out onto the tarmac, and frog-marched her to a man-sized doorway. The man-door was opened from inside, she was bundled through it. A third, freckle-faced, younger woman with a boy's haircut was waiting to help out. They were in a harness room without harnesses. Iron pegs and saddle racks sticking out from the walls. An old horse bucket with a regimental number stenciled on it. A low padded bench with a single blanket. A hospital basin of water. Soap. Towels. Rubber gloves.

Each woman was guarding a third of her. The freckled woman's eyes were the same color as Annabel's. Perhaps that was why she was the one delegated to address her. She was a woman of the south, perhaps from Baden-Württemberg, where Annabel came from, another reason. You have a choice, Annabel, she was explaining. We are following standard procedure for those who consort with terrorists. You can either submit peaceably or you can be placed under restraint. Which is it to be?

I'm a lawyer.

Do you submit or not?

Submitting, Annabel recited to herself the use-less bits of last-minute advice that she handed out to clients before they faced their tribunals: *be truthful . . . don't lose your temper . . . don't weep . . . keep*

your voice down and don't try to flirt with them . . . they
don't want to hate you or love you, they don't want to
pity you . . . they want to get their job done, get paid and
go home.

The lift door opened, revealing a small white room, like the room they had put her grandmother in when she was dead. At the bare wooden table where her grandmother should have been lying sat the man who this morning had called himself Herr Dinkelmann, puffing at a Russian cigarette; she recognized the smell immediately. The same cigarette her father had smoked in Moscow after a good dinner.

And next to Herr Dinkelmann, a tall wiry woman with graying hair and brown eyes who, though nothing like her mother in looks, had the same sagacity about her.

And on the table before them, the contents of her rucksack, laid out like court exhibits but without their plastic bags and labels. And on the side of the table nearest to her a single chair for Annabel, the accused. Standing facing her judges, she heard the thumps and plonks of the cattle lift as it descended.

"My real name is Bachmann," Dinkelmann said, as if contradicting her. "If you're thinking of suing us, it's *Günther Bachmann*. And this is

Frau Frey. *Erna* Frey. She sails. Spies and sails. I spy, but I don't sail. Sit down, please."

Annabel walked to the table and sat down.

"You want to register your protest now and get it over?" Bachmann inquired, drawing on his cigarette. "Rant about your special status as a lawyer, all that shit? Your amazing privileges, your client confidentiality? How you could get me thrown out on my ear tomorrow? How I've broken every rule in the book, which I have? Trampled on the very essence of the Constitution? Are you going to spout all that crap at me, or do we just assume it? Oh, and by the way, when's your next appointment with the wanted terrorist Issa Karpov, whom you've secreted in your apartment?"

"He's not a terrorist. You are. I demand to speak to a lawyer immediately."

"Your mother, the big judge?"

"A lawyer who can represent me."

"How about your illustrious father? Or maybe your brother-in-law in Dresden? I mean you've *really* got clout. A couple of phone calls, you can bring the entire legal establishment down on my head. The question is—do you *want* to? You don't. It's all bullshit. You want to save your boy's neck. That's all you want out of this. Sticks out a mile."

Erna Frey added her own, more thoughtful contribution.

"Your choice is between us and nobody, I'm afraid, dear. There are a lot of people not far from where we're sitting who'd like nothing better than to make Issa the subject of a dramatic police arrest, and claim the credit for it. And of course the police would be thrilled if they could arrest the people who would be seen as his accomplices. Leyla, Melik, Mr. Brue for all we know, even your brother, Hugo. It would be splendid headlines for them, whatever the outcome. Did I mention Sanctuary North? Imagine what poor Ursula's backers would say. And then there's you. Herr Werner's *official object of investigation*, to use the disagreeable terminology Herr Werner so enjoys. Abusing your lawyer status. Knowingly harboring a wanted terrorist. Lying to the authorities and the rest. Your career over at—what?—call it forty by the time you're out of prison."

"I don't care what you do to me."

"But you're not the one we're talking about, are you, dear? Issa is."

Bachmann, whose attention span was apparently limited, had already lost interest in the conversation and was picking his way through the things from her rucksack: her ring-backed notebook, diary, driving license, identity card, her headscarf—lifting it ostentatiously to his nose as if checking it for perfume that she never wore. But it was Tommy Brue's check that he kept returning to, tilting it to the light, scrutinizing it back and front, poring over the figures or the handwriting and shaking his head in studied mystification.

"Why didn't you pay this in?" he demanded.

"I was waiting."

"For what? Dr. Fischer of the clinic?"

"Yes."

"Wouldn't have lasted long, would it? Fifty grand. Not at that place."

"Long enough."

"For what?"

Annabel gave a hopeless shrug: "To try. That's all. Just try."

"Did Brue say there was going to be more where this came from?"

About to answer, Annabel abruptly changed her mind. "I need to know what makes you two think you're different," she said defiantly, turning to Erna Frey.

"Who from, dear?"

"The people you say want to have him arrested by the police and sent back to Russia or Turkey."

Replying for both of them, Bachmann once more took up Brue's check and studied it as if the answer lay there.

"Oh, we're different, okay," he growled. "That's for sure. But you're asking us what we intend to do with your boy." He laid the check before him,

but not to lose sight of it. "Well, I'm not sure we
know that, Annabel. In fact, I'm sure we *don't*. We
like to think we make the weather here. We hang
loose. We wait as long as we can. And we see
what Allah provides," he added, poking at the
check with his finger. "And if Allah comes
through—well, maybe your boy will end up a free
soul, living in the West and able to indulge his
wildest hopes and dreams. If not—if Allah *doesn't*
come through—or *you* don't—well, it's back to
where he came from, isn't it? Unless the Americans put in a bid for him. In which case, we won't
know where he is. And probably he won't either."

"We're trying to do the best for him, dear,"
Erna Frey said with such patent sincerity in her
voice that Annabel was for a moment driven to
believe her. "Günther knows that too, he just
doesn't say it very well. We don't think Issa's
bad. We're not making that kind of judgment at
all. And we know he's a bit cranky; well, who
wouldn't be? But we do think he may be able to
help us get to some very bad people all the
same."

Annabel tried to laugh. "As a spy? Issa?
You're mad! You're as sick as he is!"

"As a whatever the fuck," Bachmann retorted
irritably. "Nobody's part in this play is written yet.
That includes yours. What we *do* know is, if you're
on board with us, and we get to where we want to

get, between us we'll be saving a whole heap more innocent lives than ever you would feeding the fucking rabbits at Sanctuary North."

Picking up the check from the table, he rose impatiently to his feet. "So the first thing I want to know is: What in God's name is a Russian-speaking, not very successful, ex-Viennese British banker doing, turning out on a Friday night to pay his respects to Mr. Issa Karpov? You want to go somewhere more civilized, or are you going to stay at that table and sulk?'"

But Erna Frey had a gentler message: "We won't tell you all the truth, dear, we can't. But whatever we do tell you will be true."

It was long past midnight and still she hadn't wept.

She had told them everything she knew, half knew, guessed and half guessed, down to the last dregs, but she hadn't wept, she hadn't even complained. How come she had sided with them so quickly? What had happened to the rebel in her—to her fabled powers of argument and resistance so prized by the family forum? Why hadn't she woven another web of lies of the sort she had woven for Herr Werner? Was this Stockholm syndrome? She was reminded of a pony she once had. He was called Moritz, and Moritz was a delinquent. He was unbreakable and unrideable. Not a family in all Baden-Württemberg would have him—until Annabel heard about him and, to exert her power, overrode her parents and raised money among her school friends to buy him. When Moritz was delivered, he kicked the groom, kicked a hole in his stall and broke his way into the paddock. But next morning when Annabel in trepidation went out to him, he strolled towards her, lowered his head for the halter and became her slave forevermore. He'd had a bellyful of opposition and wanted somebody else to take charge of his problems.

So was that what she had done now? Chucked in the towel and said, "All right, damn you, have me," the way she'd said it to men a couple of times when the sheer crassness of their persistence had reduced her to furious submission?

No. The devil was in the logic, she was convinced of it: in the willed detachment with which the lawyer in her stepped back and recognized that she hadn't got even the prayer of a case to argue, let alone win—not on behalf of her client, nor herself, though she was the last person she cared about. It was the hard-nosed lawyer in her—so she desired adamantly to believe—that told her that her one hope was to throw herself on the mercy of the court: which was to say, her handlers.

Yes, she was emotionally wiped out. Of course

she was. Yes, the loneliness and strain of keeping such a huge secret to herself for so long had taken her to the limits of her endurance. And there was a certain relief, even pleasure, in becoming a child again, in handing the big decisions of her life to people wiser and older than herself. But even when she had put these factors into the balance, it was still the lawyer's logic—so she determinedly reassured herself—that had persuaded her to make a clean breast of all she knew.

She had told about Brue and Mr. Lipizzaner and the key and Anatoly's letter, about Issa and Magomed, and then about Brue again: how he looked and spoke, and how he had reacted to this moment or that one, in the Atlantic, in the café before going to Leyla's house. And what was that again about studying in Paris? And all that money he gave her suddenly—*why*? Was it to get into your knickers, dear? Erna Frey asking this question, not Bachmann. Where pretty women were concerned, he was too susceptible.

But this was not a confession dragged out of her by stealth or threats or inducements. This was Annabel shamefully indulging herself: a cathartic release of knowledge and emotions that had been locked up in her too long, a sweeping away of all the barriers she had erected in her mind: against Issa, Hugo, Ursula, the plumbers and decorators and electricians, and most of all against herself.

And they were right: she had no choice. Like Moritz she was exhausted by her own opposition. She needed friends not enemies if Issa was to be saved, whether they were truly different from the others, or only pretending to be.

A narrow corridor led to a tiny bedroom. The double bed was made up with fresh sheets. So tired that she could have gone to sleep standing, Annabel peered round her while Erna Frey demonstrated how the shower worked, and tut-tutted as she whisked away the dirty towels and replaced them with fresh ones from a drawer.

"Where will you two sleep?" Annabel asked, without knowing why she cared.

"Now don't you worry, dear. Just get yourself some good rest. You've had a very hard day of it, and tomorrow is going to be just as hard."

If I sleep, I shall return to prison, Annabel.

Tommy Brue was not in prison, but then neither was he sleeping.

By four o'clock of the same morning, he had stolen from the marital bed and tiptoed barefoot down the stairs to the study where he kept his address book. There were six numbers listed under "Georgie." Five were crossed out. The sixth was marked "K's cell phone" in his own hand. *K* for Kevin, her last known address. It was three months since he'd called it, and much longer since he'd succeeded in getting past Kevin. But this time something was urgently wrong with her and he knew it.

Don't call it premonition. Don't call it a panic attack. Call it what it is: a father's fear.

Using his cell phone so that no telltale pin light should appear on the bedside phone at Mitzi's head, he touched Kevin's number, closed his eyes and waited to hear the slack-mouthed drawl informing him that, yeah, well, sorry about that, Tommy, but Georgie doesn't feel like speaking to you right now, she's okay, she's great, but she kinda gets upset. But this time he was going to *demand* to speak to her. He was going to insist on his paternal rights, not that he had any. A burst of rock music entrenched his resolve. So did the recorded voice of Kevin advising him that if you really have to leave a message, man, maybe just leave it, but since nobody picks up messages much around here, why not hang up and call another time—until that message itself was cut short by a woman's voice.

"Georgie?"

"Who is this?"

"Is that really Georgie?"

"Of course it's me, Dad. Don't you recognize my voice?"

"I just didn't know you answered the phone. I

wasn't expecting it. How are you, Georgie? Are you all right?"

"I'm just great. Is something wrong? You sound awful. How's the new Mrs. Brue? Jesus, whatever time is it over there? Dad?"

He was holding the phone at arm's length while he collected himself. The new Mrs. Brue, eight years new. Never *Mitzi.*

"Nothing's wrong, Georgie. I'm great too. She's asleep. I was just desperately worried about you for some reason. But you're fine. You're more than fine, I can hear. I was sixty last week. Georgie?"

Don't challenge her, the odious Viennese shrink used to say. When she enters one of her silences, wait for her to come back.

"You didn't sound *right* just now, Dad," she complained, as if they had been chatting every day of the week. "I thought you were Kevin calling from the supermarket, but you were you. It just threw me."

"I had no idea you used supermarkets. What's he buying?"

"The whole store. He's gone mad. This is a forty-year-old man who's been living on pine nuts for ten years and says kids are the end of life as we know it. Now all he can think of is changing mats, Babygros with bunny ears, a cradle with frilly sides and a buggy with a sun visor. Is this how you went when Mum got pregnant? And me telling him we're broke and he's got to give all the stuff back."

"Georgie?"

"Yes?"

"That's amazing. That's wonderful. I didn't know."

"Neither did I till about five minutes ago."

"When's it due, for heaven's sake? If you don't mind my asking."

"Not for about fifty years. Can you believe it? And Kevin acting like a pregnant father already? He even wants to marry me now that his book's been accepted."

"Book? Nobody told me he was even writing one."

"It's a how-to. Brains, diet and contemplation."

"Marvelous!"

"And happy birthday, okay? Come see us some time. I love you, Dad. It's going to be a girl. Kevin's decided."

"Can I send you some money? To help you along? For the baby? For the frilly cradle and stuff?" It was on the tip of his tongue to suggest fifty thousand euros, but he restrained himself and waited for her to come back.

"Maybe later. I'll talk to Kevin and call you. Maybe frilly cradle money's okay. Just not money like money instead of love. Give me your number again."

For the nineteenth or ninetieth time in the past ten years, Brue spelled out his numbers: cell phone, house, the one that rings on my desk at the bank. Had she written them down? Maybe this time she had.

He poured himself a scotch. Wonderful, incredible news. The best he could have dreamed of.

Pity Annabel couldn't tell him she was all right too. Because actually, as he now realized, it was Annabel, not Georgie, that he had been so worried about when he woke with a jump and crept downstairs.

In short then, what you might call a case of misdirected paranoia, as the odious Viennese shrink might have said.

This staircase is an imbecility.

I should never have bought the place.

All these perilous little nooks and twists and half landings: I could break my neck.

This rucksack weighs a ton. What the hell did we put in it?

The straps are cutting into my shoulders like wire.

One more flight, I'm there.

She had slept. After two wide-awake nights in

her flat staring at the ceiling, a deep, dream-free, child's sleep.

"Issa's going to be very pleased with you, dear," Erna Frey had assured her, waking her with a cup of coffee and then sitting on her bed. "You'll be bringing him *just* the news he's hoping for. *And* a lovely breakfast."

She had said it again into the driving mirror, while Annabel crouched in the back with her bicycle, waiting to be launched down the hill to the harbor front. "Just remember there's nothing in the least deceptive or dishonorable about what you're doing, dear. You're his bringer of hope and he trusts you. I put the yogurt in last. Your key's in the right-hand pocket of your anorak. All set? Off you go, then."

The new padlock sprang open, the iron door took both hands to push, soft music was playing over the radio, she thought Brahms. She stood in the doorway, filled with fear and shame and a sickening, hopeless sadness for what she was about to do. He lay prone beneath the arched window, on the bit of floor where he had his bed, his long body wrapped head to toe in a brown blanket with the top of his skullcap peeping out one end, and Karsten's designer socks the other. Neatly arranged beside him lay everything he needed to accompany him to his next prison: the camel-skin bag, the black coat folded small, Karsten's loafers and designer jeans. Was he naked apart from the socks and hat? She closed the door behind her but remained there, leaving the length of the loft between them.

"We shall depart for the clinic immediately, please, Annabel," Issa announced from under the blanket. "Has Mr. Brue provided an armed guard and a malodorous gray bus with barred windows?"

"No bus, no armed guard, I'm afraid," she called back cheerfully. "And no clinic either. You're not going anywhere after all"—sidestepping towards the kitchen—"I've brought us an exotic breakfast to celebrate. Do you want to join me in here when you've got up? Maybe you want to pray."

Silence. Shuffle of stockinged feet. She crouched to the fridge, opened the door, set the rucksack beside it.

"No clinic, Annabel?"

"No clinic," she repeated, not hearing his footsteps anymore.

"Yesterday you tell me I must go to a clinic, Annabel. Now I must not go. Why?"

Where was he? She was too frightened to turn round. "It just wasn't such a good move as we thought," she said loudly. "Too much *bureaucracy*. Too many *forms* to fill in, awkward *questions* to answer"—Erna Frey's suggestion—"we decided you were better off where you are."

"We?"

"Mr. Brue. Me."

Keep Brue between you, Bachmann had advised. If Issa sees him as a higher being, keep him that way.

"I do not understand your motivation, Annabel."

"We changed our minds, that's all. I'm your lawyer, he's your banker. We looked at the options and decided you were best off here in my apartment, where you want to be."

She found her courage and looked round. He was standing in the doorway, filling it, swathed in the brown blanket, a monk with coal dark eyes, watching her unpack the rucksack that had everything in it she'd told Erna Frey he liked: a six-pack of fruit yogurts, poppy-seed rolls oven-warm, Greek honey, sour cream, Emmental cheese.

"Was Mr. Brue depressed by the knowledge that he must pay a lot of money to the clinic, Annabel? Is this the reason why he changed his mind?"

"I told you the reason. Your own safety."

"You are lying to me, Annabel."

She stood up abruptly and swung round to face him. There was only a meter between them. At any other time she would have respected the invisible exclusion zone that kept them apart, but this time she held her ground.

"I am *not* lying to you, Issa. I am telling you that, for your own good, there has been a change of plan."

"Your eyes are bloodshot, Annabel. Have you been drinking alcohol?"

"No, of course I haven't."

"Why *of course,* Annabel?"

"Because I don't drink alcohol."

"Do you know him very well, this Mr. Tommy Brue, please?"

"What are you talking about?"

"Have you been drinking alcohol with Mr. Brue, Annabel?"

"Issa, stop this!"

"Do you have a relationship with Mr. Tommy Brue which is comparable with the relationship you had with the unsatisfactory man in your previous apartment?"

"Issa, I told you, *stop!*"

"Is Mr. Tommy Brue the successor to this unsatisfactory man? Does Mr. Brue exercise a disproportionate power over you? I watched how he regarded you lustfully at Leyla's house. Do you succumb to Mr. Brue's base desires because he is materially rich? Does Mr. Brue believe that by keeping me here in your house, he is subjugating you to his will and also ensuring that he will not be obliged to pay big sums to the KGB clinic?"

She had regained control of herself. We don't

want you compliant, Bachmann had said. We want you creative. We want your ice-cold head and your larcenous legal mind, not a lot of callow emotional shit that can't go anywhere.

"Look, Issa," she said coaxingly, turning back to the rucksack. "Mr. Brue doesn't just want to feed your body. Look what he's sent you."

A Russian one-volume softback edition of Turgenev's *Torrents of Spring* and *First Love.*

The Tales of Chekhov, also in Russian.

A miniature disc player to improve on her old tape recorder, classical discs of Rachmaninov, Tchaikovsky and Prokofiev, and—because Erna thinks of everything—spare batteries.

"Mr. Brue likes and respects us both," she said. "He is not my lover. That's in your imagination, nowhere else. We don't want to keep you here a day longer than is necessary. We would do anything on earth to set you free. You have to believe that."

The yellow van stood where it had dropped her. The same boy was at the wheel. Erna Frey was still sitting in the passenger seat. She had the car radio on and was listening to Tchaikovsky. Annabel slung her bike in the back and the rucksack after it, jumped in and slammed the doors shut behind her.

"That's the filthiest thing I ever had to do in my life," she remarked, staring out of the windscreen. "Thank you very much. I really enjoyed it."

"Nonsense, dear. You did it beautifully," said Erna Frey. "He's happy. Listen."

The Tchaikovsky was still playing over the radio, but the reception seemed strangely ragged, until Annabel recognized the sound of Issa clumping round the loft in Karsten's moccasins, singing discordant tenor at the top of his voice.

"So I did that too," she said. "Perfect."

10

Wisteria overhung the timbered porch. The tiny but immaculate garden was groomed in the Romantic manner, with a rose shrubbery and a lily pond fed by ornamental frogs. The house itself was small but very pretty, a Snow White house with rustic pink roof tiles and whimsical chimneys, set beside one of Hamburg's most desirable canals. The time was precisely seven o'clock in the evening. Bachmann knew the importance of punctuality. He was dressed in his best bureaucratic suit and carrying an official briefcase. He had polished his black shoes and, with the help of Erna Frey's spray, flattened his rebellious mop of hair into temporary submission.

"Schneider," he murmured into the entry phone and the front door opened at once only to be swiftly closed after him by Frau Ellenberger.

* * *

In the eighteen or so hours since Erna Frey had marched Annabel off to bed, Bachmann with Maximilian's help had laid siege to the Service's central computer for all the Karpovs known to man, phoned a contact in the Austrian Security Service and obliged him to unearth the unhappy history of Brue Frères of Vienna in its declining years, buttonholed Arni Mohr's prickly head of street surveillance concerning the perceived lifestyle of the bank's surviving principal, dispatched a researcher to storm the archives of Hamburg's finance office and—by midafternoon—assailed Michael Axelrod of Joint for a full hour on the encrypted line to Berlin before calling up all files on a highly respected Muslim scholar living in north Germany and known for his moderate views and pleasing television manners.

For some of the files, Bachmann was obliged to seek special clearance from Joint's money-laundering section. To Erna Frey there had been something almost demented about him as he shambled back and forth between the researchers' den and their own, puffed at innumerable cigarettes, plunged into the files strewn across his desk or demanded sight of some memo he had sent her, forgotten about, and which now lay buried in the bowels of her computer.

"Why the bloody Brits of all people?" he had demanded to know. "What makes a Russian

crook go to a Brit bank in an Austrian city? All
right, Karpov senior admires their hypocrisy. He
respects their gentlemanly lies. But how the fuck
did he *find* them? Who *sent* him to them?"

And at three o'clock this afternoon: *Eureka!* He
had it in his hand, a flimsy brown file plucked
from the catacombs of the public prosecutor's office. It was marked for destruction but by a miracle had escaped the flames. Bachmann had once
more made the weather.

They sat in flowered armchairs, facing each other
in the window bay of her spotless drawing room
that was a piece of England, drinking Earl Grey
tea from the finest Minton bone china. On the
walls, prints of Old London and Constable land-
scapes. In a Sheraton bookcase, editions of Jane
Austen, Trollope, Hardy, Edward Lear and Lewis
Carroll. In the bay, fluffy spring buds in Wedg-
wood pots.

For a long while neither spoke. Bachmann
smiled kindly, mostly to himself. Frau Ellenberger gazed at the lace-curtained window.

"You object to a tape recorder, Frau Ellenberger?" he inquired.

"Emphatically, Herr Schneider."

"Then let there be no tape recorder," Bachmann announced decisively, dropping one in-

strument back into his briefcase while leaving the other running.

"But I may make notes," he suggested, setting a notepad on his lap, and keeping his pen poised.

"I shall require a copy of whatever you propose to place on file," she said. "If you had allowed me more notice, my brother would be here to represent me. Unfortunately he has business elsewhere tonight."

"Your brother is welcome to inspect our files at any time."

"It is to be hoped, Herr Schneider," said Frau Ellenberger.

When she had opened the front door to him, she had blushed. She was now spectral pale, and beautiful. With her wide, vulnerable eyes, swept-back hair, long neck and young girl's profile, she was to Bachmann one of those beautiful women who pass unnoticed into middle age, and disappear.

"I may begin?" Bachmann inquired.

"Please."

"Seven years ago you made a voluntary sworn statement to my predecessor and colleague, Herr Brenner, regarding certain concerns you had regarding the activities of your employer at that time."

"I have not changed my employer, Herr Schneider."

"A fact of which we are aware, and shall respect," Bachmann replied reverentially, making an ostentatious note to himself by way of reassuring her.

"It is to be hoped, Herr Schneider," Frau Ellenberger said again, to the lace curtains, while she gripped the arms of her chair.

"May I say I admire you for your courage?"

He might, he might not, for she gave no sign of having heard him.

"Probity too, of course. But courage foremost. May I ask you what moved you to make it?"

"And may I ask *you,* what you are doing here?"

"Karpov," Bachmann replied promptly. "Grigori Borisovich Karpov. Valued former client of Brue Frères Bank, Vienna, now of Hamburg. Holder of a Lipizzaner account."

While he spoke, her head swung round to him, partly—as it seemed to Bachmann—in disgust, but partly also in spirited if guilty pleasure.

"Don't tell me he's still up to his old tricks," she exclaimed.

"Karpov himself, I do not regret to inform you, is no longer with us, Frau Ellenberger. But his works live after him. As do those of his criminal associates. Which, without breaching official secrecy, is why I am here tonight. History doesn't pause for breath, they say. The deeper we dig, the deeper we seem to go back in time. Allow me to ask you: Is *Anatoly* a name to you at all? Anatoly, consigliere to the late Karpov?"

"Distantly. As a name. He was the fixer."

"But you never met him."

"There were no intermediaries." She corrected herself. "Apart from Anatoly, of course. Karpov's fixer extraordinaire, Mr. Edward called him. But Anatoly wasn't just a *fixer,* mind. He was more like a *straightener.* Always picking up Karpov's crooked bits and making them look straight."

Bachmann stored this egregious comment but did not pursue it.

"And *Ivan?* Ivan Grigorevich?"

"I know of no Ivan, Herr Schneider."

"Karpov's natural son? Later to call himself *Issa?*"

"I know of no issue of Colonel Karpov, natural or otherwise, although I have no doubt there were many. Mr. Brue Junior asked me the same question only the other day."

"He did?"

"Yes. He did."

And again Bachmann let the observation pass. A halfway-decent interrogator, he liked to preach, on the rare occasions when he was let loose on new entrants to the Service, doesn't smash the front door down. He rings the front doorbell, then goes in at the back entrance. But this was not the reason he held off, as he later confessed to Erna Frey. It was *the other music* that he was hearing: the feeling that, while she was telling him one story, he was listening to a different one, and so was she.

"So may I ask you, Frau Ellenberger—going back in time again, if I may—what prompted you, seven years ago, to make that very courageous statement in the first place?"

It took a while for her to hear him.

"I'm German, don't you see," she replied irritably, just when he was about to repeat his question.

"Yes, indeed."

"I was returning to Germany. My homeland."

"From Vienna."

"Frères was about to open a *branch* in Germany. My Germany. I wished—yes, well, I *wished,*" she said angrily, and frowned through the net curtains and all the way into the garden, as if the fault lay there.

"You wished to draw a line, perhaps? A line under the past?" Bachmann suggested.

"I wished to reenter my own country in a *pure state,*" she retorted, with sudden animation. "Untainted. Don't you understand?"

"Not quite yet, but I'm getting there, I'm sure."

"I wished to make a clean beginning. *With* the bank. *With* my life. Is that not human nature? To wish a new beginning? Perhaps you don't think so. Men are different."

"It was also the case, I believe, that your distinguished employer of many years had passed away, and Brue Junior"—using her own term for him—"had recently taken over the bank," Bachmann suggested, lowering his voice in submission to her didactic tone.

"That is the case, Herr Schneider. You have done your homework, I am pleased to note. So few do their homework these days. I was *extremely* young," she reported, in a tone of unsparing self-diagnosis. "Younger than my years by *far,* remember. If I compare myself with modern youth, I was a total *infant.* I came of a poor family, and had no experience of the larger world *whatever.*"

"But you were a raw recruit, first time in the field, allow me!" Bachmann protested, matching her indignation. "The orders came down from *above* and you obeyed them. You were young and innocent, and in a position of trust. Aren't you being a little *hard* on yourself, Frau Ellenberger?"

Did she hear him? And if she did, why then was she smiling? Her voice was changing. It was younger. As she started speaking again, a brighter cadence entered it, a softer, fresher, more Viennese lilt, that put a forgiving gloss on even her severest observations. And to the younger voice, a younger figure: still prim, still respectfully upright, but more active and flirtatious in its gestures. Stranger still was the fact that her very style of speech seemed chosen to please the ear of someone superior to her in both age and station, whereas Bachmann was neither; and that, by an unconscious act of retrospective ventriloquism, she was evoking not merely the voice of her vanished youth, but the voice in which the relationship with the person she was describing had been conducted.

"There *were* those around me who were *forward*, Herr Schneider," she remembered, fondly nonetheless. "*Very* forward, provided it secured them the attention of *Mr. Edward*." A name to prize and own. A name to savor. "But that wasn't my style *at all,* oh no. It was my reticence, not my forwardness, that commended *me* to him. He told me so himself. 'Elli, when you're scouting for a Girl Friday, better to pick the one from the back of the crowd.' That was the *rough* side of him speaking," she added dreamily. "It took me by surprise at first, the *rough* side. It took getting used to. You didn't expect it of a gentleman of Mr. Edward's refinement. Then it was all right. It was *real,*" she said proudly, and fell silent again.

"And you were a mere—*what* at that time?" Bachmann inquired at length, but very delicately, determined not on any account to break the spell.

"Twenty-two years old, and with the *highest* secretarial grades. My father had died when I was young, you see. A cloud hangs over the manner of his death, I don't mind telling you. Hanged himself, I *heard,* but never officially. We're Catholics. My mother's brother was a priest in Passau and kind enough to take us in. What else could you be in Passau? Unfortunately, with the years, my uncle became overaffectionate towards me, and I felt it prudent, at the risk of upsetting my mother, to remove myself to secretarial college in Vienna. Yes. Well. There we were. He violated me, if you want to know. I hardly realized at the time. You don't, not if you're innocent."

And again she fell silent.

"And Brue Frères was your first appointment," Bachmann suggested.

"I can only tell you," Frau Ellenberger resumed, in answer to a question he hadn't put, "that Mr. Edward treated me with *exemplary* consideration."

"I would have no doubt of that."

"Mr. Edward was a model of propriety."

"My office does not dispute that. We feel he was led astray."

"He was English in the best sense. When Mr. Edward confided in me, I felt flattered. When he invited me to accompany him socially, for example, to just a little dinner"—she was using the English words—"after a long day's work before he went home to relax with his family, I felt proud to be selected."

"Who wouldn't? Nobody."

"That he was not merely old enough to be my uncle, but practically my grandfather, did not arouse my undue concern," she resumed sternly, as if for the record. "Having already become accustomed to the attentions of an older man, I accepted them as normal for one in my position. The difference was, Mr. Edward had zest. He was *not* my uncle. When I told my mother what had occurred, she did not view my situation as unfortunate, but to the contrary advised me not to endanger it by petty considerations. Mr. Edward, having only one son to remember, would surely not forget a pretty young girl who had shown him loving friendship in his declining years."

"And he didn't forget, did he?" Bachmann prompted, casting an appreciative eye round the room, but he had lost her again—and almost, it seemed to him, she had lost herself.

"So at what point, exactly, would you say, Frau Ellenberger," he resumed brightly, making a fresh start, "did the intrusion of *Colonel Karpov* cast a blight over your shared happiness, if I may put it thus?"

Had she really not heard him?

Still?

She raised her eyebrows to their fullest extent. She tilted her head attentively to one side.

Then she launched on another statement for the file.

"The arrival of Grigori Borisovich Karpov as a major Frères client coincided with the full, improbable flowering of my relationship with Mr. Edward. I could not then, nor can I now, determine which event preceded the other. Mr. Edward had entered what I can but describe as his second or third youth. He was positive in his attentions to me, and in spirit a great deal more adventurous than many of the younger men of the Viennese banking community." She mused for a while, started to say something, shook her head and gave a roguish smile of reminiscence. "*Very* positive, if you want to know." The moment vanished. "You asked *when,* I believe. *When* he appeared on the scene, I suppose you mean. Karpov. Yes?"

"Something like that."

"Let me tell you about Karpov, then."

"Please do."

"It would be tempting to describe Karpov as the archetypal Russian bear. But that's only *half* the story. On Mr. Edward he acted like a revitalizing drug. 'Karpov is my Spanish fly,' he once remarked to me. Karpov's irreverence towards the conventional norms of life struck a kindred spark in Mr. Edward's heart. In the weeks preceding the inauguration of the Lipizzaner system,

Mr. Edward had traveled to Prague, Paris and East Berlin for the sole purpose of meeting our new client."

"With you?"

"With me sometimes, yes. With me often, in fact. And sometimes little Anatoly came along with his briefcase, bless him. I always wondered what he kept in it. A gun? Mr. Edward said it was his pajamas. Imagine a briefcase in a nightclub! And he paid for simply *everything* out of it! Just from one pocket at the front where he kept the cash. We never saw inside the *main* part. It was top secret. Being bald made it funnier somehow."

She allowed herself a little girl's chuckle.

"Not one dull minute, not with Karpov. Every encounter a blend of anarchy and culture and you never knew which you were going to get." She pulled a sharp frown, correcting herself. "I will say this, Herr Schneider. Colonel Karpov was a genuine and passionate admirer of all forms of art, music and literature, also physics. And women too, of course. That goes without saying. In Russian he would describe himself as *kulturny*. Cultured."

"Thank you," said Bachmann, writing diligently in his notebook.

The same strict tone: "After carousing until dawn in a nightclub, and availing himself of the upstairs rooms—twice or even three times, I may say—*and* discoursing about literature in between visits—he would need immediately to explore the art galleries and visit the city's cultural sites. Sleep as we understand it was not a concept to him. For Mr. Edward, and for myself personally, it was an unrepeatable journey of education."

Her severity left her and she began laughing softly and rolling her head. To keep her company, Bachmann gave her his clown's smile.

"And were the Lipizzaner accounts openly discussed on these occasions?" he inquired. "Or was it all hush-hush, secretive—just between the two men alone? And Anatoly when he was there?"

Another unnerving silence as her face turned suddenly bleak with memory.

"Oh, Mr. Edward, even at his most liberated, was never less than *secretive*, I grant you!" she complained, acknowledging the question without directly answering it. "In banking matters, well, that was natural, I suppose. But also in matters relating to the *private sphere.* Sometimes I wondered whether I was the only one, quite *apart* from Mrs. Brue. But then she died," she added with a pout. "He was distraught, I'm sure. So sad, really. I'd thought we might marry, you see. It turned out there wasn't a vacancy. Not for Elli."

"And he was also secretive about his British

friend Mr. *Findlay,* I seem to recall from your statement," Bachmann reminded her, advancing featherlight on the question he had come to ask.

Her face had darkened. She thrust her jaw forward in rejection, lips clamped together.

"Wasn't that his name? *Findlay?* The mysterious Englishman?" Bachmann lightly insisted. "That's how it stands in your statement. Or have I got it wrong?"

"No. You have *not* got it wrong. *Findlay* got it wrong. Very wrong indeed."

"Findlay the *evil genius* behind the Lipizzaner accounts, even?"

"*Nobody* should be interested in Mr. Findlay. Mr. Findlay should be relegated to oblivion forthwith and forever, is what should happen to *our Mr. Findlay,*" she said, adopting a furious nursery-rhyme voice. "Mr. Findlay should be *chopped up in little pieces and put in a pot until he's done!*"

The sudden spurt of energy with which she delivered this pronouncement confirmed what Bachmann had for some time been suspecting: that while they might be drinking English tea out of fine china cups on a silver tray, with a silver strainer and a silver milk jug and a silver pitcher of boiled water, and nibbling tastefully at homemade Scottish shortcake, the fumes that came to him sporadically on her breath derived from something a lot more potent than mere tea.

"He was that bad, eh?" Bachmann marveled. "*Chop him up. Give him what he deserves.*" But she had retreated into her own memories, so he might as well have been talking to himself. "Mind you, I do see your point. If somebody took *my* employer for a ride, I'd be pretty angry too. To sit there watching your boss being led up the garden path." No response. "Still, he must have been quite a character, our Mr. Findlay. Mustn't he? Anyone who was able to lead Mr. Edward off the straight-and-narrow—introduce him to Russian crooks like Karpov and his *fixer extraordinaire*—"

He had broken the spell.

"Findlay was *not* quite a character, thank you!" Frau Ellenberger retorted furiously. "He wasn't a *character* at all. Mr. Findlay was assembled *entirely* from characteristics *stolen* from other people!" Then promptly put her hand to her lips to shut them up.

"What did he look like, Findlay? Give me a word picture. Mr. Findlay."

"Sleek. Wicked. Shiny. Dry nose."

"How old?"

"Forty. Or he pretended to be. But his shadow was much, *much* older."

"Height? General appearance? Any physical characteristics you remember?"

"Two horns and a long tail and a very *strong* odor of sulfur."

Bachmann shook his head in wonder. "You really didn't like him much, did you?"

Frau Ellenberger underwent another of her abrupt metamorphoses. She sat up as straight as a schoolmistress, pursed her lips and fixed him with a look of stern reproach. "When a man is deliberately excluded from your life, Herr Schneider— *one's* life—somebody to whom you are emotionally attached, to whom you have revealed yourself in all your womanhood—it is not unreasonable to regard that man with loathing and suspicion, the more so if he is the seducer and corrupter of your—of Mr. Edward's banking integrity."

"Did you meet him often?"

"Once, and once was quite enough to form a judgment. He made an appointment, posing as a normal potential client. He came to the bank and I engaged him in light conversation in the waiting room, which was a part of my duties. That was the only time he appeared at the bank. Thereafter, Findlay worked his evil magic and I was excluded utterly. By both of them."

"Could you explain that?"

"We could be in the middle of a private moment, Mr. Edward and I. Alone. Or a dictation, it made no difference. The phone rang. It was Findlay. Mr. Edward had only to hear his voice and it was 'Elli, go and powder your nose.' If Findlay wished for a *meeting* with Mr. Edward, it occurred in the town, *never* at the bank, and I was again excluded. 'Not tonight, Elli. Go and cook a chicken for your mother.' "

"Did you complain to Mr. Edward about this shabby treatment?"

"His reply to me was that there are some secrets on earth that not even I could be party to, and Teddy Findlay was one of them."

"Teddy?"

"That was his first name."

"I don't think you mentioned that."

"I had no wish to. We were Teddy and Elli. Only on the telephone, of course. And on the strength of one encounter in the waiting room during which we discussed nothing of substance. It was all *pretend*. That was what Findlay was about: pretense. Our supposed familiarity on the telephone would never have survived reality, you may be sure. Mr. Edward wished me to be amused by his impertinence, so naturally I was."

"What makes you so sure Findlay was behind the Lipizzaner operation?"

"He set it up!"

"Set it up with Karpov?"

"With Anatoly, acting on Karpov's behalf,

sometimes. So I understood. From afar. But the brainchild was his alone. He boasted about it. *My* Lipizzaners. *My* little stable. *My* Mr. Edward, was what he was really saying. It was all planned. Poor Mr. Edward never had a chance. He was *lured.* First the facetious phone call, very charming, requesting the appointment—private and personal, of course, no third parties, nothing on the file. Then the flattering invitation to the British embassy and a drink with the ambassador to make it all *official.* Official *what?* may I ask. *Nothing* about the Lipizzaners was official! They were the *opposite* of official. They were doped and hobbled from the start. Bandy-legged imposters posing as blood horses is what they were!"

"Ah yes, the *embassy,*" Bachmann agreed hazily, as if the *embassy* had momentarily escaped his memory—because a halfway-decent interrogator does not smash the door down. But in reality the British embassy was complete news to him and would be to Erna Frey. Nothing in her statement of seven years ago had prepared them for the involvement of the British embassy in Vienna.

"Now just where *did* the embassy come up?" he asked, in simulated embarrassment. "Run that by me again, if you would, Frau Ellenberger. Perhaps I didn't do my homework as well as we thought."

"*Mr.* Findlay had initially represented himself

as some kind of British diplomat," she replied scathingly. "An *informal* diplomat, if there *is* such a breed, which I doubt."

To judge by Bachmann's face he doubted it too, although he had been one himself.

"Later he reinvented himself as a *financial consultant*. If you ask me, he was never either one of them. He was a charlatan and that was all he ever was."

"So the Lipizzaners began their lives courtesy of the *British embassy in Vienna*," Bachmann mused aloud. "Of course they did! I remember now. Forgive my little lapse."

"That was where the whole Lipizzaner plan was cooked up, I've no doubt of it. On the night Mr. Edward returned from that first meeting at the embassy, he outlined the entire arrangement to me. I was shocked, but it was not my place to appear so. Thereafter, whatever refinements or *improvements* were proposed invariably followed consultations with Mr. Findlay. Whether in a foreign town, or in Vienna, but well away from the bank, or over the telephone in an artfully disguised form that Mr. Edward insisted on referring to as their *word code*. It was a term I had never heard him use before. Good night, Herr Schneider."

"Good night, Frau Ellenberger."

But Bachmann didn't move. And neither did

she. In his entire career, he afterwards confided to Erna Frey, he had never come so close to a moment of psychic intuition. Frau Ellenberger had ordered him to leave but he hadn't left, because he knew she had more she was dying to tell him, but she was afraid of telling it. She was grappling with her sense of loyalty on the one hand and her outrage on the other. Suddenly, the outrage won.

"And now he's *back,*" she whispered, her eyes widening in astonishment. "Doing it all over again to poor Mr. Tommy, who isn't half the man his father was. I *smelled* his voice the moment he telephoned. Sulfur, that's what I smelled. He's a Beelzebub. *Foreman.* This time he called himself *Foreman.* Boss of the show, he has to be, always did. Next week it'll be Fiveman!"

Just a hundred meters along the road from where Bachmann's car was waiting stood a clump of lakeside woodland with a public footpath winding through it. Handing his briefcase to the driver, he was seized with a spontaneous desire to saunter there alone. A bench offered itself, and he sat on it. Dusk was falling. Hamburg's magic hour had begun. Deep in thought, he gazed at the darkening lake and the lights of the city rising round it. For a moment back there, like a thief with a conscience, he had had a sense of having robbed the wrong person. Shaking his head at this momentary weakening of purpose, he hauled a cell phone from a pocket of his bureaucratic suit and selected Michael Axelrod's direct line.

"Yes, Günther?"

"The Brits want the same as we do," he said. "Without us."

On the phone, Ian Lantern couldn't have been sweeter, Brue had to hand it to him. He was apologetic, he fully accepted that Tommy had a frightfully busy schedule and he wouldn't dream of trespassing on it for the world except that London was breathing down his neck.

"I can't say any more on the open line, unfortunately. I need a one-to-one with you by yesterday, Tommy. An hour should do it. Just tell me where and when."

No fool, Brue was at first guarded. "Would this be on the same matter that we discussed at length over lunch, by any chance?" he suggested, not giving an inch.

"Related. Not totally, but near. The past rearing its ugly head again. But unthreatening. Nothing to anyone's discredit. Actually to your advantage. One hour and you're off the hook."

Reassured, Brue glanced at his diary, although

he didn't need to. Wednesday was Mitzi's opera night. She and Bernhard both had *abonnements*. For Brue it was cold cuts from the fridge or supper and a game of snooker at the Anglo-German: on Wednesdays he could take his pick.

"Would seven-fifteen at my house be any good to you?" He started to give the address but Lantern cut him short.

"Fab, Tommy. I'll be on the dot."

And he was. With a car and driver waiting outside. And flowers for Mitzi. And that damned smile he kept in place while he sipped sparkling water with ice and a slice of lemon.

"No, I'll stand, if you don't mind, thanks," he said affably when Brue offered him a chair. "Three hours flat out on the autobahn, it's nice to stretch the old legs."

"You should try the train."

"Yes, I should, shouldn't I?"

So Brue remained standing too, with his hands behind his back, and what he hoped was the courteous but huffy air of a busy man who has been intruded upon in his own house, and is entitled to an explanation.

"We're very tight on time, Tommy, like I said, so I'll describe the predicament *you're* in first, and after that perhaps we can take a look at the predicament *we're* in. Are you comfortable with that?"

"Please yourself."

"I do terror, by the way. I don't think we mentioned that over lunch, did we?"

"I don't think we did."

"Oh, and don't worry about Mitzi. If she and her boyfriend decide to chuck it in at the interval, my lads will be the first to tell us. Why don't you sit yourself down and finish up that whisky you were drinking?"

"I'm fine as I am, thank you."

Lantern was disappointed about this, but he went on anyway.

"Not a very nice feeling it was, I can tell you, Tommy, hearing from my German opposite number that, far from being ignorant of the whereabouts of one Issa Karpov, you'd sat up half a night with him in the company of witnesses. That left us looking a bit stupid. It's not as if we didn't ask you, is it?"

"You asked me to inform you in the event that he made a claim. He had not made a claim. He still hasn't."

Lantern took Brue's point, as he would from an older man, but it was clear that he wasn't wholly satisfied all the same. "There was a lot of information out there, frankly, that you possessed and we could have done with. It would have put us ahead of the game, instead of having to eat a very large helping of humble pie."

"What *game*?"

Lantern's smile became faintly regretful. "No comment, I'm afraid. It's need-to-know in our business, Tommy."

"It is in mine too."

"We've conducted a small study on your motivation, actually, Tommy. Us and London. Your family background, the daughter by the first wife—Georgie, is it—daughter to Sue? Nobody could quite understand why you two split up, which is sad, I always think. A kind of death really, unnecessary divorce is, in my opinion. *My* parents never got over it, I know *that*. Neither did I, I suppose, in a way. Anyway, she's pregnant, which is nice. Georgie is. You must be very chuffed."

"What the hell are you drooling about? Mind your bloody business, can't you?"

"It's only us trying to sort out just why you were quite as obstructive as you were, Tommy, and what you were protecting. Or who. Was it just yourself? we asked ourselves. Or Brue Frères? Was it young Karpov: Did you take a shine to him one way or the other? I mean that was some *lying,* Tommy. You really had us fooled. Talk about grudging admiration."

"I seem to recall that you weren't exactly over-generous with the truth yourselves."

Lantern chose not to hear this. "However," he

continued blithely, "once we had taken a look at the somewhat dicky state of Brue Frères's finances, and made a rough calculation of what old Karpov must have stashed away, we felt we understood you better: Ah, *that's* what Tommy's about! He's hoping that old Karpov's millions are going to see him very nicely into his old age. No wonder he doesn't want anybody claiming them. Would you like to comment on that at all?"

"Why don't we just assume you're right?" Brue snapped. "Then get out of my house."

Lantern's young smile widened in sympathy. "Can't do that, Tommy, I'm afraid. Nor can you, if you follow me. Plus there's a young lady in the case, we hear."

"Nonsense. I have no young lady. Utter drivel. Unless you're referring to the boy's lawyer"— desperately pretending to search his mind— "Frau *Richter*. Russian speaker. Representing his asylum application and so on."

"Quite a dish too, judging from all we hear. If you like them small, which I do."

"I hadn't noticed. I'm afraid that at my age my eye for the ladies isn't what it used to be."

Pondering Brue's need to make a disowning reference to his age at this moment, Lantern strolled to the sideboard and in the most relaxed manner poured himself more sparkling water.

"So that's *your* predicament, Tommy, which I

shall expand upon further in due course. But meantime, I'd like to acquaint you with *my* predicament, which frankly, thanks to you, is not much better than yours. May I?"

"May you what?"

"I just told you. Describe the depth of the crock of shit you've landed us in. Are you listening or not?"

"Of course I am."

"Good. Because *tomorrow morning* at *nine o'clock* exactly, here in Hamburg, I shall be walking into an extremely *delicate* and highly *secret* meeting of which the subject will be none other than Issa Karpov, whom you pretended you had never set eyes on. Whereas you had."

He had become somebody else: didactic, unstoppable and Napoleonic, his voice striking at unexpected words like notes on a badly tuned piano.

"And *at* that meeting, Tommy, where thanks to you I expect to have my back *somewhat* against the wall, I need—my *office* needs—all of us who are trying to do the right thing in this extremely delicate situation—London, the Germans, plus other friendly services I will *not* bother to mention at this juncture *need*—that *you,* Mr. Tommy Brue of Brue Frères Bank—being a good British patriot and an avowed enemy of terrorism—are not only prepared but *keen* to collaborate with me in any manner, shape or form, *as* dictated by this top secret operation, of which pro tem at least you will remain totally ignorant. My question therefore to you is: *Am* I right? *Will* you collaborate, or will you as before *obstruct* us in the war on terror?"

He allowed Brue no time to fire back. He had ceased to bark and was already commiserating.

"You see, quite *apart* from your goodwill, Tommy, which is what we're appealing to here, look at what's against you. You're one small step from the Receiver, even without a charge of money laundering. *Plus* what the Germans might have to say about a British resident banker playing footsie with a known Islamic terrorist on the run, which doesn't bear thinking about. You're fucked. So why not come quietly and enjoy it? See what I mean? I'm not sure I'm getting through to you. Want me to talk about Annabel?"

"So it's blackmail," Brue suggested.

"Stick-and-carrot, Tommy. If we bring it off, the bank's past sins forgotten, a more friendly opinion of you in the City and Brue Frères will live to fight another day. What could be fairer than that?"

"And the boy?"

"Who?"

"Issa."

"Ah. Right. Your altruistic bit. Well, that will depend on how well *you* play your part, naturally. He's German property of course. We can't interfere with their sovereignty, basically they'll have to decide. But nobody's going to hang him out to dry after this, no way. Nobody around here does *that*."

"And Frau Richter? What's she supposed to have done?"

"Annabel. Oh, she's in shit too, theoretically: consorting with him, spiriting him out of sight, getting her rocks off with him probably."

"I asked you what will become of her."

"No, you didn't. You asked what she'd done. I told you. What they'll do with her is anyone's guess. Dust her off and put her back on her feet, if they've got any sense. She's frighteningly well connected, as I'm sure you know."

"I didn't."

"Top lawyer family, old established, German foreign service, titles they don't use. Estates in Freiburg. Slap her wrist and send her home, be my advice, the way this country operates."

"So I'm to give you a blank check on my services, is that what you're saying?"

"Well, it pretty much is, frankly, Tommy. You sign on the dotted line, we let bygones be bygones and move forward together proactively. And recognize we're doing a great, worthwhile job. Not just for us. For all of *them out there,* as we say in the trade."

And extraordinarily to Brue, there was indeed a document to be signed, and on examination it had many of the aspects of a blank check. It was contained in a thick brown envelope residing inside Lantern's jacket, and it committed Brue to unspecific "work of national importance" and drew his attention to the many draconian clauses of the Official Secrets Act, and to the penalties awaiting him if he transgressed them. Mystified by himself, he peered first at Lantern, then round the sunroom in search of help. Not finding any, he signed.

Lantern had gone.

Transfixed with anger, too angry even to finish his scotch as Lantern had so thoughtfully suggested, Brue stood in his own hall, staring at the closed front door. His eye fell on the bouquet of flowers that lay, still in their tissue, on the hall table. He picked them up, sniffed them, put them back where they came from.

Gardenias. Mitzi's favorite. Decent florist. No skinflint, our Ian, not when he's lashing out his government's money.

Why had he brought them? To show he *knew*? Knew what? That gardenias were Mitzi's favorite? The way they *knew* that I ate fish at La Scala? And how to get Mario to open up for Monday lunch?

Or to show he *didn't* know—that she had gone to the opera with her lover, which of course he *did* know; but then in the logic of his trade, what you know is what you pretend you don't. So officially he didn't.

And Annabel? *Oh, she's in shit too.*

Brue was not of a mind to credit much of what Lantern had said, but he believed that bit. For four days and nights he had contemplated every which way of getting in touch with her discreetly: a hand-delivered note to Sanctuary North, via the Frères courier; a bland message to her office machine or cell phone.

But out of delicacy—Lantern's word—or plain cowardice, however you parsed it, he'd held off. At all odd moments in the office, when his mind was supposed to be on high finance, he'd catch himself, chin in hand, gazing at his telephone, willing it to ring. It hadn't.

And now, exactly as he had feared, she was in trouble. And no smooth talk from Lantern would persuade him that she was going to slide out of it unscathed. All he needed was the reason to call her and, in his anger, he had hit on it. *Lantern can go hang himself. I've got a bank to run. And a scotch to finish.* He drank it at a draft, and dialed her number on the house line.

"Frau Richter?"

"Yes?"

"This is Brue. Tommy Brue."

"Hullo, Mr. Brue."

"Have I caught you at a bad time?"

Judging by her flat tone, he must have done.

"No, it's fine."

"Only I thought I'd better call you for *two* reasons. If you've really got a minute. Have you?"

"Yes. Yes, I have. Of course."

Is she drugged? Bound? Is she taking orders? Consulting someone before she answers?

"My *first* reason—I don't want to go into details over the phone, obviously—there was a *check* issued recently. It doesn't seem to have been paid in anywhere."

"Things changed," she said, after another interminable wait.

"Oh? How?"

"We decided on a different set of arrangements."

We? You and who, actually? You and Issa? It hadn't seemed that Issa was part of the decision-making process.

"But changed for the better, I trust," he said, striking an optimistic note.

"Maybe. Maybe not. It's whatever works, isn't it?" The same blank tone, a voice from the abyss. "Do you want me to tear it up? Send it back?"

"*No, no!*"—too emphatic, take it down—"not

if there's a chance you might still have a use for it, of course not. I'd be perfectly happy for you to pay it in while all this is pending, so to speak. And if nothing comes of it, well, pay back whatever part of it you don't use later." He hesitated, unsure whether to risk the second reason. "And regarding the *other* banking question. Have things moved at all on that front?"

No reply.

"I mean, regarding our friend's presumed entitlement." He made a stab at humor. "That performing horse we talked about. Whether our friend proposes to take it over."

"I can't discuss this yet. I have to talk to him again."

"Will you call me then?"

"Maybe when I've spoken to him some more."

"And meantime, you'll pay in that check?"

"Maybe."

"And you're all right yourself? No difficulties? Problems? Nothing I could help with, I mean?"

"I'm fine."

"Good."

Long silence of both their making. On his side, impotent anxiety; on hers, a seemingly profound indifference.

"So we'll have a good talk soon?" he suggested, summoning the last of his eagerness.

They would or they wouldn't. She had rung

off. They're listening, he thought. They're in the
room with her. They're conducting her choirboy
voice.

Her cell phone still in her hand, Annabel sat at
the small white writing desk in her old apartment, peering out of the window into the dark
street. Behind her, in the only armchair, sat Erna
Frey, watchfully sipping her green tea.

"He wants to know whether Issa's claiming,"
Annabel said. "And what happened to his check."

"And you stalled," Erna Frey replied approv-
ingly. "Very neatly too, I thought. Perhaps next
time he calls, you'll have better news for him."

"Better for him? Better for you? Better who
for?"

Putting her phone on the desk and her head in
her hands, Annabel stared intently at it, as if it
held the answers to the universe.

"For all of us, dear," Erna Frey said, starting to
her feet as the cell phone rang a second time.
But she was too late. Like an addict, Annabel
had already snatched it up and was saying her
name.

It was Melik, wanting to say good-bye to her
before he and his mother left for Turkey, but
also needing to find out how Issa was, because he
was feeling guilty.

"Listen, when we come back—you tell my brother—you tell our friend—*any time*. Okay? As soon as he gets himself tolerated, he's welcome. He can have his own place back, eat the whole house down. Tell him he's a great guy, okay? Melik says so. He could knock me cold in one round, okay? Not in the ring, maybe. But out there. Where he's been. Know what I'm saying?"

Yes, Melik, I know what you're saying. And give my love to Leyla. And tell her to have a great wedding, a traditional one. And have a great one yourself, Melik. And long life to your sister and her husband-to-be. Much happiness to them. And come back safe and sound, Melik, be sure to look after your mother, she's a brave, good woman and she loves you and she was a fine mother to your friend . . .

And more of the same, until Erna Frey gently prised the cell phone from Annabel's rigid fingers and switched it off, while her other hand rested tenderly on her shoulder.

11

Neither her disproportionate response to Melik, nor her frigid response to Brue, was an isolated episode in Annabel's new existence. With each day that passed her spirits lurched between shame, hatred for her handlers, luminous, irrational optimism and sustained periods of uncritical acceptance of her plight.

At the Sanctuary, despite the fact that Herr Werner, under Bachmann's prompting, had made a duty call to Ursula informing her that the matter of Issa Karpov was no longer of active concern to the authorities, she had adopted a Carmelite silence.

Erna Frey was now her neighbor as well as guardian. Within a day of delivering Annabel to the harbor front by yellow van, she had taken up residence on the ground floor of a steel and concrete *Apartotel* not a hundred meters away. Bit by bit, the flat became Annabel's third home. She stopped by before each visit to Issa, and returned

afterwards. Sometimes, for comfort, she slept
there too, in a children's bedroom that never
went quite dark because of the neon advertisements in the street.

Her twice-daily visits to Issa were no longer
risky adventures, but rehearsed pieces of theater
under Erna's meticulous direction and—as the
days passed—Bachmann's also. In the curtained
privacy of the little drawing room of the safe flat,
singly or together, they briefed her before and
after each ascent of the twisted wooden staircase.
Old scenes were replayed and analyzed, new ones
projected and refined, all with the same intent of
persuading Issa to claim his inheritance and rescue himself from the horrors of expulsion.

And Annabel, though dimly, if at all, understanding their larger purpose, was tacitly grateful
for their guidance, realizing to her despair that
she had become dependent on it. For as long as
the three of them were hunkered together over
the tape recorder, it was Erna and Günther, not
Issa, who were her touchstone with reality, and
Issa who was their absent problem child.

Only when she walked the hundred-meter *via
dolorosa* along the crowded pavement, and reen-
tered Issa's presence, did her stomach churn and
her tongue become gluey with shame, and she
longed to trample on every dirty undertaking she
had given to her manipulators. Worse still, it

seemed to her that Issa, with his prisoner's powers of empathy, was able to sense her altered state and the extra confidence that, resist it how she would, she derived from being under their control.

"Give him as much of yourself as you can, dear, as long as it's from a safe distance," Erna advised. "Just lead him gently to the water. His decision, when it comes, will be more emotional than rational."

Annabel had played chess with him, listened to music with him and, under Erna's prompting, touched on subjects that even two days ago would not have been discussible. Yet curiously, as their relationship eased, she found herself a lot less willing to let him get away with his snipings at her Western lifestyle, and in particular his disapproving references to Karsten, whose expensive clothes he seemed only too happy to wear.

"So have *you* ever loved a woman, Issa, apart from your mother?" she demanded, with the whole length of the loft between them.

Yes, he conceded, after a long silence. He was sixteen. She was eighteen and already an orphan: a full Chechen like his mother, devout, beautiful and chaste. There was no physical expression of their feelings, he assured Annabel, only pure love.

"So what happened to her?"

"She disappeared."

"What was her name?"

"It is immaterial."

"Disappeared *how*, then?"

"She was a martyr to Islam."

"Like your mother?"

"She was a martyr."

"What *kind* of martyr?" Silence. "A willing martyr? You mean she deliberately sacrificed herself for Islam?" Silence. "Or was she a reluctant one? A victim, like you? Like your mother."

It was immaterial, Issa repeated after an infinity. God was merciful. He would pardon her and receive her in Paradise. Nevertheless, the simple admission that Issa had loved at all represented an undermining of his defenses, as Erna Frey was quick to point out.

"That's not a dent in his armor, dear, it's a *hole*!" she exclaimed. "If he'll talk love, he'll talk *anything*: religion, politics, the whole gamut. He may not know it yet, but he *wants* you to talk him round. The best way to help him is to keep tapping." Followed by the habitual piece of sugar that Annabel had become dependent on. "You're doing marvelously, dear. He's very lucky."

Annabel kept tapping. Breakfast next morning, six o'clock. Coffee and fresh croissants courtesy of Erna Frey. They are seated in what by now are their usual positions: Issa beneath the arched window, Annabel huddled in the farthest corner, her long skirt pulled down to her clunky black boots.

"Bombings in Baghdad again today," she announced. "Did you put the radio on this morning? Eighty-five died, hundreds wounded."

"It is God's will."

"You mean God approves of Muslims killing Muslims? I don't think that's a God I understand very well."

"Do not judge God, Annabel. He will be harsh with you."

"Do *you* approve?"

"Of what?"

"The killings."

"You cannot make Allah happy by killing the innocent."

"Who's innocent? Who *can* you kill, and make Allah happy?"

"Allah will know. He knows always."

"How will *we* know? How will Allah *tell* us?"

"He has told us through the holy Koran. He has told us through the Prophet, peace be upon Him."

Wait till you're sure his guard's down, then go for it, Erna had advised her. She was sure now.

"I've been reading a famous Islamic scholar. His name is Dr. Abdullah. Have you heard of him? Dr. Faisal Abdullah? Lives here in Germany? He's on television from time to time. Not often. He's too devout."

"Why should I have heard of him, Annabel? If he appears on Western television, he is not a good Muslim, he is corrupt."

"He's nothing of the kind. He's devout, he's an ascetic and he's a highly regarded Islamic scholar who has written important books on Islamic faith and practice," she retorted, ignoring the sneer of suspicion that was already forming on his face.

"In what language has he written these books, Annabel?"

"Arabic. But they've been widely translated. Into German, Russian, Turkish and practically every language you can think of in the world. He represents a lot of Muslim charities. He's also written extensively on the Muslim law of giving," she added with innuendo.

"Annabel."

She waited.

"Is it your purpose in bringing to my attention the work of this Abdullah to persuade me to accept Karpov's filthy money?"

"What if it is?"

"Then please take to your heart the information that I shall never do this."

"Oh, I do!" she retorted, losing patience with him. "I do take it to my heart." Did she? Or was she faking it? She no longer knew. "I take it to my heart that you're never going to be a doctor, or whatever it is you want to be today. And that

I'm never going to get my life back. And that Mr. Brue is never going to get back the money he gave me to look after you, because any day now they're going to come here and find you and send you back to Turkey or Russia or somewhere even worse. And that won't be God's will. It'll be your own stupid, stubborn choice."

Breathing heavily, one part of her furious with him, another part ice-cold, she saw that he had risen to his feet and was gazing through the arched window at the sunlit world below him.

If it comes naturally, lose your temper with him, Bachmann had advised her. *The same way you lost it with us the night we pulled you off the street and made you grow up.*

Returning to the safe flat, Annabel found Erna Frey and Bachmann exuberant but undecided. Erna Frey's praise knew no bounds. Annabel had done superbly, she had exceeded all their expectations, things had advanced far more quickly than they had dared anticipate. The question now was whether to let Issa sweat it out for another whole day or to bring Annabel back from the Sanctuary at lunchtime under a pretext and press home the advantage by presenting him with Abdullah's books.

But this was not to reckon with a sudden downturn in Annabel's morale in the wake of her achievement. At first, in their absorption, they failed to notice her change of mood as she sat head in hand at the end of the table. They assumed she was breathing out after her ordeal. Then Erna Frey reached out and touched her arm, and she withdrew it as if it had been bitten. But Bachmann was not given to pandering to his agents' moods.

"What the hell's that about?" he demanded.

"I'm your tethered goat, aren't I?" Annabel replied into her hand.

"You are *what*?"

"I lure Issa. Then I lure Abdullah. Then you destroy Abdullah. That's what you call saving innocent lives."

Bachmann was round the table, standing over her.

"That is *total bullshit*," he shouted into her ear. "For as long as you play ball, your boy gets a free pass. And for your information, I do not propose to touch one hair of Abdullah's venerable fucking head. He's an icon of loving tolerance and inclusiveness and I'm not in the business of causing riots!"

They settled for the lunchtime option. Annabel would make a flying midday visit to Issa, drop in Abdullah's books, plead pressure of time and return this evening to hear his reaction. She agreed to all of it.

"Don't go soft on me, Erna," Bachmann said, when they had seen Annabel into the yellow van with her bicycle. "There's no space for it in this operation."

"Tell me one where there was," said Erna Frey.

Annabel and Issa were seated as usual at opposite ends of the loft. Evening had come. She had made her lightning lunchtime visit and deposited Dr. Abdullah's three little books in Russian. Now she was back. From her anorak, she drew a sheet of paper. Until now, they had barely spoken.

"I downloaded this. Want to hear it? It's in German. I'll have to translate it."

She waited for an answer and, receiving none, spoke loudly enough for both of them:

"'Dr. Abdullah is Egyptian-born, aged fifty-five. He is a world-renowned scholar, the son and grandson of imams and muftis and teachers. In his turbulent youth as a student in Cairo he was swept up by the doctrines of the Muslim Brotherhood, arrested, imprisoned and tortured for his militant convictions. On his release he risked death again, this time at the hands of his former comrades, by preaching the path of brotherliness, truthfulness, tolerance and respect for all God's creatures. Dr. Abdullah is a reformist orthodox scholar who stresses the example of the Prophet and his companions.' "

And again waited: "Are you listening to me?"

"I prefer the works of Turgenev."

"Is that because you refuse to make up your mind? Or is it because you don't want a stupid unbelieving woman bringing you books telling you what a good Muslim does with his money? How many times do I have to remind you that I'm your *lawyer*?"

In the speckled half-darkness, she closed her eyes and reopened them. Does he have no sense of urgency anymore? Why should he bother with big decisions when we take all the small ones away from him?

"*Issa, wake up, please.* Devout Muslim people *everywhere* ask Dr. Abdullah for advice. Why won't you? He represents a lot of important Muslim charities. Some of them send help to Chechnya. If a wise Muslim scholar like Dr. Abdullah is willing to tell you the right way to use your money, why the *hell* won't you listen to him?"

"It is *not* my money, Annabel. It was stolen from my mother's people."

"Then why don't you find a way to give it back to them? And while you're about it, *really* become a doctor so that you can go home and help them? Isn't that what you want to do?"

"Does Mr. Brue regard this Abdullah favorably?"

"I shouldn't think he knows him. Maybe he's seen him on television."

"It is immaterial. The opinion of a nonbeliever in regard to Dr. Abdullah is of no significance. I shall read these books for myself, and with God's help form a judgment."

Was his last barrier finally falling? In a moment of unexplained dread, she prayed it was not.

It was another age before he spoke again: "However, Mr. Tommy Brue is a banker and may therefore consult this Dr. Abdullah from a secular perspective. First he will establish with the assistance of other oligarchs whether the man is regarded as honest in his secular dealings. The oppressed people of Chechnya have been robbed many times, not only by Karpov. If he is honest, Mr. Brue will then propose certain conditions to him on my behalf, and Dr. Abdullah will interpret God's commands."

"And after that?"

"You are my lawyer, Annabel. You will advise me."

The little restaurant was called Louise and it was number three in the Maria-Louisenstrasse, which was the main artery of a cozy urban village of antique shops and health shops and shops for grooming the many rich dogs that inhabited this desirable neighborhood. Back in the days when Annabel had reckoned herself a free soul, Louise was the place where she had liked to roost on a Sunday morning, to drink latte, read newspapers and watch the world go by. And this was the place she had selected for her appointed tryst with Mr. Tommy Brue of Brue Frères Bank, in the confidence that he would not feel ill at ease in such a well-heeled and protected environment.

At Erna Frey's suggestion she had proposed midmorning as the hour when the restaurant was at its least busy, and Brue most likely to be available at short notice. Because as Erna had rightly said, if your Mr. Tommy's any sort of banker *at all,* he's sure to have a luncheon appointment. To which Annabel did not reply, as she might have done, that from everything she suspected of Brue's feelings, he would have passed up lunch with the president of the World Bank in order to accommodate her.

Nevertheless at her own suggestion—made to herself, on a whim, after a long, unimpressed stare into the mirror—she decided to dress up for the encounter. Mr. Tommy Brue would like her to. Nothing over the top, but he was a good man and in love with her and he deserved the compliment. And it would be nice to present herself to him as a Western woman for a change! So to hell with the gear forced on her by Issa's Muslim sensitivities—her prison uniform, as she was beginning to think of it—and how about her best jeans for a change and the white cross-banded silk blouse that Karsten had bought for her and she'd never worn? And her new, not-so-clumpy shoes that were okay to bicycle in as well? And while she was about it, a bit of makeup to brighten up those sickly cheeks and pick out the hidden highlights? Brue's frank enthusiasm when she had called him from the captivity of Erna's flat, first thing this morning after seeing Issa, had really touched her:

"Marvelous! Fantastic! Well done, you've talked him round then. I was beginning to feel you'd never manage it but you have! Just name the place and the hour," he had urged. And when she'd hinted at Abdullah, though not mentioning him by name because Erna thought it would be premature: "Ethical and religious concerns? Dear lady, we bankers deal with them every day! The vital thing is, your client claims. Once his claim is settled, Frères will move heaven and earth for him."

In another man of his age, such enthusiasm might have made her apprehensive, but after her lackluster performance on the last occasion they had spoken, she felt intensely relieved by it, even ecstatic. For wasn't the whole world dependent on her behavior? Wasn't her every word, smile, frown and gesture the personal property of those who owned her: Issa, Bachmann, Erna Frey and, at the Sanctuary, Ursula and the whole of her former family, all of whom deliberately avoided her eye while covertly observing her?

No wonder she couldn't sleep. She had only to put her head on the pillow to experience in vivid replay her day's many and varied performances: Did I exaggerate my concern for the Sanctuary switchboard girl's sick baby? How did I come over when Ursula suggested it was time I put in for some holiday? And why did she suggest it anyway, when all I'm doing is keeping my head down and my door closed, and giving every impression of going diligently about my duties? And why is it that I have come to think of myself as the proverbial butterfly in Australia, which only has to flap its wings to start an earthquake on the other side of the earth?

Back in her own flat last night, fired up by Issa's agreement to make his claim, she had revisited Dr. Abdullah's website and watched extracts from his television appearances and interviews, and she was very pleased indeed to know that Günther Bachmann did not intend to harm a hair of his venerable fucking head, not that he had any hair to harm anyway: he was small, bald and twinkly—and *erhaben,* a favorite word of her divinity teacher at boarding school that had drifted back to her, suggesting the sublime. His *sublimity,* like Issa's, encompassed everything she wanted to hear from a good man: purity of mind and body, love as an absolute and recognition of the many paths to God or whatever we may choose to call Him.

It puzzled her, she had to admit, that he made no reference to what others might perceive as the downside of Islam as it is practiced, but his benign, scholarly smile and quick-witted optimism effortlessly overrode such carping criticisms. All religions had believers who were led astray by their zeal and Islam was no exception, he had said; all religions were subject to misuse by evil men; diversity was God's gift to us and we should praise Him for it. In the circumstances, she liked best Abdullah's references to the need for generous giving, and his moving references to Islam's wretched of the earth, who were her clients as well as his.

Mysteriously comforted by these scattered thoughts, she fell at last into a profound sleep and woke up bright and ready.

And she felt comforted again when she saw Brue's unexpectedly happy face as he breezed through the glass doors of Louise's restaurant and stepped towards her with both hands held out to her like a Russian. She even had a spontaneous urge to ditch the restaurant and give him a coffee back in her flat, just to show him how much she valued him as a friend in need, but then she counseled caution on herself, because she had a feeling that she was keeping so much inside her head that, if she let go at all, everything would come tumbling out at once, and she would immediately regret it, and so would all the people she owed her loyalty to.

"Now what are we having? Well, I don't think that's quite *me,* is it?" he said, pulling a comic face at her glass of vanilla-flavored milk, and ordered himself a double espresso instead. "How are the Turks, by the way?"

Turks? What Turks? She knew no Turks. Her mind was in so many other places that it took her a moment to retrieve Melik and Leyla from the faces crowding in on her.

"Oh, fine," she said, and glanced rather stupidly at her watch, thinking they must be in the air by now, and on their way to Petersburg. She meant Ankara.

"They're marrying off my sister," she said.

"Your *sister*?"

"*Melik*'s sister," she corrected herself and heard herself laughing hilariously with him at her slip of the tongue. He looks so much younger, she thought, and decided to tell him. So she did, and with a come-on look that she was immediately ashamed of.

"Good lord, do you really think so?" he replied, coloring rather sweetly. "Well, I've had a bit of rather good family news, to be honest. *Yes.*"

The *yes* apparently to indicate that he wasn't at liberty to say any more at present, which she completely understood. He was an honorable man, she knew, and she really hoped they could become lifelong friends, though not of the sort he probably had in mind. Or was the thought in *her* mind rather than in his?

Either way, she decided it was time to be severe. At Erna's suggestion she had brought a copy of the printout that she had shown to Issa, plus a second printout of Dr. Abdullah's phone number, home address and e-mail, also freely available on the Internet. Remembering it all in a rush, she whipped the pages out of her rucksack and handed them to him while she watched herself in the mirror.

"So that's your man, anyway," she said in her severest voice. "And he's all about Muslim giving." And while he looked at the pages in some puzzlement—since she had still to explain their purpose to him, she hadn't quite got around to it but she would—she dived gaily for her rucksack again and this time came up with his uncashed check for fifty thousand euros, for which she felt obliged to thank him yet again, so profusely that she completely put him off reading about Dr. Abdullah, which made them both laugh, straight into each other's eyes, which she wouldn't normally have allowed to happen, but it was all right with Brue because she trusted him, and anyway she was laughing louder than he was, until she got hold of herself and checked herself in the mirror for decorum.

"So there are complications, right?" she said, still straight into his face, and she was sad to see some worry lines starting to appear in it, because until now it had been so lit up with this bit of rather good family news he'd had, but there you go.

The complication *was*, she explained, that basically her client would like to give away everything to good Muslim causes and to this end proposed to solicit instruction from the great and good Dr. Abdullah about the right way to do this, except that owing to our client's *extremely* delicate status—which we both know about, so I won't enlarge on it any further for obvious reasons—he *wasn't* in a position to make the approach directly and *therefore,* once he had successfully established his claim to his father's money—which you imply won't be a problem— he would be looking to Mr. Tommy, as he calls you affectionately, to make it for him.

"If that's an acceptable way to go as far as Brue Frères is concerned?" she ended, still looking into his eyes, and giving him her most luminous smile, which, sadly again for her, he seemed unable to reciprocate with any conviction.

"And our client is—*all right*?" he inquired doubtfully, his eyebrows nearly going through his head in his concern.

"In the circumstances, he is well, thank you, Mr. Brue. *Very* well. Things could be far, far worse, I'll put it that way."

"And he's still—he hasn't been—?"

"No"—cutting him short—"no, Mr. Brue, he has *not*. Our client is *exactly* as you saw him, thank you."

"And in safe hands?"

"As safe as they can be in the circumstances, yes. A *lot* of hands actually."

"And what about *you,* Annabel?" he asked, with a dire change of voice, and leaning urgently across the table grasped her forearm and held it while he stared at her with such a loving tenderness in his eyes that her first instinct was to share his concern and burst into floods of tears, and her second to recoil sharply, and seek the shelter of her professional status. By now she had also registered, with disapproval, that he had permitted himself the liberty of her Christian name, and more shamelessly still the intimate *du* form, both without her consent. And for this there was really no excuse whatever. She had gone rigid, she discovered, and she blamed him for that too. Also for the fact that she was speaking from between her teeth. Her chest was hurting, but who gave a shit what hurt her and what didn't? Certainly not some middle-aged banker who had presumed to paw her forearm.

"I don't break down," she announced. "Got it?"

He got it. He was already pulling back, looking ashamed of himself, but somehow he was still holding her wrist.

"I never break down. I'm a lawyer."

"And a very good one," he was agreeing, with his absurd alacrity.

"My *father*'s a lawyer. My *mother*'s a lawyer. My *brother-in-law*'s a lawyer. My boyfriend was a lawyer. Karsten. I threw him out because he was working for an insurance company, delaying asbestos claims so that the plaintiffs would die off. We are not *allowed*, in my family, as a profession, to be emotionally led. Or swear. I swore at you once. I regret it. I apologize. I referred to your fucking bank. It's not a fucking bank. It's just a bank. A perfectly decent, honorable bank, insofar that is possible for a bank to be."

Not content with clinging onto her wrist, he was trying to get an arm across her back. She shook him off. She could stand on her own feet, and did so.

"I'm a lawyer without a negotiating position, Mr. Brue, which is about the most stupid, useless thing in the universe. Just don't tell me anything soothing. I am *not* available for ingenious schemes. We go through with this, or Issa's dead meat. This is the *Save Issa Society*. This is *do the only possible, rational thing, for Issa's sake*. Am I making myself totally clear?"

But before Brue could produce an appropriately appeasing answer, she had sat down with a bump on the chair behind her, and the two women on the far side of the room were scurrying towards her. One was putting her arm where Brue had tried to put his, and the other was flapping her fat hand at a Volvo estate car illegally parked at the curb.

12

Günther Bachmann was preparing to set out his stall. Since nine this morning, the big buyers from Berlin had been trooping into Arni Mohr's anteroom in their twos and threes, sampling his coffee, snapping orders to their underlings, barking into cell phones and scowling at their laptops. In the car park stood two official helicopters. Common motorists must make do with the stables area. Bodyguards in bad gray suits prowled the courtyard like lost cats.

And Bachmann, the cause of it all, the man who had made the weather, the case-hardened fieldman in his only respectable suit, was working the room, now earnestly conferring in undertones with a bureaucratic baron, now shoulder-slapping an old buddy from way back. Ask Bachmann how long his product had been in the making, and if he knew you well enough, he'd pull his clown's smile and murmur *twenty-five fucking years,* which was how long, one way or another, he'd been laboring in the secret vineyard.

Erna Frey had deserted him. She must be close to that *poor child,* as she now called Annabel. If she needed a second excuse, which she didn't, she would cross the earth rather than breathe the same air as Dr. Keller of Cologne. Deprived of her steadying influence, Bachmann moved faster and spoke more brightly—but perhaps too brightly, like an engine with a missing cog.

Which of these men and women with their affable smiles and sideways glances was his friend for the day, and which his enemy? Which dark committee, ministry, religious persuasion or political party owned their allegiance? Only a tiny handful, to his knowledge, had ever heard a bomb explode in anger, but in the long, silent war for the leadership of their Service, they were case-hardened veterans.

And that was another lecture Bachmann would have dearly loved to give to these swiftly risen managers of the post-9/11 boom market in intelligence and allied trades—another Bachmann Cantata that he kept up his sleeve for the day when he was invited back to Berlin. It warned them that however many of the latest spies' wonder toys they had in their cupboards, however many magic codes they broke and hot-signals chatter they listened to, and brilliant de-

ductions they pulled out of the ether regarding
the enemy's organizational structures, or lack of
them, and internecine fights they had, and however many tame journalists were vying to trade
their questionable gems of knowledge for slanted
tip-offs and something for the back pocket, in the
end it was the spurned imam, the love-crossed secret courier, the venal Pakistani defense scientist,
the middle-ranking Iranian military officer who's
been passed over for promotion, the lonely sleeper
who can sleep alone no longer, who among them
provide the hard base of knowledge without
which all the rest is fodder for the truth benders,
ideologues and politopaths who ruin the earth.

But who was there to hear him? Bachmann, as
he was the first to know, was a prophet banished
to the wilderness. Of the entire Berlin espiocracy
assembled here today, only the tall, languid,
clever, slightly aging Michael Axelrod, who was
at this moment stooping to address him, could
be described as an ally.

"All well, so far, Günther?" he inquired, with
his habitual half-smile.

The question was not without its purpose. Ian
Lantern had just strolled in. Last night, at a shot-
gun wedding hosted by Axelrod himself, the
three of them had had a really friendly drink together, in the bar of the Four Seasons Hotel. Little Lantern had been so English and embarrassed

about fishing in Günther's waters, and so frank and open about what London had been planning to do with Issa if they ever hooked him—"and quite honestly, Günther, he was such a *tiny* twinkle in our eye, I'm absolutely *convinced* that in the end we'd have come to you guys and said, 'Look, let's get together on this one and do whatever you're doing'"—that Bachmann knew he had distrusted Lantern all his life.

But what he hadn't bargained for was Martha, who sailed into Arni Mohr's anteroom on Lantern's heels almost as if he were her appointed herald, which perhaps he was: majestic Martha, the Agency's formidable number two in Berlin— two out of God only knew how many—dressed like the Angel of Death herself in a crimson satin kaftan covered in black sequins. And sidling after Martha, and so close on *her* heels that he could have been using her bulk for cover, none other than six-foot-something Newton, alias Newt, onetime deputy chief of operations at the U.S. embassy in Beirut and Bachmann's opposite number there, who at the sight of his old comrade broke ranks and loped over to him, and embraced him while he yelled, "Holy shit, Günther, I last saw you stretched out in the bar of the Commodore! What the fuck are you *doing* in Hamburg, man!"

And Bachmann, while he joshed and laughed and generally acted like a good fellow in return, silently asked Newton the same question: What in heaven's name is the Berlin station of the Central Intelligence Agency doing in Hamburg, horning in on my patch? Who invited them and why? And as soon as Martha and Newton had gone off in search of other prey, he asked it again of Axelrod, heatedly and urgently.

"They're harmless observers. Calm down. We haven't even begun yet."

"Observing *what*? Newt doesn't observe. He slits throats."

"They feel they have a stake in Abdullah. They believe he cofinanced an attack on one of their housing compounds in Saudi Arabia, plus another that misfired against a U.S. listening base in Kuwait."

"So what? For all we know, he cofinanced the Twin Towers. We're trying to recruit him, not judge him. How did they get here? Who copied them in?"

"Joint. Who d'you think?"

"*Who* at Joint? Which part of Joint? Which of half-a-dozen *parts* of Joint? Are you saying *Burgdorf* copied them in? *Burgdorf* fed my operation to the *Americans*?"

"Consensus," Axelrod snapped, which was precisely the moment that Martha chose to cast herself off from Arni Mohr and like a great liner set course for him, towing Ian Lantern in her wake.

"Why, Günther Bachmann as I live and breathe!" she bellowed, in her ship-to-ship voice, as if she had only now caught sight of him on the horizon. "Why the hell are you still doing jail time in *this* neck of the woods?"—gripping his hand and drawing him into her ample body as if she needed him all to herself. "You met my little Ian already? Of course you did. Ian's my British poodle. I walk him in Charlottenburg every morning, don't I, Ian?"

"Religiously," said Lantern, drawing up gratefully beside her. "And she cleans up after me too," he added with a wink for his new friend Günther.

Axelrod had removed himself. Across the room, Burgdorf was murmuring to his satrap Dr. Otto Keller but eyeing Bachmann, so perhaps it was Bachmann they were discussing. Men of the unbending right should look the part, but Burgdorf at sixty resembled to Bachmann a disgruntled child, sulking because his siblings got more mother love than he did. The double doors had opened. Chest out, arms respectfully to his sides, Arni Mohr the impresario was bidding his guests to the feast.

Perturbed by the American presence, as well as mystified by it, Bachmann took up his pre-appointed seat at the end of the long conference table. Mohr had awarded him pride of place—or was it the dunce's chair? True, Bachmann was the originator of the operation and its petitioner; but also, if things went wrong, the culprit. The Joint Committee's decisions despite the infighting that preceded them were, as Axelrod had just reminded him, by iron policy collective. Freelance suitors such as Bachmann were therefore objects of common risk, as well as profit, to be accepted or rejected by consensus. It was in this awareness, perhaps, that the rival camps of Burgdorf and Axelrod appeared to have closed ranks in mutual defense at the farther end of the table, leaving their bureaucratic dependents to take up the space between themselves and the aggressor.

To emphasize their observers' role, Mohr had supplied Martha and Newton with a separate table all their own—but, compounding Bachmann's consternation, the two had unaccountably become three, thanks to the addition of a square-shouldered woman in her forties with perfect teeth and long, ash-blonde hair. And if that were not enough, in the short space of time since the six-foot-something Newton had embraced Bachmann, he had grown a beard, or perhaps Bachmann had failed to spot it in the clinch: a perfectly trimmed spade-shaped dab of black, perched on the point of his chin, just where you would aim to land your punch, except that Newton would by then have knocked you cold.

The sweetly courteous Ian Lantern, though a foreigner, was a co-opted player. He had been

placed at the main table, but at a point near
enough to the observers' table to whisper in
Martha's ear. At Lantern's left sat Burgdorf, but
well apart from him, for Burgdorf, so dapper,
fresh and personable, did not relish physical
proximity. Two down from Burgdorf sat a couple of female obsessives from Berlin's money-
laundering team. Their vocation was to drive
themselves into premature old age resolving
such riddles as how a ten-thousand-dollar bank
transfer raised in good faith by a Muslim charity
in Nuremberg could turn itself into five hundred liters of hair dye in a back garage in
Barcelona.

The rest of the faces arranged before Bachmann were ministerial or worse: top men from
Treasury; a funereal woman from the chancellor's
office; an absurdly young departmental chief
from the Federal Police service and the former
foreign editor of a Berlin newspaper whose ex-
pertise was killing press stories.

Should Bachmann begin? Mohr had closed the
door and locked it. Dr. Keller scowled at his cell
phone and shoved it in his pocket. Lantern tipped
Bachmann his gritty smile that said, Go for it,
Günther. Bachmann went for it.

"Operation Felix," he announced. "May I take
it that everyone here has seen the material? Nobody short-changed?"

Nobody short-changed. Every face turned to him.

"Then Professor Aziz will please provide us with a profile of our target."

Hit them with Aziz first, and leave the hard part till the end, Axelrod had advised.

For twenty years, Bachmann had loved Aziz: when Aziz was his head agent in Amman; when Aziz was rotting in a Tunisian prison with his network hanged and his family in hiding; and on the day Aziz hobbled out of the prison gates on his thrashed bare feet into the German embassy car waiting to take him to the airport and resettlement in Bavaria.

And he loved Aziz now, as a side door opened and Maximilian by arrangement briefly showed himself, and the diminutive, soldierly, dark-haired, dark-suited, mustachioed figure marched softly into the room and took his place on a raised dais at the far end of the table: Aziz the resettled spy, Joint's leading expert on the by-ways of jihadism—and on the acts and meditations of his former fellow student from Cairo days, Dr. Abdullah.

Except that Aziz doesn't call him Abdullah. He calls him Signpost, this being the whimsical codename selected by Axelrod in veiled reference to the spiritual handbook of all Islamic militants, called *Signposts Along the Way* and written by their mentor Sayyed Qutub while sitting out his sentence in an Egyptian prison. The voice of Aziz is grave, and underscored with pain.

"Signpost is in all ways but one a man of God," he begins, assuming the role of counsel for the defense. "He is an entirely genuine, erudite scholar. He is unquestionably devout. He preaches the peaceful path. He sincerely believes that the use of violence in overthrowing corrupt Islamic governments is contrary to religious law. He recently published a new translation into German of the sayings of the Prophet Mohammed. It's a pretty excellent translation. I don't know a better one. He lives simply and eats *honey*." No one laughs. "He is a passionate *honey eater*. Among Muslims, he is known for this passion for *honey*. Muslims like to typecast people. He is a man of God, of the Book and of *honey*. But unfortunately it is our perception that he is also a man of the bomb. The case is not proven. But the evidence is persuasive."

Bachmann steals a quick look round the table. Honey, God and bombs. Every eye on the soldierly little professor, former friend of the honey-eating bomber.

"Until five years ago he wore tailored suits. He was a dandy. But once he started to appear on German television and take part in public debates, he adopted a more humble attire. He wished to become conspicuous for his humility. For his abstemious lifestyle. It is a fact. I don't quite know why he did this."

Neither does his audience.

"All his life, Signpost has sincerely struggled to override sectarian distinctions within the Umma. For this I suggest he is to be admired."

He hesitates. Most of those present, but not quite all, know that by *Umma*, he is referring to the community of all Muslims worldwide.

"In his fund-raising activities, Signpost has sat on the board of charities of many persuasions, some bitterly opposed to one another, for the purpose of promoting and distributing *zakat*," Aziz continues, and takes another quick read of his audience.

"*Zakat* is the two and a half percent of a Muslim's earnings that, under Shariat law, should be devoted to good causes such as schools, hospitals, providing food for the poor and needy, scholarships for students and *orphanages*. Muslim orphanages. These are his great love. For our orphans, Signpost has declared, he will travel the earth for the rest of his life without sleep. And we should admire him for that too. Islam has many orphans. And Signpost from an early age was himself an orphan: the product of strict, very strict Koran schools."

But there is a downside to this commitment, as the tightening of his voice indicates:

"*Orphanages,* I would suggest to you, are one of the many points at which social and terrorist causes cannot help meeting. Orphanages are sanctuaries for children of the dead. Among the dead are martyrs, men and women who have given their lives defending Islam, whether on the battlefield or as suicide bombers. It is not the business of charitable donors to inquire into the particular *form* of martyrdom. I am afraid, therefore, that links with the purveyors of terrorism are in this context inevitable."

If the congregation had murmured a rapt *amen,* Bachmann would not have been surprised.

"Signpost is *intrepid,*" Professor Aziz insists, resuming his role as defense counsel. "In pursuit of his life's mission he has witnessed the plight of his Muslim brothers and sisters in some of the worst places on earth, I would say the *absolute* worst. In the last three years he has traveled at personal risk to Gaza, Baghdad, Somalia, Yemen, Ethiopia; also to Lebanon, where he experienced at firsthand the Israeli devastation of that country. That does not, I am afraid, excuse him."

He draws a deep breath, as if filling himself up with courage, although courage, in Bachmann's memory, is the last thing Aziz lacks.

"I must tell you that in these cases there is, for

Muslims and non-Muslims alike, always the same question: If the persuasive evidence is correct, is a man like Signpost doing a little *good* in order to do *bad*? Or is he doing a little *bad* in order to do *good*? Signpost's purpose in my submission was always to do *good*. Ask him about the acceptable uses of violence and he will tell you that in addressing the issue of terror, we have to distinguish between legitimate revolt against occupation on the one hand, and outright terrorism, which we do not endorse, on the other. The United Nations charter *allows* resistance against occupation. We *share* that view, as do all liberal Europeans. *However*"—he appears suddenly wistful—"*however, what we have learned in these cases*—and Signpost on the strength of persuasive evidence is no exception—is that *good* men accept a little bit of *bad* as a necessary element of their work. For some it may be as much as twenty percent. For others twelve or ten. For others again, even as little as five. But five percent bad can be very bad indeed, even if the remaining ninety-five percent is very good. They know the arguments. But in their heads"—he is tapping his own—"they consider them *unresolved*. They have a *place* for terror in their minds and it is not an entirely *negative* place. They regard it"—is he searching his own conscience and pretending it is Abdullah's?—"as a *painful but necessary* tribute to the great diversity that is the Umma. Unfortunately, that does *not* constitute an excuse. But it constitutes, I would venture to suggest, an *explanation.* Therefore while Signpost may be sure in his own *mind* of what he considers the right path, he would not actually go so far as to tell the militants to their faces that they are wrong. Because in his *heart,* he is not totally sure. That is his insoluble paradox, and he is not alone. For are not *all* true believers looking for the right path? And are not God's commands difficult to comprehend? Signpost may deeply dislike what the militants do. Probably he does. But who is he to say that they are less pious, or less guided by God, than he is himself—assuming always that the persuasive evidence persuades us?"

Bachmann glances at Burgdorf, then quickly at Martha, because the American top spy and the would-be German intelligence czar are sharing the same stare, and it is directed at each other. It is a stare without expression, signaling nothing beyond the existence of a private bond. Then watchful Lantern sees the stare too and, straining to be part of it, leans backward in his seat until he is as close as he can get to Martha's bejeweled ear, and whispers something into it that makes no impact on her features either.

If Aziz has witnessed this interaction, he ignores it.

"We must also consider *this* possibility," he continues. "That Signpost, owing to his provenance and the connections that have sprung from it, is under *moral pressure* from his fellow believers. That can happen. His cooperation is not merely *assumed,* it is *demanded.* 'If you don't help us, you are betraying us.' Perhaps Signpost is subject to other forms of coercion also. He has an earlier wife and beloved children from a previous marriage, now living in Saudi Arabia. *We do not know,*" he insists, with painful emphasis. "We shall *never* know. Perhaps Signpost himself will never know just how he became what he is—assuming that *is* what he is." He steels himself for what sounds like a final appeal to their unlikely understanding. "Maybe Signpost doesn't *want* to know—maybe he genuinely *doesn't* know—where the five percent ends up. Right down to the last link, maybe *nobody* knows. A mosque needs a roof. A hospital needs a wing. And by merciful Allah's grace, there's a go-between who gives them the money. But the poorest outposts of Islam are not exactly renowned for their meticulous bookkeeping. So the go-between is able to keep enough back to buy explosives for a couple of suicide belts." He has a last message. "Ninety-five percent of Signpost knows and loves what he does. But five percent of him doesn't want to know, and can't. I'm sorry."

Sorry for *what*? Bachmann wants to ask him.

"So what is he?" an impatient male voice demands abruptly. It is Burgdorf's.

"By his actions, Herr Burgdorf? In his *effect,* you mean? Assuming the evidence is correct?"

"Isn't that what we're dealing with here? Once we have made that assumption? His actions?"

Burgdorf the grumpy man-child is famous for his loathing of liberal equivocation. "Just give me one-armed advisors, Michael," he is reputed to have shouted at Axelrod in the course of an unseemly public spat. "Don't give me any more people who tell me, 'on the one hand, on the other hand!'"

"Signpost is a *hub,* Herr Burgdorf," Professor Aziz admits sadly, from the rostrum. "Not in the substance of what he does, but in the detail. A little bit shaved off here, a small diversion there—the sums are not *large.* At the level at which terror currently operates, they don't need to be. A few thousand dollars can be enough. In the worst places, a few hundred will do the trick. If we are talking Hamas, less."

He seems about to add something. Perhaps he is remembering what just a few hundred did. Burgdorf cuts him short:

"So he finances terror," he retorts loudly, spelling matters out for the benefit of the many.

"In effect, Herr Burgdorf, yes. If what we believe is true. Ninety-five percent of him does not. Ninety-five percent of him supports the poor and sick and needy of the Umma. But five percent of him finances terror. Consciously, and with ingenuity. He is therefore an evil man. That is his tragedy."

Axelrod has seen this moment coming and prepared for it.

"Professor Aziz, aren't you suggesting something different? From what we've been hearing between the lines, wouldn't you agree that—given the right inducements, shall we say, and the right convergence of pressures and misfortunes—Signpost is ideal material for recruitment to the peaceful path—much as you yourself were, many years ago, back in the days when you were a Muslim brother supporting direct action?"

Professor Aziz bows farewell to his audience and is escorted out. He is security-cleared—but why take the risk? Watching him depart, Bachmann overhears Martha's deliberately ill-concealed aside to Lantern: *Tell you what, Ian. I'll settle for five percent right now.*

A flurry of uncoordinated activity followed the departure of Aziz. Martha rose and sailed out of the room with her cell phone to her ear, sweeping

Newton and the big-shouldered blonde along with her. Mohr, it appeared, had set aside an office from which the Agency could do its harmless observing. Burgdorf was leaning over the seated Keller, murmuring in his ear while they looked in opposite directions. And Bachmann, struggling to quell the anxieties that were banking up in him, was praying to himself in the language of his unsung Cantata:

We are not policemen, we are spies. We do not arrest our targets. We develop them and redirect them at bigger targets. When we identify a network, we watch it, we listen to it, we penetrate it and by degrees we control it. Arrests are of negative value. They destroy a precious acquisition. They send you scrabbling back to the drawing board, looking for another network half as good as the one you've just screwed up. If Abdullah is not part of a known network, I personally will make him part of one. If need be, I will invent a network, just for him. It worked for me in the past, and it will work in the case of Abdullah, just give me the chance. Amen.

In the hands of a legendary woman researcher called Frau Zimmermann whom Bachmann had encountered on her fleeting visits to the Beirut embassy, Signpost is transforming himself from honey-eating religious academic with a five percent flaw into a red-toothed terrorist paymaster.

On a screen above Frau Zimmermann's squat head, diagrams like family trees have appeared, demonstrating which of the highly reputable Muslim charities under his control Signpost is believed to misuse in order to syphon money and matériel for terrorists. Not all his five percent transactions are financial. The wretched of Djibouti are crying out for a hundred tons of sugar? One of Signpost's charities will make sure a consignment is dispatched at once. On its way to Djibouti, however, the mercy vessel happens to put in at the humble port of Berbera on the north coast of war-torn Somalia in order to deposit other cargo, she explains, jabbing irritably at the screen with her pointer as if to rid it of an intrusive insect.

And in Berbera, it transpires that ten tons of sugar are unloaded by mistake. Well, such things happen, whether we're in Berbera or Hamburg. The trivial error is not discovered until the ship is once more under way. And when the ship reaches its official destination of Djibouti, the recipients are so hungry and so grateful to receive their ninety tons that nobody complains about the odd ten that have gone missing. Meanwhile back in Berbera, ten tons of sugar are buying detonators, land mines, hand guns and shoulder-held rocket launchers for Somali militants whose aim in life is to spread mayhem and slaughter at bargain-basement prices.

Yet who can pin the blame on the honorable charity that, in its unquestioned goodness, supplied sugar for the starving of Djibouti? And who would dare pin the blame on Signpost, the ninety-five-percent pious champion of tolerance and inclusiveness among peoples of all religions?

Frau Zimmermann would, for one.

She would also refer her audience to their Felix dossiers, which provide the detailed reasoning behind her findings. Meanwhile, for dummies, she has another diagram, even simpler than the first. It consists of an archipelago of commercial banking houses, small and large, scattered across the globe. Some are familiar names, others more likely to have their headquarters in the shanties of a hill town in Pakistan. Nothing connects the one with the other. All they have in common is a pin light, which comes on when Frau Zimmermann shakes her pointer at them, the way an angry little lady shakes her umbrella at a departing bus.

One fine day, a moderate sum of money is paid into this bank, she says. Let's say in Amsterdam. Let's say ten thousand euros. A kind man comes off the street and pays it in.

And the money stays in this bank. It can be to the credit of an individual or a company or an institution or a charity. But it doesn't budge. It remains to the credit of the lucky account holder. Maybe for as long as six months. A year.

Then a week later, lo and behold a sum in the same amount is paid into *this* bank thousands of kilometers away in—let's say—Karachi. And it too stays where it is. No phone call, no wired transfer. Just a different kind man from the street.

"Until one month later a very similar sum finally arrives *here*," Frau Zimmermann says, her sharp voice rising in indignation. The tip of the pointer rests on northern Cyprus. "At the place it was intended for all along, paid in by silent barter, which without detailed operational intelligence we cannot hope to trace. Countless transactions of this sort take place every hour. Only a tiny few support terrorist acts. Combined sources and computerized data occasionally show us the way: but only *one* way. That's the dilemma. If we trace the chain this time, who's to say we'll trace it next time? Next time it could be completely different. That's the beauty of the system. Unless of course the chain master becomes complacent, or lazy, and starts to repeat himself. Then a pattern forms and, over time, certain presumptions can be made. The optimum is to identify the chain master and his first link. Signpost is a chain master who has gone lazy."

A pin light is burning over the city of Nicosia. The pointer gives it an accusing tap, and rests there.

"As with decoding, so with invisible transfers," the legendary Frau Zimmermann resumes in her schoolmarm's South German. "Repetition is what the investigator dreams of. On the strength of three years' observation of *this* extremely insignificant shipping firm which has a long record of unloading food and other commodities to dubious places by mistake and not bothering too much about getting it back"—the innocuous name of the SEVEN FRIENDS NAVIGATION COMPANY is suddenly splurged in red across the top of the island while the pointer remains resolutely at its post—"and on the basis of Signpost's first-link payments into *this* charitable account at *this* bank"—Riyadh lights up, together with the name of the bank, in Arabic and English—"and matching money is paid into *this* bank"—the pointer has moved to Paris—"and the same sum goes into *this* bank"—we are in Istanbul—"all to accounts that we have now been able to preidentify, then *we* say that is a very clear assumption of Signpost's involvement in terrorist finance. If Signpost was clean, it is our conviction that he would never *ever* have had direct contact with this low-grade, one-off shipping company. Yet he personally has hired this company on more than one occasion, although aware—and maybe *because* he is aware—that on more than one occasion it has delivered goods to the wrong place. Proof it isn't. But as a basis for assumption, it screams out loud."

As the screen withdraws itself into the rafters, Frau Zimmermann's meticulous voice is interrupted by majestic Martha's ship-to-ship loudhailer booming out across the room.

"When you say *clear assumption,* Charlotte"— how the hell does she know the woman's first name, wonders Bachmann, and how the hell did she get back in here without my noticing?—"are you talking like *evidence* here? He makes the move we want him to make—the first-link move—and then we have the *evidence*? Evidence that would stand up in an American court of justice?"

The flustered Frau Zimmermann is protesting that the question is above her pay grade when Axelrod deftly takes it from her.

"Which of your courts are we talking about here, Martha? Your military tribunals behind closed doors, or the old sort when the accused was allowed to know what he was accused of?"

A few of the freer souls laugh. The rest pretend they haven't heard.

"Herr Bachmann," Burgdorf snaps. "You have an operational proposal. Let us hear it, please."

A man who makes the weather does not take kindly to having the uninitiated peering over his shoulder while he performs his magic. Bachmann had the artist's sensitivities about sharing the process of creation. Nevertheless he struggled to oblige his audience. In unpretentious layman's language designed to appeal to those at the fringes of the spy trade, he set out the arguments that, with editorial assistance from Erna Frey and Axelrod, had formed the core of his hastily written submission. The operational aim, he explained, was to deliver the proof of Signpost's guilt, but at the same time to leave his reputation and eminence unchanged and, in the long term, even enhanced, with all his charitable connections intact. It was to take over his five percent and use him as a duct and a listening post. Against his better inclinations, Bachmann forced himself to use the term "war on terror." Therefore the first move was the most vital: it must be to compromise Signpost absolutely, to let him know he was compromised and offer him the choice between remaining a distinguished, leading spirit of the Umma, or—

"Or *what* exactly, Günther? Tell us." Martha, the harmless observer, interrupting.

"Public humiliation and possible imprisonment."

"Possible?"

Axelrod to the rescue: "This is Germany, Martha."

"Sure. It's Germany. You try him and let's say for a change the case sticks. How long does he sit for? Like six years, three of them suspended?

You people don't know what jail *is*. Who gets to interrogate?"

Axelrod had no doubt who did. "He'd be German property and he'd be interrogated under German law. That's if he refuses to play ball. Much better, however, he stays in place and collaborates with us. We believe he will."

"Why? He's a fanatical terrorist. Maybe he'd rather blow himself up."

Bachmann again: "That's not our reading of him, Martha. He's a family man, settled, respected all across the Umma, admired in the West. It's thirty years since he's done prison. We don't ask him to become a traitor. We offer him a new definition of loyalty. We entrench his position here, we promise him German citizenship, which he's applied for half a dozen times without success. All right, maybe at first we threaten him. But that's foreplay. Then we befriend him. 'Come over to us and let's work together creatively for a better and more moderate Islam.' "

"And how about an amnesty for past terrorist acts?" Martha suggested, now appearing to join the argument rather than contest it. "Would you throw that in too?"

"Provided he made a clean breast of them. Assuming Berlin sanctioned it. As a necessary part of the package. Yes."

The shadow of mutual hostility had passed.

Martha was grinning broadly. "Günther, darling. How old are you, for fuck's sake? A hundred and fifty?"

"A hundred and forty-nine," Bachmann replied, playing her game.

"And to think I had my last ideal removed when I was seventeen and a half!" Martha cried, to a burst of general laughter, led by Ian Lantern.

But Bachmann's case was far from won. A covert survey of the faces round the table confirmed what he had feared from the start: that the prospect of a loving friendship with a terrorist paymaster did not suit every palate.

"So we are giving our enemies *citizenship* today," a known wag from the Foreign Ministry suggested acidly. "We are opening our arms, not only to Signpost, who is an identified international terrorist, but to our good friend Felix, an escaped Russian criminal jailbird with a string of convictions for Muslim-inspired acts of violence. Our hospitality towards foreign criminals seems to be unlimited. We have the man at our complete mercy, so we offer him German citizenship as an inducement. One wonders how much further our gallantry can go."

"It's for the girl," Bachmann growled, coloring.

"Ah, of course. The lady in the case. I forgot."

"The girl would never have worked for us if we hadn't given her our solemn promise Felix would go free. Without the girl, we would never have brought Felix to the water. The girl befriended him, the girl persuaded him to go to Signpost."

Realizing that his words had been greeted by an unbelieving, if not downright skeptical silence, Bachmann lowered his head belligerently into his shoulders. "I gave her *my word*. The one we never break, agent runner to agent. That was the deal. Approved by Joint." This last sally being directed straight at Burgdorf while Axelrod frowned uneasily into the middle distance. "She's his lawyer"—addressing the whole room now. "As his lawyer she's pledged to do whatever it takes to protect her client. She cooperates because we have assured her that her client will benefit. He'll go free and he'll be left alone to study and pray, which is all he wants to do. That's why she plays along with us."

"We're also told she's in love with him," the same acid voice suggested, quite unrepentant. "Maybe the question is: How much love is left for *us*?"

And Bachmann, despite a warning glance from Axelrod, might well have responded to this jibe in terms he would afterwards have regretted, had not Lantern deftly stepped into the breach to defuse the tension.

"Might I wave my little Union Jack here, Ax?"—picking on Axelrod as the recipient of his British wit—"I feel I *should* just point out that without the involvement of a certain blue-chip British bank, there'd be no Felix to inherit his father's money, and no Signpost to help him spend it!"

But the ensuing laughter was uncertain and the tension did not ease. Martha was heads down with Newton and her ash-blonde mystery woman. Now her head came up with a jolt.

"Günther. Ian. Ax. Okay. Answer me this, please. Are you boys really telling me you can pull this thing off? I mean, Jesus Christ, let's just see what we've got here. One goofy liberal woman lawyer on the verge of a nervous break-down. One semidefunct British banker who has the hots for her. And one semi-Chechen free-dom fighter on the run from Russian justice who flies paper airplanes, listens to music and thinks one day he'll be a doctor. And you boys truly think you can put them all together in one room, and they're going to nail a dyed-in-the-wool Islamist money launderer who's spent his entire life seeing round corners? Do I have this right? Or am I being a little soft in the head by any chance?"

To Bachmann's relief, Axelrod was this time able to respond from strength.

"Felix doesn't come out of blue sky, as far as Signpost is concerned, Martha. If you look at the material, you'll see we've given him quite a write-up on the Islamist websites we control, and the signals people tell me our efforts have paid off. The Swedish wanted notice and the Russian police report didn't do us any harm either. Websites we've never heard of have picked him up and billed him as this great Chechen fighter and escape artist. By the time they all meet up, Felix's fame will have gone ahead of him."

Somebody was asking about operational procedure. How long, once Signpost had been compromised and secured, could Bachmann hold on to him without arousing concerns as to his whereabouts?

Bachmann said it all depended on Signpost's arrangements for that night. Time was against them. The girl and Felix were both getting frayed.

The focus turned to Arni Mohr. Desperate to make his presence felt, he was describing his last night's visit to police headquarters, where to a select gathering he had outlined a part, not all, naturally, of the planned operation.

As Bachmann listened, despair overcame him like a sickness. The police proposed to place shooters round the bank against the possibility that Signpost was wearing a suicide belt, Mohr announced proudly.

And since it must be assumed that Signpost would arrive armed, they also proposed to cover the crucial encounter at Brue Frères Bank from all five directions: the Alster shore, both sides of the street and both ends.

Also the rooftops, Mohr went on. His master plan was to close off the area as soon as Signpost was admitted to the bank, and repopulate it with his own version of humanity: in cars, on bicycles, on foot. With police assistance, all nearby houses and hotels would be evacuated.

Keller agreed.

Burgdorf did not disagree.

Martha, though only an observer, was pleased to offer her approval.

Newton said anything they could do to help: toys, night-vision stuff, any small thing at all.

The ash-blonde mystery woman signified her agreement with a tight-lipped nod of her hatchet face.

In an effort to moderate Mohr's grandiose scheme, Axelrod reminded him that the precautions he and the police were advocating should leave no footprint, either before, during or after Signpost's visit to Brue Frères. If word got out— to the media, to the Muslim community that held him in such esteem—all hope of Signpost acting as a high-value informant was scuppered.

And yes, Axelrod conceded, as far as he was concerned, Arni Mohr himself could be present when the police technically arrested Signpost, but only if Bachmann thought an arrest desirable as a means of intimidating him before beginning the befriending process. Was everyone comfortable with that?

Everyone except Bachmann apparently was. Suddenly the meeting was over. The jury—assisted by its observers—would retire to consider its verdict, and Bachmann, not for the first time, could go back to his stable and sweat it out.

"Excellent work, Bachmann," Burgdorf told him, patting his shoulder in a rare gesture of physical contact.

To Bachmann's ear, the plaudit sounded like an obituary.

Bachmann sat at his desk, head in hands, while opposite him Erna Frey toiled methodically at her computer.

"How is she?" he asked.

"As well as can be expected."

"How well's that?"

"As long as she thinks Issa's worse off than she is, she can hold out."

"Good."

"Is it?"

What more could Bachmann say? Was it his fault if Erna too had fallen for the girl? Was it Erna's? Everyone else seemed to have fallen for her, so why shouldn't Erna? Love was whatever you could put up with and still do the job.

Elsewhere in the stables the mood was just as glum. Maximilian and Niki were decrypting and checking the day's incomings, doing whatever they did instead of going home. But not a human voice reached Bachmann's ear, not a laugh or exclamation, whether from the researchers next door or the listeners along the corridor, or the little band of drivers and street watchers on the floor below.

Standing at the window and filled with a sense of déjà vu, Bachmann watched Keller's official helicopter lift off for Cologne, then Burgdorf's for Berlin with a covey of officials and Axelrod; last aboard was Martha without her Newton, or her ash-blonde.

A line of black Mercedes headed for the main gate. The boom rose and stayed risen.

The encrypted phone was ringing on Bachmann's desk. He put it to his ear and grunted an occasional "yes, Michael," "no, Michael."

Erna Frey remained at her computer.

Bachmann said, "Good-bye, Michael," and rang off. Erna Frey continued with her work.

"We've got it," Bachmann said.

"Got what?"

"The green light. With conditions. We can go ahead. As soon as possible. They're worried we're sitting on a volcano. I get the first eight hours of him."

"*Eight.* Not nine."

"Eight will do it. If he hasn't taken the bait after eight hours, Arni can have the police arrest him."

"And where will you be taking him for your eight hours, if I may ask? The Atlantic? The Four Seasons?"

"To your safe flat down on the harbor front."

"You'll drag him there by the short hairs?"

"Invite him. As soon as he comes out of the bank. '*Herr Doktor,* I represent the German government and we would like to talk to you about certain illegal financial transactions you have just made.' "

"And he says?"

"He's in the car by then. He can say what he likes."

13

She's catatonic.

They're driving her mad.

Another week of this, she'll do the full Georgie on them, if she hasn't done it already. She probably thought I was mad too.

When we met at the Atlantic, I was dear old Tommy Brue, failing scion of a failing bank and a failed marriage, a balloon adrift.

At the house of the Turks, I was a guilt-ridden old fart buying himself into her life for fifty thousand euros she never touched.

And what am I now, as I drive northwest at a regulation one hundred and thirty kilometers an hour? The blackmailed servant of my late father's corrupters on my way to sweet-tongue a venerable Muslim scholar who's five percent bad into saving the skin of the boy she probably loves.

"You are merely responding to the wishes of another rich client," Lantern had assured him in

the course of yesterday evening's otherwise torrid
briefing session at his odious safe flat that stank
of chlorine from the communal swimming pool in
the courtyard six floors below. "Albeit from the
darker side of your bank, which explains why
you're exercising particular discretion. And you
are about to consult the investment manager of
his choice, never mind of what stripe, and you're
in for a fat commission whichever way he cuts the
cake," he added, in the assertive tones of a miniature head prefect at Brue's detested public school.
"It's your perfectly normal banking situation,
Tommy."

"Not in my book, it isn't."

"Also in the line of normal banking practice,"
Lantern persisted, magnanimously ignoring this
impertinence, "you have undertaken to explore—in accordance with your client's wishes,
as conveyed to you by his legal advisor—whether
or not the gentleman you are about to visit is an
appropriate fit. Is that a fair summary?"

"It's a summary of a sort, I suppose," Brue
said, helping himself uninvited to a generous
scotch.

"You will be shrewd and you will be objective.
You will decide, in the fullness of your professional wisdom, what is the best way forward for
both parties: for your client, and for your bank.
The interests of the elevated Muslim gentleman

you are consulting are of secondary concern to you, if at all."

"And in the fullness of my professional wisdom, I shall decide that he's the right elevated Muslim gentleman for the job," Brue suggested in similar coin.

"Well, it's not exactly as if you were spoiled for choice, is it, Tommy?" said little Lantern, turning on his winning smile.

Twelve hours earlier, Mitzi had had her own spot of news for him.

"Bernhard's being a bore," she remarked, while Brue was deep in his *Financial Times*. "Hildegard's leaving him."

Brue drank some coffee, then dabbed his lips with his napkin. In the games they played, the first rule of life was never to be surprised by anything.

"Then surely *Hildegard*'s the one who's being a bore," he suggested.

"Hildegard's *always* a bore."

"So what's poor Bernhard done that's making *him* a bore?" Brue inquired, taking the man's part.

"Proposed marriage to me. I'm to leave you and get a divorce and go to Sylt with him for the summer while we decide where to live for the rest of our lives," she said indignantly. "Can you *imagine* sharing Bernhard's old age with him?"

"It's hard for me to imagine sharing *anything* with Bernhard, to be frank."

"And Hildegard thinks she's suing you."

"*Me?*"

"Or me, what's the difference? For luring her husband away from her. She thinks you're rich. So you'll have to sue Bernhard to shut her up. I'm going to ask your buddy Westerheim who's the best lawyer."

"Has Hildegard considered the publicity?"

"She *adores* publicity. Wallows in it. It's the most vulgar thing I ever heard."

"Have you accepted Bernhard's proposal?"

"I'm thinking about it."

"Ah. And how far have you got in your deliberations?"

"I'm not sure how much use we are to each other anymore, Tommy."

"You and Bernhard?"

"You and me."

Over the flat, uninviting countryside the sky was black. The autobahn shone like glass. Headlights of oncoming cars lunged at him. So we're no use to each other anymore. Good. I'll be fine on my own. I'll sell the bank while there's still a bit to sell, and get myself a life. Might even pop over to California for old Georgie's wedding. He still hadn't told Mitzi he was going to be a grandfather, which pleased him. Maybe he never would.

Had Georgie let her mother into the secret? He hoped so. Old Sue would be happy as a sandboy. All bark and no bite, old Sue was, once you got past the fierce bit. Rather wished he'd realized that a bit earlier, to be frank. Before Mitzi, rather than after Mitzi, so to speak. Nothing to be done about it now, mind. Not with Sue tucked up safe and sound with her Italian wine grower. Nice chap, by all accounts. Perhaps they'll name a cuvée after the baby.

Then whatever exultation he had briefly felt vanished into the clatter of the wet road, and he was back with Annabel, revisiting his protective anger at what they had turned her into: the robotic walk, the remoteness of her choirboy voice, so far from the fervor with which she had assailed him in Melik's bedroom: *without your fucking bank, my client wouldn't be here!*

"The bank *owes* you, Frau Richter," he proclaimed aloud to the windscreen, aping his own pomposity. "And so I am pleased to say, the bank is about to pay its debt."

The bank loves you, he continued in his mind. Not to possess you, but to help you find your courage again so that you can live the life I con-

spicuously failed to live myself. Are you in love
with Issa, Annabel? Georgie would love him instantly. She'd love you too. And she'd tell you to
take care of me, which is the way Georgie thinks.
Everybody should take care of everybody. That's
why she gets let down so much. Does it even
matter whether you're in love with Issa? *Love* in
the dictionary sense? It emphatically does not. It
matters that you set him free.

"What happens to Annabel at the end of all this
jollity?" Brue had demanded of Lantern at the
same extended briefing as he sipped his scotch,
by no means his first, and Lantern his umpteenth
glass of sparkling water. It had been a day of
days, even by Brue's standards: at breakfast,
Mitzi's bombshell about Bernhard. At the office,
a full-scale revolt by the counting room concerning shift work over public holidays. Followed by
an hour talking to his revered solicitor in Glasgow, who appeared never to have heard of divorce before. Followed by two hours of
injudicious lunching at the À la Carte and being
hilariously witty for the benefit of a couple of hu-
morless rich clients from Oldenburg. Followed
by a hangover that he was now busy topping up.
    "What happens to her, Lantern?" he repeated.
    "It's a strictly German matter, Tommy,"

Lantern replied judiciously, resorting once more to his head prefect's voice. "My *guess* is, they'll leave her in place. As long as she doesn't write her memoirs, or otherwise rock the boat."

"Not good enough, I'm afraid."

"What isn't?"

"Your *guess*. Want firm assurances. Written ones. To her, copy to me."

"Copy of *what* precisely, Tommy? I think you're a bit pissed, aren't you? Maybe we should leave this subject for another time."

Brue was bestriding the grimy room.

"Who says there'll *be* another time? There may not be. Not if I withdraw my labor. How about that? What?"

"Well, in that case, Tommy, London might have no option but to use certain sanctions that we have regarding your bank."

"Use them, old boy, my advice. Enjoy them to the full. Be my guest. Frères goes down the tube. Much moaning at the bar. But for how long? And from who? Whom?" It was hardball at last. Long overdue, in Brue's opinion. The knives were out, and fuck 'em. "Banks go down the tube every day. Specially the old, inefficient ones like mine. Not the same as what happens to you boys when your dream operation goes pear-shaped, is it? I can smell a big deal a mile off, and this is a big deal. *Pity about young Ian: we used to think highly of him. Let's hope he'll find him-self a decent job on the outside.* Cheers. Bloody good health to you and all who sail in you."

He waited for a "cheers" back, and was pleased not to receive one.

"Just tell me what it is exactly that would put your mind at rest, Tommy," Lantern suggested, in a voice as flat as a speaking clock's.

"An OBE, for starters. Tea with the Queen. And ten-million-quid compensation for turning Frères into a Russian laundromat."

"That's a joke, I take it."

"Absolutely. A hoot, same as this whole oper-ation. I have more demands. Break points, actu-ally."

"And what would they be, Tommy, these de-mands?"

"*Number one*—want to write this down or do you think you can remember 'em?"

"I'll remember, thank you."

"An official letter. Addressed to Frau Annabel Richter, copy for me. Signed and sealed by the competent German authority, thanking her for her cooperation and assuring her that no legal or other actions will be taken against her. That's for starters, all right? The nitty-gritty to follow." And catching Lantern's expression of near-incredulity: "I'm not fucking around, Lantern. I'm deadly serious. Nothing on God's earth is going to get me through Abdullah's front door tomorrow if I don't have total satisfaction. *Number two*: an advance sight of Issa Karpov's brand-new German passport, valid as soon as he signs over his loot. I want it *in my hand* to show to Annabel, ahead of hostilities, as proof incontrovertible that whoever is pulling her strings is going to stick to his promises and not welsh. Got the message or would you like subtitles?"

"That's plain impossible. You're asking me to go to the Germans and get his passport out of them and *lend* it to you? You're in cloud-cuckooland, man!"

"Bollocks. Arrant, fully attested ordure, if you'll forgive my crudeness. You're in the magic wand business. Wave it, be it never so small. And I'll tell you something else."

"What?"

"Re that passport."

"*What,* re that passport?"

"Passports are a dime a dozen in your business, I understand. They can be faked, canceled, withdrawn and impregnated with nasty messages to the authorities of other countries. Correct?"

"So?"

"I have a lien on you. Kindly remember that. It will not expire with the issue of Issa's passport. If I ever hear that you've done the dirty on him, I shall blow the whistle on you. Very loud and very long and very clear. Lantern of the British embassy, Berlin. The spook who rats on his promises. And by the time you catch me, it will be too bloody late. I'm going home now. Call me when you've got an answer, I'm open all hours."

"What about your wife?"

What about her indeed? He lay in bed watching the ceiling sway, and waiting for it to right itself. Note from Mitzi: *Summit conference with Bernhard.*

Good luck to her. Everyone should have a summit.

It was midnight when Lantern called.

"Can you talk?"

"I'm alone, if that's what you're asking."

Lantern had waved his magic wand.

Brue signaled right and looked in his driving mirror. The slip road was approaching and they were still behind him: two men in a BMW who had been following him ever since he left his house. *Someone to watch over you,* Lantern had said, with a smirk.

The town was a cluster of red brick dumped onto misted fields. A red church, a red railway station, a fire station. A row of semi-bungalows down one side of the main street. On the other side, a petrol station and a steel-and-concrete school. There was a football field, but nobody was playing.

Parking in the high street was forbidden, so he found a side street and walked back. Lantern's minders had vanished. Probably having a coffee in the petrol station, pretending to be other people.

Two stocky Arab-looking men in baggy brown suits stood watching his approach. The elder was swinging his prayer beads, the younger smoking a foul-looking yellow cigarette. The elder shuffled a pace towards him, holding out his arms. Fifty meters up the road, two uniformed policemen stepped out of the shadow of a hedge to take a look.

"You permit, sir?"

Brue permitted. Shoulders, lapels, armpits, side pockets, back, hips, crotch, calves, ankles, all his zones, erogenous and otherwise. And on the insistence of the second man who had stamped out his cigarette, the contents of his breast pockets. *It's an ordinary fountain pen,* Lantern had said. *It looks like a pen, writes like a pen, listens like a pen. If they take it apart, it's still an ordinary fountain pen.*

They didn't take it apart.

A burst of sunshine made the place beautiful. In the overgrown front garden a heavily covered woman in black roosted in a deck chair cuddling a baby. Georgie, seven months from now. The front door stood open. A small boy in a skullcap and white robe peered round it from halfway up. Maybe she'll have a boy.

"You are most welcome, Mr. Brue, sir," he declaimed in English, and grinned from ear to ear.

From the porch, Brue stepped straight into a living room. At his feet three small girls in white were building a Lego farmyard while a silent television showed golden domes and minarets. At the foot of a staircase stood a bearded youth in long striped shirt and chinos.

"Mr. Brue, sir, I am Ismail, private secretary to Dr. Abdullah. You are most welcome," he said, and laid his right hand against his heart before extending it for Brue to shake.

If five percent of Dr. Abdullah was bad, as Lantern had insisted, then it was five percent of very little. He was tiny, twinkly, fatherly, bald and benign, with bright eyes and thick eyebrows and a dance to his tread. Springing round his desk, he whisked Brue's hand into both of his and kept it there. He wore a black suit and a white shirt with a closed collar, and sneakers with no laces.

"You are the great Mr. Brue," he piped, speaking English very fast and very well. "Your name is not unknown to us, sir. Your bank had Arab connections once, not good ones, but connections. Perhaps you have forgotten. That's one of the great problems of our modern world, you know. Forgetting. The victim *never* forgets. Ask an Irishman what the English did to him in 1920 and he'll tell you the day of the month and the time and the name of every man they killed. Ask an Iranian what the English did to him in 1953 and he'll tell you. His child will tell you. His grandchild will tell you. And when he has one, his great-grandchild will tell you too. But ask an Englishman—" He flung up his hands in mock ignorance. "If he ever knew, he has forgotten. *'Move on!'* you tell us. *'Move on! Forget what we've done to you. Tomorrow's another day!'* But it isn't, Mr. Brue." He still had Brue's hand. *"Tomorrow* was created yesterday, you see. That is the point I was making to you. And by the day *before* yesterday, too. To ignore history is to ignore the wolf at the door. Please. Take a seat. You had a safe journey, I hope?"

"Fine, just fine, thank you."

"It was not fine, it was raining. Now we briefly have sunshine. In life we must face the realities. You met my son Ismail, my secretary? This is Fatima, my daughter. Next October, God willing, Fatima will begin her studies at the London

School of Economics and Ismail will in due course follow in his father's steps to Cairo and I shall be a lonelier fellow but a proud one. You have children, sir?"

"One daughter."

"Then you too are blessed."

"But not as blessed as you are, by the look of it!" said Brue heartily.

Like her brother, Fatima was taller than her father by a head. She was broad-faced and beautiful. Her brown *hijab* fell over her shoulders like a cape.

"Hi," she said and, dipping her eyes, placed her right hand to her heart in salutation.

"The Americans are worse than you British but they have an *excuse*," Dr. Abdullah ran on in the same jolly style, guiding Brue towards the one luxuriantly stuffed visitors' armchair, but without releasing his wrist. "Their excuse is *ignorance*. They don't know what they're doing wrong. But you English know very well. You have known it a long time. And you do it all the same. You don't mind a joke, I suppose? Humor will be my undoing, I'm told. But don't mistake me for a philosopher, I beg you. Philosophy is for *you,* not for me. I am a religious authority, yes. But philosophy is for the secular and the godless. Our part of the world is in a bad state, don't tell me. Whose fault is that? I wonder. One thousand years ago, we had more hospitals per capita in Córdoba than the Spanish do today. Our doctors performed operations that still defeat your modern doctors. What went wrong? we ask ourselves. Foreign involvement? Russian imperialism? Or secularism? But we Muslims too were to blame. Some of us had lost faith in our faith. We weren't true Muslims anymore. That was where we hit the buffers. Fatima, we need tea, please. I was one year at Cambridge. Caius College. I expect you know that too. With the Internet and TV there are no secrets anymore. Information is not knowledge, mind you. Information is dead meat. Only God can turn information into knowledge. And cake, Fatima, Mr. Brue has driven from Hamburg in the rain. You are too hot, too cold, sir? Be frank with us. We are hospitable people here, trying our best to fulfill God's commands. We wish you to be comfortable. If you are bringing us money, we wish you to be *very* comfortable! The more comfortable, the better, we say! This way, please, sir. Allow us to conduct you to our consulting room! You are a kind man. You have a good *visage,* as we say."

Five percent bad *how?* Brue was thinking angrily in his nervousness. Lantern, when he asked him the question, had refused to elaborate: *Just take my word for it, Tommy. Five percent is all you need to know.* So tell me who *isn't* five percent bad?

Brue demanded of himself as, with all the family in attendance, they trooped down a narrow corridor. Brue Frères, with its dodgy investments, dodgy clients and Lipizzaners? Plus a bit of insider dealing when we can get away with it? I'd give us more like fifteen. As to our gallant president and managing director, me, what are we looking at there? Divorced a good wife, one leftover child I'm learning to love when it's too late, screwed the field, married a tart and now she's throwing me out: I'd give me more like fifty percent bad than five.

"So what does he do with the other ninety-five of himself?" he had asked Lantern.

Good works was the evasive answer.

What do I do with mine? Bugger all. Tot us both up, look at the bottom line, and you begin to wonder which of us is five percent more bad than the other.

"And so, sir, kindly begin. At your leisure but in English, please. For the children it is most important they learn English at every opportunity. This way, please, sir. Thank you."

They had moved to a humble scholar's den overlooking the back garden. Where there were no books, there was calligraphy. Dr. Abdullah sat at a plain wood desk, leaning forward over his

folded hands. Fatima must have had the tea prepared, for she arrived with it instantly, together
with a plate of sugar biscuits. Scurrying after her
came the small boy who had opened the front
door to him, accompanied by the bravest of his
three small sisters. Climbing the stairs behind Ismail, Brue had felt a single bead of sweat trickle
down his right side like a very cold insect. But
now they were settled he was calm and professional. He had entered his element. He had
Lantern's brief well rehearsed in his head, and a
job to do. And always out there in front of him
somewhere, Annabel.

"Dr. Abdullah. Forgive me," he began, striking
a note of authority.

"But, sir, what have I to forgive?"

"My client, as I mentioned to you on the
phone, insists on a high degree of confidentiality.
His situation is, to say the least, delicate. I feel we
should conduct our business alone. I'm sorry."

"But you don't even propose to tell me his
name, Mr. Brue! How can I put your esteemed
client at risk if I don't know who he is?"

He murmured a few words in Arabic. Fatima
rose and without a glance at Brue left the room,
followed by the small children and finally Ismail.
Waiting till the door had closed behind them,
Brue drew an unsealed envelope from his pocket
and placed it on Dr. Abdullah's desk.

"You have come all this way to write to me?" Dr. Abdullah asked humorously; then, seeing Brue's earnest expression, pulled on a pair of scratched reading spectacles, opened the envelope, unfolded the sheet of paper and studied the column of figures typed on it. Then he took off the spectacles, passed his hand across his face and put them on again.

"Is this a joke, Mr. Brue?"

"A rather expensive one, wouldn't you say?"

"Expensive for you?"

"For me personally, no. For my bank, yes. No bank enjoys saying good-bye to sums that size."

Unpersuaded, Dr. Abdullah took another look at the figures. "I am not accustomed to saying hullo to them either, Mr. Brue. What am I to do? Say thank you? Say no thank you? Say yes? You are a banker, sir. I am a humble beggar for God. Are my prayers being answered or are you making a fool of me?"

"However, there are conditions," Brue warned severely, choosing to ignore the question.

"I am very glad to hear it. The more conditions the better. Do you have any idea how much money all my charities put together collect in this hemisphere in one year?"

"None at all."

"I thought bankers knew everything. One-third of this sum at the very most. More like one-quarter. Allah is all-merciful."

Abdullah was still staring at the sheet of paper on his desk, his hands placed proprietorially either side of it. In a long banking life Brue had been privileged to witness men and women of all conditions awakening to the scale of their newfound wealth. Never had he seen a more radiant picture of innocent rapture than the good doctor now.

"You have no concept of what such a sum would mean to my people," he said, and to Brue's embarrassment his eyes filled with tears, causing him to close them and lower his head. But when he lifted his head again, his voice was sharp and to the point.

"Am I permitted to inquire where so much money originated—how it was obtained—how it came into your client's hands?"

"Most of it has been lodged with my bank for a decade or two."

"But the money did not *begin* with your bank."

"Obviously not."

"So where did it *begin,* Mr. Brue?"

"The money is an inheritance. In my client's view it was dishonorably obtained. It has also been earning interest, which I understand is contrary to Islamic law. Before my client lays formal

claim to it, he needs to be assured that he is acting in accordance with his faith."

"You said there were conditions, Mr. Brue."

"In asking you to distribute his wealth among
your charitable institutions, my client wishes
Chechnya to be given principal consideration."

"Your client is Chechen, Mr. Brue?" As his
tone of voice softened again, so his eyes hardened
and fine wrinkles formed around them, as if
against a desert sun.

"My client has a deep concern for the plight of
the oppressed Chechen people," Brue replied,
again declining to answer the question. "His first
priority would be to provide them with medicine
and clinics."

"We have many Muslim charities dedicated to
this important work, Mr. Brue." The dark little
eyes still fixed on Brue's.

"It is my client's hope that one day he will
himself become a doctor. In order to heal the
wrongs done to Chechens."

"God alone heals, Mr. Brue. Man only assists.
How old is your client, if I may ask? Are we looking at a man of mature years? A man perhaps
who has made his own fortune in a legitimate
sphere?"

"Of whatever age and social standing he or
she is, my client is determined to study medicine,
and wishes to be the first beneficiary of his own

generosity. Rather than make direct use of money that he regards as unclean, he asks that a Muslim charity finance a full course of medical training for him here in Europe. The cost would be negligible by comparison with the donation. But it would give him the assurance that he is acting ethically. On all of these matters, he would like to receive guidance from you personally. In Hamburg, at a time and place convenient to you both."

Dr. Abdullah's gaze returned to the sheet of paper before him, and then to Brue.

"May I appeal to your best instincts, Mr. Brue?"

"Of course."

"You are an honorable man, it is plain to me. Kind and honorable. Never mind what else you are. A Christian, a Jew, I don't care. Only that you are what you appear to be. You are a father like me. You are also a man of the world."

"I like to think so."

"Then advise me, please, why I should trust you."

"Why should you not?"

"Because there is a bad taste in my mouth regarding this magnificent proposition."

You're not leading anyone to the slaughter, Lantern had said. *You're giving him a chance to go straight and do the decent thing. So no need to get into the* mea culpa *stuff. A year from now he'll be grateful to you.*

"If there's a bad taste, it's not of my making, and it's not of my client's. Perhaps it's to do with how the money was derived."

"So you said."

"My client is fully aware of the money's unhappy origin. He has discussed it at length with his lawyer, and you're the solution they came up with."

"He has a lawyer?"

"Yes."

"Here in Germany?"

The questioning had again taken a sharper turn, to which Brue was grateful to respond.

"Yes, indeed," he said heartily.

"A good one?"

"I assume so. Since he chose her."

"A woman, then. They are the best, I am told. Did your client take advice on choosing this woman lawyer?"

"I assume so."

"Is she a Muslim?"

"You would have to ask her that yourself."

"Is your client a trusting man like me, Mr. Brue?"

This is what you tell him and no more, Lantern

had said. *A flash of ankle, enough to lead him on, and stop it there.*

"My client is a man of tragic experience, Dr. Abdullah. Many injustices have been perpetrated against him. He has endured. He has resisted. But they have left him scarred."

"Therefore?"

"Therefore he has instructed my bank, through his lawyer, that the contaminated monies, as he regards them, will be transferred *directly* to the charities that you and he have agreed upon. In his presence and yours. From Brue Frères to the recipients. He wishes for no go-betweens. He is aware of your eminence, he has studied your writings and wishes for your guidance alone. But he needs to witness the transactions with his own eyes."

"Does your client speak Arabic?"

"Forgive me."

"German? French? English? If he is Chechen, he must speak Russian. Or maybe only Chechen?"

"Whatever language he speaks, I assure you that an appropriate interpreter will be provided."

Dr. Abdullah wistfully fingered the paper before him and, fixing his gaze on Brue once more, relapsed into his thoughts.

"You are jocular," he complained at last. "You are like a man freed. Why? Your bank is saying good-bye to a fortune and you smile, which makes you paradoxical. Is it your perfidious English smile?"

"Perhaps my English smile has a reason."

"Then perhaps it is the reason that troubles me."

"My client is not the only one who finds the origin of these monies distasteful."

"But money has no smell, they say. Not to a banker, surely?"

"All the same, I think I may say that my bank is breathing a small sigh of relief."

"Your bank's morality is to be admired then. Tell me something else, please."

"If I can."

The single bead of sweat had returned, this time on the other side of Brue's ribs.

"There is an *urgency* about all this. What *is* this urgency? What strange engine is driving us, exactly? Come, sir. We are two honest men. We are alone."

"My client is living on borrowed time. At any minute, he may cease to be in a position to authorize these donations. What I need as soon as possible from you is a list of your recommended charities and a description of the causes they serve. I'll then pass this to his lawyer, who will submit it to our client for his approval, and we can conclude our business."

As Brue rose to leave, Dr. Abdullah was once more his energetic, impish self.

"So I have no time and no alternative," he complained accusingly, shaking Brue's hand with both of his, and smiling up at him with his twinkly eyes.

"And neither have I," Brue agreed with equal good humor and in the same tone of complaint. "Until very soon, I hope."

"Then I wish you a most safe journey home, sir, to the bosom of your family, as we say. Allah be with you."

"And you look after yourself, too," said Brue with equal warmth as they awkwardly shook hands.

Returning to his car, Brue discovered that the sweat had drenched his shirt and made a wet band of the collar of his jacket. As he reached the autobahn, his two minders fell in behind him, grinning like idiots. Brue didn't know what he had done to amuse them. Or when he had hated himself more.

Ever since Brue's departure from Abdullah's house eight hours ago, Erna Frey and Günther Bachmann have barely exchanged a word, although they are sitting only inches apart behind Maximilian's bank of screens. One screen is

linked to the signals intelligence center in Berlin,
another to satellite surveillance, a third to a mo-
torized five-man team of Arni Mohr's watchers.

At 15:48 hours, in dead silence, they had listened with half-closed eyes to the Brue-Abdullah
exchange as relayed by Brue's listening fountain
pen to Lantern's watchers in the garage across
the road, and passed through to the stables after
encryption. Bachmann's one response was a
soundless clapping of his hands. Erna Frey made
no response at all.

At 17:10 hours came the first of a string of in-
tercepted phone calls from Abdullah's house. A
simultaneous translation from Arabic into German scrolled down the signals intelligence screen.
For Bachmann, the Arabic speaker, the translation was redundant. For Erna Frey and most of
Bachmann's team, it was not.

With each call, the name of the person contacted appeared at the bottom of the screen. A
parallel screen provided personal particulars and
trace details. The calls, six in all, were exclusively
to respectable Muslim fund-raisers and charity officials. None of the personalities contacted, according to side comments offered by the
researchers, was under current investigation.

The message to each person called was identi-
cal: We are in funds, my brothers, merciful Allah
in His infinite bounty has deemed us worthy of a

great, an historic gift. A quirk common to each conversation was that Dr. Abdullah pretended—not very convincingly—to be talking about a gift of American rice rather than U.S. dollars. By this simplistic code, millions then became tons.

His reason for dissembling, according to the side comment, was precautionary: he wished not to arouse by accident the appetite of any local employee who chanced to be listening in. There was little variation between the conversations. A single transcript could have done for all six.

"Twelve and a half *tons* best quality, my dear friend—*American tons*—have you got that?—yes, indeed, *tons*. Every grain of it to be distributed among the faithful. Yes, you old moron! *Tons.* Has God clapped His merciful hands over your stupid ears? There are conditions, you understand. Not many, but conditions all the same. Are you still listening? Our oppressed brethren in Chechnya receive the first consignment. Their hungry will be the first to be fed. And we shall train more doctors, *Inshallah.* Is that not wonderful? In Europe also. We have one candidate already!"

This particular call was made to one Shaykh Rashid Hassan, a longtime friend and former fellow student of Abdullah in Cairo, now residing in the English town of Weybridge in Surrey. Perhaps for the same reason it was the longest and

most intimate. However it ended cryptically, a
fact noted by the researchers.

Our good friend will no doubt call you later to dis-
cuss whatever is to be discussed, Abdullah promises.
The reply is a noncommittal grunt.

At 19:42 hours, the first live images appear:

Footage of Signpost emerging from his porch
looking very European in a pale Burberry raincoat and English-style country cap. He is alone.
A black Volvo waits at his front gate, its rear
door open to receive him.

Researchers' side note: The Volvo is registered to a
Turkish-owned car rental company in Flensburg, a
full hundred and fifty kilometers north of Hamburg.
Nothing is recorded against the company or its owners.

Signpost enters the back of the Volvo, assisted
by the elder of his two bodyguards, who sits
himself beside the driver. The surveillance camera changes point of view, falls in behind the
Volvo and follows it. Pious men drive themselves
unwillingly, Bachmann reflects. He is watching
the bodyguard in the front seat, who is watching
the rear and side mirrors.

The Volvo reaches the autobahn, continues
northeast for twenty, forty, fifty-seven kilometers.
Dusk is falling. The camera assumes the furry
green of a night-vision lens. For all this distance,

the silhouette of the bodyguard's head has continued to rotate between the car's mirrors. As the Volvo pulls into a rest area, his vigilance increases.

Bodyguard exits front of car and takes a pee while he appears to check the rest area for any unwelcome presence. He stares at camera, presumably checking Mohr's surveillance vehicle parked about fifty meters behind him.

Returning to the Volvo, the bodyguard opens the rear door, speaks into the car. Signpost emerges and, clutching his cap against the wind, advances on a glass phone booth at the eastern end of the rest area. He enters the booth and immediately inserts a check card that he has ready in his hand. *Idiot,* thinks Bachmann. But perhaps the card, like the Volvo, is not Signpost's own.

As Signpost dials, a name appears at the foot of one of Maximilian's screens. It is the same Shaykh Rashid Hassan of Weybridge whom Signpost has called from his house earlier this evening. But something odd has happened to Signpost's voice in the meantime as, belatedly, and a little out of sync, Berlin signals center picks it up.

At first, even Bachmann can barely disentangle what he is hearing. He has to turn to the simultaneous translation on the next-door screen for help. Signpost is talking Arabic all right, but in a heavy colloquial Egyptian dialect that he presumably believes will defeat the ear of any chance eavesdropper.

If so, he is mistaken. The simultaneous translator, whoever he is, must be a genius. He doesn't falter:

SIGNPOST: Is this Shaykh Rashid?

RASHID: I am Rashid.

SIGNPOST: I am Faisal, the cousin of your distinguished father-in-law.

RASHID: So?

SIGNPOST: I have a message for him. Can you convey it to him?

RASHID: (delayed reply) I can. *Inshallah.*

SIGNPOST: There has been a delay regarding delivery of artificial limbs and wheelchairs to his brother's hospital in Mogadishu.

RASHID: What of it?

SIGNPOST: The delay will be rectified immediately. Then he will be free to take his holiday in Cyprus. Can you give him that message? He will be happy.

RASHID: My father-in-law will be told. *Inshallah.*

Shaykh Rashid rings off.

14

"Frau Elli," Brue began, signaling the familiar routine.

"Mr. Tommy," Frau Ellenberger replied, preparing herself for another of their ritual exchanges. She was mistaken. This time, Brue was in executive mode.

"I'm pleased to say that as of this evening we shall be closing down the last of the Lipizzaner accounts, Frau Elli."

"I am relieved, Mr. Tommy. It is high time."

"I shall be receiving the claimant this evening after banking hours. That is his express wish."

"I have no engagements this evening. I shall be happy to remain behind," Frau Elli replied, with mysterious avidity.

Was she pressing to see the back of the Lipizzaners—or to meet the bastard son of Colonel Grigori Borisovich Karpov?

"Thank you, that won't be necessary, Frau Elli. The client insists on total privacy. However,

I would be grateful if you would exhume the appropriate papers and place them on my desk."

"I take it the claimant has a *key,* Mr. Tommy?"

"According to his lawyer, he has a very appropriate key. And we have *our* key. Where?"

"In the oubliette, Mr. Tommy. In the wall safe. Under double combination."

"Beside the safe boxes?"

"Beside the safe boxes."

"I always thought it was our policy to keep the safe-box keys as far away from the safe boxes as possible."

"That was in Mr. Edward's time. In Hamburg you adopted a more relaxed policy."

"Well, perhaps you'd be good enough to release the key for me."

"I shall have to ask the chief cashier for her assistance."

"Why?"

"She is the keeper of the other combination, Mr. Tommy."

"Of course. Do you have to tell her what it's about?"

"No, Mr. Tommy."

"Then kindly don't. And we're closing early today. I would like the bank cleared of everybody by three o'clock this afternoon latest."

"Everybody?"

"Everybody but me, if you don't mind."

"Very well, Mr. Tommy," she said.

But the anger in her face unsettled him, the more so since he couldn't understand it. By three in the afternoon the bank had been cleared, as instructed, and Brue telephoned Lantern to confirm. Within minutes came a ring at the door. Alone in the building, Brue trod cautiously downstairs to find four men in blue overalls standing on the doorstep, and parked behind them in the bank's forecourt a white van purporting to belong to the Three Oceans Electrical Company of Lübeck. In the trade, unsurprisingly, we call them buggers, Lantern had confided, preparing him for their invasion.

The eldest of the four had two piratical gold teeth.

"*Mr.* Brue?" he inquired, teeth flashing.

"What do you want?"

"We have an appointment to check your system, sir," he said in laborious English.

"Well, come on in," Brue replied grumpily in German. "Do whatever you have to do. Just don't muck up the plasterwork, if you don't mind."

He had told Lantern till he was blue in the face that Frères was stiff with video cameras inside and out. If Lantern's *buggers* really needed to put in more of the same, why didn't they simply adapt the existing wiring? But this wasn't good enough for the people Lantern now referred to as "our German friends." For the next hour, Brue prowled his office impotently while the men went about their work: hall, reception area, staircase, the computer room where the cashiers sat, the secretaries' room, the lavatories, the oubliette, which he had to unlock for them with his personal set of keys.

"And now, please, your own room, Mr. Brue, sir. If you permit," said the man with the gold-toothed smile.

Brue hung about downstairs while they defiled his office. Yet, search for damage as he might, nowhere did he find a trace of their handiwork. And when he repossessed his own quarters, they too appeared untouched.

With meaningless expressions of respect, the men departed and Brue, alone again and suddenly feeling it, slumped in a heap at his desk, unwilling even to stretch out his hand towards the stack of aging Lipizzaner papers that Frau Ellenberger had left there for his attention.

But soon a different Brue asserted himself, whether the old one or a new version was irrelevant. He was Brue redux. Striding across the room, hands thrust into his pockets, he peered intently at the original, hand-painted Brue family tree that for thirty-five years had been the daily reminder of his inadequacy. Have our German friends stuck one of their bugs behind it? Is the great founder himself spying on my every move?

Well, let him. In a few weeks from now he'll be spying from a green wheelie bin.

Swinging on his heel he glared back into the room: *my* room, *my* partners' desk, *my* wooden bloody clotheshorse by Randall's of Glasgow, *my* bookcase: not my father's, not *his* father's and not *his* father's. And the books in it, even if I've never opened them: mine too. And it is time they knew that; time I knew it myself. Mine to do what I like with. To burn, or sell or donate to the wretched of the earth.

So bugger them. As *I* have just been *buggered,* ha-ha.

And having thought this little obscenity— and mulled it over, and savored it—he repeated it aloud, courteously and in good English, first for Lantern's sake, then for Lantern's German friends, and finally for all his listeners everywhere. Were they switched on yet? Bugger that too.

Then with great deliberation he went about setting the scene: Issa sits here, Abdullah there and I'll be sticking here behind my desk.

And Annabel?

Annabel does *not* get relegated to the back of

the class, thank you. Not in my house. She's here as my guest and she'll bloody well get the treatment *I* say she deserves.

And so thinking, he spotted his grandfather's chair lurking in the darkest corner to which he had consigned it, the hideous, overcarved chair with the Brue crest on its top, and the Brue tartan embroidered on its faded upholstery. Dragging it out of retirement, he tossed a couple of cushions into it and stood back to admire his handiwork: that's how she likes to sit, bolt upright, disturb me at your peril.

As a last touch, he marched to his fridge in the alcove, fetched a couple of bottles of still mineral water and set them on the coffee table so that they would be at room temperature by the time she arrived. He thought of pouring himself a scotch while he was about it, but resisted. There was one last vital piece of business to transact before the evening's conference began, and he was really looking forward to it.

Brue had insisted on the Atlantic without supplying any reason. Lantern, having made a reconnaissance, had meekly approved his choice. The time was seven o'clock, the same hour exactly at which he and Annabel had first met. The same scents pervaded the lobby. The same Herr

Schwarz was on duty. The same babel issued from the bar. The same unappreciated pianist was playing tunes of love as Brue took up his same position beneath the same mercantile paintings, and kept his eyes trained on the same swing doors. Only the weather was different. A low spring sun was beating down the street, freeing the passersby and making them taller. Or so it seemed to Brue, perhaps because he felt freer and taller himself.

He had arrived early, but Lantern and his two boys had arrived earlier and were seated like three middle executives between Brue's corner and the swing doors, presumably to head him off in case he made a dash for it with Issa's passport. Across the aisle and short of the entrance to the grill room sat the two women who had hurried to Annabel's aid at Louise's restaurant. They looked ready to do it again: unsmiling and methodical as they engaged in unconvincing dialogue over a city map.

She had shed her rucksack.

It was the first thing Brue noticed about her as she navigated the swing doors. No rucksack, a slower tread, no bicycle. A sand-colored Volvo had delivered her to the door and it wasn't a taxi, so it must have been her minders' car that had delivered her.

She was wearing the same scarf round her neck

that she had worn as a *hijab* at Leyla's house. The stern legal-black skirt and long-sleeved blouse and jacket at first came as a mild surprise to him. They suggested a lawyer who was about to make a court appearance, or had just made one, until he remembered that he too had selected his darkest suit for tonight's appointment with Dr. Abdullah.

"Water?" he suggested carefully. "No lemon? Room temperature? The mixture as before?"

She said, "Yes, please," but didn't smile.

He ordered two waters, one for himself. Shaking hands with her, he allowed himself only a sideways glance at her face for fear of what he might see. She looked drawn and sleepless. Her lips were pressed together in self-control.

"And I think you have your escorts here, do you not?" he said, deliberately jovial. "We could send them over a drink, if you like. Bottle of champagne."

A Georgie-like shrug.

He was camping for her deliberately. He was playing the English bloody fool. He was using comedy in a way it had no business to be used, but it was the only way he knew. He was an old ham actor, preparing her for her big scene, and wanting to show her that he loved her.

"I reckon you're a bit underprotected, actually, Annabel. Given what we seem to be worth to our handlers. You've only got two of the beasts, whereas I've got three. Mine are over there, if you'd care to take a look." He gestured pointedly in their direction. "The undersized young fellow in the suit is their leading intellect. Lantern, his name is. Ian Lantern of the British embassy in Berlin, you can check him out with the ambassador any time. The other two are— well, a bit *sub,* frankly. Not a lot between the ears. I assume you also are wearing a listening device?"

"Yes."

Had he seen the beginning of a smile? He believed he had. "Good. Then we're sure of a decent audience. Or do you think"—as if a sudden anxiety had struck him—"or do you think your beasts only hear *you,* and mine only hear *me?* No, that simply *can't* be, can it? I'm no electronic whiz, but they can't be on different *wavelengths.* Or can they?" He peered to left and right over her shoulder, affecting to check. "One really shouldn't worry about them so much," he said, shaking his head in self-reproach. "After all, *we're* the stars tonight. They're just audience. All *they* can do is listen," he explained, and was rewarded with a smile so heartening, so utterly undefended, that it was like a whole new world to luxuriate in.

"You've got his passport," she said, still with the smile. "They told me you were being kind."

"Well, kind I don't know, but I thought you'd

like a sight of it. I thought *I'd* quite like a sight of it too. These days, one simply has no idea who one's dealing with. I can't *give* it to you yet, unfortunately. I can only show it to you, then hand it back to young Mr. Lantern on our right, who will hand it back to one of *your* people, who will then *activate* it, if that's the expression, once our client has done what he intends—and is intended—to do."

He was holding the passport out to her. Not covertly, just offering her a passport across the table with an ostentation that caused both groups of watchers to abandon all pretense of doing anything except watch them.

"Or are there variants on your side of the house?" he went on breezily. "Vital to *compare versions* with these people, I find. They're not what we might call overburdened with truthfulness. Here's how they described it to me. You bring our client to the bank, he makes his dispositions and is then taken—*directly,* I am assured—to an establishment of which I am not permitted to know the address, where he will fill in some forms in triplicate and be handed his German passport. This very one we have here, which will then come immediately to life. Does that accord? Or do we have a problem?"

"It accords," she said.

She took the passport from him and examined

it. First the photograph, then a few innocent entry and exit stamps, nothing too new. Then the expiry date, three years and seven months from now.

"I'll need to go with him to collect this," she said, delighting him with her old decisiveness.

"Of course you will. As his lawyer, you'll have no choice."

"He's sick. He needs time out."

"Of course he does. And after tonight, he can take all the time out he wants," said Brue. "And I have a little document for you *personally*." He took back the passport and placed an unsealed envelope into her waiting hand. "Don't bother to look at it now. It's not an embarrassing jewel, I'm afraid. Just a bit of paper. But it sets *you* free too. No vindictive prosecutions or anything of that sort, provided you don't do it again, though I naturally hope you will. And it thanks you for being *aboard,* so to speak. That's about the nearest they come to a proposal of marriage in this business."

"I don't care about being set free."

"Well now, I really think you should," he replied.

But this time he spoke in Russian, not in German, which to his pleasure caused a violent flutter in the two camps either side of the aisle. Heads whipped up, heads consulted each other desperately across the aisle: Is there a Russian speaker among us? By their mystified expressions, there wasn't.

"So now that we have each other alone for a few minutes—or I hope we have," Brue went on in his classical Paris-learned Russian, "there are a couple of highly personal and top secret matters I should like to take up with you. May I do that?"

To his joy, her face had brightened magically.

"You may do that, Mr. Brue."

"You said about my bank. My fucking bank. Without it, he wouldn't be here. Well, now he's here. And he can stay here, we believe. Do you still wish he hadn't come?"

"No."

"I'm relieved. I also wish you to know that I have a much-loved daughter named Georgina. I call her Georgie for short. She is the child of an early marriage I contracted at a time in my life when I didn't understand the nature of marriage. Or for that matter, love. I was unfit for marriage and unfit for fatherhood. That is no longer the case. Georgie is going to have a baby and I shall learn to be a grandfather."

"That's wonderful."

"Thank you. I've been waiting to tell someone, and now I have, so I'm pleased. Georgie is a depressive. I mistrust jargon of that kind, but in her case I am persuaded that the diagnosis fits the condition. She has to be *balanced*. I think that's the term. She lives in California. With a writer. She was also in her time anorexic. She became like a starved bird. There was nothing one could do. So it was a bad story. The divorce didn't help. She wisely took herself to America. To California. Where she is now."

"You said."

"I'm sorry. My point is, she has got herself into clear water. I spoke to her just a few nights ago. I sometimes think, the greater the distance on the telephone, the easier it is to hear whether she's happy. She did have a baby before, but it died. This one won't, I'm sure of it. I know it won't. I'm losing my point. Forgive me. It occurred to me that, when this is over, I'd give myself some time off and slip over and see her. Maybe stay awhile. The bank is dying, frankly. I can't say I'll miss it. Everything has its natural lifespan. And then I thought: once I'm there and installed for a bit, and you're in clear water too, you might care to join us for a few days—at my expense, obviously—bring someone if you wish—and get to know Georgie a bit, and her baby. And her husband, who I'm sure is appalling."

"I'd like to."

"You don't have to answer now. It's not a pass. Just think about it. That's all I meant to say. So now we can go back to German before our audience gets too restive."

"I'll come," she said, still in Russian. "I'd like to. I don't have to think about it. I know I would."

"Excellent," he resumed in German now, checking his watch as if establishing how long he'd been away from his desk. "I have one other piece of business, and that is Dr. Abdullah's wish list for Chechnya. He has general proposals concerning the Muslim community at large, but this is a shortlist of his recommendations for Chechnya. He thought our client might care to run his eye over them ahead of tonight's conference. Perhaps it will make the time go by more easily. May I say, I look forward to seeing you both at ten o'clock this evening?"

"You may," she said. "You *may,*" and with a vigorous nod to emphasize the words, turned and walked stiffly towards the swing doors, where her escorts were already waiting for her.

"Nothing seditious, Ian," Brue assured Lantern lightly, as he handed back Issa's passport. "Just taking our free will for a walk."

It was half past eight when Annabel's women dropped her at the harbor front to climb the stairs alone to her attic apartment for what she now thought of as the last time: the last time Issa was her prisoner and she was his, the last time they would listen to Russian music by the harbor lights flickering in the arched window, the last time she would have him as her child to feed and humor, as her untouchable lover and as her tutor in unbearable pain and hope. In one hour, she would deliver him to Brue and Dr. Abdullah. In one hour, Bachmann and Erna Frey would have what they wanted. With Issa's help, they would have saved more innocent lives than the Sanctuary could save in a lifetime—except how do you ever count the unkilled?

"These are Dr. Abdullah's recommendations?" Issa inquired, in a somewhat imperious tone, standing beneath the downlight at the center of the room while he read.

"A few of them. He's put Chechnya at the top of the list. As you asked."

"He is wise. This charity he names here is well known in Chechnya. I have heard of this charity. It takes medicines and bandages to our brave fighters in the mountains, also anesthetics. We shall support this charity."

"Good."

"But first of all we must save the children of Grozny," he said, as he read further. "And afterwards the widows. Young women who have been

defiled without their complicity will not be punished but, God willing, accommodated in special
hotels. Even if their complicity is in question,
they will be accommodated. That is my wish."

"Good."

"Nobody will be punished, even by their fami-
lies. We shall appoint expert caretakers for these
women." He shuffled a page. "Children of the
martyrs will be favored, that is Allah's will. But
provided only that their fathers have not killed
the innocent. If they have killed the innocent,
which is not permitted by Allah, we shall nevertheless accommodate them. You agree with this,
Annabel?"

"It sounds great. A bit confused, but great,"
she said, smiling.

"Also *this* charity I admire. I have not heard of
it, but I admire it. The education of our children
has been neglected in our long war for indepen-
dence."

"Why not put a tick against the ones you like?
Have you got a pencil?"

"I like all of them. I like you also, Annabel."

He folded up the list and shoved it in his
pocket.

Don't say it, she was begging him from her
place at the far end of the loft. Don't make me
promise. Don't paint the unlivable dream. I'm
not strong enough for this. *Stop!*

"When you have converted to God's faith, which is the religion of my mother and my people, and I am an important doctor with a Western qualification and a car like Mr. Brue's, I shall devote all my nonprofessional time to your comfort. That is my assurance to you, Annabel. When you are not too pregnant, you will be a nurse in my hospital. I have noticed you have great compassion when you are not being severe. But first you must be trained. A legal qualification is not sufficient to become a nurse."

"I don't suppose it is."

"Are you listening, Annabel? Please concentrate."

"I'm just watching the clock, that's all. Mr. Brue wants us there well ahead of Dr. Abdullah. You need to make your claim first, even if you don't want to accept the money."

"I am aware of this, Annabel. I am conversant with such technicalities. That is why his limousine is coming to collect me here in good time. Are Melik and Leyla coming to the ceremony?"

"No. They're in Turkey."

"Then I am sad. They would draw comfort from what I am about to do. I shall provide our children with a wide and varied education. Not in Chechnya, unfortunately, it is too hazardous. First they will study the Koran, afterwards, literature and music. They will aspire to the Five Excellences. If they fail, they will not be punished. We shall love them, and pray with them many times. Personally, I am not proficient in the steps that are necessary to your conversion. A wise imam must undertake the task. Once I have formed a personal opinion of this Dr. Abdullah, whose writings I respect, I shall consider whether he is appropriate. I have never insulted you, Annabel."

"I know."

"And you have not attempted to seduce me. There have been moments when I feared you were about to. But you controlled yourself."

"I think we should start to get ourselves ready, don't you?"

"We will play Rachmaninoff."

Crossing to the arched window, he switched on the disc player. It was set at the high volume that he liked when he was alone. Huge chords boomed into the rafters. He turned to the window and she watched his silhouette as he methodically dressed himself for the journey. Karsten's leather jacket no longer appealed to him. He preferred his old black coat and woolen cap, and the yellow saddlebag across his shoulder.

"So Annabel. You will follow me, please. I will protect you. That is our tradition."

But at the door he stopped dead, and stared at her with such unprecedented frankness that for a moment she really believed he was about to close it again and keep her inside with him, in order to continue forever the life they had shared up here alone in their own world.

And perhaps she half hoped he would, but by then he was heading down the stairs and it was too late. A long black limousine was waiting. The driver was holding open the rear door. He was young and blond, a boy in his prime. She climbed in. The driver waited for Issa to follow her, but he declined. The driver opened the passenger door and he got in.

Brue led the way to his sanctum, followed by Issa then Annabel in her legal black suit and headscarf. Issa, he had at once observed, was a changed character. The pious Muslim fugitive had become a Red Army colonel's millionaire son. Entering the hall, he glowered round him with disdain, as if the bank's noble premises weren't quite what he was accustomed to. Seating himself uninvited in the chair Brue had intended for Annabel, he folded his arms and crossed his legs, waiting to be addressed, thereby incidentally relegating Annabel to the end of the row.

"Frau Richter, do you not wish to come a little nearer to us?" Brue asked her, in the Russian they all spoke.

"Thank you, Mr. Brue, I'm very comfortable," she replied with her newfound smile.

"Then I'll begin," Brue announced, swallowing his disappointment.

And began, despite the curious sensation of speaking to a packed hall rather than two people sitting six feet away from him. On behalf of Brue Frères, he welcomed Issa formally as the son of a long-standing client of the bank—but tactfully refrained from offering his condolences for the client's passing.

Issa bridled, but nodded his acknowledgment. Brue cleared his throat. In the circumstances, he said, he proposed to keep formal proceedings to a minimum. He had been advised by Issa's lawyer— with a small bow in Annabel's direction—that Issa proposed to claim his inheritance on condition that, immediately thereafter, he dispose of it to selected Muslim charitable organizations.

"I am further informed that for this purpose you will be guided by the noted religious authority Dr. Abdullah, to whom I have referred your instructions. Dr. Abdullah is pleased to be joining us shortly."

"It will be the guidance of Allah," Issa corrected him in a surly growl, addressing not Brue but the golden Koranic bracelet he was clutching in his hand. "It will be God's will, sir."

To which end—Brue continued undeterred—

he would under more normal conditions require the claimant to identify himself. However—thanks to the persuasive powers of Frau Richter, he said with emphasis—he felt able to dispense with that formality, and proceed without delay to the claim—again addressing Annabel—if that was still her client's wish.

"It is, sir! I claim," Issa cried before she could reply. "I claim for all Muslims! I claim for Chechnya!"

"Well, in that case, perhaps you'll follow me," said Brue. And picked a small, cleverly engineered key from his in tray.

The door to the oubliette creaked open. After the technicians' departure, Brue had engaged only one of its systems. The safe boxes were stacked along one wall, dark green, two keyholes apiece. Edward Amadeus, who adored silly names for things, had called it his dovecote. Some of the boxes, Brue knew, had not been opened for fifty years. Now perhaps they never would be. He turned to Annabel and saw that her face was alight and filled with cautious eagerness. Her eyes full on him, she presented him with Issa's letter from Anatoly, with the number of the box inked in heavy numerals. He knew it by heart. He knew the box by heart, though not its contents:

more battered than its neighbors, it put him in mind of a Russian ammunition box. The inscription on its label—a stained yellowed card held at its four corners by a miniature iron claw—was done in Edward Amadeus's own pedantic hand: LIP— a stroke, the number and then the legend: *no action without reference to EAB.*

"Your key, sir, kindly?" he inquired of Issa.

Returning his bracelet to his wrist, Issa unbuttoned his long coat and delved in his shirtfront for the chamois leather purse. Loosening its throat, he drew out the key and thrust it at Brue.

"I'm afraid this is something *you* must do, Issa," Brue told him with a paternal smile. "I've got one of my own, you see." And he held up the bank's key for Issa to look at.

"Does Issa go first?" Annabel asked, with the pleasure of a child at a party game.

"I think it's customary, don't you, Frau Richter?"

"Issa, do as Mr. Brue asks, please. Put your key in the lock and turn it."

Issa stepped forward and rammed his key into the left-hand lock. But when he attempted to turn it, it stuck. Thwarted, he pulled out the key and tried the right-hand lock. It turned. He stepped back. Brue stepped forward and, with the bank's key, turned the left-hand lock. Then he too stepped back.

Side by side, Brue and Annabel looked on as Colonel Grigori Borisovich Karpov's son, with unmixed revulsion, took possession of his late father's ill-gotten millions, as salted away for him by the late Edward Amadeus, OBE, at the behest of British Intelligence. At first look, the contents of the box did not amount to much: one large, oily envelope, unsealed, unaddressed.

Issa's emaciated hands were shaking. His face, under the overhead light, was once more a prison face of pits and shadows, cast in an expression of disgust. With his forefinger and thumb, he fastidiously drew out a length of engraved paper like a large banknote. Tucking the envelope under his arm to reuse another day, he unfolded the document and, with his back turned to Brue and Annabel, examined it—but as an artifact rather than for any information it might contain, since the writing on it was in German, not Russian.

"Perhaps Frau Richter would care to do the translating upstairs," Brue suggested softly, after a minute or more had gone by without Issa stirring.

"Richter?" Issa repeated, as if he had never heard the name.

"Annabel. Frau Richter. Your lawyer. The lady to whom you owe your presence here tonight, and a great deal else, if I may say so."

Returning from wherever he had gone, Issa passed the document to Annabel, then the envelope.

"This is money, Annabel?"

"It will be," she said.

Upstairs once more, Brue went out of his way to appear perfunctory, fearing that Issa, confronted with the physical reality of his father's monstrosity, might recant. Annabel, perhaps sharing his anxiety, was quick to take her cue from him. She briskly marched her client through the terms and conditions of his bearer bond, and asked him whether he had any questions, to all of which Issa shrugged in vague acquiescence. He had no questions. There was a receipt for him to sign, and Brue handed it to Annabel, inviting her to explain its purpose to her client. Quietly and patiently, she told Issa what *receipt* meant.

It meant that, until he gave the money away again, it was his. If on signing the receipt he wished to change his mind and keep the money, or look for some other use for it, he was free to do so. And it occurred to Brue that, in saying this to Issa, Annabel was placing loyalty to her client above loyalty to her handlers and manipulators; and that this was a matter of principle to her as well as a considerable act of courage, risking everything she had been brought here to do.

But Issa had no intention of changing his mind. With the pen waving in his right hand, and the bunched fingers of his left hand pressed to his brow, and the gold chain peeking from them, Issa signed the receipt in a series of angry slashes. Momentarily careless of her Muslim manners, Annabel reached out to take the pen from him, inadvertently brushing her hand against his. He recoiled, but she took it all the same.

A financial statement had been prepared by the manager of the Liechtenstein foundation. By virtue of the bearer bond and now the signed receipt, Issa was the foundation's sole owner. The sum total of all his assets, as relayed by Brue to Dr. Abdullah, was twelve and a half million American dollars; or as Dr. Abdullah had preferred to describe it to his friend in Weybridge, Surrey, twelve and a half tons of American rice.

"Issa," said Annabel, in an effort to wake him from his trance.

Staring at the bearer bond, Issa passed his palms over his hollowed cheeks, as his lips moved silently in prayer. And Brue, who knew of old all the little signs of sudden acquisition—the suppressed light of greed, of triumph, of relief—looked in vain for them in Issa, just as he had looked in vain for them in Abdullah; or if he saw them at all, saw them first transmit themselves to Annabel, then vanish as soon as they appeared.

"So then," he said brightly, "on the assumption that we have no further matters to discuss, what I have suggested to Frau Richter that we *do*—and indeed what we have provisionally *done* subject to your approval, Issa—is place this entire sum temporarily on account with our own bank, in such a way that it can be *instantly* transferred, by wire, to the beneficiaries that you and Dr. Abdullah, in the light of your ethical and religious concerns, decide upon"—he shot out an arm and glanced at his costly watch—"in, well, seven minutes from now, say. Less, if I'm not mistaken."

He was not. A car was pulling up in the forecourt. A muted exchange of Arab voices followed. The driver and his passenger were saying good-bye to each other. Brue caught an *Inshallah* and recognized Dr. Abdullah's voice. He caught a *salaam* in farewell. The car drove away and a single pair of footsteps approached the front porch.

"Forgive me one moment, please, Frau Richter," he said officiously and bustled downstairs for the next act.

Arni Mohr was proud of his new surveillance van, and had parted with it only on condition that it be deployed outside the exclusion zone that he and the police had drawn around Brue's bank. Inside the zone: Arni's street watchers and police shooters; outside the zone, the van, Bachmann, his team of two, and one empty cream-colored taxi, plastered with advertisements. That was the deal approved by Keller and Burgdorf, unsuccessfully contested by Axelrod and accepted under protest by Bachmann.

"I can't afford to fight them on every pissy point of detail, Günther," Axelrod had insisted with more desperation in his voice than Bachmann would have wished. "If I've got to give away a few pawns for their queen, that's all right by me," he added, recalling the games of chess that Bachmann and Axelrod used to play in the air-raid shelter underneath the German embassy in Beirut.

"But the queen *is* ours, right?" Bachmann had insisted anxiously.

"On the terms described, yes. If you can get Signpost to your safe flat and if you can talk to him on the lines we agreed, and if he shows signs of playing ball, he's ours. Does that answer your question?"

No. It doesn't. It makes me ask why you need three ifs to say yes.

It doesn't explain what Martha was doing at the meeting, or why she brought Newton the throat-slitter of Beirut along with her.

Or who the hatchet-faced ash-blonde with broad shoulders was.

Or why she had to be smuggled into the conference room like forbidden goods after everybody had sat down and smuggled out afterwards like a hotel hooker.

And why Axelrod, who resented the American presence as much as Bachmann did, had been unable to prevent it; and why Burgdorf had apparently condoned it.

The van, unlike the rest of its kind, was not got up as a pantechnicon, or a removals van or a container lorry, but as the lumbering gray street-cleaning leviathan it once had been, complete with its original fittings. It was also, Arni liked to boast, invisible. Nobody questioned its presence, least of all late at night when it was crawling round the city center. It could operate in movement as happily as when stationary. It could patrol a street at three kilometers an hour and nobody could say a thing.

For its location, Bachmann had chosen a lay-by between the Alster shore and the main road, just half a kilometer from Brue's bank. Under the glow of the orange streetlights, his team could admire a coppice of chestnut trees through the windscreen and, through concealed arrow slits in the rear, the bronze statue of two little girls eternally about to launch their kites.

In contrast to Mohr, Bachmann had kept his numbers to a minimum and his game plan simple. To monitor the bank of video screens and satellite imagery, he had recruited, in addition to Maximilian, his inseparable girlfriend, Niki, who spoke fluent Russian and Arabic. To give himself backup in any unforeseen emergency, he had posted two of his street watchers in a souped-up Audi, to sit just outside the exclusion zone until summoned. Bachmann alone, for as long as he remained in the van, would handle all contact with Arni Mohr and with Axelrod at Joint in Berlin. He had implored Erna Frey to accompany him, but once again she had resolutely refused to be talked round.

"That poor child has had all she can take of me, and much more than she knows," she had replied. And conscious of his stare upon her, after a prolonged delay: "I lied to her. We said we never would. We said we would never tell her the whole truth, but whatever we did tell her would be true."

"And?"

"I lied to her."

"So you said. What about?"

"Melik and Leyla."

"And what, pray, did you tell her about Melik and Leyla that was a lie?"

"Don't interrogate me, Günther."

"I *am* interrogating you."

"You may have forgotten that I have a Deep Throat in Arni Mohr's camp."

"The bad tennis player. I have not forgotten. What has the bad tennis player to do with lying to Annabel about Melik and Leyla?"

"Annabel was worried about them. It was the middle of the night. She came to my room and wanted my reassurance that Melik and Leyla were not going to suffer for taking in Issa. For being decent people doing the right thing. She said she'd been dreaming about them. But I think she'd just been lying awake, worrying."

"And you said?"

"That they would enjoy Leyla's daughter's wedding, and come back refreshed and happy, and Melik would beat all comers in the boxing ring, and Leyla would find a new husband and everything would be wonderful for them ever after. It was a fairy tale."

"Why was it a fairy tale?"

"Arni Mohr and Dr. Keller of Cologne have recommended that their permit of residence be withdrawn on the grounds that they have violated its conditions by harboring an Islamist criminal and encouraging militancy in the Turkish community. They propose that the authorities in Ankara be informed. Burgdorf is in agreement, provided their detention in Turkey does not take place in such a way as to endanger the Signpost operation."

Upon which she had demonstratively closed down her computer, locked her papers in the steel cupboard and removed herself to the safe flat on the harbor front to prepare for Signpost's late-night arrival.

Alone and sick with anger, Bachmann appealed once more to Axelrod. The response was as bad as he feared.

"For Christ's sake, Günther! How many battles do you want me to fight up here? Do you want me to barge in on Burgdorf and tell him we've been spying on the protectors?"

Over the past two hours operational intelligence had been flowing into the van at a steady rate and all of it was good.

Signpost's tour of the previous night had evidently been an aberration, since according to his known behavior pattern he did not use pay phones. Neither was it his habit to leave his house, wife and children unguarded in the hours of darkness. Tonight he proposed to follow his customary practice of calling on the services of a retired civil engineer, obliging friend and neighbor: a Palestinian named Fuad, who liked nothing better in life than to chauffeur the great

religious scholar on his rounds and exchange pro-
fundities with him. Last night, Fuad had been attending a lecture at his local cultural institute.
Tonight he was free, and Signpost's two minders
could remain on guard at the house, where they
belonged.

But where would Signpost stay the night in
Hamburg after his conference at the bank—or
where did he *think* he was going to stay? If
friends were awaiting him—if he had booked a
hotel—if he proposed to drive home late and
sleep in his own bed—Bachmann's license of
eight hours with him might be reduced to three
or four.

But on this point at least the gods had smiled
on the planners. Signpost had accepted an invitation to sleep at the house of Fuad's brother-in-
law, an Iranian named Cyrus, where he often
stayed, and Cyrus had provided Fuad with a
house key since he and his family were visiting
friends in Lübeck and would not be back till
morning.

Better still, Signpost would make his own way
there once his business at the bank was con-
cluded. Fuad had begged to be allowed to wait
outside the bank for him, but Signpost had been
adamant.

"You will please go immediately to your
dear brother-in-law, whom God preserve, and

be at ease, Fuad," he had urged him over his house telephone. "That is my command to you, dear friend. Your heart is too large for your breast. If you are not careful, Allah will pluck you to Him before your time. I shall order myself a taxi directly from the bank, don't worry yourself."

Hence the empty taxi, parked alongside the van.

Hence Bachmann's mug shot mounted in cellophane on the city license above the taxi's dashboard.

Hence Bachmann's humble jacket and seaman's cap hanging on the door to the belly of the van. If everything went according to plan, this was the garb he would be wearing when he delivered the hijacked Signpost to the safe flat on the harbor front for his forced conversion to the path of righteousness.

"I need three wishes to come true by first light," Erna Frey had told him, before she made her demonstrative exit. "I need Signpost in the bag. I need Felix and that poor girl to be put back into the wild and I need you sitting in the train with a one-way ticket to Berlin. Economy class."

"And for yourself?"

"My pension and my oceangoing yacht."

*   *   *

Signpost was due at Brue Frères at 22:00 hours.

At 20:30, according to incoming reports from Mohr's watchers, Fuad had driven up to Signpost's door in his brand-new BMW 335i coupe, the pride of his life. Word of its intended use had arrived too late for it to be bugged.

Emerging from his house, Signpost appeared in good spirits. His instruction to his wife and family, picked up from directional microphones across the road, was to be vigilant and praise God. The listeners claimed to detect a "sense of occasion" in his voice. One said "foreboding," another that he spoke "like he was going on a long journey and didn't know when he'd be back."

At 21:14, helicopter surveillance reported the safe arrival of the BMW in a northwestern suburb of the town, where it pulled into a parking area for the presumed purposes of prayer and killing time until Signpost's appointment at the bank. Contrary to Arab custom, Signpost was known to be obsessively punctual.

At 21:16—two minutes later, therefore—Bachmann's street watchers signaled the safe pickup of Felix and Annabel for transfer to Brue's bank by the limousine that Felix had insisted on, and Arni Mohr had been happy to provide.

From his exclusion zone Mohr confirmed their safe arrival. This was totally unnecessary, since

Bachmann had watched it on Maximilian's screen, but then Arni Mohr had never been a stranger to duplication.

At 21:29, Bachmann learned from no less a source than Axelrod in Berlin that Ian Lantern had contrived to wangle himself inside the exclusion zone and was parked in a cul-de-sac with a ringside view of the bank and one *unidentified passenger* in the front seat of his Peugeot.

Aghast, but by now in operational mode, Bachmann knew better than to scream in outrage. Instead, he asked Axelrod over the encrypted phone, quietly and collectedly, on whose precise authority Lantern had been invited to attend the party.

"He's got as much right to be there as you have, Günther," Axelrod pointed out.

"More, apparently."

"You've got your girl to worry about, he's got his banker."

But this explanation made no sense to Bachmann. Granted Lantern was Brue's controller. But was he also on standby to hold Brue's hand and help him with his lines if he fluffed? The only job left to Lantern that Bachmann was aware of was to scoop up his joe as soon as the meeting finished, mop his brow, debrief him and tell him how great he was. And for that, he did *not* need to hang around like a pregnant father just a hundred meters from the target house. And who in heaven's name was his passenger? How did he or she get in on the act?

But Axelrod had rung off, and Maximilian was holding up his arm. Fuad the retired engineer had delivered Signpost to Brue Frères Bank.

15

Inside Tommy Brue's upstairs sanctum, the preparations he had made were at last paying off. By assigning his grandfather's chair to Our Esteemed Interpreter, as he insisted on calling her, he had been able to wheedle her into center position. She sat, exactly as he had wanted her to, bolt upright on the cushions. To her left sat Issa and to her right Dr. Abdullah, facing Brue across his desk. At the sight of him, Issa had once more become a changed man, uncertain, shy and confused to discover that he possessed no common language with which to address his newfound mentor. Dr. Abdullah had greeted him first in Arabic, then French, English and German in quick order. He even found a few words of Chechen for Issa, who for a moment sparked, then stared shamefully downward as his fluency ran dry.

Dr. Abdullah too was in Brue's eyes a changed man since yesterday. Nervous himself, Brue had not imagined Abdullah could be more nervous still. Advancing gingerly on Issa with his arms lifted for the Arab embrace, he had seemed until the last minute uncertain whether he should go through with the greeting. His speech, once he had settled for German and Annabel's translation, displayed a guarded reverence, but it was also searching.

"Our good friend Mr. Brue rightly declines to reveal your name to me, sir. And so he should. You are Mr. X, I may not know where from. But you and I need have no secrets from each other. I have my sources. You too have your sources, or you would not have sent your English banker to examine me. Well, what you have heard of me is true, Brother Issa. I am before and after all things a man of peace. That is not to say I stand aside from our great struggle. I am no friend of violence, but I respect those returning to us from the battlefield. They have seen the smoke. As I have. They have been tortured for the Prophet and for God. They have been beaten and imprisoned, as I have, but not broken. The violence is not of their making. They are its victims."

Waiting for an answer, he peered at Issa, examining with both compassion and curiosity the impact of his words. But Issa, having listened to Annabel's translation, only bowed his head.

"Therefore, I must believe you, sir," Abdullah went on. "It is my duty before God. If God

wishes to endow us with such riches, who am I,
His poor servant, to refuse them?"

But then, exactly as Brue remembered it from
the day before, Abdullah's voice hardened.

"Therefore tell me, brother, be so kind. By
what munificence of Allah, by what ingenious
means, are you at liberty in this country? How is
it that we are able to sit with you and speak to
you and touch you when, according to certain information that has reached me over the Internet
and by other means, half the world's policemen
would like to clap you in irons?"

Issa turned to Annabel for her translation,
then back to Abdullah while she herself supplied
the answer that Brue suspected her handlers had
prewritten.

"My client's situation in Germany is precari-
ous, Dr. Abdullah," she said, first in German,
then afterwards, sotto voce, in a Russian précis.
"By German law, he may not be returned to a
country that practices torture or exacts the death
penalty. Unfortunately, it is a law that the German authorities, in common with other Western
democracies, frequently ignore. We shall nevertheless apply for asylum in Germany."

"*Shall*? How long has your distinguished client
been in this country?"

"He has been ill and is only now recovering."

"And meantime?"

"Meantime, my client is pursued, stateless and in great peril."

"But by God's mercy he is here among us," Dr. Abdullah objected, unpersuaded.

"*Meantime*"—Annabel continued firmly—"and until we receive binding assurances from the German authorities that my client will in no circumstance be expelled to Turkey or Russia, he refuses to place himself in their hands."

"In whose hands, then, has he placed himself *now,* if I may inquire?" Dr. Abdullah insisted, eyes darting from Annabel to Issa to Brue and back. "Is he a trick? Are you? Are *all of you* a trick?"—including Brue now in his sweeping gaze—"I am here in the service of Allah. I have no choice. But in whose service are *you* here? I ask this question from the heart: Are you good people, or are you out to destroy me? Are you here, in some way I do not understand, to make a fool or a knave of me? If my question offends you, pardon me. These are terrible times."

Determined to leap to Annabel's defense, Brue was still assembling his response when she came in ahead of him, and this time she dispensed with a translation.

"Dr. Abdullah," she said, in a voice that suggested either anger or desperation.

"Madam?"

"My client has come here tonight at great risk

to himself in order to present your charities with a very large sum of money. He asks only that he may give, and you receive. He asks for nothing in return—"

"God will reward him."

"—beyond the assurance that his medical studies will be paid for by one of the charities he endows. Will you give him that assurance or do you propose to continue questioning his intentions?"

"With God's will his medical studies will be provided for."

"He does however insist on your absolute silence regarding his identity, his situation here in Germany and the source of the monies he is about to hand over to your charities. Those are the terms. If you will honor them, so will he."

Dr. Abdullah's gaze returned to Issa: the haunted eyes, the haggard face, stretched taut in pain and confusion, the long, starved hands cupped together, the threadbare overcoat, the woolen skullcap and quarter-beard.

And as Abdullah looked at him, his own gaze softened.

"Issa, my son."

"Sir."

"Am I correct to believe that you have not received much instruction regarding our great religion?"

"You are right, sir!" Issa barked, his voice leaping out of control in his impatience.

But Abdullah's small, bright eyes had homed on the bracelet that Issa was nervously passing through his fingers.

"Is that made of gold, Issa, the ornament you are wearing?"

"It is the best gold, sir"—with an apprehensive glance at Annabel while she translated this.

"The small book that is attached to it: It is a depiction of the Holy Koran?"

A nod from Issa, well before Annabel had finished translating the question.

"And is the name of Allah—are those His holy words—engraved upon its pages?"

To Annabel only, and only after a long pause following her translation, came Issa's "Yes, sir."

"And has it not reached your ears, Issa, that such objects, and such display, being merely poor imitations of Christian and Jewish practice—for example, the golden Star of David or the Christian cross—are forbidden to us?"

Issa's face darkened. His head fell forward and he stared intently downward at the bracelet in his hand.

Annabel came to his rescue: "It was his mother's," she said, unprompted by any word from her client. "It was the tradition of her people and tribe."

Ignoring her interjection as if it had never happened, Abdullah continued to reflect upon the gravity of Issa's offense.

"Put it back on your wrist, Issa," he said at last. "Pull your sleeve over it so that I am not obliged to look at it." And having listened to Annabel's translation, and waited until his command had been obeyed, he resumed his homily.

"There are men in the world, Issa, who care only for the *dunya*—by this is meant money and material status in the short life we lead here on earth. And there are men in the world who care nothing for the *dunya* but everything for the *akhira*—by this is meant the eternal life that we lead afterwards, according to our merits and failures in the eyes of God. Our life in the *dunya* is the time given to us for sowing. In the *akhira* we shall see what our harvest is. Tell me now, Issa, what it is that *you* are renouncing, and for whom?"

Annabel had barely completed her translation before Issa rose to his feet and shouted: "Sir! Please! I am renouncing my father's sins for God!"

Crouched at Maximilian's side, fists braced on the worktable that ran beneath the rows of screens, Bachmann had watched every inflection and gesture that passed between the four players. Nothing he had seen of Issa surprised him: he felt he had known him ever since his arrival in Germany. A first scrutiny of Signpost had also shown him what he expected to see, and had seen countless times in television replays and in press photographs accompanied by editorials extolling the wit, moderation and inclusiveness of one of Germany's leading Muslims: a man in his late prime, darting, charismatic and intelligent, caught between his cultivated image of reclusiveness and his love of self-promotion.

Yet it was Annabel who held center stage for him. Her artful juggling of the interrogation by Abdullah had left him mute with admiration, and he was not alone. Maximilian sat rigid, his hands spread in midmovement over his keyboard while Niki watched the screen from between her fingers.

"Heaven protect us from lawyers," Bachmann breathed at last to their relieved laughter. "Didn't I say she was a natural?"

And to himself: Erna, you should have seen your poor girl just now.

The mood in Brue's office remained solemn but, to Brue, tedious rather than tense. Having discovered the gaps in Issa's learning, Dr. Abdullah was lecturing him on the nature of the broadly based Muslim charities he championed and the system that financed them. Brue was leaning back in his bank manager's leather chair, listening to him with what he hoped looked like keen interest while admiring Annabel's translation.

Zakat, Dr. Abdullah went on indefatigably, was defined in Muslim law not as a *tax* but as an *act of serving God.*

"That is very correct, sir," Issa muttered when Annabel translated this. Brue put on an expression of pious approbation.

"*Zakat* is the *giving heart of Islam,*" Dr. Abdullah continued methodically, and paused for Annabel to translate. "The giving of a portion of a man's wealth is prescribed by God and the Prophet, peace be upon Him."

"But I shall give all!" Issa cried, again rising to his feet, even before he had heard Annabel out. "Every *kopeika,* sir! You will see! I will give one hundred percent. To all of my brothers and sisters in Chechnya!"

"But also to the Umma at large, because we are all of one great family," Dr. Abdullah patiently reminded him.

"Sir! Please! Chechen are my family!" Issa cried, catching Annabel in the full flood of her translation. "Chechnya is my mother!"

"However, since we are in the West tonight,

Issa," Dr. Abdullah continued firmly, as if he hadn't heard this, "allow me to inform you that many Western Muslims today, rather than give their *zakat* to personal friends or blood relations, prefer to hand it to our many Islamic charities to be distributed within the Umma as need demands. I understand this to be also your personal wish."

Pause for Annabel's translation. Another pause while Issa digests it, head down, brows together—and signifies his concurrence.

"And it was on this understanding," Abdullah went on, coming to the point at last, "that I prepared a list of charities that I considered deserving of your generosity. You have received that list, as I understand it, Issa. And you have made certain selections from it. Is that true?"

It was true.

"So were you content with that list, Issa? Or should I explain to you more precisely the function of the charities I have recommended?"

But Issa by now had had enough. "Sir!" he blurted, yet again springing to his feet. "Dr. Abdullah! My brother! Assure me of only one thing, please! We are giving this money to God and to Chechnya. That is all I need to hear! It is the money of thieves, rapists and murderers. It is bad profit from *riba*! It is *haraam*! It is profit from alcohol and pork and pornography! It is not the money of God! It is the money of Satan!"

Having listened implacably to Annabel's translation, and assisted her with the Arabic words, Abdullah delivered his measured response.

"You are giving the money to perform God's will, my good brother Issa. You are wise and right to give it, and when you have given it, you will be free to study, and to worship God in modesty and chastity. Perhaps it is true that the money was stolen, and put to usury and other purposes forbidden by God's laws. But soon it will be God's alone, and He will be merciful to you in whatever comes after the earthly life, since none but God can judge how you will be rewarded, whether in heaven or in hell."

Which was when Brue at last felt able to make his move.

"Well then," he said brightly, also rising to his feet in company with Issa. "May I suggest we now adjourn to the cashier's office and complete our business there? Assuming Frau Richter approves, of course."

Frau Richter approved.

"Go now, sir?" Maximilian asked Bachmann, as the three of them watched Brue and Signpost head for the door, followed by Issa and Annabel.

He meant: Is it time for you to get into your

taxi, and for me to signal your two watchers to follow you in the Audi?

Bachmann jabbed a thumb at the screen that linked the van to Berlin.

"No green light," he objected, and did his best to pull a raw smile at the wondrous ways of those Berlin bureaucrats.

No positively last, final, irrevocable, undeniable, unqualifiable, *fucking* green light. Not from Burgdorf, from Axelrod, not from the whole overinflated, suited, tight-arsed, divisive lawyer-driven pack of them together, he meant. Was the jury *really* still out? Was Joint *even now* looking under its lush leather sofas for yet another way of saying no? Were they perhaps debating whether five percent bad was really bad enough to justify upsetting the bruised sensitivities of our moderate Muslim community?

I'm offering you the way out, for God's sake! he screamed at the pack of them in his mind. Do this my way, nobody will even know! Or maybe I should turn this whole thing in, and helicopter up to Berlin and explain to you fellows just what *five percent bad* means out there in the real world that you're so diligently protected from: slaughterhouse blood washing over your toe caps, and the hundred percent dead scattered in five percent bits over a square kilometer of the town square?

But his worst fear was the one that he scarcely dared express, even to himself: it was of Martha and her kind. Martha who observes and doesn't take part, as if that were ever a role she would settle for. Martha who is Burgdorf's neo-conservative soul mate. Martha who laughs aloud at the Felix operation as if it were some fancy European party game mounted by a bunch of liberal German dilettantes. He imagined her now in Berlin. Was the cutthroat Newton at her side? No, he'd stayed behind in Hamburg with the ash-blonde. He imagined Martha in the Joint ops room, telling Burgdorf what was good for him if he wanted the top job. Telling him how Langley never forgets its friends.

"No green light, sir," Maximilian confirmed. "Stand by till advised."

She was his lawyer and she knew nothing but her brief.

And her brief, imposed on her by Issa's desperate situation and rammed home by Erna Frey, was to bring her client to the table, let him sign over his money and get him his passport to freedom.

She was not a judge like her mother, or a diplomatic bigot like her father. She was a

lawyer and Issa was her mandate and whether
this gentle Muslim sage was right, wrong, innocent or guilty, was no part of that brief. Günther had said he did not intend to harm a hair of
his head and she believed him. Or so she was
telling herself as the four of them descended the
fine marble staircase of Brue's bank, with Brue
leading and Abdullah following—why so shaky
suddenly?—and Issa and Annabel bringing up
the rear.

Issa was leaning backwards, trailing his right
arm for her to take hold of, but only the cloth,
only ever the cloth. She could feel the heat of
him through it, and she fancied she could feel his
pulse beating, but it was probably her own.

"What's Abdullah *done?*" she had asked Erna
Frey yet again at lunchtime, hoping that the im-
minence of action might loosen her tongue.

"He's one small part of a big untidy boat,
dear," Erna the impassioned sailor had replied
enigmatically. "A bit like a cotter pin. And if you
don't know your way round the boat, about as
difficult to find. And about as easy to lose
again."

Peering past Issa, she could see Dr. Abdullah's
white skullcap bobbing precariously six stairs
below her: one small part of an untidy boat.

The door to the cashier's office stood open.
Brue, father to Georgina, was standing over the

computer. Could he work it? If he needs my help, he'll get it.

In the van, Bachmann and his crew of two were gripped by the same silence that had descended over the group of four gathered in the cashier's office. One camera set in the end wall of the cashier's office provided the fish-eye master shot, a second the close-up of Brue seated at the keyboard, laboriously typing with two fingers the sort codes and account numbers supplied from a printout by Dr. Abdullah and scanned by a third camera that was concealed in the overhead light fitting. On a separate screen relayed from Joint in Berlin, the same list was being reproduced to the faltering rhythm of Brue's typing. Charities not included in the group that Dr. Abdullah had already submitted for Issa's approval were highlighted in red.

"For God's sake, Michael," Bachmann pleaded over the direct line to Axelrod. "If not now, when?"

"Don't get in your taxi, Günther."

"We've nailed him, for fuck's sake! What are they waiting for?"

"Stay where you are. Don't go any nearer to the bank till I personally give you the word. That's an order."

No nearer to the bank than who? Arni Mohr? Lantern and his unidentified passenger? But Axelrod had once again rung off. Bachmann stared at the screens, caught Niki's eye and looked away. An order, he had said. An order who from? Axelrod? Burgdorf? Burgdorf with Martha whispering into his ear? Or a consensus order from a committee that was at war with itself and lived in a capsule where the smell of warm blood never entered?

His gaze returned sharply to Niki. A black, incongruously old-fashioned telephone that sat on a ledge above the screens was ringing out its homely tone. Niki's features didn't flicker. She didn't raise her eyebrows to him in question, or exhort him or join him in his hesitation. She let the phone go on ringing out, and waited for a sign from him. Bachmann nodded to her: take it. She tipped her head, waiting for the spoken word.

"Take the call," he said aloud.

She lifted the receiver and spoke in a brisk, half-singing voice that was relayed over the van's speaker system. "Hansa Taxis! Thank you for calling. Pickup where, please."

Sounding more relaxed than they had heard him all evening, Brue spelled out the bank's address at dictation speed.

"Phone number?"

Brue gave it.

"One second, please!" Niki sang and, making a pause to indicate that she was consulting her computer, put her hand over the mouthpiece of the black phone while she again waited for Bachmann's instruction. For a moment longer, he deliberated. Then, standing up, he picked the seaman's cap from the hook on the door and clapped it on his head. Then the workman's jacket, sleeve by sleeve. Then a last tug to make it sit tight on his shoulders.

"Tell him I'm on my way," he said.

Niki took her hand from the mouthpiece.

"Ten minutes," she said, and rang off.

From the door, Bachmann took a last look at the screens.

"It's just *go*," he said, to Maximilian and Niki both. "If the green light comes through, that's all you have to say to me. *Go*."

"What if it doesn't?" Niki asked for both of them.

"Doesn't what?"

"Doesn't come through. If the green light doesn't."

"Then you don't say anything, do you?"

Brue hated the very sight of the cashier's office with its wall-to-wall high-tech toys, and not

only for reasons of his own incompetence. One
of the saddest moments of his life had been
standing before the bonfire in his garden in Vienna with his first wife, Sue, one side of him and
Georgie the other, watching the fabled Brue
Frères card index go up in smoke. Another battle lost. Another past destroyed. From now on,
we'll be like all the rest.

Dr. Abdullah smells of baby powder, he noticed as he laboriously touched in one set of figures. Back there in his house, Brue hadn't noticed
it. Perhaps the old boy had put on a double dose
for the occasion. He wondered if Annabel had noticed it; when this was over, he'd ask her.

Abdullah's white shirt and skullcap were
burning bright under the strip lighting, and he
was leaning into Brue, nudging up against him
with his shoulder while he obligingly pointed
with his index finger, now a sort code, now the
amount of cash to be electronically transferred.

To be honest, Abdullah was getting a bit too
much into Brue's airspace for his liking, what with
the body contact, and the baby powder and the
heat inside the room. But Arab men, Brue had
read, made nothing of it: perfectly happy to walk
down the street or sit in cafés holding hands with
each other, and they can be the butchest chaps on
the block. All the same, he wished Abdullah would
ease off a bit, he was putting him off his stroke.

Ismail. Why was he thinking of Ismail suddenly? Maybe because he'd always wished he'd been able to provide Georgie with a brother. That was some boy. If I'd looked like that at his age, I'd have cut quite a swath. Or perhaps I *did* look like that, but failed to cut a swath. Way it goes. Fatima, off to—where was it?—Balliol?—London School of Economics, that's it. Georgie never ascended to those heights. Bright as paint, see through you in a flash, nothing gets past old Georgie, but not the kind of mind you can educate. *Born* educated in a lot of ways. But not a learner in the formal sense, not Georgie.

Another waft of baby powder. Abdullah was pressing in on him. Next thing I know, he'll be sitting on my bloody lap. And all those small ones—three? Four? Plus one in the garden? Must be an extraordinary thing, to breed like that. To breed without thinking, practically. Just hammering away, doing God's will.

Abdullah's index finger had slipped down a couple of lines. Some shipping company in Cyprus. What the hell has *that* got to do with anything? One minute a world-renowned Muslim charity with headquarters in Riyadh, and the next some Mickey Mouse shipping company in Nicosia. Partly to escape Abdullah's proximity, and partly for reassurance, Brue swung round to Annabel.

"This one okay for you two?" he asked in German. "Doesn't seem to have a tick against it. All I've got is the amount. Fifty thousand U.S. The Seven Friends Navigation Company, Nicosia."

"Ah. Now this one would be very essential for the afflicted of Yemen," Abdullah explained to Brue before Annabel could put the question to Issa. "If your client is concerned to distribute medical relief throughout the Umma, this is a most efficient means of achieving his objective."

His hands resting either side of the keyboard, Brue listened to Annabel's translation into Russian: "Dr. Abdullah says the people of Yemen are greatly afflicted by poverty. This trusted shipping company has long experience of getting assistance to them. Do you want to do this one, or not?"

Issa deliberated, now yes, now no, now a shrug. Then enlightenment came to him. "In my Turkish jail there was a Yemeni who was so sick he died! Now this will not happen again. Do it, do it, Mr. Tommy!"

Obediently, Brue typed in the shipping company's particulars, and in his imagination followed them into the ether: first to the clearing bank through which Frères was obliged to make its transfers—in precomputer days, the name Brue alone would have been enough—then to Ankara, then to some flea-bitten Turkish-Cypriot bank in Nicosia that probably looked like an outside toilet with a lot of mangy dogs sunning themselves on the doorstep. Annabel was tapping his shoulder. Other than a handshake, she had never touched him before.

"That's an ampersand. You've put a slash."

"Have I? Where? Good lord, so I have. Too stupid of me. Thanks."

He put an ampersand. He had done his job. Fourteen bloody banks and one pissy shipping firm. All he needed to do now was press the GO tit.

"Have we done the deed then, Frau Richter?" he asked jovially, his hand hovering over the keyboard, his middle finger protruding.

"Issa?" she inquired.

Issa gave a distracted nod and returned to his musings.

"Dr. Abdullah, no worries?"

"Thank you, sir, I am naturally most content."

All hundred percent of you? Brue wondered.

Still peering down at the GO key, he deliberated what gesture he should make, and what mood his face should be expressing as he touched it.

Was he a happy banker because he was about to unload twelve and a half million dollars' worth of his bank's assets? Scarcely.

Was he happy to be performing a service for the son and heir of a long-standing client of the bank?

Or happiest to be rescuing Annabel from a god-awful jam and Issa from endless incarceration and worse?

Actually the last, but for safety's sake he put on his boardroom face and in his anticipated relief hit GO harder than he meant to.

Bang goes the last Lipizzaner. Good-bye, Edward Amadeus, OBE. And good-bye Ian Lantern and God help you and all who sail in you.

He had only one more duty to perform.

"Dr. Abdullah, sir. Allow me to call you a taxi at the bank's expense."

And without waiting for the good doctor's answer, dialed the number that Lantern had given him for this moment.

Driving through the invisible cones of Mohr's exclusion zone, past mysteriously immune cars at street corners, and burly pedestrians with nothing to do but look innocent and engineers with night lamps toiling unpersuasively at junction boxes, Bachmann parked his taxi in the raised forecourt of Brue Frères Bank, pulled up the collars of his workman's jacket and, like any waiting cabbie, settled down to listen to his radio and stare vacuously through the windscreen—and less vacuously at the satellite navigation panel discreetly flickering low down on his dashboard.

He had image, but at the last minute Mohr's technicians had screwed up, and failed to provide him with sound.

No sooner had he parked his taxi than his two watchers parked their Audi in the street half a level below. They were there for the unwelcome eventuality that Signpost did not take kindly to being hijacked to an unfamiliar destination. Their remit, drummed into them by Bachmann, was to remain inside their car until he called on them. No muddling with Mohr's men on pain of excommunication.

Bachmann made a covert survey of the houses up and down the row and was horrified to discern two shadowy figures on a rooftop and two more at the opening to a cul-de-sac running up from the Binnen Alster shore. The silent pictures on his navigation panel showed Annabel and Felix dawdling in the hall while Brue first escorted Signpost to the downstairs cloakroom, then went upstairs, presumably for the same purpose, or maybe he needed a quick drink.

On-screen Annabel and Felix are facing each other two yards apart and laughing a little fixedly. It's the first time Bachmann has seen Annabel in a headscarf. It's the first time he has seen her laugh. Felix spreads his arms, raises them above his head and performs a little jig. Bachmann assumes it is a bit of Chechen dance.

Annabel in long skirt cautiously partners him. Dance ends before it has begun.

Bachmann closed his eyes and opened them, and yes, he was still here, still waiting for the positively last green light, still in direct default of Axelrod's orders, but Günther Bachmann was a famous chancer and nothing was ever going to change that. The man on the ground knows best: Bachmann's Law. But why oh why the delay, and more delay, why, why? Unless Berlin had fucked up—which admittedly was always entirely possible—Abdullah was compromised to hell and back and the operation was a triumph. So why wasn't the orchestra playing full blast, and why wasn't he getting the green light with only minutes to go?

His cell phone was ringing. Niki, speaking for Maximilian: "It's a written order. It's just come in."

"Read it," Bachmann murmured.

"'Project delayed. Evacuate area now and return to Hamburg station.'"

"Who signed it, Niki?"

"Joint Steering. Your symbol at the top, Joint Steering's at the bottom."

"No name?"

"No name," Niki confirmed.

A consensus decision then, the only kind Joint took. No matter who was pulling the strings.

"And *project, right? Project* delayed? Not *operation* delayed?"

"Project is correct. No reference to operation."

"And nothing about Felix?"

"Nothing."

"Or Signpost?"

"Nothing about Signpost. I've given you the whole message."

He tried to call Axelrod on his cell phone and got voice mail. He tried the direct line to the Joint Committee and got engaged. He tried the switchboard and got no reply. On the screen at his knees, Brue is returning from upstairs. Now all three of them are standing in the hall, waiting for Signpost to come out of the cloakroom.

Project delayed, they had said.

For how long? Five minutes, or forever?

Axelrod's been outmaneuvered. He's been outmaneuvered but they let him draft the order and he deliberately obscured the wording so that I could misunderstand.

Not Signpost, not Felix, not *operation,* just *project.* Axelrod is telling me to use my own initiative. *If you can go, go, but don't say I told you, just say you didn't understand the message. No repeat yes.*

Issa and Annabel and Brue were still waiting for Signpost to come out of the cloakroom, and so was Bachmann.

What the hell's he *doing* in there all this time?

Preparing himself for martyrdom? Bachmann remembered the look on his face as he advanced on Issa for that first embrace: *Am I embracing a brother or my own death?* He'd seen the same expression on the faces of the crazies in Beirut before they went out to get themselves killed.

He's out. Signpost has at last emerged from the cloakroom. He is wearing a fawn Burberry raincoat but no white skullcap. Has he left it in the cloakroom, or put it in his briefcase? Or is he telling us something? Is he saying what he has been thinking all along: Take me. I have knowingly walked into your baited trap, because how else could I reconcile myself with God, so take me?

Signpost has placed himself in front of Issa and is staring up at him, adoring him. Issa peers down at him in puzzlement. Signpost reaches out his arms and warmly embraces Issa, patting his shoulders: *my son.* Signpost strokes Issa's face, cradles his hands, holds them tenderly against his breast while the two Westerners watch across the cultural divide. Issa is belatedly thanking and honoring his guide and mentor. Annabel Richter is interpreting. It's becoming a long good-bye.

"No word, Niki?"

"It's dead. Our screens, everything."

I'm on my own, where I always am. The man on the ground knows best. Fuck them.

But Bachmann's screen is still miraculously functioning, even if it has no sound. The hall is empty. All four have vanished. Mohr's technicians strike again. No video coverage of the entrance lobby.

The bank's front door opening. Cameras and screen irrelevant. Naked eye takes over at last. Overbright intruder lights illuminate the steps and surrounding pillars. First out is Signpost. Unsteady walk. He's frightened shitless.

Issa has noticed his frailty too, and is walking at his side, one hand under the master's arm. Issa grinning.

Annabel behind him grinning too. Free air at last. Stars. A moon even. Annabel and Brue bringing up the rear. Everybody, Brue included, grinning now. Only Abdullah looking unhappy, which is fine by me. First I'll tell him that his worst fears have come true, then I'll be his best and only friend in need.

They're heading towards me. Issa and Annabel are chatting away to him and he's smiling somehow, but he's wobbly as a leaf.

Bachmann slowly lifts his capped head to the little group approaching his cab, a studied performance. I'm a sleepy Hamburg taxi driver, one more job and that's it for the night.

Brue leading now. Brue the English gentleman thrusting his way ahead of the group in order to usher his departing guests.

Bachmann in his cap and shabby jacket—who only fifteen seconds earlier switched off his satellite navigation system—lowers his window and gives Brue the kind of none-too-deferential greeting that any late-night taxi driver might give.

"Taxi for Brue Frères?" Brue inquires merrily, leaning into Bachmann's open window, one hand to the rear door handle. *"Fantastic!"* And, turning back to Signpost in the same hearty manner—"So where are we off to tonight, Doctor, if I may ask? If it's all the way home, that's perfectly all right by the bank. I just wish all our business could be conducted in such a friendly manner, sir."

But Abdullah had no time to answer, or if he had, Bachmann never heard him. A high-sided white minibus had careered into the forecourt, smashing into Bachmann's cab, skewing it sideways, starring the side window and crumpling the driver's door. Showered with broken glass and sprawled across the passenger seat, Bachmann had a slow-motion vision of Brue leaping for safety, the jacket of his suit billowing as if floating on water. Hauling himself half upright, he saw one black-windowed Mercedes pulling up tight behind the minibus, and a second reversing at high speed and taking up a position directly in front of it. Dazed as he was by the impact and the headlights, he saw as if by broad daylight the hatchet face and ash-blonde hair of the woman seated beside a masked driver in the windscreen of the first Mercedes as it shrieked to a halt hard behind the white minibus.

First Annabel dreamed it, then she knew it was for real. She took a step and discovered she was alone. Abdullah too had stopped dead and was standing with his little feet together and turned inward, while he stared past her down the street. If he hadn't been a great Muslim scholar she'd have obeyed her instincts and grabbed him by the forearm, because he had started swaying, and she feared he was having a seizure of some kind and was about to keel over.

But he didn't.

To her relief he righted himself, only to go on staring down the street with a look of anguished recognition and horror on his face, the look of a man whose worst fears have come to visit him. She noticed also that his skinny head had sunk into his shoulders in a self-protective cringe, as if he imagined that someone was already hammering blows on him from behind, although there was nobody behind him to do it.

By now she was looking across Abdullah to

Issa, wanting to catch his eye and refer her anxiety
to him, but instead she found herself looking past
him in the direction that both Issa and Abdullah
were staring already, and she saw at last what
they saw, although the sight didn't immediately
strike terror into her in the way it had struck terror into Abdullah.

In the course of her work at the Sanctuary, it
was true, she had heard reports of men who had
to be physically restrained and a few who had to
be beaten to make them submit to expulsion.
And the memory of Magomed waving from the
window of his departing plane would stay with
her till she died.

But that was about the limit of her experience
of such matters, which was why her mind wasn't
quick enough to grasp the unimaginable yet entirely concrete fact: not only that the forecourt
had become the scene of a complicated traffic
accident involving a parked cream-colored taxi
and two stray Mercedes with blackened windows, but that the white minibus that had
clearly caused the accident was standing sideways to her with its doors wide open, and
four—no, five—men in balaclavas and black
tracksuits and sneakers were climbing out of it
at their leisure.

And because she was so slow on the uptake, it
was sheer child's play for them. They had

snatched Abdullah from beside her as neatly as if they were snatching her handbag; whereas Issa, being more advanced in his awareness of brute force, clung onto his mentor for dear life, binding his spindly arms round him and sagging to his knees with him, to give him extra protection.

But that was only until the four or five masked men formed a cluster round the pair of them—a kind of testudo as the Romans had called it in her Latin lessons—and dragged and carried them to the minibus, threw them inside and jumped after them, then slammed the doors on themselves for privacy.

She saw Brue come running up beside her and heard him shouting after the masked men in English at the top of his voice, and she wondered why English. Then she remembered that the masked men had spoken staccato curse words to each other in American English, which would explain why Brue chose English to shout back at them, though he might as well have saved his breath for all the notice they took of him.

And it was probably Brue's presence beside her that enabled her to recover her wits, and set her free to run full pelt at the minibus as it pulled away, with every intention of placing herself in front of it, if only she could get between its dented bonnet and a Mercedes that had backed itself up against it.

*　　*　　*

Clawing himself out of the passenger door with his right arm, Bachmann half ran, half limped along the side of the minibus, beating its white wall with his good fist. Flopping onto the bonnet of the leading Mercedes, he punted himself feet-first across it to the indifference of two men in balaclava helmets seated in the front. The minibus was pulling away, its side doors were sliding shut, but not before Bachmann had a glimpse of standing men in black balaclavas and jumpsuits and two prone bodies spread-eagled facedown on the floor at their feet, the one in a long black overcoat and the other in a fawn Burberry. He heard screams and realized they were Annabel's, and saw that she had grabbed a side door handle and was allowing herself to be pulled along while she yelled, "Open the door, open the door, open the door," in English, on and on.

The chase Mercedes with the masked driver and the hatchet-faced ash-blonde in the passenger seat had pulled alongside and was trying to edge her out of the way and the minibus was accelerating but Annabel was still hanging on, shouting, "Bastards, bastards," also in English. Then he heard her screaming again, *I'll get you back!* —but in Russian, and realized that this time she was addressing Issa, not his abductors. "I'll get you back if it's the last"—and presumably she was going to say if it was the last thing she did in her whole life, but by then she was quite literally beating the air, for Brue had grabbed hold of her, and broken her grasp on the door handle. But even when he stood her on her feet, her arms were stretched out to the minibus in an effort to bring it back.

Bachmann made his way down the forecourt's slipway to the main road, where his two watchers sat motionless in their Audi, still waiting for his call. Continuing along the pavement, he kept walking as best he could until he reached the cul-de-sac where he had spotted Arni Mohr's control car. It had gone, but Arni Mohr was standing on the pavement under a street lamp, chatting with Newton from Beirut days. Next to them, waiting to be let in, stood little Ian Lantern, smiling as usual, so Bachmann assumed that Newton had been the unidentified passenger in Lantern's car.

At Bachmann's approach, Arni Mohr assumed an expression of studious detachment and needed to make a phone call that required him to walk away down the road, but Newton with his spade of new black beard stepped affably forward to greet his old mate.

"Well, *Günther Bachmann,* for Christ's sakes! How come *you* got your nose under the wire? We thought you were Mike Axelrod's little boy. Did Brother Burgdorf give you a ringside seat after all?"

But as Newton drew nearer to Bachmann, and saw his smashed arm and disheveled state, and the wild look of accusation in his eyes, he realized he had mistaken his man, and came sharply to a halt.

"Listen. Sorry about your cab, okay? Those hillbillies from the Farm drive like shit. Now go have that arm fixed. Ian drives you to a hospital. Now. Yes, Ian? He says yes. Go now."

"Where have you taken him?" Bachmann asked.

"Abdullah? Who gives a shit? Some hole in the desert, for all I know. *Justice has been rendered, man. We can all go home.*"

He had spoken these last words in English, but Bachmann in his dazed state failed to get his mind round them.

"*Rendered?*" he repeated stupidly. "What's rendered? What justice are you talking about?"

"*American* justice, asshole. Whose do you think? Justice from the fucking hip, man. No-crap justice, *that* kind of justice! Justice with no fucking lawyers around to pervert the course. Have you never heard of *extraordinary rendition*? No? Time you Krauts had a word for it! Have you given up speaking or what?"

But still nothing came out of Bachmann, so Newton went on:

"Eye for a fucking eye, Günther. Justice as

retribution, okay? Abdullah was killing *Americans*. We call that original sin. You want to play softball spy games? Go find yourself some Euro-pygmies."

"I was asking you about Issa," Bachmann said.

"Issa was *air*, man," Newton retorted, now seriously angry. "Whose fucking money was it anyway? Issa Karpov bankrolls terror, period. Issa Karpov sends money to very bad guys. He just did. Fuck *you*, Günther. Okay?" But he seemed to feel he hadn't quite made his point: "How about those Chechen militants he hung out with? Eh? You're telling me they're a bunch of pussycats?"

"He's innocent."

"Bullshit. Issa Karpov was one hundred percent complicit, and a couple of weeks from now, if he lasts that long, he'll admit it. Now get out of my face before I throw you out."

Hovering in the shadow of the tall American, Lantern seemed to agree.

A crisp night wind was whisking off the lake, bringing a smell of oil from the harbor. Annabel stood at the center of the forecourt, peering down the empty street after the departed minibus. Brue stood next to her. Her scarf had fallen round her neck. Absently, she lifted it over her head and retied it under her throat. Hearing a footstep, Brue turned and saw the driver of the smashed taxi hobbling towards them. Then Annabel turned also, and recognized the driver as Günther Bachmann, the man who made the weather, standing ten meters from her, not daring to come nearer. She scrutinized him, then shook her head and began to shudder. Brue put his arm round her shoulders where he had always wanted to put it, but he doubted whether she knew it was there.

THE AUTHOR WISHES
TO THANK:

Yassin Musharbash of Spiegel Online, for his tireless and painstaking researches; Clive Stafford Smith, Saadiya Chaudary and Alexandra Zernova with the U.K. charity Reprieve* and Bernhard Docke† in Bremen for their legal wisdoms; the writer and journalist Michael Jürgs of Hamburg, for his fruitful introductions and close reading of the early drafts; Helmuth Landwehr, former private banker, for initiating me into the ways of his less-scrupulous erstwhile colleagues; Anne Harms and Annette Heise of flucht•punkt,* Hamburg, for allowing me to create in Sanctuary North a fictional sister organization to their own, complete with fictional staff and fictional clients; and the writer and Middle East expert Said Aburish, for his wise promptings. And Carla Hornstein who, by an accident of life, started me on the journey and provided me with invaluable introductions and advice.

*Reprieve uses the law to deliver justice and save lives, from death row to Guantánamo Bay. flucht•punkt provides legal and other assistance to asylum seekers and stateless persons in the region of Hamburg. Both organizations are registered charities.
†Bernhard Docke is the pro bono legal representative of Murat Kurnaz, the Turkish German Muslim unjustly imprisoned in Guantánamo Bay for four and a half years.

ABOUT THE AUTHOR

JOHN LE CARRÉ was born in 1931. After attending the universities of Berne and Oxford, he spent five years in the British Foreign Service. *The Spy Who Came in from the Cold*, his third book, secured him a worldwide reputation. He is the author of twenty-one novels, including *Tinker, Tailor, Soldier, Spy*; *A Perfect Spy* and *The Constant Gardener*. His books have been translated into thirty-six languages. He lives in England.